THE

ICE

SWAN

ALSO BY J'NELL CIESIELSKI

Beauty Among Ruins

The Socialite

Among the Poppies

The Songbird and the Spy

THE

ICE

SWAN

J'NELL
CIESIELSKI

THOMAS NELSON
Since 1798

The Ice Swan

Copyright © 2021 J'nell Ciesielski

Published in Nashville, Tennessee, by Thomas Nelson. Thomas Nelson is a registered trademark of HarperCollins Christian Publishing, Inc.

Thomas Nelson titles may be purchased in bulk for educational, business, fundraising, or sales promotional use. For information, please e-mail SpecialMarkets@ThomasNelson.com.

Publisher's Note: This novel is a work of fiction. Names, characters, places, and incidents are either products of the author's imagination or used fictitiously. All characters are fictional, and any similarity to people living or dead is purely coincidental.

Library of Congress Cataloging-in-Publication Data

Names: Ciesielski, J'nell, author.
Title: The ice swan / J'nell Ciesielski.
Description: Nashville, Tennessee : Thomas Nelson, [2021] | Summary: "Amid the violent last days of the glittering Russian court, a Russian princess on the run finds her heart where she least expects it"-- Provided by publisher.
Identifiers: LCCN 2020056021 (print) | LCCN 2020056022 (ebook) | ISBN 9780785248422 (trade paper) | ISBN 9780785248439 (epub) | ISBN 9780785248446 (downloadable audio)
Subjects: GSAFD: Love stories.
Classification: LCC PS3603.I33 I28 2021 (print) | LCC PS3603.I33 (ebook) | DDC 813/.6--dc23
LC record available at https://lccn.loc.gov/2020056021
LC ebook record available at https://lccn.loc.gov/2020056022

Printed in the United States of America

21 22 23 24 25 LSC 5 4 3 2 1

Kim
How dull my life would be without your sparkle.

We know what lies in the balance at this moment, and what is happening right now. The hour for courage strikes upon our clocks, and courage will not desert us.

—AKHMATOVA

PROLOGUE

The night burned red with the flames of revolution.

Shots ringing out. Cannons exploding. People screaming. The Bolsheviks came intent on death with anarchy in their iron fists.

Her Serenity the Princess Svetlana Dalsky hurried down the corridor of the Blue Palace carrying a travel case that had been packed for weeks should this very scenario arise, not daring to use a single candle lest it draw attention. The dozens of windows reflected the red sky, turning the drapes and carpets and ancestral portraits to stains of blood. The rebels would soon be at their front door, and not even her father's protection unit of White Guards could hold them back. The time for that was over.

She slipped into her younger sister's chamber still cloaked in darkness and moved to the bed. A weak candle on the bedside table illuminated Marina's sweet face relaxed in worriless sleep.

Svetlana set her case down and shook her sister's shoulder. "Get up, Marina." Marina moaned and flipped over, her hair like dark honey across the lacey pillow. "Get up!"

"What for?" Marina rolled back and cracked open an eye. Taking in her sister's dark travel clothes, she bolted upright. "It is happening?"

"Yes."

Marina sprang out of bed and rushed to her wardrobe to change while Svetlana stuffed her sister's personal items into the waiting travel

1

bag. Father had told them this day would come and they had prepared well.

Svetlana scrounged through the jewelry box. "Where are the rubies?"

Marina patted her stomach as she jammed her feet into thick stockings. "Finished sewing them into my corset last week."

Another preparation. Their carried items were bound to be searched or confiscated, but their most precious items, the ones that would keep them alive, would never leave their bodies and hopefully slip right under the rebels' noses.

Dressed in heavy layers and thick coats to withstand the malevolent Russian weather, the sisters grabbed their two small cases and left the chamber, stealing down the corridor of their family's home as swift as shadows. The light beyond the windows grew brighter as if a bonfire had ignited just outside the palace gates. Gunfire ricocheted off the surrounding buildings.

Soon. They would be here soon.

A cry of despair echoed down the corridor. "The day has come!" Their mother's wail reached them a split second before she hurtled around a corner clutching her fur coat and *kubanka* hat. "They will kill us all!"

Marina gasped. Svetlana placed a steadying hand on her shoulder to ward off their mother's hysterics. "They will not find us, Mama. Where is your travel case?"

"Well, I . . ." Mama looked around as if the bag would appear by sheer willpower. "I see no reason to pack as if we are leaving forever. Your father will fight. We'll return in a matter of days. They have no right to be here!"

Svetlana stepped forward until she was inches from her mother's pale face. "We may never return."

"The tsar cannot abandon us to these madmen!"

Glass shattered.

Mama screamed, clutching her cross necklace. "Saint Peter preserve us!"

Voices shouted from the foyer. Boots pounded across the marbled floors.

A dark figure flashed around the corner leading up from the back staircase. "Svetlana! This way. *Toropis!*" Sergey. One of her brother's oldest friends.

"No. This way." Svetlana turned away from the front of the palace and down a twist of passageways to a small closet in the servants' hall. She pushed a back panel to reveal a hidden staircase. "Go down. Quickly!"

Marina and Mama disappeared into the secret entrance. Svetlana and Sergey followed and sealed the door behind them.

"Sergey, what are you doing here? Where are Nikolai and Papa?"

"Called to defend the Winter Palace. The Bolsheviks have broken in. I knew it was only a matter of time before they came here. I've come to take you to safety." His heavy breathing echoed in the tight space as they fumbled their way down the darkened stairs. The barest light seeped through the cracks to keep them from complete treachery. "Where is this leading us?"

"To the gardens." If they weren't caught.

The tunnel grew steadily brighter, but the night they emerged to was far from clear. It was red, exploding with horror and treason. Behind them, the palace, their home, shimmered with rage as dark figures raced along the windows. Their torches and guns refracted against the glass. Mama sobbed as Marina whimpered. Svetlana turned them away and out through a rusty gate. The street was quiet and slick with rain from the day before.

The day before their world ended.

Sergey herded them away. "We must hurry to the train station." He took Svetlana's hand and tucked her close to his side.

It was only a few blocks to the train station, but the distance seemed a hundred lifetimes as they darted around buildings and ducked behind carts to avoid the roaming mobs of citizens crying hateful threats of violence to anyone daring to cross their path.

A mass exodus of nobles swarmed the train platforms as women in jewels and men in fur hats crammed their panicked selves into already full cars.

"This way! Up front." Tall, with long arms and legs, Sergey pushed his way through the crowd holding tight to Svetlana. Marina and Mama hooked their arms through hers as they wound through the sea of desperate humanity.

Svetlana's travel case was ripped from her hand. A young woman with frayed clothing clutched it tight in triumph. "Give that back at once!"

The woman grinned, revealing rotting teeth. "It belongs to the People now. Your time is over, *Printsessa*."

Grubby hands reached out and snagged Marina's case. "Long live the People! Long live the Revolution!" They disappeared like smoke.

Svetlana caught glimpses of the train through the teeming bodies. Of people standing cheek to jowl inside. Of men kicking women off the ladder as they attempted to board the crammed cars. All of Petrograd was fleeing, but not all would make it. Fear curled cold and hissing in Svetlana's stomach. They would make it. She would ensure her sister and Mama made it.

The crowd thinned to allow for a gasping draw of breath as the engine belched its black smoke. A whistle trilled. The crowd screamed and plunged toward the train in final desperate flings to find space.

Sergey pushed them to the front car. Grabbing Marina, he shoved her onto the ladder before hoisting up Mama. The train wheels started to turn.

Tweet! Tweeeet!

Soldiers with red arm bands flooded the platform, striking at men and woman alike with clubs and trampling anyone knocked under their black boots. The Bolsheviks. "Get them! Don't let them flee like rats."

The soldiers rushed forward and ripped people off the train as it started to move. Sergey grabbed Svetlana, kissed her on both cheeks, and threw her up the ladder. "Paris. I will find you."

"Sergey!" Svetlana hoisted herself to the rail and held out her hand, begging him to take it. "Sergey!"

Arms striped with red bands locked around him and dragged him back where he was swallowed into the rioting of chaos.

CHAPTER 1

JULY 1918
PARIS, FRANCE

Edwynn MacCallan poised his scalpel over the beating heart. A wonder of sheer beauty with its miraculous chambers and thin veins coursing with life. The bullet pointing directly at the left ventricle threatened to end it all.

"Heart rate is falling, Doctor." Gerard Byeford, Wynn's colleague and surgical assistant, shifted uneasily on the opposite side of the operating table.

"A minute more."

"We don't have a minute."

"Fifty seconds, then."

"Wynn. You arrogant—"

Wynn heard nothing more as the bullet slipped free from its place of intended death, captured in the forceps' unrelenting grip. It clanged a solid peal of demise as it dropped into the sterile metal tray, rolling back and forth until it came to a final stop among the smears of blood.

Gerard wiped the blood trickling from the incision as Wynn handed the forceps to a nurse who then placed a needle driver with a suturing hook into his hand. Wynn made quick work with the catgut thread in a neat row of stitches that would leave the patient with a slightly puckered scar for his Blighty badge. Proof of honor earned on the battlefield. Lucky blighter. Too many of the Tommies claimed theirs with an eternity box or a mud pit in no-man's-land.

The next patient was not so lucky. Sent from a casualty clearing station near Amiens, his tag reported shrapnel to the abdomen, but with the mass moving of the wounded at such places his kidney contusion had been missed. The soldier, no older than twenty, died before the first incision was made.

Wynn ripped off his surgical mask and gloves and tossed them into the bin of soiled linen, then made his escape from the taunting smells of death and failure. And thousands more coming as the wretched war dragged them into its fourth year of death and destruction.

If he allowed the sobering thought to settle for too long, it would drive him straight out of his senses. A batty medical officer was the last thing the army needed at the moment, so he would have to reserve his mental breakdown for another time.

He slipped out the back door of the Parisian hotel turned hospital and dropped onto the stone steps. The bright orange ball of sunlight hung low in the sky, skimming the tops of Parisian buildings that had yet to crumble beneath the weekly barrage of Hun guns. Most days he couldn't tell if the sun was rising or falling as each day blurred into another. Only the smell wafting from the kitchen—congealed eggs to announce breakfast or boiled beans for supper—kept him straight. Neither a pleasant marker of time, but at least the food was hot.

"Here you are."

Wynn scrounged up a grin at the familiar voice. "Thought I smelled carrots."

Hair blazing like the ripened root vegetable, Gerard plopped next to him on the step. His once bleached surgical apron was covered in all manner of operating byproduct. Then again, so was Wynn's. "Ha-ha. That joke never gets old, does it, my lord?"

Wynn scowled at the title he tried to shuck off every chance he got. As the second son of the very wealthy Duke of Kilbride he never had to worry about the pressures of title and land hefted onto his brother, Hugh, the first born and heir. Surgeon was the only position Wynn cared about. "Told you not to call me that."

"Pardon me, Doctor Marquess."

"Another joke that never gets old."

"Never. Just when we uppity surgeons start to think too highly of ourselves, we find our elbows rubbing against nobility. Come to find out, you're not such a bad lot. In small doses."

"Don't let the others in the rank and file hear you. They'll think I'm not pulling my weight to keep the commoners down. As if we need one more thing."

Gerard hunched forward, his freckled hands clenched between his knees. "How many today, Wynn?"

The question had become common enough among the doctors at the end of their shifts. Not because it was some sick competition or morbid curiosity, but so they could spot who most needed a break. So busy caring for others, medical staff often forgot to care for themselves. This was one small way they could look out for each other.

Wynn took a deep breath of the humid evening air that hung over the small garden. Once a fashionable patch of grass for hotel guests to stroll, the area had quickly filled with hospital supplies and cleaning tents. Hopefully the smell of jasmine and orange trees would blossom again here soon instead of canvas and bleach.

"Six. Two hemorrhages. Kidney contusion. One loss of blood during an amputation. Seizure under the knife, and another infection. That lad had been left in a mud pit carved by a mortar for seventy-two hours. He didn't stand a chance when they put him on my table. I didn't even have morphine to give him." He rubbed a hand over his bleary eyes. "They keep coming. Wave after wave, and half of them never reaching my table. The ones who do . . . Well, you know."

"Yes. I know. Lost two myself."

After four hard years, there was nothing left to say. All that remained was the hope that it would end soon.

Wynn slapped Gerard on the shoulder, jostling the thinner man who not only had the misfortunate of carrot-colored hair but the build of one too. "Tomorrow will be better. Bet my best retractor on it."

"Retractor, you say? I could use a new one."

"Tired of having the nurses hold incisions open with their fingers?"

"We do what we must, mate. Pardon, my lord."

"That's Doctor Lord to you, commoner." Wynn yawned and stretched to his aching feet, checking his wristwatch. Nearly eight hours since he last sat down. Once he stepped into the operating theater, time no longer qualified for concern. All that existed was the patient before him. A moment off duty was quick to remind him of the mundane aches and pains of mere humans in need of rest. "I best be off to my bunk. Nestor needs to know where to find me when the cases start piling up in a few hours."

Gerard rolled his eyes at the mention of the hospital's administrative director. "I'll keep him at bay long enough for you to get a few minutes of shut eye this time."

"Thanks, mate. If you see me go down, prop me up with a broom."

He walked around to the side of the building where large pots of boiling water had been set up for disinfecting stained aprons, gloves, and masks. A good soak in bleach and a vigorous scrubbing with lye and the surgical items would be ready to greet the next patients with medical cleanliness. Hurrying back inside, he was careful to stay out of view. If he were spotted by a militant nurse he'd never find his bed.

He quickly checked out. The nurse on duty tipped her head as Wynn signed the logbook. "See you in six hours, Doctor MacCallan."

"Aren't you the wishful thinker?" Wynn slipped his arms into his constricting jacket, not bothering with the tie.

"Someone has to be."

"Too right about that. Good night."

"Good night, Doctor."

Leaving the hospital, Wynn turned down the empty Boulevard

de Courcelles and started walking the two blocks to where he and the other doctors were quartered. He was grateful his special pass allowed him out after curfew or he'd be forced to pitch a tent in his office until morning. The cobblestone street was lined with tall maple trees in the full bloom of green. Quintessential Parisian sandstone buildings with tiny wrought iron balconies and intricate carvings stood guard against the slow passing of time as hurried generations passed before their solemn gazes. Gas lamps rested silently from their hooks on street poles as the City of Light was forced to extinguish her glow while surrounded by war. She sighed now after the exhaustion of a washed-out day as her beauty sparkled under the brilliant coaxing of moonlight.

The air was heavy with summer, a blessing after one of the coldest winters in France's history. The people of Paris had taken to chopping down doors and furniture that had withstood innumerable revolutions to keep fires going in their homes, but it couldn't prevent the numerous deaths from exposure. Conditions on the battlefield were a thousand times worse. It was a miracle any of the soldiers had survived. Injuries of shell fragments, shattered bones, and bullet holes had turned to frostbite and hypothermia.

"*Non!*" The shriek carried down the empty street. Three doors ahead, a woman stood in the entrance shouting in French at a person standing on her front steps.

The person, draped in a long shawl that covered their head, took a step back and held up their hands as if pleading. A woman by the slender shape and fringe of her covering.

"*Non!*" The Frenchwoman grabbed a bottle from behind her and raised it as if preparing to hurl it.

The shawl woman stumbled to the footpath, blocking her face and head with her arms. With a vicious screech, the Frenchwoman lobbed the bottle into the street, then turned and slammed the door behind her. Glass shattered. The panicked woman turned away but caught her foot on the edge of her shawl, tripping her into the street and the broken glass. As she cried out in pain, her hood toppled back to reveal a sheen of silver hair and face that could have been carved from exquisite ice. Yanking the covering back in place, the woman stumbled to her feet and lurched forward.

"Miss!" Wynn hurried toward her. "You're hurt. Let me help you."

Clutching her shawl, the woman hobbled across the street and slipped between the gates to the Parc Monceau. Wynn raced after her. She was quick, darting among the trees and their shadows until breaking through the tall black gate on the opposite side. By the time he reached the gate, she had vanished across the five-point intersection of Rue de Courcelles and Avenue Hoche. Commonly filled with the clatter of carriages and carts and pedestrians, it lay empty in the hours after curfew.

How could an injured woman move that fast? The injury was most likely bleeding. He scanned the ground. Drops of blood leading down Avenue Hoche. Feeling all too much like a hound, he followed the wet trail until it turned down an alleyway. The tall, surrounding build-ings closed around him as he slipped down the narrow passage and emerged into a small courtyard behind a squat building with conical roofs topped by gold balls and crosses. A church. A Russian Orthodox church, to be exact. He'd never been in this neighborhood before.

The woman crept from a dark corner of the courtyard. Her limp had worsened and she was breathing hard. She needed medical attention.

A siren exploded in the distance. Hospital alarm. Wounded con-veys incoming, which meant all hands to the operating theater.

There were other doctors. Wynn wasn't needed despite the urging in his veins. He stepped into the courtyard and collided into a set of rubbish bins. The metal lids clattered to the stone ground.

The woman dashed across the courtyard and yanked at a cellar door at the back of the church.

"Wait!" Wynn called.

The woman rushed inside and slammed the door behind her. The sound of a rusty lock clicked in place.

The siren sounded again. He could ignore it no longer. With one last frustrating glance to the door, Wynn took off running back to hospital.

The operating theater bustled with activity until the wee hours of the morning. Soldiers from the offense exploding around Reims. Sometime around five, after his last patient was carried off to a recovery room, Wynn dozed off in a corner chair only to be awakened by the gentle shaking of a nurse.

"Doctor, there's no need for you to remain. Please go home and rest."

A flock of Voluntary Aid Detachment nurses had descended to clean and tidy the once grand dining room that was now filled with operating tables, surgical tools, and apparatuses imperative to his work. Only a bin filled with filthy and bloody bandages served as proof to the night's frantic endeavors.

Wynn came awake in an instant. A habit forged in occupational necessity. "I'll check on my patients first. There was one head case—"

"Doctor Byeford is doing a round and has promised to alert you if there is a need. Shoo, Doctor."

"Aye-aye, Sister." Pushing to his feet, he gave her a mock salute. One never argued with the Sisters. The medical staff would be hopeless without them.

After discarding his surgical apron, mask, and gloves and a good scrubbing of the hands, Wynn made for the front door with his bed calling to him. This time he might actually make it.

"We don't take your kind here. Find the All Saint's Chapel. They're taking on cases likes yours." A baby-faced lieutenant straight out of medical school blocked the front steps to what appeared to be two women wrapped in colorful shawls despite the summer air.

"Please. She cannot make it so far," said the taller one. Russian. And highly cultured from the sound of it.

"I'm sure you've a mystic in your traveling caravan to chant over your troubles. What was that chap's name? Rasputin? I hear he took real good care of your Imperial family. Especially the tsarina."

"You know nothing of which you speak, impudent *slovach*." The woman's tone was brittle as an icicle.

Wynn stepped forward before the lieutenant could further prove his worthlessness. "May I be of assistance?"

The little man whipped around and paled. "Doctor MacCallan. I was telling these people that their needs will be better assisted at the refugee chapel in Paris. Where their kind are."

"That's over eight kilometers from here."

"Yes, sir, but they can't—"

Wynn sidestepped his blethering. "What needs have you, ladies?" Any further words stuck in Wynn's throat as the woman turned to face him. The early gray morning light sculpted her like white marble just as she had appeared a few hours before, falling in the street. In a word, breathtaking. "You!"

"I beg pardon?" She didn't recognize him. Her ice blue gaze held him with a haughtiness that bespoke a life of bowing down to no one. Tall and slender, she held herself like an aristocrat.

He wanted nothing more than to get to the bottom of her midnight escapade, but not standing on the front steps for all of France to see. He dragged his attention to the other woman with a face full of wrinkles and a wrapped hand cradled to her bosom. The one in need of medical attention. "Come inside. Please."

The lieutenant moved to block the steps. "But, sir—"

Wynn pinned him with a superior look of disgust. He hated throwing his rank around, but in this weasel's case he was willing to make an exception. "You may resume your duties. Bed pans, was it?"

Scowling, the lieutenant scurried off. Wynn stood aside and swept his arm toward the hospital entrance. "Ladies. After you."

Anchoring her arm around the older woman, the younger lady

guided her up the remaining steps and glided into the hospital. Or glided as best she could while favoring her right leg.

The Voluntary Aid Detachment nurse, or VAD, glanced up from reception. A welcoming smile on her young face. "Back so soon, Doctor?"

"Can't keep me away. I'll be in my office for examination."

"Yes, sir."

Under ordinary circumstances Wynn would never allow a patient into the private sanctum of the medical staff, but every available room was stuffed to the brim with wounded Tommies. Plus, there was one other rather alarming reason he didn't wish to open his work quarters. At least not to ladies.

Wynn swung open the door and winced. Shoved together in the center of the room were two desks, littered with clamps, linens, and glass bottles of carbolic lotion and disinfectant. Maps of France, battlefields, and train depots were tacked to the walls, and an overflow of charts were stacked on the desks. The results of doctors being too busy binding up patients to hassle with paperwork.

"Excuse the mess. This is what happens when you throw in two bachelors and hope for the best."

The young woman's gaze scanned around the room before cutting to him and revealing a razor-sharp intellect. "Are you a doctor?"

"Hope so. Otherwise I'm going to be in trouble when they find me in here." Her expression didn't crack. *Tough crowd.* Shuffling the papers off his chair and abandoning them to the abyss of Gerard's desk, Wynn pulled out a chair and indicated for the old woman to sit.

She shuffled forward and plopped down, clinging to her injured hand. Wynn gave her a quick assessment: ashy skin, cracked lips, dry eyes, onset of arthritis. Frizzy gray hair receding under a black shawl tied under a sagging chin. Worn but sturdy clothes. Cracked boots and hunched back. Diagnosis? Accustomed to hard work and plain food. A meager lifestyle, but not poor. Until now.

Kneeling, he took her hand and gently unwrapped the cloth to reveal a cut forefinger and thumb. Bright red blood trickled from the cuts as air hit the skin. He quickly rewrapped it. "Squeeze to keep pressure on it." Rummaging through the supplies, he scrounged up fresh gauze, linen strips, lysol swabs, and ointment and set them on the desk next to her. "How did you cut yourself?"

Neither woman said a word.

Wynn reached for the stained cloth around the old woman's hand. She slapped him away and pointed at the younger woman, speaking in fervent Russian. The younger woman shook her head, seeming to argue as she tried to draw attention back to the old woman's hand. Exasperated, the old woman yanked at the young woman's skirt. It was then that Wynn noticed the tear and the stain of blood.

The injury from when she fell before running away from him. An injury she was now trying to hide in favor of her elder companion's wound. Admirable, but pride had no function in the medical ward.

"I'd like to exam your leg," Wynn said.

"See to her first."

"Miss, you're bleeding and limping, which is a more serious case. Your companion is well enough for now."

Those ice blue eyes cut into him, assessing his capability of determining such a conclusion no doubt. Only with a tug from the old woman did she acquiesce and take a seat in the chair Wynn pulled out from Gerard's desk.

Though dressed simply in blue and gray, her clothes were of a fine quality despite the hole torn over her shin. Ladies were not often found begging in the streets. If she wanted to maintain a sense of mystery, she had perfected the art.

Attend to her medical issue. He was a doctor first, for crying out loud. "Will you lift your skirt, please?"

Lips pursed in distaste at his choice of words—he hated saying them himself—she lifted the hem of her skirt to just below her knee.

Thin, cotton stockings covered her shapely legs, but one had been rolled down to expose a piece of glass embedded in the shin. A thick, green paste had been applied to the area, but bright red dots of blood trickled down her leg. The fragment had most likely loosened during her walk to hospital.

"You're in luck," he said. "We won't need to amputate after all."

She gasped. "It is not so bad."

"No, it's not."

"You are funny."

"Thank you."

"I did not mean it as a compliment."

"Well, that's put me in my place." Moving to the stack of supplies, Wynn found an extraction kit complete with forceps, iodine, gauze, linen, and suturing needle. He'd used these on shrapnel patients more times than he cared to count. This would be the first on a woman.

"How did you come by the injury?" He was fairly certain he knew the answer, but how far to prod? Forthcoming with information the woman was not.

Panic flashed across her face. She quickly smoothed it over. "I fell."

"On a bottle?"

"There are many things on the ground that should not be there and I tripped."

Clearly she didn't want to confess the true origin of her injury. He would respect her desire for privacy. For now. Rubbing his hands with a few drops of iodine, Wynn quickly laid out his tools in order of necessity, then patted the top of his desk.

"Apologies for not having a proper examination table, but this will have to do."

Maneuvering gracefully to sit atop the desk, she then straightened out her legs with toes pointed and back straight as a board. Impeccable posture considering the pain she must be in.

Using the forceps, Wynn dipped a pad of gauze into the iodine.

"This will sting a wee bit." He swabbed the area around the wound. She didn't flinch. Good. That was the easy part. "Now, with your right forefinger and thumb I want you to pinch the skin between said fingers on your opposite hand. Pinch as hard as you dare."

"This will help my leg how?"

"It's part of the procedure. Trust me." It had nothing whatsoever to do with the procedure but gave patients a task to occupy them for the seconds he needed to extract the foreign object. No one had ever questioned him before. Taking a firm grip on the forceps, Wynn pinched the glass and tugged. It moved slightly. The woman made a slight noise in her throat. "Are you squeezing?"

"Yes." Her voice was tight. He knew how painful it must be, brave girl.

Steadying himself for the required exertion, Wynn gave a mighty yank. The glass pulled free. Bright red blood spilled out. He wiped the area clean as best he could, then made a neat row of quick sutures before dabbing on more iodine and wrapping a clean bandage around her leg. He pulled her skirt down for modesty and stepped back.

"All done."

The woman's white fingers were latched around the edges of his desk, her mouth a colorless slash across her pale face.

Wynn gently touched her shoulder. "You can breathe now."

She took a deep breath, breaking free from the protective shell of silence the wounded often enclosed themselves within to endure a procedure. "Thank you."

"Care for the souvenir?" Wynn pointed at the jagged bit of bottle. Dirty piece of work that. The Frenchwoman who threw it ought to be forced to crawl over the fragments herself.

"It is common to keep an object of such torment?"

"Many of the soldiers do with their shrapnel and bullets. I wrap the items in a strip of cloth and tie it around the patient's arm after surgery. It's a badge of honor that they like to show the folks back home."

"It is not a reminder I need." Smoothing her skirts, she eased off the desk in one fluid movement.

Wynn turned to his other patient with an encouraging smile. "Now, madam, it's your turn." Kneeling, he quickly unwrapped the older woman's hand. The bleeding had stopped to reveal clean but deep cuts. The kind only slivered glass or metal could inflict. "How did she receive this?"

The young woman hesitated. "She tried to remove the glass from my leg. In Russia she is considered a great healer."

"It was you who concocted that green paste." Wynn held up the linen he'd used to clean away the mixture. The old woman nodded in a knowing manner and replied in Russian.

"A mash of yarrow mixed with comfrey water," the young woman translated.

"Good work," Wynn said.

The young woman translated softly in Russian, each word brightening the old woman's face. She seemed to ask a question in return.

The young woman nodded. "*Da, babushka.*"

Grinning to reveal a missing tooth, the old woman patted Wynn's cheek with her free hand. Dabbing more iodine onto a clean swatch of gauze, he cleaned her cuts. A hiss of air escaped her cracked lips.

A thick braid of pale blond slipped over the young woman's shoulder as she bent close to the old woman's ear. "*Uspokoysya, babushka.*"

Wynn nodded in encouragement. "You're doing fine, Mrs. Babushka."

The young woman's eyebrows drew together. "Why do you call her this?"

"Is that not her name?"

"*Babushka* is Russian for 'grandmother.'"

"Oh. Forgive me. I meant no disrespect."

"It is very respectful to call older generations this in recognition of their wisdom."

"What a relief. My own grandmother would've skelped me if I

dared to call her something so informal in public. A great protector of propriety, she was."

The old woman looked up at the younger lady and asked something. Nodding, the younger lady spoke quickly, gesturing to Wynn a few times. As she finished translating, the old woman's face crackled into a smile.

She patted Wynn's cheek. "*Golubchik.*"

"Mrs. Varjensky says you are sweet."

Wynn bowed over the injured hand still in his grasp. "A pleasure, Mrs. Varjensky. I'm Edwynn MacCallan, but I prefer Wynn."

"*Golubchik.*" Mrs. Varjensky patted his cheek again, then indicated the younger woman. "*Yeyo Spokoystviye Printsessa* Svetlana Dmitrievna Dalsky."

Did she say princess?

The young woman blanched and placed a hand on Mrs. Varjensky's shoulder. "Svetlana Dalsky. Please."

Brow wrinkling, Mrs. Varjensky rattled off a string of Russian, which Svetlana's response quickly combated.

Taking it as a conversation on the forgoing of noble titles that he wasn't intended to hear, Wynn grabbed a bandage and quickly wrapped Mrs. Varjensky's hand.

"It may take a few days to heal, but if the pain worsens you and your grandmother—"

"She is not my grandmother," Svetlana said.

"No? I thought . . . Well, that's me with both feet in my mouth now."

She glanced down at his feet. "What does this mean with feet still on the ground? They are too large and unsanitary for such a task."

"It's an expression. Means I don't know when to keep my mouth shut."

"We are speaking. Why would you wish to remain silent?"

"I don't translate into Russian very well, do I?" Wynn laughed and set about tidying the used supplies before Gerard could come in and question the impromptu surgery. "It means I say the wrong thing sometimes. Not usually on purpose. Don't tell me you've never slipped and said something you shouldn't."

"No."

"Never?"

"I have been trained out of the habit." Taking Mrs. Varjensky's arm, she helped the old woman to her feet. "How much do we owe you?"

Wynn waved his hand. "On the house." At Svetlana's confused look around the room, he clarified. "We don't charge for patients in need at wartime."

"*Spasibo*. Thank you."

"*Spasibo, golubchik*," repeated Mrs. Varjensky with another pat to Wynn's cheek.

Wynn followed them out into the grand lobby turned waiting room. The smell of eggs and bacon drifted from the industrial-size kitchen as breakfast was readied for the patients.

With the immediate distraction of wounds and blood taken care of, Wynn's curiosity about the previous night swung back at full force. "Allow me to escort you. I would call for a carriage or one of those new motorcars, but most of them have been commandeered to support the frontlines."

Svetlana pulled her colorful shawl over her head. "That is not necessary. We can find our way on foot."

"You may be able to find your way, but I'd rather not find you tottered off into a gutter come morning. Doctor's orders." That and he had no intention of allowing two injured women to wander down the road alone. Paris was far enough from the frontline, but that didn't make the streets safe.

"If you insist." Without waiting, Svetlana took Mrs. Varjensky's arm and left the building, leaving Wynn to follow in their wake.

As he hurried to take the older woman's other arm, she winked up at him and hobbled around to the other side of Svetlana, leaving him to walk next to the princess in hiding. Seemed no matter the culture all grandmothers and *babushkas* maneuvered the same way. Not that he minded walking next to a beautiful woman. He just preferred one who spoke to him without frowning.

The sun peaked over the blue and gray slate roofs of buildings, dusting the world with brilliant orange light that reflected off the hundreds of windows lining the sandstone facades, rousing the sleeping inhabitants within from slumber. Paris was a city of life, but here in the quiet one could take a deep breath before the bustle seized it away. His favorite time of day.

"How long have you been in France?" he asked.

"Six months."

"Traveling in the middle of winter. That must have been difficult. I hear Russian winters are brutal."

"Yes." With each limping step her mouth pressed tighter and tighter. Wynn reached for her arm. "Lean against my arm. It'll take the pressure off your leg."

She pulled away. "I can manage alone."

She could manage her stubbornness sure enough. If the pain grew to be too much, he'd have to carry her. He could imagine the protests at that prospect.

"Did you travel alone?"

"No."

"With family?"

"Yes."

Like trying to crack a wall of ice with his bare hands. Wynn changed tactics as they bypassed Parc Monceau and with it the memories of last evening's chase through the foliage.

"My brother and I used to travel all the time together. Growing up in Scotland, it's easy to lose your way for a day or two. Of course, we were never lost. We knew every tree and rock by heart on MacCallan land. Got into all sorts of trouble." Sadness pricked at the bygone days of carefree youth. "That was back before the war."

A cat scampered by, its ribs poking against its skin. Not one element of life had been spared the hunger of war. It stared at them a moment with ancient eyes, then with a flick of its mangy tail, disappeared down an alleyway.

Svetlana dared a glance at him. "You have been in France long?"

"Ever since the war broke out. I had just finished my second year at Edinburgh Hospital. My brother was the first to sign up, but I felt I was of better use remaining a civilian. Most of my days are spent here at hospital. No military red tape to bother with there. I've been swabbing the mud ever since."

"Your brother is here?"

Wynn turned them off the boulevard and onto Rue Daru, into the neighborhood he was unfamiliar with. And for good reason. In the clear light of day he noted the signs over the doors were written in Cyrillic. Men in thick leather boots and long tunics smoked cigarettes in doorways as hunched old women in faded black scarfs ambled along with baskets tucked over their arms. Russians. A few blocks more and they'd be in front of the mystery church that Svetlana had conveniently found a back door to.

"Hugh's commanding a battalion somewhere near Verdun. Haven't seen him in over two years, but we promised to meet up right here the day peace is called."

"A strange place to meet."

Wynn thought of their family's townhouse located in the fashionable 8th Arrondissement and all the times they had spent summer holiday there wandering the Jardin des Tuileries and listening to concerts at the Petit Palais. He and Hugh would always sneak off to search for treasure buried by Napoleon rather than listen to another woodwind quartet.

"You could say it has sentimental value to us."

"Sentiments are not always practical."

"True, but the world grows tedious and life hopeless without them."

"You may keep your hope. I know better." Her voice held a thousand lives of bitterness, too many for one so young.

At last the church rose into view among the gray and beige sandstone structures, the rising sun glancing off its onion domes in shots of orange and gold. Svetlana stopped cold.

"Where are you leading us?"

She couldn't outrun him now. "This is where you're going, isn't it?"

CHAPTER 2

Panic rang in Svetlana's ears, drowning out the pain in her leg. She willed her expression to remain impenetrable as she stared at Alexander Nevsky Cathedral with its golden cupolas shining in the brilliant and indomitable morning sun. How did he know? They'd been so careful to hide here.

"You are mistaken. I do not know this place."

"Not at all? Mayhap it looks different in daylight."

She never should have allowed this man to walk with them. "I have no interest in a church."

"Not even for moonlight strolls?" He leaned closer, the scent of lye soap and cotton heavy on him. "After having a bottle hurled at you by an obnoxious Frenchwoman. A cheap bottle of red wine, I might add."

With that her mask crashed to the ground. "You are the man."

Last night rushed back in hideous remembrance. Desperate, she'd gone to seek new sanctuary for her family as their presence grew tedious to the other Russian émigrés taking refuge in the church cellar. Mama's presence in particular. She complained to all that the conditions were unacceptable for a noblewoman. That horrible Frenchwoman didn't even allow Svetlana time to offer the diamond brooch in exchange for renting a room before the bottle came at her head. Memories of fleeing Petrograd and all the shouting voices had come flooding back.

Then a voice had called out from the dark. His voice. And she'd fled. "Will you report me for remaining out after curfew?"

"No. I only wanted to make sure you were all right. That was a nasty fall."

She waited for the trick. Her family had existed within the false sense of safety for months as they escaped the madness choking Russia behind them, but always ready for the trap to spring. Their troubles would not allow them to leave so easily. This doctor may not wear a red armband, but it did not sanctify him from a new sort of traitor that would drag them back to a Petrograd firing squad. And yet she found nothing treasonous in his eyes. Only kindness and, dare she imagine, understanding.

Nothing seemed to slip by him. She'd felt his quiet assessment at the hospital, not in a manner calculating profit and risk. More in a way that peered past the apparent to find the heart of the matter hidden beneath the veneer. He did it again now with that golden-green gaze—colors that reminded her of an autumn sun setting over the Crimean Mountains.

It would be insulting to both of their intelligence to continue the farce.

"Very well."

Skirting around the main entrance, meant only for believers to enter the holy place, Svetlana circled around to the back of the church where her kind entered through the cellar. The heavy door groaned under protest as she opened it. A draft of cool stone, mold, and compacted bodies drifted up, evoking a loathing visceral enough to make her spit. Here they lived like rats.

With an agility belying her age, Mrs. Varjensky waddled down the creaky steps and disappeared into the dimness. Svetlana counted the steps with hesitation as the pain in her leg throbbed. She'd danced *en pointe* with a broken toe before. She could manage this. Taking the first step, her injured leg buckled. She grabbed for the handrail. A strong arm anchored around her waist before her fingertips brushed the wood.

Embarrassed at her loss of composure, she stiffened and pulled away. "Thank you."

"All in a day's work. Women are always falling for me. I'm quite charming that way." Wynn grinned to reveal a full show of white teeth.

Svetlana hesitated, considering the meaning of this Englishman's strangely phrased words. "You are funny again."

He winced. "Only to myself it seems. Again."

"You are easily amused."

"And you are not."

"Nothing is amusing in Russia. Not anymore." She limped down the remaining steps, hating the sudden weakness in her trained body. His hand never left the small of her back. By the time she reached the floor, a sheen of sweat dotted her brow and fires of pain danced up her leg. How would she ever perform on stage again if a flight of stairs defeated her?

She pulled away from the doctor's touch and straightened herself. "Say nothing. They are wary of strangers."

His brow furrowed. "Who are they?"

With the unavoidable at hand, Svetlana guided him through another door and into the cellar proper stuffed to the brim with Russian émigrés. It was a small space no bigger than her family's dining room back in their Petrograd home, the Blue Palace. A narrow path wound through the maze of blankets and luggage spread across the cold stone floor. Clothes cleaned as best they could from the two wash buckets were strung over rope anchored from wall to wall. Children dressed in the worn peasant clothing of the countryside huddled close to their mothers and fathers, their Russian dialects spread as wide as the plains to the Altai Mountains. The Reds had covered much ground in displacing their people.

Conversations hushed and questioning glances followed as she guided Wynn through the confusion to the back rows where crass voices melted into elegant French, the language of Russia's upper class. Here blankets had been hung as dividers for privileged privacy. Narrow windows cut high in the back wall beckoned in a timid light that barely scratched the peasant rows. The blanket wall in the back corner rustled and out rushed her mother and sister with identical expressions of concern.

"Svetka! Here you are at last. What has happened to take so long?" Her mother stumbled to a halt at the sight of Wynn, as he'd so informally introduced himself back at the hospital. "Who is this man?"

While her mother spoke in their customary French, Svetlana kept to English for the courtesy of their guest. "Allow me to present Doctor MacCallan of the English hospital here in Paris." Drawing her shawl close to hide the exerted beating of her heart from the painful walk, she gestured to her mother. "My mother, Ana Dalsky, and my sister, Marina."

Mama's mouth twisted in her way of displeasure. "Her Serenity the Princess Ana Andreevna Dalsky." She held out her hand to be kissed as if they were standing once more in St. George's Hall in the Winter Palace.

"Mama! We cannot be so blatant about our titles in this unfamiliar place," Svetlana said in French. It was rude to cut their guest so obviously from the conversation, but it was safer to trust no one, hunted as they were simply for being nobility. The old life was gone and clinging to it—as desperately as she wanted to—was a death sentence, in soul and body. Mama could never make things easier when it went against her will.

"This man is of little consequence and absorbed in a war little to do with our situation. I will not lessen myself, nor should you." Mama waggled her waiting fingers, once glittering with rings but now bare, the rings having been sold for scraps of food on their escape.

With only the slightest show of surprise, Wynn bent over Mama's fingers as any gentleman of standing was required. "A pleasure, Your Serenity."

Other nobles of ranking—counts, barons, and countesses—peeked around the corners of their blanket walls. Scowls creasing their wane faces, they whispered to one another as Mama smiled in triumph. Once upon a time a visiting physician was nothing to draw jealousy, but here, to host a visitor of any kind was an occasion harkening back to the privileges they all once possessed and grappled to grasp once again.

"Won't you come in?" With a change back to English, Mama swept into their chamber that was little more than three dividing blankets and a stone wall.

"I'll see Mrs. Varjensky settled first. She needs to rest." Smiling in that English manner of politeness, he retraced their steps, seeming not the least bit affected by the stares and scowls.

Mama rounded on Svetlana as soon as she hobbled into their cordoned-off space. "Have you taken complete leave of your senses? That man does not belong here."

Svetlana kept her voice low. "Then why did you receive him so happily?"

"I may have lost my home, my clothes, and my jewels, but I have not forgotten the simple manners of receiving a visitor no matter how unexpected or unwelcome he is. Good breeding would not allow me to. Good breeding should have taught you not to go to such a hospital and drag back the help."

Marina helped Svetlana to a bundle of scratchy blankets serving as their shared sleeping pallet. "Mama, Svetka was injured. She had no choice but to go." A younger version of their mother with dark blond hair and a petite frame that was quickly filling out with her fourteen years, Marina was always the one to seek peace.

"She had a choice not to bring him here. He'll report us. We'll be cast out and then where will we go?" Clutching the gold cross dangling from her neck, Mama draped herself across the pallet and turned her face away with a soft sob.

Ignoring the theatrics, Marina knelt next to Svetlana and took her hands. New callouses had developed on her tender palms from carrying in buckets of water each morning. A task once suited to a servant, but Marina never complained.

"Are you all right?"

Svetlana stretched out her leg, flexing and curling her toes. One by one the cramps eased from the tightened muscles. "Yes. He pulled the piece from my knee and bandaged it before dressing Mrs. Varjensky's hand."

"Do you think we're in trouble for staying here? Will he tell the authorities who we are? I tire of running."

Svetlana smoothed the hair from her sister's thinning face. Their once impeccably tailored clothes were fitting a bit looser these days. She tried to keep her family fed as best she could, but food was scarce all over Paris. Not to mention shelter. Pain cut into her leg, scuttling guilt across her conscience. If her family were safe enough in this refuge cellar, she never would have gone off last night, and none of the transpiring events would have happened. That insistent man could have stayed at his hospital sharpening scalpels and not be here intruding on their peace of mind.

None of this could she tell Mama or Marina and so she summed a serene smile. "There is nothing to worry yourself about, *kotyonok*. We are safe."

"I wish Papa and Nicky were here."

"They will join us soon enough or send for us when they've defeated the revolutionaries. In the meantime we will make ourselves as discrete as possible." Svetlana stretched out her other leg, easing the strain from having to put all her weight on one side. She had not been in this amount of pain since she twisted her ankle on a difficult *jeté* landing during rehearsal for *La Sylphide*. It was the first summer she had danced before the tsar and the tsarina. The White Nights of Russia's summer had cast a golden glow across the stage as dozens of gossamer ballerina wings flapped in rhythm. If she could have but one more carefree summer such as that— She pushed the longing away. There was no point in dwelling on impossibilities when survival demanded her every minute.

"The Reds will not find us here. Not this far from Russia, will they?" Fear quaked in Marina's eyes. Terror of the Reds was a fear they had never known until a year ago when the revolutions began. They had come to live with the anxiety ever since. God willing, the White Army would win back the throne for the tsar and they could all return home.

"Papa and Nicky will not allow them. You'll see."

"Hello? May I come in?" Wynn stood on the other side of the blanket serving as their door.

Like a spring, Mama bounced up from her prostrate position dry eyed and pink cheeked. She scooted to the edge of the pallet and arranged her skirts into regal folds before clasping her hands in her lap. "Enter."

Wynn took a single, polite step into the chamber, but it was enough to take up all remaining space. He was tall, taller than Papa, who was considered the tallest of the tsar's guards, and could easily brush the ceiling if he were to push to his toes. A thick, broad chest that foretold of well-shaped muscles beneath his clothes. Unlike most lanky physicians she'd seen before. His hair that had appeared a dark blond in the morning light now shone light brown; the long locks on top were parted to the side and cut much shorter around his ears.

He was a man at ease with himself and the world and his place in it. Would Svetlana ever feel that way again or would the revolutionaries strip away that hope as well?

"Doctor, how might we thank you for your services?" Mama

reached for her handbag, which contained a few coins they'd managed to trade an heirloom brooch for upon arriving in France.

Wynn held up his hand. "As I told your daughter, there is no charge in wartime."

For the first time, Mama dared to relax her face into what others might be fooled into considering as a friendly look. "Are all physicians as noble as you?"

"I wouldn't call it noble, ma'am, but we do what we can for those in need."

Mama glanced away and touched the bottom slanted bar of her Orthodox cross. "How these times make us all suffer. Some more than others."

"You're right about that, but you'll never hear those Tommies complaining. I think they're all out for the medal of suffering in silence."

Mama's lips pursed at his not taking her pitying bait. "Yes, well, we have seen a great deal of suffering on our travel here."

"Do you plan to remain in Paris or travel on to a final destination?"

"Any final destination for a Russian is in Russia, though the circumstances do not allow for it at present. Here we shall stay with nothing but our dignity until such a time as we may return."

"I believe we all feel that way about going home." The easy light in his eyes flickered.

It was the slightest break in an illusion of well-being that Svetlana felt all too keenly. She didn't want to believe that of him. Couldn't allow herself to believe it. No one was to be trusted. Not even kind doctors who pulled glass from her leg.

Svetlana shifted on the hard floor. "Is Mrs. Varjensky comfortable?"

Wynn nodded, looking once more the confident doctor. "She's resting now, as you should be doing. Keep your leg elevated and only put weight on it if you must. A bit of valerian root or white willow bark in scandal water should help relieve any pain for the both of you. Tomorrow I'll try to get you proper medicines."

"What is this scandalous water?"

"Tea. Because ladies often use it as social lubricant for gossip."

Svetlana's gaze dropped to the wrapped package in his hand. "What do you have there?"

"Pastry of some sort." Unwrapping the muslin, he held up a ring of baked dough with cheese in the center. "Mrs. Varjensky insisted."

"*Vatrushka*."

"*Vatrushka*." His pronunciation was terrible, but it didn't keep him from grinning. A habit he so easily allowed. "Breakfast. Now, if you'll excuse me, it's been a long night and my next round of duties begins in eight hours. I'll bring the medicines after my shift."

The panic from earlier came swooping back. They didn't need him returning and drawing attention. "We can make do without and will trouble you no further."

"As my patient it's your prerogative to trouble me. Let's me know I'm still needed."

"But the soldiers—"

"I should warn you now that I've perfected the art of ignoring patients' gallant notions of martyrdom. Part of a physician's training." He sketched a short bow and backed out of the chamber. "Ladies, I bid you all a pleasant morning and remainder of the day."

Svetlana struggled to her feet in a last desperate attempt. Her leg cramped in protest. "Marina can collect the medicine instead of you coming so far to deliver it."

Wynn stuck his head back in and cocked an eyebrow at her. "You're going to be a difficult one, aren't you? Rest." With a quick flash of his eye, he disappeared.

Mama gasped. "That man winked at you."

"No, a mere twitch," Svetlana said. It was very much a wink, but admitting so brought no favors.

"He could be dangerous."

"As dangerous as using titles in front of him?"

Huffing, Mama surged to her dainty feet. The fraying hem of her once fashionable skirt swished around her ankles. "Whatever he is, he's proven the English have nothing of court protocol. Mrs. Dalsky. As if I would answer to such a commoner's name. Blessed be he's a simple physician and not expected to circulate within higher society."

"I think he's nice," Marina said, patting Svetlana's hand. "He took care of you. And Mrs. Varjensky."

He did. When no one else would.

Mama sniffed and pulled at a loose thread from her shawl. "Hmph. Another commoner. I don't know why you insisted on bringing her."

"Her sons were killed in the February Revolution last year and her husband died while they were escaping from the Bolsheviks," Svetlana said, ignoring the sting that came with her mother's criticism of her judgment. It came more often than not at Svetlana's expense. "She has no one left. We couldn't leave her in that miserable church with people crawling on top of one another."

While making their way through Belgium they had heard of a church on the outskirts of Paris that was taking in White émigrés, but upon arrival there had only been space enough in the basement for them to sit back to back in hopes of sleeping. Mama had demanded—loudly—that serene princesses of relation to the tsar himself deserved an entire corner to themselves. It hadn't taken long for threats to come. Svetlana had sneaked out her family and Mrs. Varjensky in the middle of the night and led them into the city only to find themselves beneath the floor of another church.

"How is your leg?" Mama's expression softened, but the sunlight streaming through the window was not kind to the lines on her face. Her skin was soft and smooth as a young girl's in Petrograd, but the passing months had left their wearisome marks.

"It will heal."

"God give you strength. Rest now."

Svetlana took Marina's offered hand and lowered herself once more to the pallet. Marina folded her shawl and propped it under Svetlana's ankle. "I'll see if I can find something to make the tea for you and Mrs. Varjensky. Try to close your eyes."

Every fiber in Svetlana's body cried out for rest the way it did after a long day of dancing. But unlike the familiarity of a ballet barre to push her onward, nothing of comfort was to be found here. Nothing but unrest and danger. They could stay no longer.

CHAPTER 3

Svetlana Dmitrievna Dalsky. Princess. A Russian princess. Princess Svetlana of the silver hair and arctic eyes who didn't smile. Svetlana of the too many names who wanted no one to find her.

But Wynn had found her and she'd been a constant on his mind ever since.

"Wake up, Your Excellency. You're in a daze." Gerard ribbed him.

Wynn blinked. Drying soap suds covered his hands. "Sorry. Mind elsewhere." He quickly rinsed off the lather and dried his hands with a fresh cloth. The sounds of cleanup from the surgery thumped in the room next door.

"Let me guess. Somewhere far north of here with the strains of a balalaika playing in the background." At Wynn's frown, Gerard rolled his eyes and stuck his hands under the steaming stream of water. "If you're to woo a lady of Russian origins, you might as well start learning her culture. Women appreciate that sort of attention to detail. I'll lend you my copy of Pushkin."

"I see the rumor mill is already churning."

"How can it not? I hear the lady puts a glittering diamond to shame."

"Was it also mentioned that said lady had a large glass fragment embedded in her tibialis anterior muscle?" Wynn tossed a clean towel directly at his mate's head. Or that she'd had the strength of a soldier not to cry out in pain when he'd yanked said glass from her leg?

The towel knocked Gerard's glasses sideways. "Ah, so that's why you walked her home. Going to see her again?" Adjusting the wire frames, his large eyes blinked behind the glass.

"I'm taking medicine to her and the other patient who came in with her."

"Good play. Always need a reason to make a second impression. Or so I've been told. Never gotten a chance to make one myself."

"The fact that I'm treating them for wounds makes no never mind."

"Of course, that too." Gerard tossed his towel in the bin with the other used ones and followed Wynn out of the washroom and into the carpeted hall where nurses bustled with supply trollies. "Is she staying nearby?"

Wynn stopped himself from nodding. Svetlana had taken great pains to hide her family, to the point of foregoing their titles, and had been terrified at his discovery. Whatever hunted them, they were safe enough at the church. Yet he had no desire to usher in needless fear by giving them away.

"Near enough. Seems to be quite a few of her countrymen on the run."

"Who can blame them? The people are revolting, and their tsar abdicated to a mob who is keeping him and his family locked in a palace like prisoners. The whole country is in turmoil. I hope they set it right again and soon before Germany takes advantage of the chaos. The Allies need stabilizing in this war."

They rounded the corner to the administrative hall. Hotel staff once operated within these small offices that were now overrun with dead-on-their-feet medical staff. Wynn opened the door to their designated office, switched on the light, and immediately regretted it. Ignoring the mounds of paperwork was easier in the dark.

"Speaking of stable, that first lieutenant who was brought in from machine-gun wounds has a heart stutter," Wynn said.

"He took six bullets to the chest. I'd be surprised if he didn't."

"I don't feel right about it."

"I doubt he does either." Walking around his desk, Gerard slumped into his chair. "Look, I know what you're thinking, but you need to keep your head down about this cardiac development. The surgeons around here aren't keen on these newfangled ideas."

Wynn scoffed as he did anytime those white-haired naysayers halted progress for the sake of tradition. "Just because we don't completely understand cardiology doesn't invalidate its imperative need. We as doctors should not fear it. If anything, we should work harder to refine a procedure that doesn't involve stopping a patient's heart. Permanently."

"You want to take that risk to your career? You're the best surgeon I know, Wynn, but even you have your limits." Gerard scratched his freckled hand through his red hair, sticking it up like needles in a pincushion. "Enough of the heavy. I'm off shift, but I'll see you at supper. If you can make it away from your prettier patients, that is."

Wynn grinned. "A fact I will not argue. Now go on with you."

Despite the anticipation of seeing Svetlana again, the predicament of his heart patient ate away at Wynn's peace of mind. There had to be an explanation he couldn't yet ascertain. Slipping into the white coat that signaled to one and all his doctoral status, he climbed the staircase to the third-floor post-operation recovery ward. After the Somme push two years prior, the existing walls of individual rooms had been knocked down to accommodate the influx of wounded. Privacy was at a premium and reserved for the most severe cases that needed more one-on-one attention, but here the patrol of nurses could march from one end of the corridor to the other with an attentive eye on the whole of their domain.

A nurse dressed in the pristine white apron of the Red Cross looked up from her small desk by the landing. "Good afternoon, Doctor MacCallan."

"Afternoon, Sister. I'm here to make a small round with particular interest to Lieutenant Harkin."

"He's been put halfway down the left wing next to the window."
She leaned forward and dropped her voice. "While in good spirits, he's
been complaining about a dull ache in his chest."

"Yes, that's what I'm here to see about. Thank you, Sister."

Afternoon sunlight filtered through the evenly spaced windows,
casting the ward and its lined hospital beds into a haze. Patients
swathed in all manner of bandages from head to broken toes lay sleeping or reading quietly. More than one stared blankly at the wall with
the haunted look that chased them from the trenches.

Wynn made a quick round of the more concerning cases and
found there was nothing his measly skills could do to improve upon
the nurses' tender and thorough care. Finally, he came to Harkin's bed.
Wrapped from neck to waist in bandages, the man held a letter written
in flowery script. He looked up as Wynn scanned the status clipboard
hanging from the end of his bed.

"Afternoon, Doc." Harkin's voice was rusty from the trauma
inflicted on his lungs.

"Good afternoon. How are you feeling?"

"Better than yesterday when I had more than one hole in my
bellows to breathe through." A wheezing laugh tumbled out. Harkin
grimaced and clutched his chest.

Setting down the clipboard, Wynn came around the side of the
bed and placed a steady hand on the man's shoulder. He skimmed the
bandages for pinpricks of blood. "Take it easy. We don't want those
wounds splitting open on account of humor. In this case laughter is
not the best medicine."

"Still got pains, Doc. Right here." Harkin pointed to his heart.
"Like a dull ache pressing on me."

"How often are the pains coming?"

"Steady as a second hand on a clock."

Wynn pulled out his stethoscope and placed it over Harkin's
heart. Nothing but a steady beat. Uneasiness pitted in his stomach.

He motioned over the ward matron. "Sister, send Lieutenant Harkin for an X-ray. I want to see what's going on in there."

She nodded. "I believe Major Reynolds was having a spot of trouble with it this morning. New technology is always troublesome, but he assured me it would be operational by later this afternoon, if not tomorrow morning." She made a note on her clipboard. "I'll send one of the VADs to check the status right away."

"Notify me at once with the results."

"Of course, Doctor."

Wynn gave Harkin his best reassuring smile. "We'll get this cleared up. Don't worry."

Harkin glanced down at the letter in his hand as a shadow crossed his face. "I ain't a croaker yet, am I?"

"You were mowed down by a machine gun and survived. Everything else is a walk in the park."

Or so Wynn hoped. He never lied to his patients. It promoted distrust in his sworn duties as a healer, an oath he did not take lightly, though there were times to hold back the truth. Patients often needed a glimmer of hope to cling to and if that rested in Wynn's silence, then so be it.

Signing off duty, Wynn stopped by his rented room and buttoned into a fresh shirt that didn't smell of carbolic lotion. He added a drop of *eau de cologne* that had nothing whatsoever to do with the woman he was about to visit.

Patient, he corrected. The *patient* he was about to visit.

Mayhap she would smile today. He'd never given much thought to making a woman smile. Certainly he'd endeavored to offer a pleasant evening to whichever debutante his mother cajoled him into escorting to the season's balls or theater outings, but the experiences never left a lasting impression. This woman had. Her sadness and the stubborn way she tried to overrule it tugged at him in a way he never expected. All he wished to do was relieve her of the burden.

With the challenge set before him, Wynn headed down the street to Alexander Nevsky Cathedral. Thick white clouds formed overhead, blocking out the mid-summer sky. With any luck a light rain shower would cool down the temperatures and keep the Tommies from heat exhaustion. There was nothing more embarrassing for an experienced soldier than to be brought into hospital with sunburns instead of a stray bullet.

Wynn paused at the cellar door. Smoothed his waistcoat—having foregone a jacket in the heat—and rerolled a shirtsleeve that had slipped. He chided himself for being so ludicrous. He was here as a physician. Nothing more. Before he could question the shine on his shoes, he entered.

Voices rose to meet him on the descent into the cool chamber. People milled about in states of boredom and all the variations that took on individual characters. Children running about, women folding and refolding their meager belongings, and men in heavy discussion among themselves. People caught in limbo as war raged around them. They couldn't take up arms nor could they go about the ordinary duties of hearth and home. It was a demoralizing existence of waiting while one's fate was determined elsewhere.

The whispers and stares intensified the farther he waded in. He caught snatches of one word rising with reverence above the rest: *print-sessa*. Svetlana. He'd never given much thought to titles. Nobles and peasants bled alike on the operating table, but these people had stared at her yesterday in awe. He'd witnessed a few crossing themselves— not in a devil-get-thee-behind-me way, but more as if seeing the Almighty's chosen. All of which had been wiped away the second they spotted him trailing behind.

"Good afternoon." He smiled at a little girl staring boldly at him. Her mother yanked her away. Was there something about him that Russians didn't like?

Stepping over what he assumed to be the line into aristocratic territory, disgruntled voices shifted between the blanket dividers. Svetlana, her mother, sister, and four other agitated adults stood at the far end of the last row in what could only be described as a full-blown disagreement complete with gesturing and finger-pointing. Why did they all speak French?

Unaffected as a cliff against howling winds, Svetlana stood in the center of the warring parties speaking calmly and keeping her mother from leaping forward like a pepped-up rabbit. She caught Wynn watching and hurried over. "I will be with you shortly, Doctor. Excuse us."

A hand grabbed his shoulder from behind and yanked him into a blanketed chamber littered with vials and tin pots. Mrs. Varjensky smiled up at him. "*Oy, smotrite kto prishol to. Golubchik.*" She pushed him onto a folded blanket serving as a cushion and bent over one of the pots with ladle in hand while prattling away. Spooning what smelled like an earth broth into a small wooden bowl, she pushed it into his hands and stared at him with spare eyebrows raised in expectation.

He wasn't the least bit hungry and by the looks of things the occupants of the cellar needed the nourishment more than he did, but manners were manners. He lifted the bowl to his lips and took a deep swallow. "Very good."

Mrs. Varjensky gestured for him to eat more, and he obliged. She quickly ladled in more soup.

After three more sips, Wynn put down the bowl. "It's delicious, but I'm too full to take another bite." He gestured to indicate a full belly.

Clucking, she patted his cheeks, his forehead, and his stomach, then shook her head and ladled in more. "*Kushai, golubchik.*"

"*On ne goloden.*" Svetlana stood in the doorway. Hair twisted off her neck, she was still dressed in the clothing from yesterday, but the tear in her skirt had been repaired with dainty stiches that put his own suturing to shame. Then again, material was different from skin.

Wynn scrambled to his feet. "Good afternoon."

She didn't look at him as she continued in back-and-forth Russian with Mrs. Varjensky. Wynn stood awkwardly as the conversation flowed around him without bothering to include him. Mrs. Varjensky patted his stomach again, to which Svetlana finally looked at him.

"She thinks you're too thin," she said, those pale blue eyes with the slight tilt at the outer corners taking in everything.

"That's something I've never been accused of. Handsome, funny, and charming, yes. I concede to those accusations, but never thin. My mother used to chide me for eating everything in the pantry before Cook had a chance to restock. I once ate an entire platter of game hens that were supposed to be reserved for a dinner party. Cook chased me around the kitchen for an hour with her wooden spoon."

Her expression never changed but for a slight flicker behind her eyes calculating his words. At last she clasped her hands in front of her in the tell-tale sign of a polite apology. "I am sorry we do not have meat to offer you."

So far he was losing the smile challenge. Miserably. "No, that's not what I meant. Your hospitality has been very gracious. How do you say 'thank you' in Russian?"

"*Spasibo.*"

"*Spasibo, babushka.*"

Mrs. Varjensky grinned, revealing a gold tooth in place of her left canine. "*Pozhaluysta.*"

Steering back to safer waters, Wynn emptied out his pockets. "I've brought medicine and extra bandages, as my true purpose is to check on both of you." Taking the ladle from Mrs. Varjensky before she had a chance to wield it further, Wynn directed her to the cushion.

Svetlana put out a graceful hand as if to stop him. "Doctor MacCallan. Your dedication is appreciated, but we can no longer indebt ourselves to your courtesy."

"If that's a polite way to say 'get lost,' I respectfully decline. At least until I've examined you both. If you get an infection, you'll be seeing a lot more of me whether you want to or not." He unwrapped the older woman's hand and slanted it toward the tiny window for better light. A touch of red, but not like before. Reaching into the muslin bag he'd brought, he took out a swab and dipped it in the small bottle of iodine, then blotted it across the wound. She winced but let him finish without complaint.

"Did you manage with a pain relief of tea last night?" he asked as he bandaged the hand with fresh linen.

"Yes. We found the ingredients in the church's garden. Mrs. Varjensky is very good at determining plants."

"I suspect a healer would be. You are done, my lady." Wynn patted the older woman's wrist and helped her stand before turning to Svetlana. "Your turn."

Sitting straight-backed on an overturned bucket, her head erect as if wearing a crown, Svetlana lifted her skirt as high as modesty would allow. Wynn knelt in front of her and pondered the best way to go about the examination. There was nothing for it now. Taking her foot, he propped it on his knee so that her leg was straight. She inhaled sharply but said nothing.

As a first-year medical student he couldn't cease blushing when examining a female patient, but he'd quickly grown accustomed to the professional intimacy afforded between a physician and his patient. The human body was a wondrous creation of bone, sinew, muscle, and blood that moved in a rhythm designed to perfection. A miraculous universe contained within a single entity that he gave his life to study and heal. He'd examined limbs, arteries, and tissues in all manner of construction, but never had he seen one so lovely formed as the woman sitting before him now, inducing the tiniest bit of nerves to shoot through him.

Doing his best to ignore the slender ankle and well-defined calf muscle that was anything but a professional examination, he unwrapped the bandage. A bit more red than he would've liked, but it wasn't spreading. No purulent discharge. Guilt stabbed him anew. If he hadn't called out and frightened her, she never would have been hurt. Then again, he may never have met her either.

Cleansing the area and dabbing it with iodine, he placed fresh gauze over the wound and bandaged it. "A few more days and you should be able to leave the wrap off. It's important for wounds to have fresh air, otherwise they don't heal properly." He lowered her foot to the floor.

She gracefully smoothed her skirts back into place. "How long before it is healed?"

"You'll have a scar there for the rest of your life, but I should say by the end of next week you'll be able to waltz up and down the stairs without much issue."

"That long?"

"It's not really that long. Unless you have some place to be."

"I— No."

"*Chay.*" Mrs. Varjensky announced, breaking the disgruntled spell. She traded in her ladle and held up a cracked teapot.

Shaking her head, Svetlana replied before translating to Wynn. "Tea, but we won't inconvenience you any longer. Thank you for coming."

He had been as pleasant as possible thinking her standoffishness was a cultural difference he'd yet to navigate, but mayhap her constant dismissal had more to do with him and not interpersonal courtesies.

"Is it me or visitors in general you try to kick out at the earliest opportunity?"

Her eyes widened a fraction. A sliver enough for him to see embarrassment. "You misunderstand."

It summed up the whole of their short interactions so far, but he was more than willing to get them on the right foot. Even for one simple conversation.

"*Chay.*" Mrs. Varjensky rattled an empty tin and showed him the remnants of dried leaves at the bottom. She shoved the tin into Wynn's hands before pushing him and Svetlana out of her chamber. He caught the twinkle in the old woman's eyes before she closed the blanket partition on their protests. Well, Svetlana's protests. He was doing no such thing; he was grateful to have a bit more time with her.

"Where are you going?" Her Serenity the Princess Ana stood alone in the same spot as before clutching a velvet bag to her chest. She eyed Wynn with suspicion.

"To the garden. Mrs. Varjensky wishes tea," Svetlana said.

Placated but not pleased, Ana nodded. "Tarry not. This southern sun will melt your complexion."

"Yes, Mama."

The blanket behind Ana pulled back to reveal a man with dated side chops and a pinched-face woman who stared at the bag in Ana's hands. They gestured her into the chamber and pulled taut the blanket.

"*Voleurs,*" Svetlana hissed.

Not one for languages outside of the medical Latin and the passing French he'd acquired since being in country, Wynn knew that word from traveling the overcrowded and starving streets of Paris. *Thieves.*

On edge, he stepped closer to her. "Is there something else I can be of assistance with?"

"Most of the émigrés want to find peace while others seek only advantage. Come."

Outside, a sunny haze enveloped the walled courtyard, blurring the harsh lines of stone and slate roof and filling the elm trees with golden light. They turned away from the boiling pots of laundry and soup and walked to the small garden in the far back corner hidden behind a crumbling wall. Much of the dirt patch was overgrown with tangled vines and leaves, but several rows appeared to be somewhat maintained with individual plants poking through the earth.

"The Father Superior gave us permission to use what we needed. He doubted anything of use still grew here, but Mrs. Varjensky has coaxed a few herbs from hiding in their forgotten state." Svetlana ran a hand across her puckered brow. "We picked much of the comfrey yesterday. I do not understand how we ran out."

"Mayhap she boiled a secret batch and drank it all while you slept. Ladies and their tea."

Svetlana took the few steps forward while heavily favoring her good leg. Her lips pursed into a thin line with the effort. Wynn took her hand and looped it under his arm, forcing her to lean against him as he led her to a crooked bench perched under a tree.

"Here, let me get it. You rest."

"Thank you." Smoothing her cotton skirt, she flexed and straightened her foot as a dancer might to ascertain pliability. If she was a dancer, that would explain her movements. Like water they were. "Do you know where the plant is?"

Wynn stood in the middle of the overgrown garden and did his best to tell the plants apart. He could discern the flexor carpi radialis, flexor carpi ulnaris, and palmaris longus with his eyes closed, yet the growing green stalks defied him. "Not a clue."

"I thought doctors knew all their medicines."

"From a textbook, certainly. Or ground up in tubes from the lab. It's another beast all together when foraging in the wild."

Svetlana shifted on the bench and pointed to the middle of the plot. "It is the long leaf pointed at the end. There are dead purple flowers beneath it. Do you see? Mrs. Varjensky was adamant it is this and not the plant next to it that she claimed to produce blood from the ear."

Wynn grimaced. Not a prognosis he wished to get involved with. "Stay away from that one." Picking his way to the center, he squatted next to the desirable plant and eyed the indicated fallen purple flowers. "Do you know those people your mother was speaking with?"

"Not in particular."

"Are they causing problems for your family?"

"It is of no consequence. We will not be here for long."

Two reactions pinned him simultaneously. The first, a physician's concern. "I hope you're not thinking of traveling anytime soon. Not with your injury." The other, something far more human responding to the guarded measures of her tone. "You're safe here."

"There is no place safe. Not anymore." She stiffened and looked away. Wynn had the feeling she was looking far beyond the back wall. To a place only seen in memory.

He picked a handful of comfrey sprigs as he weighed his words. "It's true the war makes such reliability obsolete, but the Germans are far from here. They'll never breach Paris."

"Who are you to guarantee such a thing?"

"I'm offering you a chance to hope. You don't seem to have much of it lately."

She looked at him fully for the first time, unashamedly in her direct perusal. He returned the directness. Hair of palest blond it was nearly white; unblemished skin kept from a lifetime of sun; and eyes the color of a wintry sea. So pale blue in the center one might lose himself in the vastness until drifting to the rim of arctic blue around the outside. *Beautiful* was not enough. Words such as *elegant* and *exquisite* were used to describe women like her, and while he felt himself affected by such attributes, it was not what held his attention.

Intelligence was not a calling card for most women he knew as society highly disapproved of such liberal notions. Her Serenity the Princess Svetlana—and all those other names he couldn't remember—displayed hers without reserve. She didn't defer or feign false modesty. She held herself with quiet pride, and nothing could kindle his admiration more.

"I had hope once." Her soft admission was snatched on a breeze of sorrow. "Such notions belong to ruins of the past."

"Back when you were a princess?" She startled and he immediately regretted his bluntness, though it was hardly a secret after her mother's brazen introduction. Surely they were far enough from Russia and its troubles to no longer remain fearful of their identities, but one look at the panic in her eyes told him the fear was rooted in death. "Don't worry. I'll keep your secret safe—as long as you don't let on that I'm a marquis."

As before, it took a moment for her panic to recede. When it did a new confusion took its place. "What is this marquis?"

"I'm the second son of a duke. Upon my father's death, my brother, Hugh, became Duke of Kilbride and I the humble Marquis of Tarltan."

She shrugged, unimpressed. "There are many dukes in Russia."

"Which makes me the only marquis of your acquaintance." Wynn stood with the picked comfrey and brushed dirt from his trousers. "Well, that's something anyway. What is that plant there?"

"A lily. Mrs. Varjensky says the boiled roots can be used in ointments for burns and rashes." A smile crossed her face. "I used to arrange them in vases once belonging to Empress Ekaterina. They filled our music room in white, pink, and yellow blooms."

"That sounds calming."

"Arranging is one of the few activities deemed appropriate for a lady to learn. Not growing them or clipping them, mind you, that was too strenuous. Placing them in decorative vases was the extent of our labor."

"Would you have liked to grow them yourself?"

Wistfulness whispered across her face, then faded like the petals of a bloom past its day in the sun. "What I would have liked is of no consequence. It was not to be for a princess then, nor for a refugee now."

A breeze ruffled the nearby elms, filling the air with scents of sweet grass and thick herbs. A pleasant departure from the cloying hospital smell of sterilization. If he closed his eyes, he could imagine he was home in Scotland enjoying the lazy days of summer and not existing on the brink of trenches and barbed wire. What those front-line lads wouldn't give for a whiff of a single blade of grass.

"My brother and I got in trouble once for whacking off rose tops with sticks in the Luxembourg Gardens when we were younger. Our parents were asked not to bring us back."

"The carefree mischief of youth," she said. "You are close with this brother, Hugh."

Wynn nodded. "Best of friends growing up, but Hugh's always had to hold himself apart as the next duke. Me? I'm the second son and can get away with murder. Though I won't because it would be breaking my Hippocratic oath. Hugh knows all the rules and lives to keep them."

"My brother, Nikolai, is the same."

"Is he here in France?"

"He stayed with Papa to defend our homeland." Her face shuttered, depriving him of her thoughts once more. "I should not be outside." She stood, favoring her unhurt leg.

Wynn strode through the weeds and captured her hand before she had the chance to take a limping step. "I don't know what you're running from in Russia, though I can venture a guess, but you don't have to be frightened any longer."

"You do not know. You do not understand what fear is."

Living the past four years in a war zone gave him every right to understand the meaning of fear, but the look blazing in her eyes spoke of something more, a crippling terror he'd not seen before. Not knowing how to root out the pain, he nodded and looped her arm around his. "I'll take you inside."

Her hand was cool against his forearm. Slight calluses rested at the base of her long fingers. Signs of refined hands adjusting to recent hardships. Likely she had never had to pick up an item a day in her life. Until now, when she was clothed in ripped skirts scrounging in a weedy garden. Yet not one ounce of dirt could diminish the regal way with which she held herself.

"Before you say 'don't come back,' know that I will come back. Tomorrow or the next time I'm off shift," Wynn said.

"You are a difficult man to say no to."

"Another trait of my profession. We're hard to refuse when a gangrenous limb hangs in the balance."

Her brow puckered in confusion, then suddenly smoothed. "Ah. Another joke."

"Medical humor. If we can't heal you, we'll kill you with terrible comedy."

"Maybe it is better you continue with medicine instead." A light sparked in her eyes. Was that the verge of a smile?

Wynn's heart rate bumped up. "Maybe you're right."

Across the courtyard, Mrs. Varjensky had pushed aside one of the other women to stir a boiling pot of soup herself. At the sight of them, she bustled over and handed him a jar filled with vegetable broth. "*Do svidaniya, golubchik.*"

Wynn glanced at her other hand that held the cracked teapot. Familiar green leaves poked out of the spout. Biting back a laugh, he stuffed the newly picked but unneeded comfrey into the teapot.

"*Spasibo, babushka.*" He grinned at Svetlana. "Getting rather good at this Russian."

"It is better you continue with medicine."

"Perhaps you're right." He pulled out the lily he had clipped secretly from the garden and handed it to her. "Until next time."

The corners of her mouth flitted up as she took the flower. It wasn't quite the smile he'd hoped for, but it wasn't a frown.

He would take it as a victory.

"He has made you smile." Mama's thin eyebrows raised in accusation as soon as Svetlana, holding the lily, stepped into their shared blanket quadrant.

Svetlana pulled the makeshift curtain tight, cutting off the smell of boiled cabbage that permeated the cellar. The elusive emotion of enjoyment and the sweet scent of the lily that had floated around her a moment earlier deflated.

"Don't be ridiculous."

"You are engaged to Sergey."

"I am not. An informal, unspoken understanding at the most."

"You are as good as engaged. Sergey is one of our kind—the only kind—and a dear friend to our family for years. Do not forget this."

How could she, when not for one moment did Mama allow it? Man after man had been paraded before her at every ball and concert, the most successful venues for finding acceptable husbands. Men with all the right titles, family wealth, and political ties, but without a bone of enticement to hold them upright. Perhaps one day a man would fit her credentials.

"I have no intention of falling in love right now. If such a thing is even possible."

Mama scoffed and batted her small hand in the air as if to chase off Svetlana's ludicrous notion. "Love has nothing to do with a successful marriage. It is a sentiment best reserved for the *nishchebrod*. This man, this doctor, is no one, otherwise he would not have a menial job as a physician. Bah. Working class."

It was doubtful the poor had more claim on matters of the heart than the nobility, but speaking of peasants would only fall on Mama's deaf ear. A mar on the otherwise glittering world she hoped to return to.

"He's—" Svetlana cut short her defense of Wynn as she reached for an empty milk jar. He'd asked her not to reveal him as Marquis of Tarltan. While she had no intention of surrendering her trust to him, she still respected a promise when given. Pouring a bit of precious water into the jar, she gently slipped the flower into the glass. How beautiful these would be planted in a garden next to roses, freesia, buttercups, and peonies. Trouble could not touch them in such a peaceful place. "He is dedicated to his profession."

"As if that concerns us. You are a princess. A blood relation to Tsar Nicholas himself."

"A third cousin twice removed, I believe."

"Still blood. We are set apart by God Himself." Mama spit over her left shoulder so as not to tempt Fate.

That inalienable truth had been infused into the very air Svetlana breathed since the first day she drew breath. The nobles and titled of the land had been chosen by God, were touched by His divine hand, and sat upon pedestals to be worshipped by the poorer masses. It had been a life of comfort, ease, and adoration. But the revolution had destroyed it all, leaving bitter ashes of all that once sparkled as diamonds. Princesses could spill blood as easily as peasants when bullets fired without prejudice on the burning streets of Petrograd.

"*Privyet.*" Without waiting for a reply, Mrs. Varjensky waddled in with a steaming bowl and ladle in her good hand. Her ever-present peasant scarf was tied tightly under her baggy chin. "Hungry, *printsessas*? There plenty of broth left."

Mama looked away and made her polite offended noise. She'd yet to grow accustomed to dining without caviar.

"*Nyet,*" Svetlana said. "I will wait until later, but please leave Marina a bowl for when she returns from her errand." With food scarce, she tried filling up on water throughout the day to carry her into the evening and the waiting bowl of thinned soup or what meager means the priest had managed to scrape together.

"That *mal'chik* needs eat more." Mrs. Varjensky waved her ladle toward the door as if Wynn were still within sight. "He waste away and then no good he be to sick."

"That man," Svetlana corrected, for there was nothing boyish about him, "can take care of himself."

The old woman waggled her head back and forth, loosening strands of gray from under her scarf. "*Nyet*. Impossible for men. Need woman to help."

Speaking of helping . . . "Where did all the comfrey go from yesterday?"

"It gone. That all I know." Mrs. Varjensky touched her head and gestured as if she had not a clue, but her avoiding eyes admitted to knowing precisely where the plants had gone. Her version of a woman helping. "You had nice time outside, *da*?" Her gaze slipped to the lily.

Meddling was the pastime of older generations. Their favorite being affairs of the young and what they hoped to conjure into romance. Svetlana refused to become another sport.

"A nice time picking more herbs since the armload we collected yesterday mysteriously disappeared."

"Mystery, *da*." With a knowing smile, Mrs. Varjensky turned back to her own quarters humming an offbeat tune.

Made of tough Volga stock, the old woman wasn't giving in without a fight. Svetlana had to respect her sheer determination.

"Speaking of mysterious disappearances . . . Mama, I want to speak with you about earlier."

Mama's face pained delicately. "Let it wait. I have a terrible headache and need to lie down." Her headaches only came on for two reasons. One for stalling and the other for sympathy. If Svetlana's hunch was correct, it was the former in this instance for the very reason she wished to discuss.

"It cannot wait."

"Very well." Mama moved to sit on a chair that had quite recently appeared, then eyed Svetlana's leg before sinking to the unoccupied pallet, deftly covering the velvet bag with her skirts. "What must you speak to me about that cannot wait until my head is better?"

"Where did the chair come from?"

"That? Oh, I traded for it with one of Marina's combs."

"We agreed to only trade or sell out of necessity. For food or clothes."

"It is a necessity for my back. You don't wish me continual suffering from sitting on this hard floor all the time, do you?"

Stilling the boil of anger to keep the peace, Svetlana took the chair. Her leg cried with relief, but she didn't allow it to detract from her intended purpose.

"What jewels did you give him?"

"Give who?" Mama's voice pitched an entire octave higher.

"Ivan Petro. Right before I left for the garden, you disappeared into that horrible man's chamber."

"He is not a man to lay your suspicions on. He was Privy Councillor to the tsar, a highly respectable position."

Svetlana's patience rattled. "The jewels?"

"His wife, on the other hand, not so respectable," her mother continued the detour as she examined her nails. "There were rumors about her and General Miller in the fountains at Peterhof."

"Mama. I am not interested in court scandals."

"That's because fun doesn't appeal to you. To think, a daughter of mine with a constitution so rigid it would put a Siberian ice block to shame." Mama clutched her gold cross as if in pain.

Svetlana remained motionless under her mother's lament of disapproval. Words meant to prick and proddle while making herself out to be the one suffering. She loved nothing more than an audience for her act, but Svetlana had witnessed it time and again over the years. The performance had long since grown stale.

Not receiving the groveling response she desired, Mama stood and fluffed a pair of silk drawers she had drying over a crate.

"It was one tiny ruby. That flawed absurdity your father's grandmother gave me as a wedding gift. She knew it was flawed when she gifted it to me." She took a deep breath in preparation for her next act. "Ivan has contacts in Paris."

"No. No mysterious contacts. If the Reds find out where we are, they'll come for us and kill us. Or drag us back to Russia and kill us there as an example of what's to be done with aristocrats. Do you not remember Prince Boris Baranov? Beat to death at a train station while his wife barely escaped disguised as a maid."

Mama flung her arms wide and stared accusingly. "At least they're not hiding in a basement. Reduced to sharing quarters and eating from a pot with these people. It's undignified."

"So is being shot in the head."

"Do not say such vulgar things to me. You are a lady of high breeding. These contacts could place us back into the lifestyle we are accustomed to—a divine apartment, food, and clothes—while we wait for this turmoil to blow over. We have lived in the same clothing for months. It is not to be endured."

Svetlana's leg cramped. Standing, she gripped the back of the chair and eased into a *demi plie* before pushing to her toes in *relevé*. The cramp slowly knotted from her calf. She focused on the precise movements and not the flood of irritation at her mother's complete lack of understanding their precarious situation. It had always been Mama's way, and Svetlana learned long ago that it would never change.

"Even if the Reds surrendered tomorrow, there is still another war raging right where we are. Do you not remember how difficult it was to travel here? Sleeping in cattle cars, hiding in the woods, begging for a crust at village doors, and you want to turn around and do it all over again."

"Our circumstances have yet to improve. Must you do that here?" Mama frowned as Svetlana added a *tendu*. "We must wait for Sergey to find us as he promised, but he will never look for us in a place like this." The frown eased from her brow, and a rare glimpse of genuine concern softened her expression. "Perhaps he will bring us triumphant news of your father and Nikolai, for they'll be too busy securing the country to come themselves."

God willing. Svetlana could not rest easy until their family was reunited. Strong, valiant Papa had always carried the familial responsibilities with soldierly dignity. A lesson she had taken to heart, drawing upon his absent strength as they carried on without him.

"I will continue to make discreet inquiries for new accommodations and news from Russia. We do not need outside help."

"Always with the fear and isolation. We are not the only émigrés here. On our journey I met a dozen duchesses and four princes. We do not need to live in this terror you insist on, not here when the country is crawling in confusion."

The knot in Svetlana's leg crawled up her spine and rooted itself into a headache. "Even so, we must take precautions, and that includes not pawning off our gems at every vacant promise that comes along. We need those to secure shelter and food. From now on, talk to me first."

"How do you propose to do a better job than Petro's contact at locating something for us? You know nothing of Paris."

Svetlana's eyes laned on the lily, and she touched one of the flower's creamy petals. The softness curled to a yellow center dusted with pollen. "Leave it to me."

CHAPTER 4

The warm drizzle soaked through the top of Svetlana's shawl and puddled in her hair before dribbling down her back. Rain should have been a relief to tamp down the summer dust, but the droplets struck the hot ground in sizzles, turning the congested city into a swamp.

Standing on the steps of a tenant building four streets over from the church and a world away in culture, Svetlana batted away an errant drop careening into her eye and met the reluctant Frenchwoman's stare.

"We will pay whatever you ask. We will not cause you any trouble."

"As I explained, *chere*, we only have room for a single occupant to rent."

"My mother, sister, and I do not mind sharing a small space. Look." Svetlana stepped onto the small stoop and pulled a bulky handkerchief from the pocket in her skirt. Inside nestled Mama's favorite citrine diamond earrings. "A gift from Empress Dowager Maria herself."

The woman's eyes widened as she ogled the precious gems. Slowly, she shook her head. "They are *très belle*, but I am sorry. There is no room. You are better to stay where you are." Stepping back into her darkened hall, she closed the door. A lock quickly echoed.

Another rejection. Ten so far, barely before noon. Each with a different reason, but all equating to no. A distasteful word that grated on the ears. Svetlana had heard it more often since escaping Russia than in the entirety of her life. She didn't care for the change one bit.

Rewrapping the earrings and returning them to her pocket,

Svetlana descended the short flight of stairs to the cracked sidewalk. A grand carriage should have been waiting for her. And a footman dressed in immaculate livery to open the door so she could sweep into the cushioned confines, dry and comfortable with perhaps a small vase filled with lavender to drive away the fusty scents drifting up from the streets. A crack of the whip would urge on the matching bays and off they would go to the palace.

This avenue was a far cry from the grandness of carriages and livery. Perhaps under the rule of the Sun King these imposing buildings had stood in refinement, but the years sagged against the structural lines as the paint chipped wearily away. Though they were not without color. Canon smoke and gunpowder drifted into the city on brisk winds, coating roofs and lampposts with black dust and drawing the war that much closer. Miles separated them from the frontline, but no matter the distance, no one was safe.

Pulling the shawl tight over her head, Svetlana hurried away with toes squishing in her soggy stockings.

"No luck from old bird, *Vashe blagorodiye*?" The formal address spoken in common Russian stopped Svetlana in her tracks. A woman dressed in pre-war fashion stepped out of the shadows of a neighboring stoop. A cigarette dangled between her fingers.

"I beg your pardon. We have not been introduced for you to address me."

"Forgive lack in manners. It is war. Takes what gentility we have and tosses to dump heap."

"In that you are correct."

The woman clomped down the steps. She appeared close in age to Svetlana, but a harsh survival etched itself into the lines around the woman's eyes and mouth. Rouge, the call sign of a less than upright woman, smudged her lean cheeks.

"What mean is, French don't know true value when see it. Not as we do. Not when you offer such lovely bauble."

"I carry no such thing." Svetlana moved to walk around her, but the woman wasn't so easily put off.

She fell in step with Svetlana. "Ladies like us always spot genuine article. Your courtly senses no disappear back in Russia, *Vashe blagorodiye*. Neither did mine."

"What court did you find yourself in? Nearer the docks or the soldiers' barracks?"

The woman laughed and ground her cigarette into the pavement with a heel in desperate need of black polish.

"That what I like about you, *Vashe Svyetlost*. Sense of humor."

At least Svetlana was moving up in the ranks. First a mere Well Born and now an Imperial Highness. If she kept the delightfulness going, she might hold the title of Empress before the conversation was over. She rounded a corner in hopes of shaking loose her undesirable companion.

"Please do excuse me. I've a rather busy schedule to attend."

"Looking for place to stay, *da*?"

An older gentleman holding an umbrella approached, his gaze casting with interest between Svetlana and the woman, who smiled enticingly in return. Svetlana raised one eyebrow in scathing rebuke, and he scuttled across the street to the opposite sidewalk.

"I need learn that trick. Old men not bathe often." Wrinkling her nose, the woman drew a fresh cigarette and match from her beaded handbag, lit the fag, and puffed. The cherry glowing end hissed as the drizzle splattered onto the paper. "I know few places. French snobs waste of time. Need you ask around Rue de la Néva and Pierre le Grand."

Those streets were within a stone's throw from the church, but Svetlana wasn't about to lead this stranger to where her family lived.

"Those streets are tiny with barely enough room for shops."

"It heart of Russian neighborhood. Always room for another son and daughter of beloved motherland. You need know who ask."

"And you do?"

"I know every Russian in Paris. It privilege of living here five years. Before I gave up duchess tiara in Moscow." The woman laughed and weaved her arm through Svetlana's as if they shared a secret.

"What is this I hear of Moscow, Tatya?" Moving like an oil-sleeked seal, a man appeared in front of them holding an umbrella. He cut a lean figure with dark hair combed to the side and a tailored blue suit with crisp edges not often seen during the war years.

Tatya's smile tightened as she tugged the front of her dress. "Pyotr, meet new friend. Russian lady of quality."

"Is that so?" Assessing and quick, his gaze cut over Svetlana like a jeweler's would a gem. He bowed before angling the umbrella over her head. Tatya was forced to make do with her drooping wool hat. "*Privyet*, gentle lady. My name is Pyotr Argunov."

"*Zdrastvuytye*," Svetlana replied in the more formal greeting. A lifetime of unfortunate circumstances could be hidden beneath a well-tailored cuff, but speech was a revelation to one's true breeding. One had it or one did not. For all his trimmed collars and buttons, Pyotr Argunov did not. All the better for her to remain guarded.

"May I ask your name?"

"You may ask if you are so inclined."

Tatya snorted through a puff of smoke. "All class, this one."

"So I see. Could do very well for us." Pyotr pulled the cigarette from Tatya's mouth and flicked it in the gutter. "Why don't I take the two most beautiful women this side of the Neva River out for a drink? Catch up on old times with the tsar, determine the best place to find stroganoff, and pour a glass of vodka for the comrades we left behind." His arm slipped around Svetlana with a light touch to the small of her back. Leading in a dance she had no desire to join.

Having reigned a lifetime in ballrooms armed with the noble art of avoidance, Svetlana sidestepped his nefarious intentions with ease.

"As I've told the duchess here, I have my own errands to see to."

Tatya leaned forward, poking her head just under the protection of the umbrella. "That right. She looks place to stay. I show her Sheremetev place."

Pyotr tilted the umbrella more over his own head and away from Tatya. "Ah, Sheremetev. The man who knows everyone and everything happening from Paris to Petrograd. Whatever you need, he has it or the ability to procure it."

Whatever Svetlana needed. The promise of hope so near at hand crooked its beckoning finger at her, enticing her with deliverance from fear. Could it be so simple as knowing the right man's name? Such information never came without a cost, but it was a fortune she would gladly pay to keep the Bolsheviks from finding them.

"Where might I find this Sheremetev?"

"A stroke of fortune in that I'm heading to the White Bear now to meet him. I'll introduce you." A smile slicked across Pyotr's wide mouth as he no doubt imagined himself landing his prize.

But she was no game piece to claim in victory. He'd overplayed his hand from first introduction, and it was high time he learned a lesson in civilized defeat.

"I will produce my own means of introduction should I find myself in need of such services. Yours are not required."

"No need to be cold, *printsessa*."

The careless tossing out of her rightful title stung. She had a right to claim it and rebuke his insolence, but no longer were they at the imperial court. No longer did her title carry clout. It was a death warrant in the wrong hands, and if her instincts were correct, Pyotr's hands were far from clean.

"If I were as cold as you claim, you would have been frozen to the spot long ago. As such, I'll thank you to remove your hand and never dare touch a lady again."

He stepped closer. Spiced wine fouled the air. "I've met *tyolka* like you before. Braying about, thinking you're better than everyone."

"I try not to presume such a claim, but in your case I'll make an exception."

"We're not in Russia anymore. Your kind are toppling."

"A shame if your kind were crushed in the rubble."

"Move away from the lady." Wynn's voice cut through the building tension. He thrust himself into the space between Svetlana and Pyotr. Anger rolled off him in heated waves. "I said, move away."

Tall as she was, Svetlana saw little beyond Wynn's wide shoulders. They blocked everything from view. She peered around him.

"Who are you to interrupt so rudely a conversation that does not concern you, *anglichanin*?" Pyotr sneered, nearly knocking Wynn in the head with his umbrella.

Wynn didn't flinch. "I'll ask you once to move along."

"Or what?"

"It'll end with broken bones and they won't be mine."

Aiming a disgusting spit at Wynn's feet, Pyotr grabbed Tatya's arm and yanked her away. Tatya's feet skipped to keep up. Passersby stared at the uncivilized behavior before shrugging it off as wont to do for a girl of her working station. She cast a pitiful look over her shoulder at Svetlana before she was hauled around a corner and out of sight.

Wynn turned on Svetlana, thick eyebrows crushed together. "Why is it I always tend to find you in verbal altercations on random footpaths? Is the church cellar so dull that you seek out entertainment elsewhere, never mind the notoriety of these little run-ins?"

She dismissed his indignation as the triviality it was. "It is none of your affair."

"A lady being assaulted on the street is my affair."

"His lack of manners was the only assault to me. It was not the first time I've deflected boorish attacks."

"This isn't some fancy salon where a rap on the man's knuckles with your fan will do the trick. Men like him don't stop at the word *no*."

"You know this how?"

"Work in enough hospitals and it's easy to learn the type when you're patching them up from pub fights." Shifting a parcel under his arm, he popped open his umbrella and angled it over Svetlana's head. The drizzle had turned into a mist that thickened the air with a cloying dampness.

"What is this pub?"

Wynn released a gusty sigh that loosened the tense line between his eyebrows. "A public house. A tavern, barroom, saloon. A place where drink inflates men's egos and they duke it out in the back alley defending said ego."

"I would never dare step foot into a place of debauchery."

"Good. That rules out half of Paris the next time I'm forced to find you out wandering on your own."

This man and his high-handed ways. As if he held the right to intrude on whoever and whatever he pleased. She had more important matters to occupy herself with than wondering when he would next show up. Or what color the light would turn his eyes. Today, touches of brown.

Svetlana plucked at the shawl clinging to her head to ward off her study of him. "No one has forced you to do anything. I do not understand why you are here in the first place."

"The chemist a block over was able to secure a specially made stethoscope for me." He jostled the package under his arm. "Upon picking up my order, whom should I see but Your Serenity making new friends."

"I did not realize that upon our brief acquaintance I am required to provide a list of names of whom I should be conversing with. Might I also note that these persons were not sought out but came to me. Most uninvited."

"Does that include me?"

"Increasingly so."

His mouth cocked up at one corner and he rocked back on his heels. The amused reaction felt far more intimate than the generated distance suggested.

"Why is that? As far as I know, I've been nothing but polite and helpful, yet you're determined to make a nuisance of me. Some might call that ungratefully snobbish."

The barb hit quick, its defiance slicing past years of defense erected against its sting. All her life she'd stood apart, followed every rule and protocol for the sake of propriety, never once accepting an offering that was said to be beneath her. It was the expected nature of a princess. It had served her well, but she was not immune to the whispers behind drawing room doors: cold, conceited, condescending. She'd taken them in stride as petty jealousies, but the man before her had no reason for spite. If she'd learned anything about him in their short association, she knew he was not a bluffing man.

She turned away. "I will not stand here and be insulted on the street."

His hand locked around her elbow, halting her departure. "Before you get on that high prancing horse, let me stop you there, Princess."

"I do not require your halting, marquee."

"It's marquis, but let's not get tangled on semantics. I said some people might call you that. I would call you a woman who's had the path ripped out from under her slippered feet and has fallen back on old world habits. The problem is, this is a different world and old habits won't survive here. We have to adapt else we lose the fight."

Svetlana flushed hot. His blatant philosophy insulted the very essence of tradition her life had been built upon. The foundation of who she was. Without it there was no purpose. *She* had no purpose. And he had the gall to make a point of it.

She wrenched from his grasp. "Who are you to speak to me thus? No one speaks to me in this manner."

"A shame because they're doing you a disservice."

"And you think you're the one in service, do you?"

"If it weren't for me, you'd be having pickle juice ladled down your royal neck to cure a leg injury. *Babushka* showed me a jar of mushrooms." He shook his head. "I never realized how many things can be pickled."

He shifted topics quicker than a tiara on wet hair. Could he not allow her righteous outrage to simmer longer?

"Peasants pickle everything. It lasts longer."

"Do they pickle humor? There seems to be a shortage of it."

"Unlike Englishmen who abound with the sentiment." She spiked her eyebrows in pointed disapproval.

"The English? No, dry as a peat bog in a drought, that lot. My charm comes from pure Scottish roots."

"I believe your roots may have hit bedrock."

Glancing up and down the street at the people hunkered into their collars against the wet, he leaned down close to her ear. "Careful, *printsessa*. Your humor is unearthing itself."

"Only with you it seems." She tugged the shawl ends closer around her neck, warding off the heat radiating from him.

"I'll take that as a compliment."

The heat threatened the logic in her head. Not to mention his clean scent of wool splashed with cologne. Svetlana moved away before it proved too great a distraction.

"And I shall take my leave."

He didn't perceive the hint and moved along with her.

"Excellent idea. I was heading that way myself."

"Your hospital is the other way."

"Some days I prefer the long route. Prettier scenery."

"I prefer to walk alone."

"If the lady insists, but I hope you don't mind me following a few paces behind. Take my umbrella. I've got a hat to cover me and you've not more than that soaked shawl. Don't need you catching a chill."

He held out the umbrella to her. "Funny how I'll take a patient with a broken arm over a fever any day. There's nothing worse than having to watch a person wait it out of their system and not be able to mend it straightaway."

"You are an impatient man."

"Only when it counts. Other things, well, I'm considering they might be worth waiting for." His gaze settled over her in a direct manner that combed through her tightly woven insides, spinning them out to singular threads humming with awareness.

She tamped the vibrations into submission. He was a stranger. No one could be trusted, especially not a self-professed charmer. The survival of her family remained paramount to any unwanted entanglements. Entanglements that confronted her with golden-green eyes that deepened under the brim of his hat.

As if delighting in the inner chaos he created, the edge of his mouth curled. He handed her the umbrella, brushing her fingers as she reached for it. The unraveled threads sang. Traitors to her very dignity. She had no better control of herself than an *ingénue* standing at her first barre.

She clutched the handle. "Thank you."

"*Pozhaluysta.*"

The Russian word rang in her ears as she turned and walked on. How did he manage to manipulate a single word—spoken in a language deemed fit only for peasants, no less—into a flirtatious invitation? More vexing, why did she notice?

She pushed the unsettling thoughts away, but the man himself was not so easily ignored. His footsteps fell in line behind her. Bits of water from the tips of his shoes sprayed against her skirt with each step he took. She dared a peek over her shoulder. He smiled and tipped his hat.

He was entirely too cheerful. Very unRussian. And also very wet. Her desire to remain distant warred with her polite breeding. She wouldn't dare claim it as a spark of humanity lest it flame out of control and she suddenly discover herself ladling at a soup kitchen. Best to pass over a few coins in such a situation, but she had no coin at present. Only a soggy man ridiculously smiling at her and, for the life of her, she could not leave him that way.

"Join me under the umbrella."

"I'm sorry. Would you repeat that?" He cocked his head to the side as if he hadn't quite heard.

Svetlana gestured impatiently. "Join me."

"Is that a command or a request? Difficult to tell in all this rain." As if to emphasize his point, he frowned and held out his hand for raindrops to plop against his palm.

He'd heard her perfectly well and they both knew it.

"Would you care to join me out of the weather under this umbrella you have so thoughtfully provided?"

"Don't mind if I do." He took shelter under the canopied protection, or rather, the right side of him did. The wide expanse of his left shoulder and back remained exposed to the elements. "Is it back to the church or do you have a few more clandestine characters to meet around the next corner?"

"I have no one to meet. Not in this neighborhood." Svetlana curled her hand around the gems in her pocket. "Snobbish French. They do not trust us Russians. They are afraid we will bring our revolution to their streets. A hypocritical concern considering their own history with Madame Guillotine."

Bam!

Gunshots. Feet pounding on pavement followed by shouts.

Bam-bam!

The terror that had scorched Svetlana's nightmares since that burning October night clawed for breath. The revolutionaries. They were coming for her. They were here.

A man barreled out of the alleyway ahead of them. His jacket flapped around him as he twisted his wild-eyed stare over his shoulder. His foot caught. Down he went, smacking the sidewalk with his shoulder. Up and down the street people scattered and screamed like pigeons in a park.

Bam!

The man jerked and cried out. Red seeped from his shoulder.

Svetlana dropped the umbrella and spun away. The revolutionaries. They'd found her.

CHAPTER 5

Wynn grabbed her and pushed her against the side of a building, covering her with his body. Svetlana didn't want to look, didn't want to see the horrible image before her, but Wynn's weight immobilized her against the wet stone with her unblinking eyes pinned on the shot man.

Scrambling backward on his hand, the man pulled a gun from his jacket and fired down the alleyway. The shot ricocheted off the walls.

"Cowards! Shooting me in back!" he shouted in Russian. Feet scuffled, growing farther away. "That is right. Run!" He collapsed, clutching his bleeding shoulder.

"Stay here," Wynn hissed in her ear. His weight lifted from her, leaving a terrible chill in his absence as he rushed to the fallen man.

The blood rushed from Svetlana's extremities until they shook from deprivation. She watched as if standing in a water bubble that deafened all sound, thought, and movement. She blinked heavily, yet her eyes could not belie what her brain tried to deceive her with. Reds. Guns. A man bleeding. Wynn bending over him, fingers prodding the wound.

He turned to her. Eyes urgent as his mouth moved. What was he saying? She couldn't hear anything beyond the thudding of her heart.

"Svetlana!" The vacuous bubble burst. Sound and understanding flooded in, shocking her with its force. "Here."

She shook her head to clear the vestiges of fog and hurried to his side on wobbly legs.

"Do you have a handkerchief?" Wynn's question rolled in her ear, but the ability to discern its meaning eluded her as she stared at the hurt man's face. Sickly pale and dotted with rain, he clenched his crooked teeth behind thin lips. Wynn's voice prodded her once more. "Svetlana. Look at me."

Slowly Svetlana turned her attention to him as the vacantness threatened its hold once more. Wynn's gaze was calm, steadying her against the trembling moving through her body.

"Do you have a handkerchief?"

She felt her head shake no.

"Your shawl. Take it off and wrap it around his shoulder while I hold him up. Do you understand?" The man moaned and convulsed. Red seeped between Wynn's fingers as he pressed against the shoulder. "Svetlana. Look at me. Do you understand?"

She felt herself nodding. So much blood.

"Do it now." His sharpness cut through the haze, severing her from the stupor it trapped her in.

Whipping off the shawl, she carefully wrapped it under the man's thick arm and over his shoulder as Wynn propped him up. She tried to focus on her task. Up, over, under. Red splattered the sidewalk. Up, over, under. It feathered out between cracks in the pavement, turning blotchy as raindrops collided with the red rivulets. A life washing into the gutter. She wrapped faster, water squeezing between her fingers.

"The material is too wet to soak up the"—she swallowed against the roil of sickness—"the blood."

"Better than nothing." Wynn steadied the man's head as it lolled to the side. "No you don't, mate. I need you awake."

Svetlana didn't blame the man. If she'd been shot, she'd rather remain unconscious throughout the ordeal as well.

"What shall I do with the ends?"

"Tie them. We don't need the dressing slipping off before we get to hospital."

"*Nyet!*" The man wrestled awake as he cried out in Russian. "No hospital! Do no take me there. *Nyet.*"

J'NELL CIESIELSKI

Fresh blood seeped out from the shawl as he flailed in an effort to throw them off. Svetlana had gone to too much trouble wrapping the wound. This fool wasn't going to undo it all now.

She slapped his pudgy cheek.

"Calm yourself. Do you not see this doctor is trying to help you?"

The man froze and stared at her in disbelief. "*Russkaya?*"

"*Da.*" She knotted the ends of the shawl and looked at Wynn, who didn't seem the least bit distressed by the terrifying situation in which they found themselves. "He says he doesn't want to go to the hospital."

"He's been shot. He doesn't get much of a choice."

"There choice, *da*," the man said in broken English, bobbing his head and sending rain from his hair streaking into his eyes.

Wynn's brow lifted. "Oh, speak English, do you? Good. Makes things easier." He glanced at Svetlana. "Not that I don't appreciate hearing your lovely interpretations. Grab the umbrella and try to keep it over his wound. Hospital is three blocks over. Can you make it, mate?" Swiping his hands against his trouser leg and leaving a swath of red on the dark gray material, Wynn stood and hooked an arm around the man's thick waist and hauled him to his feet.

Staggering, the man grimaced in pain. "There choice. Apartment street over. Mine." He jabbed his finger in the intended direction.

Wynn secured the man's uninjured arm around his shoulders while maintaining a steady arm around the man's waist. "I understand we all want the comforts of home when we've taken a beating, but this isn't going to be cured with an aspirin and a lie-down."

The man turned flat brown eyes to Svetlana. Flat face. Flat nose. Flat lips. All Russian. "You tell him. You *russkaya*. Make him understand. English hospital no good. They find me again. Only safe in apartment."

Svetlana formed a protest but snuffed it cold at the terrifying prospect of truth in his words. What was to stop those men from finishing their heinous murder at the hospital? All those innocent people. If it was the Reds, the last thing they should be offered was open grounds to exact vengeance on opposing soldiers too injured to fight back once they'd taken this man's life.

"We'll take him to the apartment," she said.

Wynn shook his head. "Absolutely not. I'm the doctor here and this man needs—"

"He needs you to attend him and you can do that anywhere. Though preferably not in the street, yes?" Walking back to where she'd dropped the umbrella, she picked it up along with Wynn's package, then stared down a curious woman watching them through her window. The woman crossed herself and made a hasty retreat behind her curtains. Others who had fled at the gunshots crept back onto the sidewalk and watched with unabashed curiosity. Ignoring them, she returned and held the umbrella over the man.

"For the safety of all your patients it is best we take this man to a quiet place. I will retrieve anything you need."

He stared at her. His stubborn need for medical superiority warring with concern for all involved patients transpired like a shifting wall across Wynn's face.

At last he settled on a decision. "Where's the flat?"

―――――――

Wynn scrubbed his hands in the basin of water and soap as his patient slowly regained consciousness on the ornate bed. The man had passed out no sooner than they had entered the building. Rather rude of him considering the four flights of stairs they had to traverse before arriving at his door with limp body in tow, but the blackout proved to be a blessing. Wynn was able to make a quick examination of the entry and exit wounds, clean away debris, and dress the injuries with a few shirts Svetlana had found in a bureau and cut into strips.

After checking his patient once more, Wynn left the bedchamber and stepped into the sitting room. Expensive furniture and artwork crammed the space with plush Aubusson rugs covering the parquet floor. Faux columns stood in the corners with spiky green plants sitting on top while a marble fireplace was half hidden behind a trolley loaded with amber liquid–filled decanters and tumblers.

Not knowing what to make of the gaudy taste, Wynn ambled to the kitchen where Svetlana brooded over a silver contraption with a spout that looked suspiciously like an oversize tea kettle. Her hair rested in a limp coil at the base of her neck with escaped silvery strands straggling off in all directions. Her dark blue dress was wrinkled and water stained, but her erect posture didn't sag under the mistreatment. Nor did her odd foot arrangement, one flat and the other pointed to the side. Snapped to the front. To the side again.

If one thing could be said for this princess, it was that she was a brick. Not once had she complained or backed away when he requested assistance. If another thing could be said, it was that this princess was no nurse. She'd managed to jab their patient in the exit wound as the dressing was applied and brought Wynn cologne water to wash his hands instead of soap, arguing he had worked up quite the "aroma" on the trudge through the streets and up the stairs. The sweat dampening the back of his shirt couldn't deny that statement.

"*Espèce de rate.*" Svetlana smacked the silver contraption with her palm.

"Having trouble?" Wynn stepped into the small yet serviceable room that didn't appear to have cooked a meal in all its existence. No dishes, no cutlery, nothing to indicate it was more than a passing thought to its occupant.

Svetlana turned to face him, her scowl giving way beneath a pink of embarrassed frustration. "I thought to make tea."

"With that? It looks more suitable to holding the remains of the deceased. Or sterilizing equipment in the surgery."

"It is a samovar. A Russian tea maker."

"Have you used one before?"

"No. Our cook always prepared our trays in the kitchen. I shouldn't think it that difficult being only hot water and tea leaves." She pointed to the curved spout etched with intricate scrollwork. "I only know the hot water comes from this spout and into the teapot where the leaves are. The leaves were difficult to find." She frowned at the matching silver teapot on the counter.

A coffee man himself, and only a good slug to get him through a grueling shift, Wynn didn't have much practice in the domestic arts, but he'd seen his mum make the watery brew often enough.

Unable to resist a challenge of inner workings, especially with a beautiful woman watching, he pried off the lid and gazed inside. It was an open chamber half filled with water and a metal pipe running vertically through the middle.

"There are burnt wood pieces in this smaller pipe. We'll need to light them to boil this water for the teapot."

"Yes, that seems logical." Svetlana reached toward the windowsill and pulled down a box of matches. With a dainty flick of her wrist, she struck the match to a fiery orange and dropped it into the kindling tube. The fire crawled down the bits of dry wood and flamed the other pieces to life. "Does that look right?"

"It'll take a few minutes, but metal is a good conductor of heat. Fanciest way I've ever seen it brewed."

Svetlana smiled faintly and gazed out the rain-speckled window, the sides of her mouth turning down. With the tea underway and nothing left to divert her attention, exhaustion traced its wearisome existence over her drawn features. The natural reaction of adrenaline leaving the body after coursing through the veins in bursts of oxygen and blood to overcome stress. How she'd managed to resist its crashing effects thus far was a miracle.

"Let's take a seat while we wait." He crossed to the small table tucked in the corner and pulled out one of the two elaborately carved chairs. She sat and he took the chair opposite. "Better?"

She nodded. "Too much standing without stretching grows the legs stiff."

Wynn settled back and propped one ankle atop his opposite knee. "Mine were like that when I first started medical school. Could hardly put one foot in front of the other at the end of the day, but you get used to it."

Her gaze dropped to the table as the warm scent of burning wood drifted around them. "Seeing a man shot in the street is not a thing to become accustomed to."

"No, it's not. Neither is war, and yet we are surrounded by it. An ugly reality brought to our doorstep that we can't turn away from."

"He was lucky to fall at your feet. A physician to save his life."

Wynn shifted as always when a compliment veered his way. Easier to deflect the discomfort with humor. "Good thing I didn't give in to that career impulse of being a chimney sweep like I wanted to when I was younger. Lot of good a blackened broom would do him."

Her gaze lifted to him with not a trace of humor to be found. "How do you remain so calm?"

"I have good training to rely on. Besides, what good will it do my patients if I give in to hysterics? A surgeon must always remain in control of himself in order to control the situation."

"Unlike myself." Her voice grew smaller, curling into itself in search of shelter.

What meager comfort he had in words, he offered to her. This amazing woman, this princess born with every luxury of life who now found herself lost in uncertainty.

"You were more composed than most would have been. It's not easy to step into a situation like that without training. With training, for that matter. I've seen many a good nurse go down or turn green after seeing a gruesome injury. It's a strength of character not forged in many people. A strength gained by trial of fire. Not everyone could have escaped a revolution in the dead of winter. You did."

She dipped her head as a single tear escaped. "Leaving Russia I had to remain resilient for Marina and my mother. Today I wanted only to run."

"But you didn't." Thinking of nothing beyond the need to ease her pain, Wynn reached across the table and placed his hand over hers. "I'm sorry I put you in that situation. You were very brave, and I'm grateful for your assistance."

Her hand moved beneath his, her little finger curling around his. Slender and finely boned, her cool fingers were soft as cream against his skin. His physician's concern for a patient warmed to desire to ease her hurt far beyond the abilities of prescription and bandages. It surprised him how easily the desire to protect came. The sentiment had always existed, it was part of his calling as a physician, but it came in increments like carefully measured pills at the dispensary. A bit given to each patient before moving to the next, never in full doses. Until her.

She tugged at something deep within him, a part yet to be unlocked, since the day he'd called to her in the street. An irresistible pull that kept him tethered to her presence. If given the chance, what might he find at the end of their rope? Dare he dwell on the possibility of a key to unlock that hidden part?

He gently squeezed her hand, drawing her eyes to his. Eyes of pale blue. Melted were the ice shards she carried day to day and in their place was a vulnerable heartbeat.

"Perhaps next time we take a walk we might avoid injuries," she said.

He curled his fingers and touched the sensitive skin inside her wrist. Elevated pulse. If he took his own, he bet it matched. "We do seem to attract them when we're together."

Steam billowed from the samovar, dousing the quiet moment they had escaped to. Svetlana yanked her hand back and jumped to her feet, the jerkiest movements he'd ever witnessed from her. She turned a knob on top of the spout and out poured hot water into the waiting teapot. Keeping her back to him, she busied herself pulling glasses with silver bottoms and handles from a cabinet.

"What business is a man about when he is shot in the street?" Gone was the tremor of vulnerability in her voice. In place once more reigned control.

Wynn rubbed his palm with his thumb, trying not to linger on the memory of her fingers curled against his. "From my experience, never anything good."

"Yet you took pity on him. For all you know he could be a criminal, a murderous zealot."

"Makes no difference if he's the Archbishop of Canterbury or Jack the Ripper. I swore an oath to preserve all human life."

"What made you choose such an oath?"

A question he'd been asked several times over on any given week. Finding his own path held far more appeal than traversing the well-laid one his title procured. Steadfast and secure was for Hugh, not him.

"As a second son there were only so many options available. Barrister. Too many rules. Clergyman. Even more restrictions and they don't appreciate a sense of humor. Soldier. Well, I'd rather put people back together than a hole in them."

The teapot gulped softly as Svetlana poured the amber brew into the glasses. "My father and brother are soldiers. The men in our family always are."

A thousand questions flooded Wynn's mind at the mention of her father and brother. "Are they still fighting in Russia?"

"They fight against those who would destroy everything, leaving nothing but a faint memory of what was once our glorious homeland."

"Have you heard from them?"

"No." She plunked the teapot on the counter, rattling the lid.

"In a war letters are difficult to—"

"Tea." Her expression drawn tight, she placed one of the glasses in front of him. The personal conversation was over. "There is no sugar or milk, if you take them in your drink."

"I've never had the luxury, at least not with the coffee I get at hospital. Faster to drink it straight and move on to the next patient. Spooning and stirring are for the gentleman at ease."

Svetlana slid into her chair and raised her glass. "*Santé.*"

One minute they spoke of Russia and the next she was speaking in French. "Why do you speak French and not your native tongue?"

"I speak several languages; French is merely one of them."

"How many is several?"

"French, English, Russian, Spanish, German, and a touch of Swedish. I can also read in Latin and Greek."

"Impressive, but you still haven't answered my question about your native tongue."

"My native tongue is French, as it is for all the nobility in Petrograd. Peter the Great was enamored with all things French. He dignified it as the height of sophistication and brought the customs to what was once Petersburg. Anything Russian was and is considered *déplaisant*. My native tongue, as you put it, is spoken only by the peasants, of which many go on to become nannies for the nobles' children. It is from the time in the nursery and our peasant nannies that we learn Russian."

He'd heard enough French in the past four years. He wanted to hear her language. "What do Russians say to cheer?"

"*Za zdarovje.*" Warm and round and husky. "To your health."

"*Za zdarovje.*" Wynn took a swallow and spit out the foulness accosting his mouth. "What's in this?"

Svetlana's eyebrows pinched in confusion. "Tea."

He smelled the so-called tea. "Where did you get it?"

"The pouch. Little was left to be found." She pointed to a small brown bag half hidden behind the samovar.

Grabbing the pouch from the counter, Wynn wafted it under his nose. "Stale tobacco. Did you not notice the smell?"

Red danced across Svetlana's cheeks as she shook her head. "I never assumed identification was required in the making of a pot of tea."

Despite her cringing with embarrassment, Wynn couldn't stop the corner of his mouth from curling. Nor could he stop the laugh building up his throat and bursting free. Svetlana's gaze lifted to his. The red slowly faded to pink across her cheeks as her lips perked up. She covered her mouth and giggled. A free, feminine sound that skipped around the room and filled it with light. And filled Wynn with the intense desire to hear it again and again.

A crash sounded in the other room.

Wynn sprinted out of the kitchen and into where his patient grappled with the bedside table in an attempt to sit himself upright. He reached out to push the man back onto the pillows, but the man knocked away Wynn's hands and shouted in Russian.

Svetlana entered and stood behind Wynn as she replied to the man's outburst before considerately switching to English. "You must stay still or do your injury harm."

The man's eyes narrowed. "Who you?"

"Svetlana Dalsky. We were on the street when those men shot you. Do you not remember?"

The man slowly raised a hand to his sagging cheek and scratched. Recognition dawned. "Angel who slap me. Like kiss from heaven." His attention swung to Wynn, all excitement dropping. "Who you?"

"Dr. Edwynn MacCallan." Wynn took his new stethoscope from the bureau where he'd left it and placed the earpieces in his ears.

"He saved your life," Svetlana added.

"Speak truth, angel? *Da*, of course do. Angels no lie. In such case I indebted you, Doctor." He loudly kissed the back of Wynn's hand before bowing his head over it.

"Er, think nothing of it." Wynn withdrew his hand and discreetly wiped it against his trouser leg before placing the stethoscope bell against the man's chest. "We've yet to get your name."

"Leonid the third. My father second, but no confuse me with him. He fat. No mention to him this. He very sensitive about waistline." Leonid pawed at his nightstand and frowned. "Where cigarettes?"

"No smoking." Satisfied with the heartbeat and lungs, Wynn unplugged the earpieces and slung the instrument around his neck. "I don't have morphine to offer you, but I can bring a bit tomorrow when I return to check on you. You're lucky the bullet went clean through. We would've had a wee mess on our hands if it hadn't."

"That good, Doctor. Appreciate you after what *durak* do me." Leonid scowled at his bandaged shoulder as if it were a minor inconvenience and not a gaping hole.

"Who were those men and why were they shooting at you?" Stockstill, Svetlana crossed her arms with the inquiring intensity of a London bobby.

"Crazies. I not know names. One minute I at café sitting reading newspaper—never pleasant stories anymore—and next they shoving me in alley with gun. Say over money." Leonid raked his hand through the wisps of hair waving like flags from a last stand atop his balding head. "No talk more about in front of lady. It rude, and one thing my *papochka* taught me never politics before breakfast. Or front of lady."

The lady didn't relent. "Were these men Russian?"

"*Da*, but everyone here Russian. *Russkiye* neighborhood. Little Neva. What say name was, angel?"

"Svetlana Dalsky."

"Dalsky. Name familiar, *da*?" He snapped his fingers near his head as if to summon wandering thoughts. "Will come to me."

Wynn cleared his throat before she had the chance to launch a formal version of the Inquisition. "I'll come again tomorrow morning to check on you, Leonid, but for now we should be leaving. I've left a list of instructions here on the table. The most important thing is to rest. No unnecessary moving about. And no smoking."

Leonid's flat face fell with disappointment. "Go? No, no, no. Cannot leave until thank proper. I know! Join name day celebration in two nights. Big party. My *papochka* want meet you. Meet other friends, listen at music, enjoy food and vodka. Fountains of vodka."

"I must insist on no vodka. Not with your injury."

Frowning, Leonid's gaze swiveled to Svetlana. "What he mean no vodka?"

Svetlana turned her head to Wynn and whispered, "I think you do not understand Russian culture and its vodka."

"Believe it or not, I do understand," he hissed back. "We have a similar epidemic where I come from, only it's whisky."

"Whisky? Ah! You make joke." Leonid's grin revealed two rows of teeth that surprisingly crowded his wide mouth. Wynn couldn't help warming to the interesting fellow. "You funny doctor, *da*? Almost fool me you serious. Here, here, take card. Show doorman. He let in." Grimacing, Leonid leaned over and pulled two cards from the bedside table drawer and handed them to Wynn and Svetlana. "If ever need help, show card. I loyal friend."

It was a thick, cream cardstock of the finest quality with a strip of gold embossed around the edges. The White Bear was printed in fine scroll on the front. On the back a name in matching font.

Svetlana inhaled. "Sheremetev?"

Leonid nodded. "Muscovy branch. You come, *da*? Both."

Wynn hesitated. "I may be on shift—"

Svetlana grabbed his wrist and squeezed. "*Da*. We will be there."

Before Wynn could decipher the cryptic vice around his hand, Leonid Sheremetev of the White Bear's infamous vodka fell back on his pillow with a loud snore.

CHAPTER 6

W*e will be there.*"

Svetlana marched across the Alexander Nevsky Cathedral courtyard, her too-short beaded skirt whipping around her ankles. What had propelled her to say such a preposterous thing? If the good doctor couldn't attend, all the better for her expressing her family's need to the Sheremetevs for their influence. Hers was a matter of delicate and deadly proportions that must be handled with discreet care. Wynn was a complication she could ill afford. Yet the moment she had the opportunity to cut him loose, she had grabbed his hand in panic and assured his continued presence lest Leonid revoke the invitation.

No more. After tonight's meeting, she would be well on her way to providing safety for her family, and the reoccurring brushes with Dr. MacCallan would be a thing of the past.

"If you hurry like that, we'll arrive before the party begins," Mama huffed behind her.

"It's a bit late for that. The party started an hour ago." A hairpin bounced off Svetlana's exposed shoulder. With no ladies' maids at hand, she'd found it exceedingly difficult to achieve a formal hairstyle based on her own talent. Or lack of.

"A lady does not arrive at the designated start of an event. It is within her best interest to be announced once all the other guests have arrived. That way all attention is given to her entrance."

It had taken less than three seconds for Mama to discover the card from Leonid Sheremetev. The woman could sniff out a societal invitation a drawing room away. She had gasped and nearly fainted in a flutter of excitement. This was it. Their fortunes were about to change as they reentered the social circle they were entitled to, and she wasn't allowing Svetlana to enter alone.

Mama had traded an emerald bracelet and two gold rings for two gowns from a countess who had managed to escape Russia with her trunks. A pearl choker was paid to a peasant seamstress to have one of the gowns fitted. Mama chose her own for the alteration, claiming Svetlana's was passable and such cheap satin wasn't worth the price of another necklace.

Rounding the front of the grand church, the fading blue of dusk settled on a carriage pulled by two white horses. A driver hopped down from his perch and opened the door.

"Compliments of Dr. MacCallan, who has been detained at the hospital and conveys his deepest regrets."

What was that discomforting feeling of disappointment settling in Svetlana's stomach?

Mama stepped into the carriage as if she were owed nothing less than a fine ride waiting for her. Like old times. Inside, she squealed at a single white rosebud on the seat.

The driver looked at her and then to Svetlana. "Apologizes, *mademoiselle*. I was told only one passenger, and the flower—"

"It's quite all right, *monsieur*. The doctor was unaware of my guest." As much as she was unaware of this tremulous expense. Carriages were not easy to come by in the city—much less horses—with all wheels and hooves needed for the war effort. Why must the man insist on surprising her? Even in his absence she could not find distance from him.

"But of course. *S'il vous plaît*." The driver offered her his hand and helped her inside. Climbing to his perch, he gave a command and the horses set off.

"The physician's manners have improved in the treatment of nobility, even if he is bourgeois." Mama anchored the rose to her gown with a pearl-tipped pin that had been secured to the shortened stem. "At least there's more room. Carriages easily become overly populated."

The fluted white petals spiraled to a ruffled center of pure cream. The sweet scent pirouetted under Svetlana's nose with images of spring gardens, rain showers, and violin strings. She could almost feel the velvetiness gliding under her finger. Had Wynn picked it out himself? Catching herself, she turned away and stared out the window as darkness descended on the streets. What did it matter if he sent a hundred roses? They meant nothing, as did this carriage. What mattered was meeting one of the wealthiest and most influential families in all of Russia that night. If anyone could help her family's dire situation, it would be them. If anyone could gather information about Nikolai and Papa, the Sheremetevs could.

The rose scent wafted closer. Svetlana clenched her hands in her lap against its enticement. She never should have bared her vulnerability to him. But the rain and fear and his soothing manner had weakened her defenses, which should have remained impenetrable. Yet the crack came as bits of her slipped through and into the solace between them. In that suspended moment she'd felt the relief of release to another who understood—understood and provided steady ground when her own feet shifted beneath her.

A flitting moment of weakness, that's all it was. She had more important matters at hand.

Before long, the carriage stopped and the door opened to a white bricked building with a green metal-and-glass awning fanning over two dark wood doors. There were no windows.

"Is this the correct address?" Mama squinted at the façade. "It looks deserted."

Svetlana moved up the short flight of stairs and read the gold plaque next to the door. The White Bear. She pulled Leonid's card from her beaded purse. The names matched.

Out of nowhere a hand plucked the card from her fingers. The hand quickly morphed into an arm and then a barrel-chested man who looked like he could stop canon fire by himself. From the looks of his face he probably did.

"You may enter," he boomed in Russian. He returned the card and opened one of the doors.

They entered a small room with dark paneling and low-lit sconces on the wall. A woman dressed in a traditional Russian *kokoshnik* and *sarafan* stood behind a counter on the left.

"Can I take your wraps?" she asked. Accepting their outer garments, the woman indicated a somewhat hidden door at the back of the room. "Have a pleasant evening."

The door swung open to a blaze of red, gold, and green. A swell of music and laughter carried them inside to an imperial palace of decadence. Red carpets sprawled across the floor to the dark green walls that swept to a gold-leafed ceiling that refracted the dozens of crystal chandeliers. Dark booths lined the walls while a step down to a lower tier was dotted with tables draped in snowy linens and candles ensconced in glass. Men dressed in formal white tie and women dripping in silk and jewels crowded every space available while cigarette smoke and music wove between the cracks, enticing couples to the dance floor.

"Are we not to be announced?" Mama complained over the din. No one noticed.

"I do not think this is the kind of place for announcing," Svetlana said as a waiter sped past them with a loaded tray of drinks. She resisted the urge to slide her feet into third position, which always produced a grounding effect.

"Then what sort of place have you forced us to?"

"Mama, remember we are not here for frivolities. We are here to assess if this Sheremetev can help us out of the church cellar and find a safer place to live in Paris, but he is not to know our true intentions or our true titles until I deem him trustworthy enough to confide in.

Mama, are you listening?" In fact, her mother was not once a tray heaped with caviar and chocolate truffles had swerved in front of them. Without warning, Svetlana's stomach rumbled with the unfilling portions of cabbage and celery stew she had sipped hours before. The last time she'd eaten a truffle . . . Her stomach rumbled louder.

"Svetlana Dalsky!" Leonid forced his way through the crowd, his flat face lifting in charismatic pleasure. "I thought you never to arrive! And look. Most beautiful woman in our place." He kissed her on both cheeks, careful to keep his cigarette from catching her hair. "But where doctor? He not saving other gunshots?"

"He was called to the hospital but sends his deepest regrets and well wishes on your name day celebration."

"That is sad, but now I smoke. Do not tell this." He took a defiant puff and looked behind her. "This is who?"

"Allow me to present my mother, Ana Dalsky."

"Princess Ana Andreevna Dalsky," Mama clarified. She angled an eyebrow at Svetlana, challenging her to object when not a minute before Svetlana had expressly told her to remain silent about their titles. They would all end up in shackled sacks at the bottom of the Seine River before long. Why did no one else see the danger of giving themselves away to perfect strangers? Had the October Revolution taught them nothing?

"Illustrious guests. Why did you no tell me you are princess, angel? Come, come. I will take you to my father." Puffing away like a steam engine, Leonid strode through the crowd that parted for him like a blade through bread.

Too late to put the proverbial cat back into the bag, Svetlana shot her mother a disapproving look, which made Ana smirk in triumph. Following Leonid, Svetlana kept her face impassive and head erect as women stared. She was accustomed to being sized up; it was a favorite pastime of the nobility at play, but she had always been armored in her own clothing and jewels. Tonight she was in borrowed hand-me-downs two sizes too large and four inches too short in a hideous shade of puce.

Elegance isn't found in one's wardrobe but in one's manner. A favored quote of her governess and one that had steeled Svetlana's spine for years. Still, a wistful part of her wished for the tiara she'd left behind in Petrograd.

Leonid led them to a large circular booth partially shrouded with thick damask drapes tied back with gold tassels. Around the booth sat thickly muscled men with a wild collection of facial scars and bulging side jackets.

"*Papochka*, she is here!" Leonid announced as they reached the table.

Taking up nearly a quarter of the booth and dressed in a black suit with gold epaulets was *Papochka* Sheremetev himself. He was round everywhere, like a ball of kneaded dough, with a drooping nose, eyes pushed into the thick skin, and bald with silver hairs wisping around the back. He smiled and his eyes disappeared into the folds.

"At last. Her Serenity the Princess Svetlana Dmitrievna Dalsky. You are welcomed with humble indebtedness for saving my son's life. Ask and it will be made yours."

It had been so long since her full title had been spoken aloud, so long since she was allowed to feel the thrilling rush it gave her. The sense of purpose it bestowed, but fear was not long in its wake. She had yet to ascertain this man's loyalties, yet he knew precisely who she was.

"The pleasure is mine, sir." She made a polite dip. "May I inquire as to how you know who I am, or rather what I am, when even your son until a moment ago did not know of my rank?"

"Nothing slips past without my knowing. Every Russian in Paris is known to me. When I hear names new to the city, it is my top priority to discover who they are. I keep a long, well-informed list from the old country." Smiling conspiratorially, he tapped the side of his head.

The cat from the bag was well and truly gone. No use in keeping up the pretense. Svetlana indicated her mother. "Allow me to introduce my mother."

Sheremetev nodded without surprise. "Welcome to you as well, Princess. Sit with me, please."

Mama settled into the booth with ease. "It's been much too long since I've been properly addressed."

"Look around you, Princess. Friends are among you. All White émigrés. Everyone here is a count or duchess or excellency of the imperial court of Tsar Nicholas." Sheremetev touched the stick pin in his neckcloth. The pin was a solid ruby carved in the shape of a double-headed eagle. The symbol of Imperial Russia. "Our new homeland until returning safe to ours."

"A delightful relief to be among our own kind again. My daughter worries so. Do you know she wants us to slink around without use of our titles as if we were common peasants?"

"Mama, please." Svetlana squeezed her fingers together to keep from slapping a hand over her mother's wide mouth.

Ana ignored her. "I believe she imagines a Bolshevik around every corner set to drag us back to a firing squad."

Did other mothers prove so difficult and shameless? "It is not unheard of."

"She is right, but Paris is safe enough," Sheremetev said. "A buffer is provided by war, but the outcome does not bring me fear. Not with men like your husband and son fighting in the White Army. Honorable and a good solider is your Prince Dmitri. Losing we cannot with men like him battling for us."

Tears sprang to Mama's eyes. She touched her ever-present cross pendant. "How do you know of my husband and son?"

"As I said, everyone and everything is mine to know, Princess. Word does not take long to cross my attention." Sheremetev twitched his finger, and a bottle of vodka and another of red wine appeared on the table along with fresh glasses. "Such as the absence of your doctor. Has the Marquess of Tarltan abandoned us?"

"Only for patients. He is devoted to them. I have the proof." Leonid raised the cigarette to his lips, hesitated, then ground it into the crystal ashtray on the table. He slid a wink to Svetlana.

"Marquess." Mama's tears evaporated as she indicated for a glass of the red to be filled. "I have never heard of this marquess. He is a physician, yes?"

"It's a noble title in Scotland where he comes from. Below a duke," Svetlana said. "Which I assume you already know, along with the holdings in his possession."

Sheremetev tapped the side of his nose. "Ahead of the competition I remain."

Mama's accusatory gaze slid to her over the top of the wine glass. She despised being absent of pertinent information. The only thing she loathed more was being intentionally left out. "Well, I see he amounts to more than what I was led to believe. Though why he continues with menial work when the respectability of a title rests on him is beyond my comprehension."

"I believe he cares more for the title of surgeon," Svetlana said.

Mama rolled her eyes with exasperation to Sheremetev. "These younger generations have no sense of tradition. Of the demands on retaining their place in society." She took a sip of her wine and leaned close to Svetlana. "This wine is delicious. When you marry Sergey be sure his shipping business imports this and not the cheap grapes from Italy."

Unable to listen anymore, Svetlana turned her attention to the crowd who bounced around to the unusual musical combination of piano, violin, tambourine, and balalaika. Drinks, one could assume vodka, flowed like the River Neva and the people mere fish swimming from one frothy bubble to the next, gulping up the offered sips of life. One might never know death, poverty, and war stalked outside.

"Dance, Angel?" Leonid whispered on a puff of cigarette breath. "Parents talk much and say little. These ears of mine are bleeding."

Svetlana nodded. "I would be delighted."

On the dance floor, Leonid swept her around in something akin to a waltz with a strange beat similar to what a *skomorokh*, or traveling minstrel, might pluck.

"Enjoying the party?" he asked as they whisked past a waiter carrying bowls of caviar. Where had they found these extravagances? It was nothing short of a return to the world she had known, one that had all but disappeared into a dank basement of merest survival. For one night she wished only to revel in the memory of what once was.

"It's very exciting."

"Everything is loud and big with *Papochka*. Love life is a Sheremetev tradition."

"I've never been to a party quite like this."

"That is because you are from old Saint Petersburg. Whole city filled with walking corpses." He pretended to snore. He was right. Her home city was one of grand architecture, watercolors, and stale conversation by aristocrats too busy imagining themselves in a French court. The only life that existed was the vein of gossip pumping to keep society upright. "We Muscovite. Know how to live!" He thumped his chest, which garnered a loud cheer from whirling couples.

A slight pain shivered on her shin. The wound from the shard of glass was healing nicely, but it would be some time before the discomfort vanished completely. "Is this what it's like every night in Moscow? Music, dancing, drinking, and general merrymaking?"

"*Da*, though drink first. First, and second, and third, and always at end." He laughed loudly in his easy manner. "It is rude ending a party before sun rises. Bad host."

"I imagine the Sheremetevs are magnanimous hosts."

"*Da*. It is noble custom to open doors at mealtime. 'On Sheremetev account' is considered other name for generosity in Moscow."

"Careful. You open those doors too wide and any ol' riffraff can walk in." Wynn stood at the edge of the dance floor, effortlessly relaxed amid a sea of jostling Russians.

"Doctor! How excellent see you." Leonid twirled them to a stop, his words bubbling out in broken English. "We think no come."

"I almost didn't, but things calmed down enough for me to slip out. I hope you'll forgive my tardiness."

"Anything for man save life."

"In that case, may I steal your partner? If the lady is agreeable, of course." Though he was dressed identical to many of the gentlemen in the room in black tails and white tie, Wynn's was tailored to show off broad shoulders and a trim waist. His hair, customarily shoved back with an indifferent hand, was combed and pomaded to the side with one defiant wave passing over his right ear. A dangerously handsome complication, if ever there was one. Why did he not stay away?

Every woman in the nearby vicinity stared at him with more than passing interest. And he watched Svetlana.

"*Da, da!* Go, go." Grinning wildly, Leonid stepped back and was immediately swallowed into the crowd of well-wishers.

Wynn held his hand out. "Shall we?"

Svetlana stepped into his arms, placing one hand on his shoulder and slipping her other into his waiting hand. Her hands and arms felt scandalously bare without proper gloves as she touched palm to palm with him. His hands were wide with long fingers that wrapped completely around her own, and his skin felt cool against hers, which had suddenly climbed several degrees.

An accordion vibrated in her ears in a clash with her beating heart.

"I don't think I know this one."

"Pardon?" The noise and rush of blood cleared. Svetlana looked around to find them the only couple standing on the floor. All others were moving back to the tables as a troupe of men and women in brightly colored *sarafans* and *kaftans* danced out to a *pliaska*, a traditional peasant dance.

"We better move before they think we want to join their circle." Still holding her hand, Wynn led her to one of the few empty tables.

Svetlana eased onto the chair he held out for her. "I do know this dance. It's traditional."

Wynn pulled his chair close to hers and sat. He smelled of shaving lotion, ironed starch, and faint metal. Like his hospital instruments. "Do all Russian children learn the traditional dances?"

"In villages, I suppose. The aristocracy are taught more courtly dances." She traced the pattern of the steps with her eyes before the dancers' feet moved. "I learned for one of our ballets."

"You're a ballerina?"

"Yes. Or I was."

"That would explain your calves."

Her gaze snapped to his. "I beg your pardon?"

"Your calves. The gastrocnemius muscles are more well-defined than most women's." He held her gaze, not the least bit embarrassed at the topic. "Apologies. Anatomy isn't the talk of polite society outside the surgery. Forget where I am sometimes. And who I'm with. You look beautiful tonight."

The straightforwardness caught her off balance, but she quickly recovered. If life in a palace had taught her one thing, it was not to be thrown off by charm. Besides, she had a course to maintain.

"The hospital must be desolate without you."

"Alas, it must survive in my absence. I needed to see for myself why you were so eager to attend tonight."

Her impulsive hand grab in Leonid's apartment hadn't gone unnoticed, as she would have preferred. "I thought it only polite when Leonid wished to express his gratitude."

"And the enticing Sheremetev name, by chance?" He'd noticed

more than she gave him credit for. Denial at this point was her worst option and likely to incur more of his curiosity.

"They are one of the most influential families outside of the Romanovs themselves."

"I wonder if the Romanovs—they're your royalty, aren't they?—carry sidearms to parties."

"It is war."

"And yet I find myself woefully unprepared for the battle before me." A half smile curved his full mouth in the manner of a man who knew precisely what he was about.

The confidence sent a tremor through Svetlana as she met him head-on. Somewhere across the room the balalaika's strings trembled as the dancers spun in colorful whirls.

"What battle might that be?"

"One of intrigue." Placing his arms on the table, he leaned forward to catch the candlelight glowing in the center of his eyes. The heart of a flame. "No matter how often I try to dispense myself of it, the allure returns me to the frontline time and again. I'll be honest. I don't know if I'm winning or losing."

Svetlana danced around the flame, refusing to be captured by it. "Perhaps you've already lost."

"Oh, no. It's just getting started."

"I should only wage war if the odds are in my favor."

The smile gained full control of his lips, tilting them up at both ends. "Diminished odds for impossible causes are my weakness."

"Some call that an honorable pursuit."

"Honorable? No. A challenge. The greater the challenge, the greater the reward."

She hiked a disinterested eyebrow that belied the fluttering in her heart. "What reward do you have in mind for this battle of intrigue?"

"I'm still deciding, but it'll be worth the patience." His gaze lingered on her, allowing the words to settle deep inside her. Given enough time they might take root. That she could not allow.

"Dr. MacCallan. Marquess, or whatever you wish to be called—"

"Wynn."

"I think it best—" A sequined hip swung into her, knocking her practically onto Wynn's lap. He steadied her, but not before her lips came dangerously close to grazing his neck. He smelled even better at this proximity. She jerked upright in her chair and smoothed her skirt before her hands could tremble. "Forgive me."

"Nothing to forgive when a lady falls into my arms." A charming quip for every situation. The flame in his eyes warmed to pure gold. "I very much wanted to escort you tonight, but I hope the carriage eased your troubles."

"It was very thoughtful for you to think of us in that way. We are grateful."

His brow creased. "We?"

"My mother insisted on attending with me." Svetlana inclined her head to where her mother lounged in Sheremetev's booth guzzling wine and preening like a peacock too long displaced from her court of honor. Some things never changed.

Wynn followed her gaze. "Ah, I see your mother got the flower I sent you."

"It was lovely." Svetlana touched the spot on her gown where she would've pinned the flower, then quickly brushed at it. Did she imagine him wooing her? Certainly not. "I wanted to correct the misunderstanding, but that often leads to greater troubles, and Mama is rather—"

"Difficult?"

"Unchangeable."

Wynn turned back to her, expression softening. "I'm almost glad you're not wearing it. You would shame any rose daring to call itself lovely."

This man and his charm!

As the dancers took their bow, a parade of chilled buckets filled with champagne, trays loaded with food, and stacks of cigarettes in silver cases arrived at their table with Leonid leading the grand procession just in time to save her. The atmosphere, having grown densely warm over the past several minutes, eased.

"Enjoy party, *da*? Eat, eat." Leonid lifted a tray lid to expose a mountain of deep red and passed it under Wynn's nose. "Delicious."

"Is that pickled beets?" Wynn's questioning gaze lifted to Svetlana.

She shrugged, sending her blousy sleeve sliding down. "Pickle everything."

Hesitating under Leonid's waiting eye, Wynn forked a single beet and tucked it into his mouth. His expression shifted as he chewed and swallowed, followed by a quick gulp of champagne.

"I've never had beets prepared that way."

"You honorary Russian now. Eat beets and cabbage. Drink vodka." Leonid tried pushing a glass of vodka into Wynn's hands.

"No, thank you. Have to stay sharp in case I'm called to operate, but in the meantime allow me to present something to you." Reaching into his jacket pocket, Wynn pulled out a small package wrapped in gauze and tied with twine. "Sorry about the wrapping. I couldn't find proper gifting paper, but I didn't want to arrive empty-handed to your name day celebration. Which I'm still not clear about."

"I named after saint. Anointed day on calendar he has. His day. My day. It same. Like birthday." Leonid tore off the gift wrapping and howled with delight at the bullet cartridge in his palm. "Is mine?"

Wynn nodded. "I found it on the footpath behind you. Thought you might like a souvenir. Many of the soldiers do when they're wounded."

"Soldiers see enemy across line, no back of alley." Words steely, Leonid's fingers curled over the bullet. "They pay."

"Do you know who attacked you?"

"*Nyet*, but soon. No have crazy streets like Moscow, or Petrograd, or Novgorod. *Papochka* bring peace here now." Leonid's expression softened as he patted Svetlana's hand. "No Bolsheviks here, Angel. Trust people, *da*? Trust me."

A look dawned across Wynn's face as he settled back in his chair and gazed at her. She glanced away as he probed into her, overturning truths she wished to remain hidden and safe.

"He is here! Here is famous surgeon saving my son's life." Sheremetev barreled through the throng with thick arms spread wide and switching to English for Wynn's sake. Anyone not coherent enough to leap from his path was knocked out by his rotund belly. Seizing Wynn by the shoulders, he hauled him to his feet and into a hug that could have cracked ribs. "Owe you everything. Tell me, what I do for you? I get anything for show appreciation. Name it only."

"Your son alive is all the gratitude I need, sir."

"Englishmen too modest. Come, come. Accept humble token." Sheremetev snapped his fingers and a finely wrapped box appeared in his fleshy palm. "For you. It great insult to refusals."

It was a Fabergé egg made of glossy emerald and gold filigree. Inside was a miniature of St. Basil's Cathedral in dazzling colors of sapphire, ruby, turquoise, tourmaline, and diamond. Wynn stared in stunned silence.

"I think he likes." Sheremetev thumped him on the back to the crowd's roar of laughter. "A toast! My son Mikhail Leonid on name day. To man who saved life, and to angel who shining between them. *Na Zdorovye!*"

"*Spasibo*," Wynn managed. The drunken audience cheered with delight at his Russian. An easy crowd to please.

Sheremetev shifted his attention to Svetlana, causing the orbit of onlookers to mimic him. "And for you, our dear princess, whatever heart's desire will be wish to grant."

As with any diplomatic service, she'd keep first introductions modest. To request his help now would be a hand overplayed. Such entreaties required a delicacy of timing. "Sir, your kindness and hospitality are more than enough. Please do not think on it again."

"I must think on it, be assured. For own good." Tweaking her sleeve so the beads jangled together, he disappeared into the haze of vodka bottles and cigarettes. Leonid trailed at his heels.

Svetlana eased a breath out. She'd done it. One step closer to safety.

The crowd bumped back to their tables jabbering incoherently over the music, leaving her and Wynn alone once more. Alone with their prize platter of beets.

"I do believe you've firmly ingratiated yourself into the White émigrés' society. Do not be surprised to find requests for house calls from them," she said.

"They'll be sorely disappointed to find I'm not a general practitioner."

"It matters not. By tomorrow morning you will achieve near-saint status."

"I'd settle for a dance with you." Smoothing his face to one of grave solemnity, he bowed and held out his hand. "My dear princess, might you honor me with this waltz that has finally played to a rhythm my feet can comprehend?"

A waltz was difficult to resist and one of her favorites, a reminder of days filled with grace and elegance. It had nothing whatsoever to do with him or the way he looked in evening dress. Or so she told herself. "A pleasure, Marquess."

Taking her hand, he hesitated with the Fabergé egg in his other hand while sizing up his jacket pocket.

"It's quite safe on the table. No one in this entire room would dare touch it under Sheremetev's protection."

Placing the egg in the center of the table, Wynn guided her to the dance floor and she once more found herself in his arms. This time his palm was warm against hers.

"Quite a party. Are all Russian get-togethers like this?"

"Truthfully, I have never entered a place such as this. It is as if they have forgotten the war exists outside."

"The extravagance is a wee bit surprising, but then again these Sheremetevs don't seem to do things in half measures. Still, it makes one wonder." He looked around with a slight frown puckering his forehead. "Are you enjoying yourself?"

"I believe so."

"Not worried about the Bolsheviks, are you?" Svetlana's hand slipped in his. He caught it and held tight, forcing her attention to him. "Is that why you won't trust me? I might be the enemy?"

Memories of that red night with Petrograd burning around her and screams renting the streets flashed through her mind rapidly as gunfire. The aftermath of horror, of starving, of freezing, of hiding among beasts to avoid capture snapped at her heels. Always the same nightmare relived each time she closed her eyes.

"You don't understand. You weren't there."

"No, I wasn't, but I can promise—"

"You cannot commit promises on things you know nothing about. Your world is of sterile hospitals, treating patients, and a home tucked safely on an island across a channel from war. This is not your world. These, the White émigrés, we are not your people. I am grateful for all you've done, truly, and I'm glad Leonid was able to express his gratitude for you saving his life, but you should take your leave after tonight."

He had the gall to look not the least bit taken aback. "And miss the opportunity to become the premier physician to the fleeing nobles of Russia? Not likely."

"This is nothing to jest about. You do not belong here. Please see to your priorities elsewhere."

"Rather snobbish of you."

"Do not make this more difficult than need be. You have your place as I have mine. I see no reason for our paths to cross again. After this evening we will say goodbye." It was for the best. It had to be. Her life was without certainty, a position she despised. She would not allow a man, a near stranger, to rock her further from the shaky ground upon which she hovered, and Wynn MacCallan came at her with every ability to distract her focus.

"No."

"I beg your pardon."

"No. It means to refuse or decline. You're familiar with the term, yes? Must be a shock when you've never been on the receiving end of such a preposterous notion." He had the nerve to wink. Right there on the dance floor surrounded by dozens of people.

"You mock me." She tried to pull away, but he held fast.

"Only because you make things much more difficult than need be." He pulled her closer until his face was inches from hers, and she could see the soft dent in his full bottom lip. "Give me a chance."

Svetlana hesitated, caught somewhere between the soft look of his lip, the persuasive charm in his eye, and an instinct of protection holding her back. "I—"

Crash!

Cymbals clashed, stopping the music as Sheremetev hauled himself onto the bandstand. Sweat dripped from his pale face as his diminutive eyes skittered around the room.

"Ladies and gentlemen! Unspeakable horror has struck our beloved motherland." A telegram shook in his hand. "Tsar Nicholas and his family have been executed. The Imperial family is dead!"

CHAPTER 7

An incision on the left side of the chest exposed the beating heart. Wynn angled his head to see where the slug had entered, but after a moment of gentle probing, the bullet refused to be located.

"Where's it gone?" he muttered.

"Right ventricle or passed to the spine?" Gerard offered as he stood opposite the operating table.

Wynn shook his head. "Not possible with the trajectory of the entrance wound. Or based on the X-ray findings. Let me see that shot again."

A nurse scrambled to put the X-ray on the light board. A fuzzy black image of bone, organs, and cavities flickered. Barely out of its infancy, this new technology in medical diagnosis was a miraculous gift to surgeons. Countless were the lives saved by its internal depictions, a view once reserved for the Creator alone.

Glancing from the X-ray to Harkin's exposed heart, attempting to merge the two images together in his mind, Wynn's frustration mounted. He worked his fingertips over the organ. Smooth muscle, bumpy interventricular artery and cardiac vein, and aortic arch. No bullet.

"It's not here."

"What do you mean? Of course it is. The X-ray shows it. Unless Harkin decided to perform his own surgery that we don't know about since the images were taken."

"It's hiding." Instinct nudged. Wynn rationalized the possibilities and outcomes, but intuition wouldn't be denied. "Breathing status?"

The anesthesiologist checked the gas apparatus that kept the patient sedated before taking his pulse. "Steady, Doctor."

"Stand by. I'm going to rotate the heart for a posterior examination."

Gerard fumbled a pair of forceps. They bounced off the floor and skittered across the room. "You can't do that! It's impossible."

"It's the only recourse to finding the bullet."

"Doctor MacCallan." Gerard took a shaky breath and lowered his voice. "Wynn. You'll kill him."

He might, but he also might save his life. The risk was worth it. "Stand by for rotation."

Clearing his mind of the assaulting doubt and apprehension, Wynn focused on the life-sustaining piece as it beat in time with the clock on the wall. His own heart calmed to follow the pace, its steady rhythm narrowing the room and all its distractions to a single moment captured in his hands. The familiar comfort of knowledge quietly settled within him. He knew what he was doing, and moreover, knew what needed to be done.

Turning Harkin's heart in minuscule fractions, he slipped his fingers around to the posterior side and closed his eyes, blocking out visual distractions. The mind often worked best in darkness as it was forced to rely on truth and not vision's desensitization. The inferior vena cava carrying deoxygenated blood from the lower half of the body into the right atrium. Pulmonary veins carrying oxygenated blood from the lungs. Right ventricle. Left ventricle. A bump.

Wynn's eyes flew open. He ran his finger over it again.

A smooth cylinder. The bullet.

"It's here. Lodged between the posterior left and right ventricle. Angle the lamp here. Doctor Byeford, take the forceps while I hold the heart steady." A small gag brought Wynn's head up to Gerard's pale face. "If you're going to be sick, there's a bucket in the corner."

"I'm a surgeon, not a green-nosed VAD. I'll hold. You extract."

Gripping the forceps, Wynn slowly withdrew the obstruction from its hiding place and held it up to the light.

"There you are, bonny beastie." A slug from a German 8mm

Mauser rifle. He'd pulled out thousands of them since the start of the war, yet it never failed to amaze him the amount of pain a single body could endure. Nor the amount of horror a human could inflict upon another. How senseless was war in its incessant drive to destruction. If the human race could see the wonders that composed their bodies, the intricacies of veins, the precise perfection of the humerus in its rotating cuff, or the delicacy of a heart pumping, they would not be so quick to sacrifice themselves at the altar of fevered battle. Sheer waste.

He dropped the bullet into a sterile dish the nurse held and then the forceps into another.

"Breathing dropping," the anesthesiologist said.

Words no surgeon wanted to hear.

"Heart stopped."

Even worse.

"Stand clear." Wynn waved back the flap of nurses and positioned himself over the patient's heart once more. Every fiber of his being tuned to the absent heartbeat.

"Begin manual resuscitation." He gently massaged. One. Two. Three. Nothing. Again. One. Two. Three. Nothing. Wynn gritted his teeth, refusing the well of panic. He hadn't given in to it before and he wouldn't start now. One. Two. Three. "Come on, laddie. Don't go out on me in front of the nurses. Bad cricket, that."

Sweat puckered his brow. One. Two. Three. Not Harkin. Not after Wynn had given the man his solemn oath of care. It was a vow given on the rarest occasion as it benefited no one but a patient's peace of mind and set the surgeon to a not-always-possible standard of achievement. A momentary lapse of weakness, or perhaps a sense of reassuring himself in the dangerous endeavor, and the vow hung suspended like a thread of hope between patient and surgeon, ready to be severed at the hand of Fate.

Fate would not sever them now.

Massage. One. Two. Three.

A pulse rippled through the heart. Another. Life thumped into a steady beat.

Wynn let out a shaky breath.

"Heart rate climbing. Breathing maintained. Closing into normal," announced the anesthesiologist in a shaky tone of his own.

Wynn glanced across the table to where Gerard stood immobilized. "Ready for closure, Doctor?"

Gerard blinked several times at the pulsing heart within reach of his fingertips and finally lifted his gaze to Wynn as a nurse placed sterilized packing gauze in his hand.

"Ready on your count."

An hour later Wynn sat on the back steps of the hospital, arms looped over his knees and head dragging down. Exhaustion wearied every bone of his body until the angles seemed to morph into one sagging mass. Yet the thrill of success could not escape him. It bounded from one fatigued muscle to the next, skipping over synapses like sparks of lightning that blazed through his nervous system with blinding excitement.

He'd done it. He'd kept his promise to Harkin.

The sheer magnitude of what had been accomplished in that operating theater deprived him of words. A rare occurrence indeed, but mere mortal words could not express the awed response demanded by this unprecedented surgery. The practice of medicine existed in closed, round rooms where the select privileged were admitted to trod. There to bloat themselves among the shelves of practices deemed favorable for centuries, hardly daring to open the door for new possibilities but for the fearless souls in search of better treatment. The doors to Wynn's medical chamber had been flung wide open. What might exist beyond the walls?

The door banged open behind him. Gerard huffed down the steps. Orange hair blazing like a crinkled carrot, he furrowed his hands through it as he paced on the grass in front of Wynn. Back and forth he strode with a determination lacking conviction of direction.

Wynn sat quietly in the fading heat of day and waited for his friend to settle on the words tossing about in his mind. It wouldn't be long. Gerard never could bottle his reactions for extended amounts of time.

Gerard stopped directly in front of him. "That was the most insane, terrifying, mad, not to mention off the chump stunt I have ever witnessed."

Wynn dropped his head. "Anything else?"

"It was bloody brilliant. I've never seen anything like that." Gerard bent over and grabbed his knees. "Don't ever do it again. My heart can't handle the theatrics."

"You call saving a patient's life theatrical?"

"The way you perform, yes. Always invoking the most drama into theater instead of sticking to the rules."

Wynn's head snapped up. "I hardly think Harkin would agree with sticking to the rules in there. He'd be shoving daisies on the table."

"You were reckless. Sometimes I think you care more for the triumph in the challenge than the actual patient."

"That's absurd."

"Is it? Then why are you always mucking about with things best left out of our grasp? Stop playing God and leave well enough alone because I won't go down with your foolish need to prove yourself." Gerard stormed back inside and slammed the door. A second later the door opened again and he huffed back out. "My apologies, chap. I should not have spoken in anger to you."

Wynn's defense deflated. As loathe as he was to hear it, his friend had a point. "Anger often reveals our truest meaning when it isn't being hidden behind good manners."

"True, but you do not deserve my censorship in so harsh a tone. Please do forgive me."

Standing, Wynn clapped him on the shoulder. A comradery of candidness was not one he wished to forsake on the grounds of his pride. "There's nothing to forgive."

"What happened in there?"

"The heart stopped. I restarted it."

Gerard gave him a sharp look. "But how did you know?"

"I've been reading medical correspondence from the frontline. A similar operation took place at the Battle of Cambrai last year. The surgeons at the casualty clearing station wouldn't touch the patient, said he was as good as dead. All heart cases are considered such, but the chief surgeon had read in a medical journal years before the war about the groundbreaking research and techniques the Germans were employed in."

"The Germans and Austrians have always ingratiated themselves to the newest fangled treatment." A hint of derision laced Gerard's tone.

"With great success. Consider the sheer number of patients admitting themselves to their spas in the mountains to take the waters. The achievement of their results cannot be denied."

"My mother goes there, or did, every June for her nerves. Personally, I think it's to spend the month away from Father when his horse betting kicks into a frenzy." Gerard grew quiet as two grizzled physicians walked by deep in conversation about a leg amputation. He lowered his voice. "I don't believe we should be trusting the Jerries when it comes to treatment for our patients. It's unpatriotic."

Wynn harbored no such discrepancies as to who heard him. Would do them all some good to open their ears. They ridiculed him enough behind closed doors. Might as well bring it out into the open.

"Disease, sickness, and death have no such boundaries of partisanship. They're indiscriminate to lines on a map. What that physician did in Cambrai was unprecedented. No one has dared to cut into the heart before to this extent. At least no British physician. Until now."

"It's dangerous. Not only for the patient but for you as well. What do you think the board will say when they find out? Or Nestor, for that matter. He's a real tartar for rule following, and it's his job as hospital director to ensure we do as well."

"Nestor should've retired decades ago. If it were up to him, we'd still be using leeches and bloodletting. We owe it to our patients to implement the newest advancements, otherwise we are signing their death sentences by not trying."

"The men in our profession do not often trust what is new. It isn't safe. By continuing with these practices they will think you aren't safe."

"Nothing in our profession is safe. Men are being ripped apart in the trenches and sent to us in pieces. What about bullets, and cannons, and bayonets seem safe to you? As physicians we are charged with seeking the best treatment for those in our care, and if that means bucking against what stuffy old men clustered around their draconian traditions declare, then by God, that's precisely what I'll do. I have no use for the doctor whose beliefs are founded on medical authority alone."

Gerard placed a steadying hand on Wynn's shoulder. "Tread carefully, Wynn. Your brilliant defiance to toeing the line may be your undoing. How will you care for your patients then?"

"If I toe the line, they might all be dead."

Dropping his hand to his pocket, a weary smile slid across Gerard's face. "Do you always have to have the last word?"

Wynn couldn't stop his own smile from creeping out. "Only if it's the right one."

"Speaking of which, how's that lady of yours?"

Smile fading, Wynn toed a rock embedded in the dirt. "She's not mine."

"I thought you were courting her."

"Courting would involve agreement from the lady. At the moment it's a one-sided pursuit."

"Then why persist?"

"Because I'd like it to become two-sided."

Gerard sighed as if the entire situation weighed him down. Which wouldn't take much in his case. The man was as lanky as a tattie bogle scaring off the crows.

"There are any number of women in this sweltering metropolis, or London or Edinburgh, for that matter, who would adore nothing more than to acquire the title Marchioness of Tarltan. Why must you chase after the one who doesn't want you?"

"Precisely for that reason."

"Because you're a glutton for punishment? Because you have to do everything the hard way?"

How many times had Wynn asked himself that very question only to be stumped by the mystery? He couldn't ignore the inexplicable draw he felt toward this woman. As if there were a piece of her calling to him, pleading for discovery. Any woman in her position would've given up long before now, but not her. There was a fierceness about her pride that refused to accept defeat. Nothing was more admirable.

Wynn kicked the rock across the grass patch. "Because she intrigues me and I need to find out why."

"Like I said, reckless." Gerard started for the door, his feet dragging on each step. Surgery was an exhausting business. "Up for a game later tonight? Your choice after you nodded off during chess last time."

"Too much sitting for me, but we'll need something to keep us awake while we adjust swinging onto the night shift." Wynn checked his wristwatch, a gift from a colonel whose leg he'd saved from being amputated after the Somme. The handy timepieces were a brilliant advancement deployed by the men in the trenches to better synchronize tactics and were far more maneuverable than bulky pocket watches. Perhaps in time, their uses would prove a trend far from battle. "I need to check on Leonid Sheremetev first. His bandages are about ready to come off."

"Odd company you keep. I realize the Russians are allies, or they were until the country turned on itself in civil war, but they're not like us. A whole other culture. Bears, beets, and a sentimental longing for misery."

"Don't believe everything you read. Leonid Sheremetev has an unbeatable zest for life in his bones." Despite his initial concerns—after all, upstanding citizens didn't get into alleyway shootouts—Wynn had come to like his gregarious patient since meeting him nearly two weeks ago. He had heart.

Gerard snorted. "Alexander Pushkin is said to be the greatest Russian poet who ever lived. If he stakes a claim of his own country, then I am faultless to believe him."

"As I am faultless if I fall asleep during your waxing of poetry. A fate I cannot succumb to for the sake of my patient who happens to serve delicious beets."

It was nearing ten o'clock by the time Wynn left the hospital. He hurried down the street as the streetlamps flickered one by one to douse the City of Light in darkness. They, too, well-served as beacons for German zeppelins and their Fokkers mounted with deadly machine guns swooping in on nighttime raids. It was an eerie experience walking through the great city in absolute obscurity when it should be teeming with life. As if he were trespassing on her hesitant breath of survival.

Arriving at Leonid's flat, Wynn reached for a note stuck between the door and the frame. He pulled the note out and scanned the uneven writing.

Mac,

    White Bear. Come join.

L

The club was the last place he wanted to go, much less attend a patient, but said patient wasn't making recovery easy. Two nights prior Leonid had engaged in a one-armed fist fight with a man who insulted the vodka being served by not taking a fourth glass. Why he'd taken three before deciding it was beneath his taste buds Wynn couldn't puzzle out, but it had earned the man a bloody nose and Leonid bruised knuckles.

Wynn glanced at his wristwatch, calculating how long it would take him to rush home, change, and get to the club. Too much time. The stuff-shirted men and glittering ladies would have to find another direction in which to look if his working clothes offended them. Hopefully he'd managed to avoid any unseen blood splatters today.

The White Bear's guard opened the door without a word, and once more Wynn found himself swept away to another world. One clogged with thick smoke, chilled bottles, glittering gold, and weeping music. A world desperately trying to spin itself into resurrection and teetering from its pinnacle like a top with a faulty axis. Truth be told, he felt a wee bit sad for them all swanning about as they once had in courts of royalty.

A woman with too much rouge painted on her cheeks and smelling heavily of violets draped herself across Wynn's arm and whispered in his ear.

Wynn turned his nose from her sour breath. "Sorry. I don't speak French."

"Buy drink." She jabbed a gloved finger into his chest, then into the creased flesh of her sagging bosom. "Thirsty, *oui*."

"*Nyet*. Em, *non*." Once more his mind had to rework itself in speaking French to a Russian.

"I countess. Command you."

"Apologies, your ladyship, but I believe you've had enough to drink and I'm fresh out of vodka."

"Never run dry in Russia. It flow like River Neva to Petersburg palaces. It still Petersburg. No call Petrograd. War never changed that. It no change me countess." She poked herself again. "Countess Pletnyovna. You kiss." She swung her hand up to Wynn's face, smearing her fingers across his lips.

"A pleasure to meet you, Countess, but I have a rather important matter to attend to."

"I many important matters in Russia. Balls, parties, operas. Here, nothing. Sit. Wait for home return. Live in palace with many jewels. All gone now."

"My sympathies for your loss, Countess. Please, excuse me." Wynn tore himself away as a far-off mist clouded her eyes. Whether from the drink or the memories of diamonds lost, he couldn't decide. Most likely both if forced to give his professional diagnosis.

Wynn angled his way to the VIP table where Sheremetev was customarily found holding court. Dodging a harried waiter with a loaded tray, he sidestepped into a cluster of men smoking cigars. He could handle all manner of smells from gangrene, to putrid flesh, to chlorine gas bubbling first thing in the morning, but being able to endure cigar smoke was not one of his nasal-suffering attributes.

"*Vrach.*" One of the men's arms landed across Wynn's shoulders and tugged him close. Much too close as he felt perspiration seeping through the man's dinner jacket. "You here, *vrach.*"

It hadn't taken long for Wynn to decipher that Russian word and the universal response being announced as a physician achieved. An unequal mixture of awe and suspicion that undoubtedly led to—

"*Vrach*, here bump. You look." Warning given, the man hiked up his shirt and pointed to a dysplastic nevus below his third rib. "It turn red."

"It's turning red because you're touching it."

"But it red."

Not wanting to give a formal examination standing next to the dance floor, Wynn gave the spot a once-over to ensure the man wasn't suffering a lethal mole, then gently tugged the shirt back down.

"I see no cause for concern. However, if you're distressed about its appearance, you may come to Hôpital du Sacré-Coeur tomorrow. Give my name, Dr. MacCallan, and one of the physicians will attend you."

Frowning dubiously at being put off, the man went back to poking his side with his cohorts as audience. Wynn moved quickly through the crowd before another potential patient required medical attention.

It never failed. Attend a party and before long he ended up in a side room taking consultations without even a glass of punch to remind him why he'd come in the first place.

At last he arrived at the circle of sidearm-strapped men guarding Sheremetev's private booth. "Evening, gents. I see you haven't moved since last I saw you." It wasn't uncommon for a club, hotel, or fancy restaurant to have discreet crowd control should the need arise, but the stipulation was always discreet. These men made no bones about their inclusion and intent to the establishment. An unsettling insight into the owner himself.

One of the guards grunted and peeled back an inch of the velvet curtain that sectioned off the private table. A few words of Russian and the curtain pulled back as a man wearing a thick coat and a tall wool hat like many of the émigrés he'd seen in the Alexander church basement slid from the booth and slunk away. The guard grunted for Wynn to enter.

"Our own savior. Come in. Come." Managing to surround himself with his own atmosphere, Sheremetev assembled himself in the center of the booth with his bulbous belly pushing against the table. He was dressed in immaculate evening clothes that were too fine for wartimes with the same double-headed eagle stickpin glistening from the folds of his white ascot. Like a drop of blood on snow. A ruby that size could feed the entire 8th Arrondissement for a month.

Wynn stepped into the cordoned-off space and remained standing. "Forgive the intrusion."

"Never could you intrude. Our business at conclusion." The folds around Sheremetev's eyes twitched as they followed the man out of the club. "Heat addling him."

"Perhaps he should have taken off his wool hat. It's nearly thirty-three degrees Celsius outside."

"Russians these days wear all worldly goods no matter temperature wherever go. One never know."

The unspoken fear hung in the air, like a basin suspended on a thread. A word, a shift could tip it from the precarious balance to rain panic on their heads. Was this the anxiety Svetlana lived each day? Never knowing one hour to the next if she was in danger. Always one eye hunting ahead while the other searched behind for threat.

"But you've found safety in Paris. The troubles of your country can't touch you here." It was not with naivety Wynn made such a statement, rather one of earnest conviction. One he was fervent to see unbroken.

"You thinking no? It presumed surface of safety. One we vigilant protecting at all costs." As with the precarious basin of fear, Sheremetev, too, held his own balancing act. A manner of ease and affability as a mask to the ring of steel within. A ring of steel that grasped tightly to the reins of control. Woe to the one standing in defiance of such a claim.

Danger lurked as Wynn's constant companion in the operating theater, but it was a danger he understood, one he could defend against to the best of his learned knowledge. Sheremetev pulsed a peril of incurability. Like a heart beating at its own time, but a closer examination detected an erraticism of the rhythm from its fixed course.

Wynn shifted the medical bag in his hand, eager to conclude his own business and be on his way. "Is Leonid about? I found a note saying to meet him here for a short exam."

Sheremetev snapped his pudgy fingers and one of the guards appeared, silent as an apparition. A quick command in Russian and the guard disappeared, presumably in search of the prodigal patient.

"Death of me that boy will be. Much play and work not enough. He on the mend, *da*?"

Wynn nodded, grateful he'd picked up the minimal Russian word for yes and even more grateful that his Russian hosts spoke enough English to communicate, otherwise there would be a lot more hand gestures. He was terrible at charades.

"I'm preparing to remove the bandages tonight. Fresh air does wonders for a wound after the initial phase of recovery has passed. Any chance of finding who did this to him?"

"I know already."

"The authorities have apprehended them? That's a relief. The people of Paris have enough to trouble themselves over without back-alley ruffians."

"No need authorities. This Russian matter. Deal with as such."

Chipped with ice and weighted with ominousness, the words sank deep into Wynn's unsettlement. The plush booths, gold trim, bejeweled women, and titled lords were nothing more than an opulent smokescreen wafted over nefarious means. He could venture a good guess to those means exactly, but he'd rather not dwell on the implications. Best to treat his patient and move on before he became embroiled in this underworld of Russian dealings.

"Do you understand meaning, Dr. MacCallan?" Despite his eyes being hidden in rolls of fat, Sheremetev watched him closely.

"My understanding goes to my patients and their medical needs only. All else I leave to others and their expertise."

"Wise. Often noses sniffing around business not their own. Some easily pushed back with little tap. Others requiring more knocking."

"Good way to earn a broken nose."

"I no broken nose. Only bruised knuckles and shoulder." Leonid loomed in front of the table. His hair was askew, and his black jacket was draped around his wounded shoulder. His infectious grin was in sharp contrast to his father's menacing one.

Grateful for the distraction, Wynn turned his full attention to his patient. "It's that shoulder I've come to see you about. Shall we find a quiet corner?"

"No, here. I wish see our fine physician at work." Sheremetev poured himself a dram of vodka, then signaled for the thick curtain to conceal them in muffled privacy. "While asking few things from son. Where have been?"

Leonid shrugged out of his jacket, then sat on the edge of the seat to unbutton his shirt. "Around."

"Around gaming tables."

"*Da*, and kitchen, and stage. All smooth running."

"No doubt including dancers. One particular with black curls."

Leonid reddened. "*Da*."

"If caring one day take over family business, you need present more attention to entirety of operation and not ongoings of backstage. Sheremetev name one of success. First in Moscow and now Paris." Sheremetev swallowed his vodka whole and plunked the crystal glass on the linen tablecloth, glaring at his son.

"Fifteen years White Bear serving as relaxation place for Russian nobles touring Europe capitals, comforting taste of home many thousand miles away. Now it sanctuary for nobles finding themselves cut from homeland. A venture no taken lightly."

Silence pulsed between father and son. From the vein throbbing in Leonid's neck, he was anything but silent internally.

Still standing, Wynn set his bag on the table and took the opportunity for a diversion as he examined the injury.

"The entry and exit have scabbed over nicely. You don't require the bandage any longer, but keep the area clean and try not to put pressure on the shoulder. You should regain full use of it soon, as long as you stay away from scrapping."

"Wound no matter for family honor," Leonid said.

"I've seen enough honor injuries to last me a lifetime. Don't add anymore to my needless count."

"Try. No promise."

"Taking good care of patients, Dr. MacCallan. Well they taught you at University of Glasgow." At Wynn's look of surprise, Sheremetev nodded. "My information gleaned from eyes and ears everywhere. Like knowing you top class four years in row, and submit thesis paper your second year with detailing surgical intervention of heart disease."

"Putting Heart Disease Under the Knife," he'd titled his two-hundred-page thesis. Congenital heart disease and damage to the four inner valves caused by rheumatic fever were difficult to diagnose at best, and most physicians remained skeptical of delving further than need be. A mystery, they said, that risk dictated remain so. Rigid old jossers. The heart was simply another part of anatomy, an unexplored territory of the human landscape. His paper lambasted their fears and stodgy practices that refused to concede evolving knowledge. His professors had been astounded. By the absurdity of such radical thinking and from a second year, no less, who believed himself capable of putting forward said absurdity.

While Leonid slid his shirt back on Wynn returned the unneeded bits of bandage to his bag and snapped it shut. "Dare I ask if you read my thesis?"

"*Nyet*, but had man on it. Consider his self expert with hearts now."

"He was probably the only one to read it. I was certain my professors burned it in the courtyard along with the other heretical texts."

"Heretics. Groundbreakers. One in the same."

"Depends on who you ask."

"Duke of Westminster? He believe in your groundbreaking theories for recommending you a position at Hôpital du Sacré-Coeur where he patron. Ties with him and your father go back to Eton College, *da*?"

"Mr. Sheremetev, has there ever been a time when your information was not mistaken?"

"*Nyet*." The confident old man poured himself another vodka and downed it. He rolled the bottom of the drained glass around in circles, leaving wet marks on the tablecloth. "I can use man like you. Never know when needing physician, and I resting easier having your talent call on. Medical attention lacking to my countrymen this far from home."

A private client list with a powerful patron at the top. Many physicians dreamed of such an opportunity, but Wynn wasn't one of them. It was too safe, too predictable. Outweighing all other considerations, he had no desire to be pinned under Sheremetev's thumb. The man was powerful, the epicenter of the Russian world he'd shrewdly created here in Paris. Wynn had seen enough to piece together precisely how this world was held together and he wanted no part of it.

He also knew better than to offend his host with outright refusal. "It's my honor to attend any in need, though my duties are prioritized at hospital with the Tommies."

The fleshy folds of Sheremetev's neck twitched as he signaled for the velvet curtains to be drawn open. "Who this Tommy demanding all your time?"

"Tommy Atkins is a common reference for British soldiers. The military loves its jargon."

In a jargon foreign yet becoming increasingly familiar to Wynn's ear, Russian peeled from an opening door that had been obscured by large potted plants. Two burly men in evening dress escorted a woman in glittering gold who swayed laughing between them. A shimmering vision of silver glided down the stairs behind them. Svetlana.

Gone were the tattered rags and ill-fitting dresses that were naught to behold in the wake of this gown that skimmed over every curve and elegant line like pouring water. A magnificent armor that made her appear all the more fragile. Pale jewels winked at her throat, ears, and scattered among the fine swirls of hair pinned up to showcase a swan-like neck. A princess in all her glory, leaving Wynn precious little room to be anything other than struck by awe.

Princess Ana tittered in French as she swatted at her handlers, who were not the least bit perturbed by her antics. Discretion no longer a viable option, having drawn the attention of most of the room, the guards did their best to shield her from curious eyes while steering her toward the exit, but she was having none of it.

"Sheremetev! *Où es-tu?*" Ana scanned the crowd until her eyes lighted on Sheremetev's table. With a cry of joy, she darted in their direction, knocking against no less than three tables while en route. She slipped around Wynn and slid into the booth, then leaned back against the cushion with a dreamy smile across her pinked face. "Such wonderful tables you have, Sheremetev. I've never played with such crisp cards. Not even in the Winter Palace. They play with the same decks since before Napoleon invaded Moscow."

Svetlana glided to the table. Her cool gaze took in nothing but the soppy woman in front of her. "Mama, please. Let us retire for the evening before the spectacle becomes too much."

"There is never too much of a good thing. Except for you." Ana turned to Sheremetev. "My daughter would have me give up all manner of fun for propriety's sake. There are days when I don't believe she knows how to smile."

Sheremetev ran his thick finger around the rim of his empty glass, considering as he looked at Svetlana. "Perhaps she not given reason to."

"Tosh. She has the world in her feet—no, *at* her feet—and it is still not good enough. When will it measure up, Svetka?"

If possible, Svetlana straightened even further. "Come, Mama."

"The evening is still young with too many exciting things waiting to be discovered. Is that vodka? A tipple if you will, dear friend." Ana took the empty glass from Sheremetev and nudged it toward the bottle.

"There has been enough drink for one evening."

"There is never enough to suit my mood, especially after that last disastrous hand. I lost a ruby ring and matching choker to a rather oily looking man. You don't serve Cossacks here, do you, Sheremetev? The beastly lot cannot be trusted."

"Enough, Mama. We are leaving."

"You leave while I enjoy myself." Ana took the glass now filled with clear liquid from Sheremetev and tipped it past her lips. "The first time in ages."

Family squabble aside, the elder princess was well on her way to a drunken stupor. Wynn stepped forward.

"Her Highness is right, Princess. More drink will bring nothing good this evening."

As if aware of him for the first time, Svetlana's attention turned to him with a shot of ice. "Dr. MacCallan. How often your presence is found here. Though in this instance it is not required."

"A gentleman should never dispute with a lady in public. This rule of engagement, however, does not impede me in a professional capacity as I've dealt with a fair share of inebriation and stand to argue that my unrequired presence may be of help. Allow me to escort you home."

Svetlana's expression never wavered, at least not to a casual observer. To one who knew where to look, indecision oscillated behind that glacier façade. An ability perfected by nobility and heightened to its zenith by her exacting standards where proper manners warred with a fuming dismissal. Which victor would he be left to contend with?

"I'm certain your services are greatly relied upon by our host, otherwise I cannot account for your continued presence when the hospital is better suited." Ah, a cold dismissal hidden behind concerned manners. Fortunately for Wynn, he was immune to such tactics.

"As I told you before, when I find something I enjoy, I stick with it. Even when it would be easier to forgo."

Leonid cleared his throat. "Sheremetev private carriage. I get." Sticking his good arm into his jacket sleeve, he tugged the other side to cover his wounded shoulder and leaned close to Wynn's ear. "Careful. Princess no appreciate hook you dangle."

Wynn grinned. "If you want the best, you have to be willing to take a risk."

"Risk eaten alive." Leonid clicked his teeth together to emphasize his point. "Luck to you."

As Leonid scuttled off to locate their transport, a waiter appeared at the table holding a bill of receipt.

"Princess Dalsky," he said.

Ana demurred as if embarrassed to handle a concept so inferior as a bill.

Coming to her rescue, Sheremetev plucked the paper from the waiter's hand and placed it facedown in front of the princess. "When you ready."

To her credit, she made a good show of fumbling through her beaded handbag until at last emerging with just the right amount of disappointment.

"How embarrassing. I must have left my coin purse behind this evening. Cumbersome little thing when one is not accustomed to traveling with the common burden."

"I understand, Lady Princess. Until next time." Sheremetev took the bill and slipped it into his inner jacket pocket with a gentle pat.

Smiling with gratitude, Ana raised the little glass of vodka to her lips. And missed. Crystal clear drops dribbled onto the golden beads of her bodice. "*Sacré bleu!* My new gown. It was my favorite from all the new ones you gave us."

Sheremetev whipped a hankie from his pocket and handed it to her. "Shed no precious tear. There many more where came from."

"But this was my favorite one. With the matching shoes."

"We will repay you at the earliest convenience, sir. For every bit of your magnanimousness shown to us." The muscles in Svetlana's throat constricted as if each word were forced from her.

"No more speak of it. Your lows are mine for shouldering as long as grant me the favor. Women of your rank and beauty no be forced to endure discards of regime that expelling you from splendor of which are accustomed to." Sheremetev's eyes cast between the bedecked women, weighing each gilded jewel in turn. "In meantime, have most pleasant evening and look forward next time you are gracing my humble doors. Doctor, you as well."

Wynn inclined his head. "Good evening to you, sir. Ladies, shall we adjourn?"

A sleek black carriage pulled by two white horses waited for them out front. Settled inside on the opposite bench from the ladies, there wasn't much room to accommodate his legs and their gowns. Every roll of the wheels brushed Svetlana's skirts against him. Ana fell promptly asleep.

The interior was dark, shrouding them in the relief of obscurity. As the carriage turned, moonlight faintly caught the beads of Svetlana's gown. Wynn resisted the urge to reach across the short distance to determine her realness or if she shimmered beyond his reach like the northern lights shifting across the sky during winter.

"I didn't expect to see you."

"There was no choice for it." From the tone of her voice, he knew she sat straight as a rod. "Choice has become an option ill-afforded. For many things."

Including wardrobes, it seemed. Jealousy pricked its tiny fangs into Wynn's sense of pride. He would have liked to be the one to obtain suitable attire for her, though he'd scarcely call a sequined gown a garment of necessity during wartime. Then again, she was a princess. She might sleep in a tiara. Whatever the case might be, she'd found benevolence in a near stranger. Certainly, Sheremetev was somewhat Russian nobility himself, and there was something to be said for instant kinship upon meeting another citizen of your homeland while traveling afar, a thread of commonality linking memory and custom unique to that place understood by those who dwell there. Wynn had no such thread to her. His only claim was being present when blood was involved. That had to count for something, didn't it?

"You're enchanting tonight," he said.

"The hour draws too late for enchanting."

"Bewitching then. It's close to midnight, which I believe is the proper time for such things, so you can't fault me there."

Her gown ruffled against his foot. "If you feel the need to remark on such things, do not sit in expectation of a swoon."

"From you? Never. It might force you to slacken the rigidity so ingrained. I'd settle for a smile or even a nod. A twitch to acknowledge the compliment."

"I never asked for a compliment."

Her reactions were nothing short of a dare. A measure he was happy to supply. "No, but when a man is faced with the truth, he's forced to confess it, be the recipient willing or not. Truth will out, as they say."

"Some truths are better left unsaid."

"Not when they rile you so easily."

"What do you mean by this rile?" He imagined her fine eyebrows slanting over narrowed eyes.

"To rile, vex, needle. To provoke into reaction."

"A game then for your own amusement. Tell me, what do other women do? Laugh and bat their lashes behind silken fans, begging for one more compliment?"

"Only the silly ones."

"Perhaps they are better suited to your game of vexation."

"I don't want a silly woman."

"A challenge for you then, considering all proper ladies are required a decorum of vacuous heads balanced precariously upon tittering laughter as they float about on clouds spun of gossip and boredom."

"I prefer a challenge." He leaned forward, eager to make out the delicate lines of her face that masked a temper. "Why else do I find myself so drawn to you?"

"A consummate need for disappointment would be my diagnosis. But then, you are the doctor."

Wynn laughed, loud and clear. She might not enjoy the game, but he certainly did. A better equipped opponent he'd yet to encounter.

The carriage slowed to a halt and bounced as the driver dropped from his perch to open the door. Ana jerked awake and stared around in confusion.

"Have we arrived at the palace? Why are the torches not lit for us?"

"There is no palace, Mama," Svetlana said. "This is the church."

Wynn climbed out before turning to help the ladies.

Ana squinted at the three pointed towers of the church. The gold onion domes gleamed dully against the ink-blotted sky.

"The driver has brought us to the wrong place." She spun around and glared at the man in question. "I shall inform my husband, the prince, of this negligence."

"Mama, this is where we are staying now." Svetlana took her mother's arm and turned them to go around the back of the church. "Let's go inside."

"Like a serf? As soon as order is restored in Russia, I shall—" Ana pressed her fingers to her forehead. "Do you know, my head feels too light for this reprimand." Her eyes fluttered closed and she wilted. Wynn caught her before she puddled on the cobblestones and hefted the unconscious princess into his arms before following Svetlana around back.

Reaching the cellar door, Svetlana eased it open as quietly as she could on its rusty hinges. It creaked like an unoiled trumpet on Judgment Day.

Ana's eyes snapped open. Heavily dilated pupils stared up at Wynn. "Unhand me at once. I will have no improprieties taken of me."

"Mama, please. You fainted," Svetlana said.

"I should think so with the ill-treatment I've received. My nerves cannot handle the upset. Now, unhand me."

Wynn set Ana on her feet. She flicked him away and started down the stairs on wobbly legs, clutching the walls for balance.

Wynn hurried to take her elbow. "Your Highness, allow me to escort you downstairs. The passage is dark and the steps less than stable."

She slapped his hand away. "How many times must I command you to unhand me? Because you are a physician does not give you the right to manhandle as you see fit."

A light flickered at the bottom of the steps as a small figure dressed in white appeared. "Mama? Svetka? *Est-ce vous?*" Marina, the younger sister.

"*Oui*." Svetlana took her mother's arm and led her down the remaining steps.

At the bottom each sister took a side to support their drooping mother and walked her into the cellar space that had become a dank home for the lost refugees. The smell of warm, unwashed bodies and linen hung pungent in the air, punctured only by snores and sleeping snuffles.

Wynn followed closely behind should the older woman's sway turn into a drunken sprawl. "She'll need plenty of water. Keep an eye on her when she sleeps and lean her on her side."

Svetlana's eyes narrowed over her shoulder as she looked back at him. "We are well-versed in the care of our mother during these times."

"She said herself it's been some time since she last imbibed. The alcohol will have absorbed into her blood much quicker."

Whispering to her sister, Svetlana released her mother's arm and turned to brush past Wynn. "A word." She headed for the stairs and didn't stop until she'd reached the courtyard. Shadows seeped through the trees and lingered over the stones with revered silence.

"It is time for you to leave."

"Your mother—"

"Is not your concern."

"You'd prefer I left her slumped in the gutter after she's been to the bottom of the glass more than once. At a less than reputable place,

I might add. Or mayhap you'd like to defend yourself against the rats prowling around after curfew in hopes of easy prey. Is that what you mean to tell me?"

"I have told— What do you mean by disreputable? The Sheremetevs are one of the most respected families in all of Moscow."

"This isn't Moscow. People do what they need to in order to stay on top. Have you not wondered why his club is able to stay open all hours of the night when the entire city is shut down for curfew? Have you stopped to take a good look at the men he surrounds himself with?" He leaned in and lowered his voice. "You need to be careful. It wasn't a stray bullet that found Leonid that day."

"You have proof of this?" She studied him, not backing down.

"It's more of a gut instinct. Or will you tell me it's no concern of mine?"

"Precisely. You, on more than one occasion when your interfering presence was not required nor desired, have not heeded my words to stay away, for here you are."

Shoving his hands into his pockets, Wynn leaned against the wall. The rigors of Harkin's surgery and Svetlana's ever-present need for a battle of wills was catching up with him.

"Yes, here I am. Doing what I thought was a kind deed only to be slapped with ingratitude."

"You harbor deep needs to be thanked with boundless applause and simpering. How do you sleep at night without accolades drifting you off?"

"First of all, something cannot drift you off. One simply drifts of their own accord. Secondly, you respond with nothing but snobbery. Is that what qualifies for manners in Russia? The ruder you are to a person the more refined that makes you? If so, you are the most refined lady I have ever met."

Her eyebrows shot up, then slanted down in a scowl.

"You are the most exasperating man I have ever met. Unable to take a simple no because your opinion on the matter outweighs all else. Pride won't allow you to admit that you have overstepped the mark, as you have done repeatedly since first we met."

"Well, that's put me in my place. You're getting rather good at it, Princess." Pursuing a woman was bound to offer a few scrapes to a man's efforts, particularly a woman such as her, but when the bruised ego tempted him to lash out, it was time to withdraw his cards from the game. He shoved off the wall and conjured a smile. "Good night to you then. Remember to eat your apples. Helps keep us pesky doctors away."

CHAPTER 8

The time had come.

Svetlana had waited patiently, putting in social appearances over the past several weeks in order to aid her cause. Delicate matters required precise timing, and the less frantic one seemed the more likely their matter was to be met with favor. She wasn't accustomed to asking favors, but there was a first time for everything.

"How is it a daughter of Russia refuses partaking in her national drink?" Sheremetev poured fresh vodka into his glass, then set the bottle back in the bucket of ice standing at the ready next to his private table.

"This daughter prefers to find culture in her homeland's tea." Svetlana raised her *podstakannik* and took a tiny sip. It was the first time since leaving her homeland that she'd been served the traditional Russian clear glass for admiring the tea's color, with an elaborately decorated silver bottom and handle to keep from burning the hand. Despite the glass's beauty, the warm liquid gurgled past the tightness in her throat. "I find it soothing."

"Is soothing what you require?"

She'd rehearsed her speech over and over, yet pride proved difficult to overcome. It scolded her to find another way. But there was no other way. She'd tried and failed, with the only recourse now to humble herself and ask for help.

She scanned the White Bear's crowded floor. Russian nobility swarmed every inch like bees in search of honey, their nectar consisting of cigarettes, drink, dalliances, and sharing sad stories of their former lives. Music set them buzzing as if the tunes could pluck them from misery and cast them into a pretense of joy for one evening. Only, these evenings were never once. They happened every night. The same people. The same drinks, dances, and mindless conversations. What so many sought as the comfort of the familiar, Svetlana found raw as sand against skin. They, too, once had their pride, but eventually found themselves where she was now. If there was any hope to be found, it was to one day find her dear friend Sergey sitting among them, for without his selflessness she never would have escaped.

Beneath the table she slid her feet to third position to steady herself. "I confess I find myself in turmoil. My family, like so many others, lost much when we fled Petrograd. I worry every day how I will keep our heads above water."

"In leaving Moscow years ago to travel the world and increase the Sheremetev prosperity, I wanted to open a place of familiarity and comfort for my fellow Russians as they traveled abroad. Then two years ago when I brought my boy to join me, it was the first time he'd left the soil of his birth. With him came the first waves of èmigrès. I knew then I could use my connections to help those of our kind who lost everything." He leaned forward, catching the light on his ruby stickpin. "A lady must never worry about such things. I have promised to help you in any way I can, and for as long as necessary I will continue to do so."

Svetlana smoothed a hand over her watered-silk dress. One of the many ways he'd helped her family, plus food supplies and silk bedding. Quite the stir it had caused among those in the church basement, not to mention jealousy. Svetlana had protested at the extravagance that would place them in debt to this man they barely knew, but Mama would hear nothing of it. The Sheremetevs are famous for their benevolence, she'd claimed. Benevolence was one thing, but running up a tab was not something Svetlana wished to carry.

"Your generosity can never fully be repaid, though I will do everything in my power to do so. I'm afraid I must ask one more tally in our account."

"It is yours for the asking, Princess."

Asking. More like groveling. Oh, how she despised it. "The place we are staying is becoming unbearably crowded. Every day refugees pour into the city and there are too few places that will take in Russians. We are forced to live atop one another. It is agony for my sister and mother."

"For yourself as well, I imagine. A far cry from the Blue Palace that church basement must be."

Svetlana refused to give in to the memories of the home she'd last seen by the torching light of the revolutionaries. Did it still stand? "Could you help us find accommodations elsewhere? It need not be grand, merely private."

Taking a sip of his vodka, Sheremetev settled against his cushion and scrunched his eyes as if in thought. They nearly disappeared into fleshy creases. "With the war on, places to rent are at a premium. Spaces not conscripted by the military or hospital are snapped up by families coming to visit their wounded or fleeing the countryside. It would be difficult."

"We're willing to pay." If Mama hadn't gambled it all away upstairs at the card tables.

"Let me see what I can do."

If her corset had allowed it, she would have sagged with relief. "Thank you, Mr. Sheremetev."

"Think nothing of it. I adore helping beautiful women. Here, you really must try these in your tea." He lifted the lid of a silver dish and scooped a spoonful of sugared cherries into her glass. "An addition of subtle sweetness."

She took a brief sip and closed her eyes, savoring the flavor. "I haven't tasted this in years. Wherever did you find the cherries during rationing?"

"Bavaria. I have a man who runs imports from there."

Right in the middle of enemy territory. Disreputable, wasn't that what Wynn had called the Sheremetevs the last night she'd seen him nearly a month ago? Worry niggled. She would tread carefully with Sheremetev and put the apprehension—and Wynn—out of her mind for now.

"My father always said the best cherries came from Bakaldy. He likes them in his tea as well."

"Has news of your father and brother come?"

Her short-term relief fizzled. "None. We pray for them daily."

"As you should now that Lenin has seized power. My contacts may have news. Their methods of delivery are secure compared to the post, where your father's letters may have been intercepted."

"Have you stopped to take a good look at the men he surrounds himself with?" Once more, Wynn's voice refused to be silenced. The man took up more space in her thoughts than he had any right to claim.

A man appeared at the table and leaned over to whisper to Sheremetev. Without expression, Sheremetev nodded and heaved himself from the booth, knocking the table with his paunch.

"I beg your forgiveness, Princess. An urgent matter has presented itself that I must see to."

As soon as he disappeared, Svetlana pushed her glass away and knotted her trembling hands in her lap. What sort of man was she dealing with? She had told herself she would do whatever it took to keep her family safe while they waited for Papa and Nikolai, but was she making a bargain with the devil? Perhaps she should find another way.

She started to rise.

"Angel! You are here." Leonid dropped into the booth next to her and grinned. "How grand tonight you look."

"*Spasibo.*" Her exit now blocked, all she could do was manage a few more polite minutes before making her excuses.

He looked around. "You seen Mac?"

Mac. MacCallan. Wynn. The topic she'd prefer to avoid yet conversation always seemed to veer around to him. "Not in some time."

"He never comes anymore."

Because of her. She'd told him to stay away, perhaps a bit harsher than she'd intended, and he'd listened. For once. It was the right thing to do. With wars and revolutions, they did not belong in each other's worlds. Though she no longer believed him a Bolshevik, the threat of discovery from those enemies hung ever present. She could truly trust no one. It was the only way to survive. Yet, at the end of the wearying days when the candles were snuffed and loneliness crept in to drape her in isolation, she wished she could trust him.

Such wishes belonged to another life. One she'd severed.

"I'm certain he's busy at the hospital."

"We play chess on day off. He always ask how you are. This makes me think you are not speaking." Pushing his father's empty glass aside, Leonid leaned his elbows on the table. "Why argue with Mac?"

"Argue? Who mentioned an argument?"

"That is what he says. Now I see it is true. You tell Leo. I fix all the problems."

Her heart thumped with more force than she liked. "I'm afraid you're mistaken."

"That is a polite way to say such business does not belong to me, but I am your friend. Your business always is mine." He settled back and spread his hands in a nonchalant manner. "If you do not tell, I find out ways that are other."

"You are relentless."

"Relentless charm." He smiled in a way that was clearly meant to be debonair but came across as childishly comedic. A far cry from his father's smooth elegance, but one Svetlana couldn't help warming to.

She sipped her tea, the cherries rich against the soured memory of her words. "I've asked him to keep a distance. Though he seems a kind man and thoughtful doctor, he is not Russian. He has his people to see to as we do ours. It's best the two do not mix."

"That is snobbish."

"I'm sorry if you don't agree. There are a great many here tonight who would."

"They are snobbish too." He waved a dismissing hand to the throngs of people crowding the tables around them. "Know what I think? You are mad he got close and now you push him away. Forgive Mac. Make things right, then we are all friends again."

"Circumstances do not allow for such easy diplomacy."

"*Papochka* partners with *russkiye*, Serb, Tatar, Mongul, Lats. Born enemies. He works with all. A good man is Mac, unlike men here."

She couldn't help smiling at his honesty. A sincere trait too often lacking in the aristocracy circles. "I see one good man before me."

Leonid puffed up his chest and nodded. "That is right. I am good."

If she stayed much longer, his amiability would have her convinced to repair the rift with Wynn, or worse, enjoy herself in this place. Exhaustion slivered in at the thought.

"It's getting rather late. I should say good evening." Rising from the table, Svetlana made for the stairs leading up to the next floor. The hidden rooms where guests disappeared for hours only to return exalted or defeated. Mama more often than not returned defeated.

As her foot hit the first stair, Leonid took her arm. "Where do you go, Angel? This is no way for a lady."

"Mama is there."

"I will fetch her."

"No. I'll collect her myself." It was high time she saw for herself what drew everyone's attention to the ongoings beyond the thick walnut doors draped in red velvet. What illusions captivated Mama to stuff her purse with unpaid bills as if Svetlana wouldn't find them along with their dwindling money supply.

He didn't let go of her arm.

At the sight of Leonid, the doormen swung wide the doors to a world of secrets and expense. Heavy drapes covered the walls, folding the large room into a muffled embrace. Gold chandeliers dripped from the ceilings to cast their golden glow across the tables covered in green felt and shuffling cards. Dice flashed around spinning wheels and tumbled across red and black numbers as chips clanked softly in eager palms. When the chips ran out, money and gems of all cut and color were pushed into betting piles.

Svetlana's stomach clenched with sickness. She'd known from the start, but to see it before her in bloated depravity was enough to make her want to scream. Had they not lost enough?

"Wait. I will find her," Leonid whispered.

"No need. I see her." Dislodging from his grip, Svetlana sailed between the tables, ignoring the appreciative glances from drunken boyars and counts, and stopped at a table near the back surrounded by four gentlemen and two ladies. "Hello, Mama."

Mama jumped from her chair, unexpected surprise registering on her face. A garish clash with her lilac gown and white hair plumes.

"What are you doing here?" She cast a glance at the jewel- and medal-bedecked people behind her at the table. Her shoulders straightened. "That is, allow me to present my daughter, Her Serenity the Princess Svetlana Dmitrievna Dalsky."

"I don't care if she's a scullery maid. Titles are worthless. You owe me eight hundred rubles." One of the men with a pointy black beard and shiny gold buttons glared at her mother. "Tonight."

"Count, if you'll only allow me to pay you tomorrow when I have the funds. You see—"

The count smacked his palm against the table, crumbling the pile of chips in front of him. "Excuses. Do not come to the tables if you do not have funds to participate."

"I did not come empty-handed, as you well know. It sits there before you."

"That was from the first two games. You owe me for the third."

Svetlana's eye moved to the table. There among the pile of chips and coins was a ruby bracelet that once belonged to her great-aunt and an egg-size topaz brooch that once graced the robes of Princess Sophia Dalsky during the coronation of Empress Catherine II. Her family's precious few heirlooms, smuggled out of Russia to be used for food, clothing, and shelter. How vulgar they looked discarded there next to the playing cards and empty glasses of vodka, as if they were another stale crumb to be tossed to the ravenous vultures.

Vicious fear twisted in Svetlana's stomach. Without the jewels they did not stand a chance to survive and escape for good. She leaned down to her mother's ear, her voice ragged. "Mama, what have you done?"

Mama swept her fan up to cover her mouth so only Svetlana might hear her. "Stop fretting. It is not the last of them, merely the only ones I brought this night."

"You will ruin us."

The lines around Mama's mouth tightened, but as a true lady of breeding, she didn't allow them to further express her inner fright. She covered that with a haughty sweep of her fan while leveling her gaze at the count.

"As you say, I should not be attending so I will take my leave for the evening and send over a bottle of champagne to soothe any ruffled spirits."

The count curled his hand into a fist on the green felt table. "Not without paying me first."

"Your rudeness is intolerable and I will not subject myself or my daughter a minute longer. Come, Svetlana."

Cursing under his breath, the count lurched out of his chair and came around the table with eyes blazing. Two muscled men with bulges beneath their jackets stepped in and blocked his path.

Sheremetev, along with Leonid, appeared behind his guards with a thin smile. "My dear count. Is there a problem?"

"The so-called princess doesn't see it fitting to pay me what's owed."

"Princess Ana is an honored guest of mine and her honor will not be tarnished." Sheremetev smiled benevolently at Mama and continued. "It is my own honor that requires all debts to be paid in full in a timely manner and as circumstances dictate by the owed."

Mama stammered and made a show of opening her beaded purse. "W-well, I don't believe I have the appropriate amount, but if you'll allow me—"

"I require payment now. As my honor and circumstances dictate," said the count. "I would hate to alert the authorities."

Everyone at the table gasped. Threats were never made against nobility. Only low-class mongrels stooped so low as to bring in the laws of commoners.

Svetlana bristled at the insinuation. Had her family not suffered enough humiliation? "Do you know to whom you are speaking? Peter and Paul Fortress would do well to show you manners."

The count's eyes narrowed to slits. His pointy beard made him all the more serpent-like. "Is that how you think to threaten me, *print-sessa*? Perhaps you should drag me back to the Reds."

"Enough. Count," Sheremetev said. "Gentleladies will not be insulted in my club. Nor do I allow outstanding debt. If you'll wait for me at the cashier's booth, your payment I will bring momentarily."

Scowling, the count grabbed his hat and cane and pushed through the crowd to the indicated booth.

Sheremetev turned to the table and the wide-eyed guests watching every move and word, no doubt savoring for gossip. "Apologies. There are free bottles of champagne for each of you at the bar. Please, enjoy after this upset." As they all scuttled away whispering to one another, he looked to Mama. "Dear Princess. What a night you have suffered, and to think the tragedy came at my club."

In an instant Mama's haughtiness softened to accommodating.

"I know that measly count does not represent you or your kindness. Think nothing of it."

"I'm afraid I must. You see, there is an outstanding debt to be paid."

"Of course, but I haven't managed a winning streak these past few nights—I do believe the count was cheating all this time—and my other funds remain back at our lodgings." Gripping her purse, she lowered her voice to throw off the listening ears around them. "I do so depend on our friendship. Might I ask for an extension of credit?"

The slightest hint of irritation flashed in Sheremetev's eyes, but he covered it quickly with a nod and pulled a slim cheque book from his inner jacket pocket. "As I told your daughter, I am here to help."

The strumming strings of a balalaika and gusli vibrated over a small dance space spread across the back wall where two traditionally dressed women stood. As one, they moved and pirouetted, dipped, and floated to a peasant tune often played among the aristocracy for amusement. Excitement buzzed through the crowd as they watched the performance, grabbing flutes of champagne and shots of vodka as waiters slipped by with full trays. An orchestra, not only on the dance floor, but masterfully played among the guests with Sheremetev's attention to detail as the conductor. If he couldn't collect their money at the tables, he'd collect it in drink.

For the briefest moment, the world's cares and her family's struggles fell away to the haunting dance steps of a life Svetlana knew before. Her feet longed to move; her legs ached to stretch and bend with the rhythm, her body stretching and twisting with elegant control. Though each step was governed, it was the only time she allowed herself to be liberated.

"You enjoy the dance?" Sheremetev's question shook her from the fantasy.

Svetlana nodded. "It's beautiful."

"Many Russian ladies are taught the cultural dances by their nannies in nursery. Do you know the steps?"

"Not these, but others like them."

Mama sidled closer to Svetlana. "My daughter was training to join the Imperial Russian Ballet."

"Is that so?" Sheremetev rolled his gold pen between his fingers as he studied her. "I imagine it has been some time since you danced. Would you like to do so again?"

Her heart tugging her, Svetlana glanced at the dancers, then looked away. "Someday perhaps. There are more pressing matters than ballet."

"So there are." He wrote Mama's name in elegant script on the To line of the cheque, then hovered over the Amount line. "You would show us perhaps."

"No, I'd rather not."

He pulled his pen away and frowned. "No?"

Leonid stepped to her side. "*Papochka*, Angel does not wish to entertain. Look at this rabble. For her they are too unrefined."

"Nothing in my club is unrefined, a point well to remember if you ever hope to succeed me." Sheremetev kept his voice even, but there was no denying the warning in his eyes.

Leonid dropped his gaze. "Remember, *da*."

"Good. Go see to the orders in the basement. Our clients are waiting."

"But, *Papochka*—"

Sheremetev jabbed him in the chest with his pen. "Go."

Leonid cast an apologetic look over his shoulder to Svetlana as he scurried away under his father's foreboding stare. Her champion gone as quickly as he'd tried to rise to her defense. He was, indeed, her good friend.

Sensing the rebuttal had weakened her cause, Mama's eyes skittered from the unfulfilled cheque to Svetlana. She clutched her arm. "Silly child. Of course she will." Her nails dug into Svetlana's skin. "Please Mr. Sheremetev with a dance."

Svetlana stiffened against her mother's restraint. She wasn't a windup toy perched on a box to perform at whim, and she certainly wouldn't lower herself to dance in front of card-playing castoffs as they guzzled drinks into oblivion. Ballet was not for casual amusement.

Across the room, the count stared with hatred as his fingers rapped against the cashier booth. If he held true on his promise to alert the authorities, Mama would be arrested with unimaginable horrors awaiting her. Mama would never recover from the humiliation, and her family may never recover from the cost of bail. Money that was to be saved for their survival.

Sheremetev's gold pen hovered once more over the Amount line. One more payment of debt to their account. He watched her, waiting.

As Mama's nails dug farther, Svetlana swallowed the knot of pride and nodded. "I will dance for you."

Smiling, Sheremetev touched his pen to the cheque. "Excellent."

CHAPTER 9

As the same question was repeated yet again in a different syntax, Wynn glanced longingly at the pitcher of water mere feet away. His throat was parched after an hour-long presentation before the hospital board and another hour in which questions and accusation had been lobbed at him from every angle in the Paris School of Médecine's lecture hall. The room seemed to shrink in on him with every passing minute. He dare not step away for a drink lest the white-haired doctors in the gallery smell weakness. He couldn't afford weakness at this crucial moment when the old dragons had to be won over.

He'd been summoned to explain his cardiological surgery on Lieutenant Harkin after his supervisor learned of the rogue procedure and reported it to the board. Following a month of paperwork, Wynn had finally been called to testify.

"It is often the practice of qualified surgeons to ascertain whether an object is best left unremoved to forgo further complications. Death for instance." From the second row, the questioning doctor squinted at him through large spectacles. "Why did you negate such a practice?"

Wynn tried not to think about the cool water as he answered the question. The same question. For the tenth time. "While this is a tried method, it is not always successful. In the case of my patient I felt he was better served to remove the object."

"You felt. How quaint. A physician's job is not determined by emotion but by studious examination, facts, and knowledge gained by those who have gone before."

"All of which I consulted before making a final decision and gaining permission from the patient."

"A patient cannot be trusted to know what is best for them. They have not the learning."

A doctor at the far end of the front row stood up. With dated muttonchops and a pristine white coat, he commanded attention. "While I am in agreement that patients do not have the learning to understand the workings of our profession, I cannot agree that their opinion is invalid. A good doctor must weigh both. It speaks well of Dr. MacCallan that this Lieutenant Harkin confided in him regarding the continuing pain."

The first doctor inclined his head, causing his spectacles to slip down his nose. "Your words are highly respected, Dr. Lehr, but a good bedside manner cannot be confused with medical aptitude."

Wynn knew his kind. Shuffling behind his medical books and claiming they held all the answers, too afraid to seek improvement beyond the sacred texts. These men lived in the Dark Ages where medical advancement was akin to witchcraft.

Wynn wasn't going to the stake based on that man's stupidity. "If you challenge my aptitude, then you challenge Romero, Williams, Cappelen, and most recently a surgeon in Malta. All performed similar successful operations. As was the surgery performed in Cambrai last year, from which medical notes I used as a basis to my decision."

"Youth's arrogance often leads to downfall."

"A physician's age does not determine his arrogance. In fact, I've found that advancing age often hinders one's ability to see past their own inclinations."

A gasp sounded around the room, the inhaled vacuum quickly filled with murmurs of outrage. Hang it all. Wynn grabbed the pitcher and poured himself a liberal amount of water. He downed the glass in one gulp and forced himself to remain calm for the sake of crowd control. He was losing them fast, and if he didn't recover the discussion they might bar him from medical practice for good.

"Gentlemen, please. I realize how heretical this may sound as the heart is considered a sacred organ, but as well-respected physicians you also know that it is another part of the body. We have an obligation to our patients and the welfare of future generations not to leave it a mystery." He gazed across the rows of the lecture hall and into the upper galleries. Half empty as many could not spare time away from their patients, but enough had come. All different ages and levels of skill, but a common purpose drew them together. It must continue to bring them together if the world was to have any hope.

"Every man here has seen the horrors of war raging mere miles from our hospital doors. Soldiers, men, boys are brought to our operating tables broken and bleeding. It is our duty, nay, our vow to heal them within our powers and do no harm. I consider it a great harm to neglect procedures that can and will save lives. Lives that we will be held responsible for at Judgment Day."

Another hour later Wynn had drained a second pitcher of water and packed up his presentation materials. He'd never talked so much in his entire life. All he wanted was to go home and pull the covers over his head until morning without saying a word to another soul.

Exiting the lecture hall, Wynn saw Gerard bounding toward him. "Brilliant."

"I'm hoarse."

"Tea with honey."

The image of a silvery princess with a hole in her dress pouring him tea hit Wynn with a force he'd tried to ignore. She was out of his life, as she'd requested. Extracting her from his thoughts proved to be a mightier challenge. One that was defeating him no matter the soreness lingering from that night.

"You won them over," Gerard said.

"Were we in the same room? I half expected a noose when I walked out here."

"Certainly some of them will take more convincing, but you got them talking. Talking will lead to thinking. Thinking leads to change."

"Changing me from a doctor to a broom pusher if some of them have their say."

"Looks like you'll keep your license another day, MacCallan." Dr. Nestor, the administrative director of Wynn's hospital, peeled himself away from a group long enough to reposition Wynn under his thumb. Or try to at any rate. "From now on you ask my approval before engaging in such a ridiculous stunt."

"I doubt Harkin considers it ridiculous from the bed where he's resting, still alive."

Nestor stepped closer, bumping the tips of his shoes against Wynn's. His breath smelled of the ham sandwich he'd eaten for lunch. "One more time. I'll have you out on your—"

"Good afternoon, gentlemen." Dr. Lehr stood smiling at them as if not having observed the confrontation. "Dr. Nestor, a pleasure to meet you. You must be very proud to have such a forward-thinking physician on your staff."

Nestor backed up and wiped a hand over his sweaty upper lip. "I, well . . . He surprises me at every turn."

"No doubt." Lehr dismissed Nestor completely and smiled at Wynn, displaying a row of squared off teeth. "My boy, I should like very much to examine your notes and X-rays. I have a few thoughts on myocardial infarction in relation to shell shock."

Wynn grasped the man's hand and shook it. "I would be honored."

"Next week?" At Wynn's eager nod, Lehr shook his hand once more. "If you'll excuse me, I must return to my hospital. We have more and more patients coming in with what looks to be a second wave of influenza. Death rates are climbing higher than the first."

Nestor elbowed his way back into the conversation. "Dr. Lehr, we've had a great many cases ourselves. I wonder if we might discuss treatment procedures. Perhaps to share your wealth of knowledge."

"I would love nothing more, but for now I suggest you pick Dr. MacCallan's brain. He seems more than up for the task."

With that, Wynn considered his day a success.

CHAPTER 10

I f she kept her eyes focused on the empty space above the audience's head, Svetlana might ease herself of the abject humiliation. Around the dance floor she spun. And *chasséd*. And *balloned*. A ballet of degradation. One she had been performing for nearly three weeks. What started as a single dance to repay that blighted count quickly turned into another night's dance for an unpaid champagne tab. The next night, a caviar tab. On and on they went until Svetlana was dizzy from the amount Mama owed. Sheremetev, ever the businessman, offered a dance for a bill, and so she danced nearly every night in hopes of clearing their debt.

The music ended and Svetlana swept behind the curtain to the crowd's thunderous applause. Her cheeks burned, even more so as she walked the gauntlet of waiters lounging in the corridor. Cigarette smoke filled the tiny space as coarse laughter and suggestive gestures followed her into the dressing room. It had been erected in her honor after one week. Sheremetev had hopes of his own.

Mama lounged on a velvet settee in a gown of fresh silk and fringe, giving an outstanding performance of not looking in debt. "Did they enjoy your performance?"

"They're too sotted to notice otherwise. I could have slumped in a chair and they would have cheered." Svetlana sat at the vanity illuminated by those fancy new bulbs a Mr. Edison had created. She preferred the soft glow of candles. They were never harsh enough to point out the dark circles under her eyes.

"But you didn't. You danced. Never something I really approved of, that was more for your father. He loved to watch you."

"I'm glad he's not here to see me. He'd be ashamed of what we've come to."

Mama had the grace to look momentarily curtailed. Watching her in the mirror's reflection, Svetlana spotted a platter and crystal cut glass. She spun around on the low stool.

"What is that?"

"This?" Mama pointed to the platter and shrugged. "A bite to eat. I get famished waiting for you back here after you banned me from sitting out front. The waiters are thoughtful to bring it for me."

No doubt they were, adding to the expense of yet another bill. Another dance. "I am trying to pay off our debt. How can I make any progress to that end when you continue to partake?"

"This isn't only for me. I've informed the waiters that what isn't consumed is to be boxed up so I may take it back for Marina. Those priests give us so little sustenance it's no wonder her clothes are hanging off her." Sighing, Mama swung her buckle-shoed feet off the settee. "If you find this dancing as distasteful as you make it sound, then sell a bracelet or two and pay the balance off. Be done with it."

"We only brought so many jewels with us from Russia. Several of which we've already sold for money, and the money, too, is dwindling. We must conserve our resources for food and shelter until Papa and Nikolai come." The war would be over someday. It had to be, and they would know what to do. She wouldn't have to shoulder the burden alone any longer.

"Then I see no recourse but for you to keep dancing until this distasteful business is behind us."

All of Svetlana's patience kept in relentless check, all acceptance of her mother's selfishly unalterable behaviors boiled over. "You are unbelievable! Will you never accept responsibility for our predicament? If you had shown restraint in your vices, I would not be forced to sell my dancing like some painted bawd on a stage for drunken voyeurs as payment of your debt."

Mama reared back as if the words had slapped her. "How dare you take that tone with me? I am your mother and a princess from one of the highest houses in all of Russia. How do you expect me to live as less than I am? I know no other way to live."

Svetlana saw her mother truly then. Not as a selfish creature but a creature of circumstance. Unquestionable privilege had molded her for nearly five decades to place her own desires first, with every need being met before she asked. It was a life Svetlana was well acquainted with, yet a revolution had forced her to alter her outlook. Perhaps it was the advantage of youth where the grasp of changeability was more mobile. Advancing years tightened its grip on the unchanging past.

Knock. Knock.

Svetlana averted her glare from her mother and took a fortifying breath. "Enter."

The door opened and Sheremetev pushed in belly first. "What are these raised voices?"

Mama was off the settee in a flash and gripping Svetlana's shoulders. "We were merely talking costumes and how I think this one could use gemstones to make it come alive."

Svetlana neatly shrugged her off with the appearance of adjusting the shoulder flounces of her dress. "I think gemstones would be hypocritical as this is traditional peasant garb."

"How fortunate I should come by at this time for I have just the thing." Sheremetev snapped his fingers, creating more of a thick meaty sound than a crisp snap. "Leonid!"

Leonid bustled into the dressing room holding a black box. He placed it on the vanity counter in front of Svetlana. "For you, Angel."

With apprehension, Svetlana untied the white ribbon and lifted the lid. Nestled within tissue paper was a ballerina costume of white gossamer tulle, feathers, and pearls.

Sheremetev moved closer, eyes glowing as he gazed at the delicate piece. "I had it created based on Tchaikovsky's *Swan Lake*. You will be my Odette. Perfect. Innocent. And beautiful above all others."

Svetlana's stomach roiled at the thought of being that man's anything. She gently pushed the box to the edge of the vanity. "Once more, you are too generous. I cannot accept this gift and am sorry for the effort you went to since I will not be dancing for much longer."

The glow in his eyes flickered like a shadow crossing the moon. "As you say. At least will you not try it on?" Sheremetev's gaze slid to Mama, then back to her. "While we are waiting, Leonid, go to my office and fetch my accounts ledger."

Leonid hesitated, knowing as well as Svetlana it was a threat to force her to do his bidding. Powerful men loved nothing more than dangling their power for all to see. Svetlana was no fool. While every fiber of her being protested, she obediently slipped behind the privacy screen and wriggled into the costume. It fit like a glove. She stepped out to a collective gasp.

Sheremetev beamed like a proud owner. "*Prekrasnaya*."

"*Da*, beautiful, Angel," said Leonid.

Tears filled Mama's eyes as she clasped her hands together. "You remind me of the night you first stepped out into society. Dripping in white and pearls for innocence. It was the night you captured Sergey's heart for good."

"Angel, are betrothed you?" Leonid's anxious face reflected in the mirror.

"No. Sergey is a dear friend." Svetlana smoothed a feather as memories tumbled one over another. Sergey's face wreathed in fire. The train station. The Reds dragging him back. "He was taken by the Bolsheviks as we escaped Petrograd. He promised to meet us here in Paris."

"And so he will," Mama said as she dabbed at a stray tear.

"Leonid, take Princess Ana to my table for a glass of sherry. On the house. It will comfort your spirits." Before a protest could be offered,

Sheremetev ushered Leonid and Mama from the room, then offered his arm to Svetlana. "Come with me."

"I should change."

"The costume maker informed me you'll need to walk in it to ensure all the stitches and boning are correct. I do not understand her meaning, but I assume it is all important to the comfort of its wearer." He adjusted his dinner jacket. The cheque book flashed from where it rested in his inner pocket. It taunted her with power, manipulating her into obedience. She hated it.

He guided her down the hall. This time the waiters cast their eyes down in respectful deference. On the other side of the curtain, a woman sang a sad love song. A catalyst, she'd learned, for the ordering of more vodka. There was only one thing Russians loved more than sadness and that was vodka to drown said sorrows in.

"The band is playing Tchaikovsky next. In honor of you."

"I have danced already this evening."

"Please, one more. The costume is already on." He motioned for her to turn around. When she did so, he slipped a mask over her eyes and tied the ribbons behind her head, then gently pushed her in front of the mirror hung for performers to check their appearance before taking the stage.

Svetlana's fingers curled into her feathered skirt as anger poured molten through her veins. It was a delicate mask made of stiffened Venetian black lace. Black diamonds studded the winged tips.

"They will come from all over Paris to see the Russian swan dance on my stage." His face hovered in the mirror over her shoulder. "You will dazzle them."

"I danced on the stages of Petersburg, not before drunken ex-aristocrats."

"Think of it as staying in practice. For when I introduce you to Sergei Diaghilev and his Ballets Russes, the epitome of Russian culture here in Paris."

A gasp sprang to her lips. The impresario Diaghilev was known for his groundbreaking artistry and collaboration with masters in choreography, composition, and dance. To dance for the Ballets Russes was to achieve the highest honor for a Russian artist outside of their homeland. Perhaps if she were to gain the approval of Diaghilev she could earn a wage to repay the debt owed Sheremetev and no longer rely on their dwindling jewels for basic survival.

"If I dance tonight, you will introduce me to Diaghilev tomorrow."

"I see this delights you. Proper introductions will be made at the earliest convenience." The corners of Sheremetev's mouth turned up, dimples in the dough. He turned to leave. "I'll inform the band you're on next."

The stage spotlight bled through the curtain, washing Svetlana in muted red as she waited. No more being coerced into dancing for others. After tonight she would secure a respectable way to settle their account at the White Bear and be done with the horrid place for good. One more dance. That was all.

A woman sat on a stool a few feet away, neatly tucked between a stack of chairs and crates of wine. Cigarette smoke curled from her lip. Her slouched posture and brightly rouged cheeks looked familiar.

"Hello again, Duchess. I see land on feet." The working woman she'd met on the street. From the looks of things, work had not been kind of late.

"Tatya, was it? A surprise to see you here."

"Not surprise when this where all Russians come for good time."

Svetlana searched for something appropriate to say, but what did one say to a girl of her station? *How does the night fare?*

"I don't believe the guests are allowed backstage. You'll enjoy the show more from the tables."

"I no guest."

"You work here?"

"*Da*. He ready in minute." Tatya took a drag of her cigarette and sank farther into the smoke. "You?"

Svetlana shook her head. Never did she wish to claim working here. "I'm doing a favor for Mr. Sheremetev."

Tatya barked with laughter that stuttered into a cough. "We all favors for Mr. Sheremetev. You prettiest yet."

One of the locked doors along the hallway opened and a jacketless man with the front of his shirt unbuttoned motioned at Tatya. The woman jumped off the stool and ground her cigarette under her heel. She sauntered by Svetlana, tweaking one of her feathers.

"Showtime, Duchess."

"Is it done?" Marina asked sleepily from her pallet on the cold floor as Svetlana and Mama slipped into their makeshift quarters.

Svetlana groped for their single candle and a match. A tiny light sprang to life, producing a halo of orange that didn't quite reach the entirety of the space. "Nearly, *kotyonok*."

Marina yawned and stretched, mimicking her nickname of little kitten. "I'll be glad when you don't go there anymore. It's lonely without you."

Guilt swelled in Svetlana's chest. There was only one way to alleviate it, but it came at the price of her pride. One look at her little sister's pale face and she moved past her spat with Mama. Svetlana would paint herself and twirl like a bawd as many times as it took to remove her sister from this place.

"You should have seen her tonight. Dressed like a swan in pearls and feathers. I've never heard such rapturous applause." Mama shimmied out of her gown and placed it in the trunk with all the others. "She has an introduction to Monsieur Diaghilev of the Ballets Russes. Think of the prestige of performing on a Parisian stage."

Svetlana slipped her aching feet out of her shoes and rubbed the dull ache in her shin. She tried forgetting about the earlier spat for Marina's sake, but Mama gave a valiant effort for resurrecting it.

"Your tune about my dancing is oddly different than a few hours ago."

"Think of those attending Ballets Russes. Nobility, gentlemen and ladies. Diamonds and evening gloves. One step closer to the world in which we belong."

"I'm sure it will be wonderful, Mama." Marina met Svetlana's eye. She had learned the patience of placating their mother long before Svetlana could even attempt it. "Only because Svetka's grace will outshine them all." She coughed and fell back on her pillow.

"That doesn't sound good." Svetlana knelt beside her and touched a hand to her sister's brow. "You're warm."

"No, it's cold in here. The nights are turning cooler, and this floor is like an ice block come morning."

Taking the blanket from her own pallet and a fur-lined cloak of Sheremetev's offering, Svetlana stuffed it under her sister. It wasn't much, but it might muffle out some of the chill. "Try to sleep. In the morning we'll help Mrs. Varjenksy make a large batch of hot soup."

"You're a terrible cook."

"I can stir, can't I?"

"Only when you remember to and half the potatoes are already stuck to the bottom of the pot."

Svetlana pulled the thin blanket up to Marina's chin, cutting off further remarks on her lack of culinary skills. "Good night."

A few hours later, when the sun was no more than a lingering consideration on the gray horizon, Svetlana awoke to a violent shuddering. She rolled over to find Marina shaking next to her. Drenched in sweat, her entire body convulsed hard enough to rattle her teeth.

"Marina! Wake up." Svetlana shook her sister. A shocking heat scorched through her nightdress. "Wake up."

Marina's eyes barely fluttered as a wheeze escaped her throat.

"Mama!" Svetlana flung the wet blanket off her sister and quickly covered her with her own dry one. "Marina is burning up. Get Mrs. Varjensky."

Mama flew out of their quarters and was back in a matter of seconds with a groggy Mrs. Varjensky in tow. The old woman took in the situation in a glance and knelt beside Marina. She touched the girl's forehead, throat, arms, and opened her eyelids to reveal a solid white.

Mrs. Varjensky's face wrinkled. "Herbs no help this. Need something more."

Panic bolted through every inch of Svetlana. The old woman was a wise healer. If she couldn't help . . . Svetlana jumped to her feet and pulled her clothes on, her decision immediate. "I know precisely the person."

CHAPTER 11

Sleep was the only thing on Wynn's mind as he made out the last of the Blighty tickets. Slips worth more than gold to send the wounded home to England for recovery or for good. He printed Harkin's name on the last ticket, which boldly stated "rest and release from formal duties." Harkin had done his bit. He was free at last. Wynn signed the bottom and added the document to the stack to be given to the patients in the morning. This time next week those lucky devils would be crossing the Channel, leaving the stench of war far behind. If only all his patients were so lucky.

Stretching out of the stiff chair, he left his office and made a final round of the post-op ward. Rumors abounded of faltering Austria-Hungary lines and Germany doubting continued victories on the battlefield. The words *armistice* and *peace negotiations* floated on prayers that were battered remnants of hope after four dragging years of war.

As Wynn made his way back downstairs and crossed the vestibule, the front doors banged open. An echo thudded down the length of his body, not from the disturbing sound but rather the sight.

Svetlana. Wide-eyed. Clothes haphazard and breathing hard.

And she was staring straight at him. "I need you."

=====

There is a sense of pride when a physician is able to diagnosis a patient correctly—not in a sense of gloating righteousness, but that his skills could be used for the betterment of his patient. Too often skills are not enough and must concede to bitter failure. It was with this knowledge Wynn grappled when Svetlana told him of Marina's symptoms. He could be wrong, but he doubted it.

Ordering an ambulance to find them at the church, Wynn grabbed his medical bag and raced with Svetlana to Marina as dawn cracked the sky. Running was faster than waiting for the ambulance to twist through the narrow streets. Even so, by the time they arrived, blood had begun to trickle from the young girl's nose. Wynn kept the diagnosis to himself as they loaded her into the ambulance and drove back to hospital with masks covering their noses and mouths. Once there, he had to block the entrance to the quarantine ward as Svetlana and her mother tried to push past him.

"This is a restricted area," he said in his calmest doctor voice, bracing his arms across the door. "Medical staff only."

"Restricted for what?" Ana shrieked, wringing her hands and fluttering about like a caged bird.

"Influenza."

With a gasp, she wilted against the wall.

Svetlana didn't flinch. "What will happen?"

It had been a long while since he'd seen her. She was thinner, with a weary countenance that had become more pronounced. Awkwardness from their ill-parting lingered in the tension between them.

"She'll be kept as comfortable as possible in a temperature-even room with other afflicted patients. She'll be sponged down and have her sheets changed as needed, and kept hydrated in hopes of staving off pneumonia. That's all we can do."

"What about medicine?"

He shook his head. "This strain is like nothing we've encountered. It defies every preconceived notion we have of the virus. There's nothing we can do but wait it out." To see if they live or die. It was the worst, most powerless situation.

"Then I will wait with my sister." Ducking, Svetlana slipped under his arm.

He caught her elbow and pulled her away as her fingers brushed the door. At times of family consultations when he had to give heartbreaking news, he relied on a reserve of professional calm and detachment. Many outside the medical field called it coldly impersonal, but it was necessary lest emotion destroy the order he was trying to keep.

All detached order shattered the moment he touched her. It was as if a live wire had been routed under his skin to his heart, jolting it alive. He'd tried to put her out of his mind and thought he was having a rather decent go at it, but that involuntary reaction told him he'd failed miserably.

"Your desire to help is admirable, but I'm short staffed and there aren't enough nurses as it is. The last thing I need is for you to come down sick, too, adding to our increasing list."

She glanced down at his hand still holding her elbow but didn't move to dislodge him. "With not enough nurses to see to proper care, you have no argument to be selective. I will nurse my sister."

He did have an argument, a very good one, but her twist of semantics wasn't the most important one at the moment. "You don't have proper training."

"Then I will learn. Quickly."

Nestor would gleefully have Wynn's head on a platter if he discovered this break in protocol, but if the Duchess of Westminster could tend the wounded in a casino turned hospital, why not a Russian princess?

Reluctantly, Wynn released her arm as nurses bustled by, their head coverings flapping behind them. This could be the best decision he ever made or the worst. Odd, how those two were often separated by a precariously thin line.

"You must do precisely as the nurses instruct without question. No privileges will be given. At the first whimper of insubordination, you're gone. Do you understand?"

She nodded, loose hair slipping from her plait. "Yes."

"You'll need a sterilized uniform before you can enter the ward. One of the VADs should do, and your regular clothing will need to be boiled and scrubbed with lye."

Ana roused herself from where she still leaned against the wall. Her face had paled by two shades. "I'm going too. My daughter needs me."

The last thing her daughter needed was a nervous mother hovering about and causing more harm than good. She'd only serve to cause upset. To everyone.

Wynn shook his head. "Your maternal feelings are commendable but will be put to greater use from a distance. You must remain strong to care for her once she is released. In the meantime, boil all of your clothing and bed materials in the hottest water you can manage. We need to stop the sickness from spreading to the other émigrés."

"You are right, of course, Doctor, but I'm not sure . . . I can't think properly." Ana clutched the golden cross necklace around her throat. "What's going to happen to my little girl? She's so young."

Svetlana slipped an arm around her mother's shoulders. "Mama, I believe Dr. MacCallan is correct. Marina will rest much easier knowing you're far from here and praying for her. Come, I'll take you back to the church." She eased the woman toward the stairs before looking back to Wynn. "I'll return shortly."

As promised, Svetlana returned an hour later sans hysterical mother. She'd changed from her rumpled clothing into a plain but clean VAD uniform—a blue dress and crisp white apron with a white handkerchief tied around her head—that Wynn had taken from the nurses' supply closet. He wasted no time in placing her under the watchful eye of Sister Elton, a no-nonsense matron of the first and second Boer War and survivor of the disastrous Gallipoli Campaign. Ironside, the younger nurses called her for her unbending tenacity.

Sister Elton didn't blink as she stared down at Svetlana from her imposing height. "I don't care if you're a princess or a chauffer's daughter. This is my ward. My rules are to be obeyed at all times."

To her credit, Svetlana met her stare boldly. "Of course."

"Yes, Sister."

"Yes, Sister," Svetlana respectfully repeated. Shoulders pulled back and chin tilted just so, one might never suspect she was not accustomed to acting the subordinate.

"We're breaking every hospital rule I know, and I know them all, having written several of them myself over the years, but I can't deny an extra pair of hands." In addition to her tenacity, Sister Elton was known for her rationality. She swept a critical eye over Svetlana. "You'll do well enough. Come." She opened the infectious ward door and motioned Svetlana in.

A look of uncertainty passed over Svetlana's ashen face. She glanced back at Wynn. "Aren't you coming?"

Her expectant reliance on him sent a thrill through his bones, instantly followed by shame that it came at the expense of her sister's illness. As much as he wanted to devote his time to them, more urgent patients required his care. "I'm needed in surgery. I'll be up to check on Marina as soon as I can." His words did little to relieve the anxiety in her eyes. "She will receive the best possible care in this ward. I promise."

It was the only thing he could promise. The outcome of that care was completely and hopelessly out of his hands.

CHAPTER 12

Hours had passed according to the sweep of shadows from one wall to the opposite, yet it was as if time stood still, holding all in its unrelenting grip. Decorated in flocked damask wallpaper with faded squares indicating where portraits once hung, the space had previously been part of the hotel's second floor of suites. The whispers of silk gowns and polished shoes were naught more than echoes of the past stifled among the coughing and moaning of the current inhabitants. The elegance surrounding them mocked the battle for life.

Svetlana used the sleeve of her dress to wipe the perspiration from her brow, careful not to dislodge the mask from her face, as she changed Marina's sheets for the third time. Every part of her body ached from standing so long and bending over so often, but it was nothing to the agony of watching her sister writhe about in delusions or lie deathly still, so still that Svetlana kept a hand to Marina's chest to ensure she still breathed. Her own heart had yet to quiet as she'd found a routine in sponging Marina off, checking her temperature, offering a sip of water, adding blankets, removing blankets, and starting the routine again until the sheets needed changing.

As Svetlana gently dabbed the wet sponge along Marina's arm, she noticed a gritty texture. Salt. Disturbed by this new development, she inched open the privacy curtain and stuck her head out in search of Sister Elton. She'd been ordered to be seen as little as possible lest she arouses suspicion in the other nurses. Catching sight of Sister Elton across the rows of beds, she motioned for her.

The matron came into the cubicle and pulled the privacy curtain closed. Svetlana didn't wait for her to ask. "There's salt."

Sister Elton swiped a finger along Marina's arm. "She's losing too much sodium from the excessive perspiration. I'll order a bowl of broth. Ladle as much as you can into her."

Svetlana managed two spoonfuls before Marina began coughing so violently that the broth and other substances came up. She quickly wiped away the mess with a napkin. Phlegm shook in Marina's lungs like a death rattle.

"She's congested." Like a summoned angel, Wynn appeared next to her.

Svetlana fought the urge to throw her arms around him in relief. He always seemed to appear when she was in need of assistance. Even if he didn't, she knew he would always come if she called. Her relief splintered. Of course he would come. He was a doctor. Their rift could be cast aside in the face of illness, but tension lingered in the perimeter.

"We need to remove the congestion before it settles into pneumonia," he said. "Retrieve the cupping trolley next to the supply station. It's the one with little glass cups no bigger than a whisky tumbler on it."

Like the day Leonid was shot, fear rang in her ears. Only this time she wasn't staring down at a bleeding stranger. This was her sister. And she could die.

"Glass cups. Yes."

She raced for the trolley and wheeled it back inside the curtain. He'd turned Marina onto her stomach with her nightgown peeled down to her waist.

"Due to the severity, I'll need to make an incision first." Wynn reached for a sharp-looking knife that fit slimly in the palm of his hand. "You can look away if this distresses you."

Svetlana swallowed against the terror of seeing her sister cut open. "Tell me what to do."

"Pour alcohol into that pan."

With a slight tremble in her hand, she did as instructed while Wynn made the shallow cut on Marina's back. Taking a rod with cotton wrapped around the tip, he dipped it in the alcohol, then lit it afire with a match. He popped the burning cotton end into one of the glass cups, then immediately yanked it out and placed the cup on Marina's back. Three more times he did this.

"The fire helps create suction, which will loosen the mucus. The Chinese have been practicing the art for centuries, and it's become popular in French hospitals." He set his extinguished cotton rod on the trolley. "It's the best option we have."

"I trust you." She did, she realized with a start. With no reservation.

It was difficult to decipher his entire expression with the lower half of his face covered by a mask, but she knew he weighed her words carefully.

"I'm glad," he said at last.

Was that relief she heard? The shame of the words spoken to him that night so many weeks before burned through her as thoroughly as the fire had those bits of cotton. Apologizing was not a task she was entirely familiar with, having done so only on limited occasions. In circles of nobility, opinions were often treated as facts and boastful comments taken as law. It was then easy to accept every instinct and word issued as the right one. Never doubt; only confidence. Until meeting a man who forced her to look beyond the shallow waters in which she'd tread her entire life.

She cleared her throat. "That night we last spoke—"

The curtain ripped open and the towering Sister Elton stared at her. "I saw you take the cupping trolley. Is there— Oh. Dr. MacCallan." Her eyes swiftly took in the scene. "Congestion, is it? She take any of that broth?"

Svetlana shook her head. "She started coughing." Marina mumbled incoherently. Svetlana dabbed a wet cloth across her fevered forehead.

"When she rouses we'll try Bovril with milk. She'll need nourishment. They all do." With that terrifying truth, Sister Elton returned to her duties on the floor. Marina's labored breathing filled the small space. She wasn't alone. Harsh breathing, hacking coughs, gasping, and cries of pain spiraled through the ward as the rows of patients struggled for life. Svetlana had overheard a nurse say six of the men had died since that morning after being struck down only the night before.

Pulling the single chair close to Marina's head, Svetlana sank onto it. "What happens next?"

Crossing his arms, Wynn leaned against the wall. His critical gaze swept over Marina, possibly analyzing every drop of sweat, shiver, and erratic breath.

"We wait. The first twenty-four hours are the worst. If she makes it through, she stands a good chance at recovery."

Svetlana followed Wynn's gaze, but instead of a patient or medical prognosis, all she could see was her sweet little sister. Always kind and trusting. The peacemaker who bound their mismatched family together. Svetlana pushed a wet strand of hair from her hot cheek.

"She doesn't deserve this. If anyone must be sick, it should have struck me."

"No one deserves this. Every patient in this hospital has been battling for far too long. Your sister in the Revolution and the soldiers in the war. To survive four horrendous years of bombing and killing only to be taken down by a fever. It's beyond reckoning."

"What is this reckoning?"

"Beyond reckoning. It means beyond understanding. Difficult to come to terms with."

The prolonged tension throbbed. "Much the same could be said of our acquaintance."

"If one was attempting to define the thing, yes, I suppose they could." His gaze moved to her, piercing skin and bone straight to the spikes of her pride. "Though I've never been called difficult a day in my life. They must be referring to you."

She opened her mouth for a retort but promptly closed it as she realized she'd been about to prove his point. If he was set on taking her down a gilded peg, then she would return the favor. After all, he wasn't completely blameless in provoking her hurtful words.

"One could say charm is rather difficult to come to terms with."

Instead of being insulted as she intended, he laughed. "Not in my case, so I'll take that as a compliment." Pushing off the wall, he stood next to Marina's bed. One by one, he popped the glass cups from her back and placed them on the trolley. Round bruises now marred the pale skin. "The bruising will go away in a few days. Her breathing should be easier."

Marina twitched away from him and mumbled.

Svetlana pulled the blanket over her sister's bare back. The sheets needed to be changed again. "She's not sleeping well."

"And likely won't until the fever breaks. It's the body's way of fighting off the virus."

"Is Dr. MacCallan here?" The voice came from the other side of the curtain.

Wynn stuck his head out of the curtain and spoke using words like *X-ray* and *cranial suture*. He popped back in and rubbed the back of his neck, bringing Svetlana's attention to the brush of whiskers trailing his jawline just below his mask, the faint red lines creeping into his eyes, and the husky tiredness coating his voice. The desire to fetch him a blanket and pillow and stroke his hair as he fell asleep swelled over her.

She tucked her hands in her lap before they got ideas. "You should rest."

"I'll rest when the work is done."

"The work of war may never be done. You'll die on your feet and then what will your patients do?"

"You're a rather morbid encourager."

"Russians are firmly rooted in the dramatic. We know no other way."

"Don't I know it." He moved to open the curtain. "Try to get some rest yourself. For your sister's sake as well as your own."

"'I'll rest when the work is done.'" The words rushed from her heart before she could stop them. Before he would be too far gone to hear them. "Dr. MacCallan. Wynn. It's good to see you."

He looked at her for a long moment. The corners of his eyes crinkled, a telltale sign of the smile beneath his mask. "It's good to see you too."

―――

Wynn stood aside, the book in his hand forgotten, as three more covered bodies were carried down the stairs to be taken out back of the hospital to await transport to the mass grave being dug outside the city. One of many constructed lately to accommodate the influenza victims. There were simply too many.

"Are these all?" he asked the last orderly.

"Two more. Civilians. We'll come back and fetch them once the Sisters have finished washing the bodies."

Dread filling him, Wynn waited until the grim procession passed out of sight before sprinting the remaining stairs to the infectious ward. Death steals boldly in the dark night of a sick ward, seizing those in rest who otherwise remain vigilant in light of day. He heard the rattles of breath and the shivers leaving bodies weak and exposed to searching Death.

The Sisters stood guard as they patrolled up and down the aisles, but none stood by the curtained bed. Wynn hurried toward it and pulled back the flimsy material. Marina lay on the bed with red blotching her cheeks. Svetlana sat in the chair next to her, her cheek resting on her arm beside her sister's hand. Asleep.

He released a shaky breath. Death had not visited. He checked the medical chart attached to the foot of the bed, then performed a quick examination of the patient, careful not to disturb her. She was still feverish, but the sheets were dry. The crucial twenty-four hours had passed, yet she remained in some danger. Patients often seemed to recover the second day only to relapse.

Wynn's attention drifted to Svetlana. Thin and pale, with purple smudging under her eyes. The months of fleeing had not been gentle to her. Would that he had a medicine or surgical instrument to alleviate the fear she must carry.

"It's good to see you." Her admission had sparked a part of him he'd all but shuttered. A place he'd allowed hope to root, only to be cut down. It had been nothing more than fanciful thinking, and for what? A woman he barely knew with foreign ideas on humor (or lack thereof) and sentimentality (also lacking). An enigma wrapped in silvery stubbornness and topped off by a challenge, that's what she was.

And there was nothing he loved more than a challenge. It was a lifelong pursuit of his, claiming the endeavors others thought out of reach and exploring them until he understood them inside and out, until he alone could reveal the hidden treasure within, like the life-pumping valves of a heart.

No cardiological study sent his heart racing the way she did. There was something about her that called to a lost part of him. She possessed a strength of character that bolstered his own. When problems seemed insurmountable in the operating theater, he would remember her fortitude not to cower at the Red Army, instead braving Russia's bitter winter to escape, and confining herself to a dank basement for the safety of her family. She inspired him.

Across the bed, Svetlana stirred awake. Her eyes widened at the sight of him and she jerked in her chair to grab Marina's hand.

"She's asleep," he reassured her.

She took a shaky breath, much the same as he had done a few minutes before, then tugged at the kerchief covering her hair. While her nurse's uniform was nothing of a shock to see on a hospital floor, she wore it with the discomfort of an unfamiliar skin.

"I didn't mean to fall asleep. Are you still on duty?"

He nodded. "Surgery is quiet for the moment. I came to see how you're doing."

"You did not return home."

An accurate observation that he felt to the weariness of his marrow. "I managed to close my eyes for a few minutes in my office."

"That is not resting."

"Neither is sleeping in a chair."

"No, but I suppose we both do what we can under the circumstances." Rising, she stretched her arms fully above her head, then straightened each leg in turn with toes pointed. "I have full admiration for your nurses. They never come off their feet."

He'd missed her unique way of phrasing words. Particularly when they weren't barbed insults aimed at him. "You seem to hold your own as a nurse."

"It is not my gift."

Taking the chair from the empty bedside next door, Wynn carried it around to sit next to her chair. His knees popped as he sat.

"Then what is? What have you always wanted to be?"

"I am a princess." She said it as if it were the only natural conclusion in the world. Her skirt rustled and peeking out from the shortened hemline were two black boots at perpendicular angles.

"Yes, but what did you want to do besides wear a tiara?"

"There is no wanting for a princess. This is what I am." So self-assured. So confident of her placement in life. So devastating not to glimpse beyond her mold.

"Forget the title for a minute. Humor me."

One eyebrow arched in regal disapproval. "Humor you? I am not some jester at court provided for your amusement."

"No, it means to pretend. Let the inhibitions go and allow yourself to dream for one unguarded moment."

She continued to eye him with questioning suspicion, but slowly her expression drifted inward as if her mind's eye caught the glimpse of a fleeting dream. "A dancer."

Spoken so low, he almost missed it, but there it was. A dream for herself outside the stuffy titles. "Ballerina?"

"The most beautiful kind there is." She spoke softly, as if the dream were fragile enough to shatter in the open air.

He glimpsed a carefree woman living under the full sun beyond the cold shadows of duty and expectation. A chill he narrowly avoided himself.

"I was six when I began ballet. Eight when I slipped on my first pair of toe shoes. I remember feeling like Cinderella in her glass slippers."

"Do you still dance?" He could have guessed given the muscle structure of her calves and her odd stretching, but he wanted to hear her tell it.

Sitting, her mouth turned down as she knotted her fingers together. "Not in the way I would like."

Whatever tension his question had provoked was ruining the moment. He scrambled to rescue it before it was lost for good.

"What is it about ballet that you love so much?"

"The controlled elegance. Some believe it too rigid and confining, but I find a freedom in the structure of steps. My feet are grounded while the rest of me is allowed to express what cannot be formed in words." Her eyes, softened by lantern light, sought his. "Can you make sense of that?"

"It's how I feel as a physician. Surgery is a precisely controlled state of elegance that must answer to the needs of the body. I never feel more myself than when I'm standing at an operating table."

"At the expense of the unfortunate person lying there."

He gave a short laugh. "From their position I suppose they might think that, but when they arise—and they will if they're my patient—they'll be alive and mended and have gifted me with knowledge I can then use for the next patient. And the next after that. Like new partners for dances ever evolving."

"I cannot comprehend your fascination with blood and cutting open people." She shuddered. "But I am glad for it. The lives you save are immeasurable. I doubt many marquises can claim the same. Russian noblemen often consider it below their rank to put their hands to work."

"I need to prove I'm something more than a title. My hands weren't created to be idle, and I'll push them to the limit every way I can."

"And your family finds this agreeable?"

"My father told me before he died not to let being the second son keep me from making my life useful, while my mother encouraged me to reach for the impossible. Their support means a great deal to me. With stalwart Hugh to carry on the family legacy, I was left free to pursue my own passions and will continue to do so for as long as I'm able. We know so little of how the heart works, despite it being the center of our living bodies. Cardiology must be taken seriously if we are to—" He stopped and rubbed the back of his neck with embarrassment. "Sorry. My excitement on the subject gets out of hand."

"I do not mind your excitement. It stems from a desire to help. I see that now." She straightened her posture and clasped her hands in her lap. "I should not have said those things to you that night, and I sincerely apologize. My desire was only in protecting my family, but that does not excuse my blatant rudeness when you have been nothing but kind."

He could see the hit the apology took to her pride. She wasn't a woman to consider herself in the wrong often. It humbled him to witness her humility.

"Do you accept my apology?" she demanded.

And then she hit him with that.

"It is customary to allow the other person to offer acceptance on their own. Since you're new at this, I'll forgo the dictates of formal apologies and acquiesce to your demand. Yes, I accept your apology in hopes that you'll accept mine. My words were harsh and ungentlemanly. I'm sorry."

"Apology accepted." She settled back in her chair looking smug. "What have you there?"

He looked down to where the book rested forgotten on his knee. "Ah, this. A book on botany I found among the research journals and periodicals. It's mostly filled with medicinal plants, but there's a chapter on creating the ideal garden from the correct type of soil—do you realize how many types of dirt there are?—to allow proper root drainage. I thought you could use it as a guide for when you plant your own garden."

She took the book, running her fingers through the pages until stopping on one with the painted picture of a small daisy.

"Chamomile. We have them all around the city and Russian countryside. They smell sweet, like apples. Whenever I was sick our cook would make tea from the crushed petals." She reverently closed the book and looked at him. "Thank you."

"Friends again?" He stuck out his hand as the final peace offering.

She stretched her hand out, palm down, in answer. Grasping her fingers, he brushed a kiss over her knuckles. Or as best he could with a mask on.

Perhaps it was the midnight hour darkening her eyes or the lantern light that melted the striking angles of her face into a pale blur. Perhaps it was exhaustion that softened the mask she held in place, for in that moment time inhaled deeply on a breath that existed only for them. In that precious space something new was forged. The shape wound ubiquitously around them, giving no hint of what it would become, only that it could become.

The corners of her eyes creased, indicating a smile beneath her mask. He had the sudden desire to see what that curving mouth felt like against his own lips.

A door banged open. Feet scurried across the floor.

"Madam, you cannot be in here!" One of the Sisters hissed. "This is a contagious ward."

"Svetlana!" Ana.

Svetlana jumped to her feet and raced out of the tiny cubicle with Wynn fast on her heels. The older princess was dressed in silk and pearls with panic seared across her face. As Svetlana reached her, Ana grabbed her shoulders and spoke in rapid French. With each word, more color leeched from Svetlana's face.

Sister Elton bore down on them like a U-boat with sights fixed. Wynn took Svetlana and Ana by their elbows and steered them out of the room.

"A sick ward cannot be treated as a hotel with guests coming and going as they please."

Ana didn't spare him a glance as she continued her screeching. Wynn's French was faulty at best, but he picked out *money*, *White Bear*, and *want*. No, that was *voulez*. This sounded more like—

"Has someone stolen from you?" he interrupted.

CHAPTER 13

One more dance for the night and she could finally rip off this wretched costume of feathers and pearls. Costumes were meant to invoke the possibility of being someone else to live out a dream. This was a straitjacket, created to restrain the wearer into submission. Svetlana had become nothing more than a dancing bear set to the tune of whatever music Sheremetev played. And play he did as her act brought in more patrons to drink his vodka and gamble at his tables than before the war broke out. All of Paris wanted to see the Swan Princess and she had no choice but to comply.

Choice required money, and money she did not have.

Influenza had decimated half the city, and only a few remained in the church basement. There was nowhere else for them to go. The walls and floors had been scrubbed and every linen boiled in hot water, but contamination was difficult to prevent in such squalid conditions. Nearly a week ago Mama had retired to their quarters after another mandatory scrubbing and discovered their cache of money and jewels gone. She'd looked everywhere, but not a ruble or franc or necklace had been spared. Their only salvation were the loose gems still sewn into their corsets. Just as the Romanov women had done before they were exiled.

After begging Sister Elton to look after Marina, which the old nurse gladly agreed to, Svetlana had swallowed what remained of her pride and gone straight to Sheremetev to beg an introduction to Monsieur Diaghilev of the Ballets Russes, but the master had traveled to America in hope of procuring new investors and wasn't expected to return for some time. With no option left, she had pleaded more dancing opportunities at the White Bear in order to hasten the payment of their debts. She said nothing of the theft. When she wasn't dancing, she was at the hospital. Marina was improving but wasn't yet well enough to be discharged. Where would she go? Back to the dank basement where newly infected cases sprang up despite the careful cleaning? By some miracle, or more likely Wynn's strict instructions on cleanliness, Mrs. Varjensky and Mama had not been touched.

Most heart-wrenching were the banknotes Wynn tried pressing into her hands each time she came to the hospital. She refused and tried to avoid him, not wishing him to see the depths to which they'd plummeted. The building, however, was only so big, and he knew every room of it. There was no hiding. She'd told him in the broadest of strokes that their funds had disappeared, not revealing how much or how little remained. She could not bear to be pitied, especially not by him.

Taking a break backstage at the White Bear between performances, she startled when a door at the end of the hallway swung open. Moonlight from the back alley spilled over darkened figures kicking a lump in the middle of their circle. The lump moaned and cried. A man! Seized with fear, Svetlana looked all around backstage for one of the security men, but found none.

Shaking now, she stepped toward them. "You there! I command you to stop beating that man."

The figures halted for a second and shouted back at her in angry Russian. Curses like she'd never heard filled her ears. Then a new figure, this one larger than all the rest, came through the door and shut it behind him with a firm click.

Sheremetev. "My dear princess. Why are you not onstage? You were to start five minutes ago." He walked toward her, his ruby stickpin glowing like blood in the backstage light and his walking stick tapping staccato on the wood floor.

"Those men need to be stopped at once."

"Those men work for me as security. They found that miscreant sneaking around."

"Beating him is not an appropriate response."

"During war it is. We can never be too careful, people in positions such as you and I. There is always the rabble lot wishing to overthrow us."

The blood drained from her head. "Is he a Bolshevik?"

Sheremetev pulled a pristine handkerchief from his pocket and wiped his hands. "Soon enough we'll know. On the stage with you. I'll handle everything, my dear."

Svetlana couldn't control the cold numbing her from head to toe as she performed to yet more shattering applause. Had the Bolsheviks found them? Barely scratching the surface of survival and with Marina bedridden, would they be forced to flee once more? How would they survive another escape?

Legs shaking as she rounded the curtain backstage, she collapsed against the wall. When would the fear finally stop?

"No well, Duchess?" Tatya sat perched on a barstool between a stack of crates smoking a stumpy cigarette. If possible she looked more haggard than the last time. "Look fainting."

Svetlana straightened. "The dance takes much out of me."

"I know feeling." Tatya laughed harshly and dropped her cigarette on the ground, grinding it out with her toe. As she leaned forward, the dim light caught blackness rimming her eye.

"What happened there?"

Tatya jerked back. "Nothing."

"Are you hurt? Do you need to see a doctor? I know a man—"

"Knight who save you from rain? With golden hair and shiny umbrella?" She laughed again, this time a hollow sound as if the energy to care had been rubbed out of her. "Knights no for me. Only duchesses. I get animals." Her fingers raised to her cheek, then dropped lifelessly into her lap.

A door along the hallway, opposite from where the ladies enter-tained, opened and out came a handful of men dressed in loose dark clothing much like the kind factory workers wore in Russia. They were the same voices she'd heard from the kicking figures. As the last man came out, he pulled a red band from his arm and shoved it in his pocket before looking down the corridor at the women.

"Tatya. Come." Pyotr Argunov. Tatya's sleazy handler of irreput-able liaisons. "Ah, Princess. Looks like you didn't need my help making introductions to Sheremetev after all. If only you'd told me you needed work. I know the perfect street corner for you."

Tatya eased off her barstool and leaned close to Svetlana. "Careful. They dangerous men. Black Claw."

Svetlana's head whirled as she was left alone in the hallway. Bolsheviks, prostitutes, merciless alley beatings. The Black Claw. It was a name she'd heard only once before, but once was enough to know of the evil men it represented and their nefarious underworld dealings. All spokes in a terrifying circle with Sheremetev at the center. Had she escaped the horrors of Russia only to run headlong into the evil lurking within what was supposed to be sanctuary?

"Here again? You make it easy for me to find you." Were his ears burning? Sheremetev stood at the top of a wide set of stairs that led to his second-floor office. He beckoned her up. "Please, join me."

Sick at the thought of going anywhere near him, she started to back away. "I must return to Marina."

"There is business I would like to discuss. It will benefit your entire family and situation." Leaving no room for argument, he turned and stepped inside his office.

Every sensible bone in her body screamed for her to run as far away as possible, while the desperate side of her fairly salivated at the mention of a benefit. If he canceled their debt, they would be free of this place once and for all. They could leave without the threat of consequences looming at their backs. She tired of being hunted like an animal.

"Anton, help the princess," Sheremetev called from the den of his office.

Anton, one of the many bodyguards, appeared from the shadows and practically shoved her up the stairs, closing the door behind her. It was a spacious room lined with dark oak panels, heavy furniture of the Rococo style, and thick red drapes. Sconces dotted the walls to cast a warm glow across the plush Persian rugs. A royal sanctum for a man of power.

Having lived in a palace and visited the Romanov estates every week for tea since she was a child, Svetlana was left unimpressed by his attempts at bought taste.

"Who were those men?"

Sheremetev paused from filling a tumbler with amber liquid poured out of a crystal decanter. "As I said before, there are numerous security risks—"

"They wore red armbands. Like the revolutionists."

He returned the stopper to the decanter and swirled his drink. "You must be mistaken. I do not allow politics to enter my premises. Bad for business. Which leads me to my proposition for you. Won't you sit?"

"I cannot stay long."

Smiling, he took his time drinking down his glass before walking behind the massive desk and pulling open a drawer. "The situation in Russia grows worse by the day. Executions, riots, theft, lack of jobs, poor rationing. It has become uncivilized. A princess of noble blood should not have to live in fear of such things, and returning is not an option. Have you considered how to support yourself and your mother and sister in the long run?"

"My father and brother will join us soon." And Sergey, God willing. She didn't want to think of him in an airless prison cell or a freezing gulag on the Siberian tundra. Or worse. "We will decide then."

"What if they do not? Forgive me. Sadness I do not wish to bring you, but you must contemplate the possibility. Gemstones will get you only so far. Once they run out . . ." He let the thought trail straight into her fears. Fears for a future she did not want to envision.

"I appreciate your concern, but my family's business is our own."

"That's not quite true, is it? Right now your family owes my business money, a business that is thriving with you at the glittering heart of my show." Pulling a small box from the drawer, he came around his desk. "There is a way to sign the debts as paid. A way to provide your sister with the medications and help she needs. To see you safely guarded, never having to look over your shoulder again. Security for the rest of your life. To continue to dance for years to come with the whole of Paris bowing at your slippered feet."

Lifting the lid to the box, he held it out to her. A ring with a ruby the size of a marble surrounded by flashes of diamonds winked blood red.

Svetlana gasped as she remembered the last time she'd seen the ring on the hand of Alexandra, empress of all Russia. "It can't be."

"Isn't it exquisite? The cost of smuggling it from Yekaterinburg was beyond reckoning, but I consider it mere kopeks to grace the hand of the most magnificent woman in my life."

Chills sprayed across her flesh. Yekaterinburg was where the imperial family had been imprisoned and executed. She stared at the ring in horror, imagining stains of blood as it was pried from the lifeless finger of the tsarina. And now this man wished to place it on her finger. Wynn was right—had been right all along. She never should have trusted Sheremetev.

"No," she whispered, backing toward the door. Her faltering footsteps were swallowed in the plush carpets.

"The prestigious name of Sheremetev and the noble bloodline of Dalsky. As my wife you will continue to dance here, drawing in crowds from all over to witness the splendid swan you are while their money is easily parted from them at my gambling tables. Think of the power we will wield together as the new king and queen of Paris."

"I see. Disappointed that you cannot grab a dowry from me, poor as I am, you wish to draw funds from me another way—by presenting me onstage every evening in your seedy club. A dancing milch cow. You have ripped the beauty from my dance and twisted it into something ugly and sordid."

Box held out to her, he followed. "There is no need to be crass. Cow, indeed. I would not make this offer to you if you were not the most striking woman I have ever seen, and I do enjoy being surrounded by beautiful things. You will be the most glorious gem in my crowning achievements, and what better than to collect a gem that pays dividends?"

"You never intended to introduce me to Diaghilev, did you?" What a fool she'd been to believe the lie, but her hope had been so wasted that she couldn't help clinging to the one sprig of dangled happiness. More than anything, she'd been a fool to believe she could pay back the debt with no strings attached. "I have no desire to be an ornament for anyone's crown, and I most certainly do not and will not stay in this place a minute longer." The doorknob jammed into her back.

"You may run, but you do not have a choice in this matter. I will catch you, make no mistake. If you proceed to be difficult, those men with the red armbands will take great pleasure in learning who you truly are. A firing squad will be the least of your troubles compared to what they will do to you. And your sister and your mother."

"You are a monster."

Quick as a snake, he grabbed her chin and squeezed. His eyes receded farther into the bags of skin, cutting them to mere slits. "I am a man who gets what he wants. By whatever means necessary. You belong to me."

"No." She fumbled for the door handle.

He squeezed harder, his breath sour in her face. "Svetlana, my Ice Swan, my princess. You *will* marry me."

CHAPTER 14

She was the most exquisite creature Wynn had ever beheld. Svetlana spun across the White Bear's floor, every step and line of her body a sweep of elegance that held him mesmerized. He braced an arm against the back wall as his heart nearly thudded from his chest. Her shell had cracked off to reveal the breathtaking life within, and he felt sole witness to its emergence.

When she twirled to a stop and dipped into a deep curtsy on a cloud of feathers, applause exploded around him. The spell broke and suddenly he was surrounded by people once more.

Her movements stilled, he saw her face. A black lace mask hid most of it, but not enough to obscure the whiteness of her lips and clenching of her jaw. Not a look he expected after hearing her describe what dance did to her. Then again, she carried the weight of a thousand worries on her slim shoulders. If he could help relieve merely one of them, he would.

She disappeared behind the stage, and Wynn edged his way through the throng of patrons clamoring to the dance floor as the band swung into a more lively tune. Several of the familiars spotted him and waved to get his attention. Wynn ignored them. He was in no mood for goiters or suspicious bunions tonight.

"Mac!" Leonid's voice cut through the cigarette haze.

Wynn followed the sound and spotted his friend standing at the far side of the room next to an empty booth. He weaved his way over.

"Good to see you, but I can't stop. I came to see Svetlana."

"She changing. We wait here." Leonid slid into the red cushioned booth and gestured for Wynn to do the same. "Her I walk home. She find me."

Eyes anxiously glancing to the curtain, Wynn took a seat. It wouldn't do to barge in on her in the dressing room. She'd avoided him for days, refusing his money and claiming she had her situation in hand. The lie had danced between them long enough.

"You and Angel speak again, *da*? *Khorosho*. I no like friends argue. I no choose sides."

"I'm glad. I feared you'd choose her over me, and I'd be out a chess partner."

"She prettier you."

"Can't argue that."

Leonid leaned forward, all traces of humor gone. "Must take care. She not do well."

Wynn's gaze darted to the curtain as a tightness constricted his chest. "I know. Her sister has been in hospital for over a week, and tensions are strained in that infectious hovel they're staying in. I want to get her and her family out." He didn't mention the stolen property. If he hadn't been standing there to overhear it, he doubted she would have told him.

Glancing over his shoulder, Leonid leaned forward until his chest nearly touched the tabletop.

"Greater danger." His eyes darted over Wynn's shoulder, then back. "Happenings . . . around."

Wynn tensed on immediate alert. "What danger?"

"Hear things. See things. Russian things."

"Are the Bolsheviks in Paris?"

"*Papochka* no involve politics, but turn blind eye to all with money. Angel need get out." He stared pointedly at Wynn, pinning him with the answer. Svetlana's living nightmare. That which had destroyed her world and sought her death had followed her.

The curtain rustled and applause exploded over the dancing music. Svetlana bobbed through the crowd as adoring fans rushed around her. She broke free and tore to the exit.

Leonid fumbled from the table. "Angel! Wait! I walk you."

"I got her." Wynn shoved through the crowd, not caring how many he knocked down in his haste. They were too drunk to protest.

Outside, he scanned up and down the footpath. Where could she have gotten to so quickly? Heel clicks sounded on the pavement. He took off running left. Her hair made a bright spot against the inkiness of midnight and shadowy buildings. In a matter of seconds, he closed in on her and reached for her hand. With a wrangled sob, she yanked away from him and shouted in French.

"Calm down. It's me."

Her face was bleached in terror and tears ran down her cheeks. With another strangled sob, she covered her face with her hands. Tiny cries shook her body. Moving on instinct, Wynn wrapped his arms around her and pulled her close. He could feel the delicate bones beneath her thin coat and the flutter of her lashes as her face pressed into his neck.

Did she know about the Bolsheviks? If so, why appear so publicly? Why would Sheremetev plaster a poster outside the White Bear advertising the Ice Swan, a beacon to her enemies? Wynn could kill the man with his bare hands. That is, if he could get his hands around that fat neck.

Svetlana pulled away abruptly. Blinking rapidly, her gaze darted up and down the dark street shooting through the heart of Little Neva.

"I must go. I must leave."

"Where? That's the wrong direction for hospital and the church."

"I must go. I must leave here."

She was in shock. He grasped her face, forcing her to focus on him, then lowered his hands to rest on her shoulders, grounding her.

If the Bolsheviks were sniffing around as Leonid claimed, they might go straight to those places in search of her.

"Where would you feel most safe?"

Her eyes came into focus as a single tear slid down her cheek. She swiped it away. "I . . . the stage, but that's not . . ." She looked back to the White Bear, then quickly away. "The gardens of the Blue Palace. There were roses in summer."

Anchoring his arm around her, he led her across the deserted street with its shuttered cafés and butcher shops long since deprived of meat and headed west toward Parc Monceau. It wasn't a palace, but it was the best he could manage in the circumstances. Curfew was still in effect, but the city had grown eerily quiet as half its citizens were struck down by influenza. The other half were left to care for them and the incoming wounded soldiers.

With the Germans losing ground on the frontlines, they had little ability or strength left to summon for night raids. A fact Wynn didn't take for granted as the full moon and shower of stars offered a brilliant amount of light by which to guide bombers to unsuspecting targets. Instead, he used it to navigate the formal pathways with overgrown shrubberies and lonely statues of writers and musicians toward the pond, half flanked by a classical colonnade. He guided Svetlana to a wrought iron bench nestled between the columns and pulled off his wool coat, wrapping it around her. Having grown up in Scotland, the early November air did little more than brisk his skin.

They sat quietly staring at the dance of moonlight off the pond's still surface.

"Do you feel safe now?" He kept his voice low and even, careful not to rattle her. An effective bedside method.

She reached for his hand. "Yes."

Wynn didn't move lest he disturb the fragile touch. Her hand was cold in his, as if her long fingers were carved of ice. "Where is the Blue Palace?"

"My family's home in Petrograd. So called for the way the winter light turns the walls to pale blue. We had the most dazzling blooms in all the city, and I could sit there for hours in the quiet."

The musty scent of dry leaves clinging to dead branches and scraggly plants left unattended in the years of war were a far cry from palace roses, but the area was peaceful as the earth slowly reclaimed man's version of nature. In all the years his family had holidayed in Paris, they'd never visited this park, preferring the Jardin des Tuileries and Jardin du Luxembourg or Mother's favorite stretching from that Eiffel Tower tangle of metal. Bit of a marvel he was only stepping foot here now, but the occasion was gratifying. It was a place where he held a memory of no other but of her and him.

"Why did you run out of the club?"

Her hand slipped from his and she tugged up the collar of his coat. He didn't take it as a rejection, merely a move to settle into a defensive position like a soldier adjusting his armor.

"Sheremetev offered to cancel my family's debt and provide security by offer of marriage."

"No." His harsh answer tore out in a contorted growl of disbelief and anger. He didn't care how fat the man's neck was, Wynn would strangle him if he ever laid eyes on the dog again. To blazes with his oath to do no harm.

"He spins a compassionate tale of rescuing the maiden in distress, but it's the title and money he's after. A princess of the proud Dalsky line would provide prestige that his own name, powerful as it is, cannot acquire. As his wife I would be forced to continue dancing to bring in waves of rich patrons. He has taken the thing I love and turned it against me." Her voice was flat. Emotional detachment. A common response to shock and one she handled with practiced skill. "Tonight I watched him sanction the beating of a man begging for his life by thugs wearing red armbands. Do you know what red represents in Russia?"

181

Wynn clenched his hands as rage poured into his veins, hot and vindictive. "I can guess."

"Then you know what I failed to see before. They were there all the time. They are here. No matter how far I ran or what I've done, they have found me."

"I won't let them hurt you. Do you understand? I will keep you safe."

"Safe?" She laughed bitterly and swiped at an errant tear. "No one is safe from a man like Sheremetev. He may not be political enough for a Bolshevik, but I believe he's part of the criminal sect Black Claw. Importing and exporting opioids, weapons, prostitution rings, laundering of money, and other illegal activities. His connections are like poisonous vines crawling beneath the surface on which we walk. At his will the vines shoot through the dirt and twist at our ankles, dragging us into his lair. No one can stop him."

Jerking off the bench, Wynn paced as he fought to keep a string of curses silent. Every blood vessel throbbed with anger.

"You cannot marry that monster."

"Do you know what he offered me? A ruby ring red as blood. It may as well have been as it was pried from the dead tsarina's finger after she was executed along with her family in a filthy basement by a group of Red soldiers. Men of whose ilk he allows to plot in his club." She pulled down the corner of his coat collar to reveal bruises on her jaw in a distinctive handprint. "He has fed on my fears and closed the circle around me."

"You cannot marry him."

"He will feed me to the Bolsheviks if I do not comply. It seems I have no other option."

He squatted before her. "There's one. Marry me."

CHAPTER 15

Y ou cannot marry him."

"Mama, I have no choice." Svetlana flipped the veil over her face as the church's organ swelled to a bridal march, jangling her nerves. "Besides, it is too late to turn back now."

She had been engaged to Dr. Edwynn MacCallan, Marquis of Tarltan, for a grand total of three days. That night in the garden she had been shocked into silence at his sudden proposal, but as her questions rose like a frantic tide she could keep silent no longer. For nearly an hour she had questioned his sanity, his reasoning, and his intentions. He had answered each one with calm logic.

She and her family would have the protection of his name and wealth with no obligations on Svetlana's part except to say I do. A marriage in name only if that was her wish. In the end, when thinking had exhausted her, she asked him why he would go to such trouble for her. He'd merely smiled in that way of his and said he could no longer stand by and watch her suffer when there was something he could do to alleviate her pain.

Mama fussed with the veil that had been borrowed from one of their neighbors in the church basement. It was one of the few treasures the woman had escaped Russia with, and she'd only agreed to loan it when Svetlana offered her daily ration of food.

"To think, a daughter of mine and princess of Russia married to a tradesman. In a borrowed dress with no proper tiara to signify her rank."

Svetlana stepped away before her mother could jab another hairpin into her scalp. If only Marina were here to bring a sense of calm, but under doctor's orders she was to remain on bed rest at his family's townhouse until her strength fully recovered. Wynn had extended his kindness by offering his mother's closet for Svetlana's perusal. She was grateful, but a wedding dress and tiara were nothing compared to the absence of her beloved sister, and more than anything Svetlana needed her soothing strength this day.

"Wynn may be a physician, but he is also a marquis, a high noble rank in Britain."

"It is a sin when you are bound to another man. Sergey will be heartbroken. He's been so good to you over the years."

"Sergey and I were never officially betrothed. I cannot wait for him to find us, if indeed he ever does." Sergey had been good to her. His parting act had been to see her to safety while sacrificing himself to the enemy. She could never forget that, but the promises made in Russia were best left to the past. She had a future to secure. "Wynn is a good man. He would not take on our troubles otherwise."

"May the saints preserve us from those black deeds." Mama crossed herself before one of the many gilded icons decorating the vestibule of the Alexander Nevsky Cathedral. A fitting place for the ceremony. Not to mention the only place to allow an Orthodox wedding. "How was our family brought to such an abyss? If only I had been stronger. If only your father were here. He would know what to do."

"He would put the well-being of our family above all else as I am trying to do. Is that not what marriages are for? A weeding out of sentiments for the betterment of an alliance. Wynn is a good alliance."

"The man is an Anglican!" Mama's trump card. No proper Russian argued with the dictates of the Holy Church, but wartime had a way of requiring one's head to be turned the other way as circumstances required.

"Due to our upsetting circumstances, the priest is willing to overlook Wynn's heresy." A few gold coins slipped into the altar coin box might have pushed the decision to more favorable means as well.

"Surely there must be another way. Perhaps you have not thought of them all. I'm certain if we were to ask Shereme—"

"No!" Svetlana took a deep breath as every fiber of anger, sadness, and fear roiled within her. Mama would never learn of what happened with Sheremetev nor of the evilness he allowed to hunt them. Wynn was their only hope now. "Go and take a seat."

"Svetka." Mama reached a hand toward the veil.

Svetlana pulled away. If one more person prodded her, she would lose her last shred of control. "I'm ready. Please go."

Ready. A rather misleading term. Certainly she was ready to put her troubles behind her and breathe for one day without the threat of financial ruin or starvation, but was she ready to marry a man she barely knew? She'd known Sergey for years, which was an anomaly in her social circles. Marriage contracts were often drawn up based on name and wealth alone with the bride and groom having met a mere afterthought. And love, well, that was best left to the fairy tales. She was under no illusion of what this marriage to Wynn meant and her gratitude to him could never be fully expressed.

A side door opened. Svetlana jumped.

"Are you prepared, my child?" The priest was dressed in robes of gold and black with a bushy beard stretching down his chest.

Heart racing, Svetlana nodded. It wasn't Sheremetev come to drag her away to the den of the Reds.

"I must ask you never to tell that this holy church allowed a man of non-faith to be joined to you, a true believer, in its inner sanctum. If rumors were to spread, anarchy could ensue. Papists will demand their own heretical services."

It could hardly be imagined that the Catholics would storm these doors when they had the magnificent Notre Dame to worship in, but Svetlana did not bother to correct him. She simply bowed her head in quiet respect as she sought to delicately defend her fiancé. "I believe Anglican is considered a righteous faith in England."

The priest snorted. "They would."

The heavy door creaked open to the inner sanctum. Hundreds of candles gleamed from their ornate brass chandeliers and altar stands, while mid-morning sun poured through the windows set high in the cupola and bounced off the golden icons painted on the panels of rich wood.

Dressed in a black-and-gray morning suit, Wynn stood waiting for her. His hair shone like gold under the shaft of sunlight, the glowing aura of a knight to the rescue. While she the maiden led a dragon to his door. Her regret cut deeper at involving him in her woes. If he thought anything of regret, he didn't show it. Together they traversed the short walk down the aisle and stopped before the iconostasis.

He grasped her elbow and leaned close to her ear. "You're lovely."

She mumbled a thank-you, or at least she thought she did. The proceedings turned to a haze as the Orthodox priest read the Epistle, repeated in English by the Anglican priest Wynn had asked to come on his behalf. Then the sacred wedding loaf, the blessing with icons, and the placing of the wedding crowns on their heads.

The cup of warm, red wine was then offered with another blessing. Wynn took a sip and passed the cup to her. As she took the cup, her fingers brushed his. He was trembling. The haze rolled back as she realized he was as nervous as she was. Unflappable Wynn who had calmed her distress time and again. Her own nerves stilled and she smiled. He smiled back. Taking the cup, she raised it to her lips.

The front door banged open. Svetlana jumped, sloshing tiny drops of red down the front of her blue silk dress. A shadowy figure inched along the back wall. Too small to be Sheremetev, but no. He would never come himself. He was a man who sent others to do his dirty work.

Wynn tugged on her hand, and she allowed him to lead her

around the lectern behind the priest as the final words were spoken and they were consecrated as man and wife.

"Who is that?" Not the most romantic words a bride had first spoken to her groom, but then again most brides probably weren't being hunted by political radicals or jilted club owners.

Wynn peered at the shadows in which the figure hovered. "A guest?"

"Everyone we invited is here." Everyone being her mother and Wynn's friend Gerard from the hospital. Even Mrs. Varjensky's cheerful presence was missing as she had volunteered to stay with Marina.

"An inquisitive parishioner?"

"I don't think so."

Taking both of her hands, he stepped close. Behind him Mama clutched her cross at the impropriety in a church. "You're safe. He can never harm you again. As Marchioness of Tarltan you are a British citizen now and answer only to British law." He pressed a kiss to her fingers. "I will keep you safe."

She nodded numbly, desperately wanting to believe him, but fear lurked deep in her heart. British or not, the Bolsheviks would never respect such laws. They were the enemy of law.

The figure moved into the flicker of candlelight. Tatya. With a breath of relief, Svetlana hurried toward her with Wynn right behind her.

"What are you doing here?"

Tatya looked her up and down before pressing a hand over her own rumpled dress. "Apology no dress up. No fine duchess like you." She winked at Wynn. "Hello, sir knight. *Pozdravlyayu*."

"*Spasibo*." Wynn gave a slight bow, his Russian lessons proving themselves at her congratulations. "You're the lady we met before in the rain."

Tatya laughed, startling the priests who were talking to Mama and Gerard. "I no lady. If were, no hearing things. Bad things."

Cold swept through Svetlana. "What things?"

"I come warn. Sheremetev. He know. Get out while can." Tatya brushed past her.

"Wait!" Svetlana hurried after her and unbuckled the sapphire brooch at her throat, pressing it into Tatya's gloveless hand. Her fingers were little more than bird claws, frozen from the November wind. "Take this."

Tatya shoved it back at her. "I no charity."

"It's not charity." Svetlana closed Tatya's fingers around the expensive piece. The last jewel she owned. "Take it. Get out while you can."

The wedding feast was a solemn affair with a few pastries and sandwiches allotted by the rations to feed the equally solemn guests as they gathered in Wynn's Parisian townhouse. More specifically, Château Sable Bleu, which sat a mere stone's throw from the grand Champs Élysées along the fashionable Rue de Faubourg Saint-Honoré, and belonged to Hugh as one of the many grand homes owned by the Duke of Kilbride. Since the war began, the house had been occupied by a major in Hugh's regiment and the man's wife. The major was killed a fortnight ago and the wife had gone back to England, returning the key to the MacCallans once again.

The night Wynn proposed to Svetlana, he'd whisked her here along with her mother, sister, and Mrs. Varjensky while he kept to his bachelor lodgings with the other doctors. That would change now.

"Congratulations, mate," Gerard said as he put on his hat and coat to meet the bitter November air. "You've a charming bride, and I wish you all the happiness in the world."

"Thank you for coming," Wynn said. "Listen, I've been going over the charts for the influenza cases, and tomorrow I'd like to—"

"Tomorrow you'll be here with your wife. Leave all hospital problems and thoughts to me."

"Yes, but there's—"

"The hospital can survive a few days without your brilliance blinding the patients. If there's an emergency, I'll know right where to find you. In the meantime, enjoy being married."

Wynn's gaze, heavy with doubt, drifted up toward the bedchambers beyond. "I'll do my best."

After seeing out his one and only guest, Wynn instructed the new maid to clear away the remaining food and then attend to her mistress upstairs. Wanting to give Svetlana as much time as she needed, he went to the study and pulled out the list of remaining expenses owed to Sheremetev that he and Svetlana had compiled the night before. Tallying them once more and throwing in a bit extra for cushion, Wynn wrote a cheque to the monstrous boar and signed it with a flourish. He then took out a blank sheet of stationary stamped with the Kilbride ducal seal and added a short note.

> This payment hereby honors and discharges all debts owed by the Dalsky family to be paid here in full on behalf of Princess Svetlana MacCallan, Marchioness of Tarltan.

He signed his name at the bottom, relishing the weight of his full title for once.

There. The whole sordid deed was done. He'd have the money delivered to the White Bear first thing in the morning, and then he could begin arrangements for Svetlana and her family to travel to Thornhill. They would be safe at last on his family's Scottish estate.

Hopefully soon the war would end and he could join them. Maybe start a new medical practice out of Glasgow. He and Svetlana would have to find themselves a new home, one with a large garden for her to plant roses in and for children to play in. He stopped himself at the fanciful dream. He'd promised her this was a marriage in name and appearance only. Yet in time he hoped it would become more. Much more.

Occupying himself for another hour, Wynn finally made his way up the winding staircase to the second-floor landing and knocked on Marina's door.

Mrs. Varjensky bustled out carrying an empty bowl of soup. She said something and pulled his head down to plant two squishy kisses on both his cheeks. "*Golubchik*."

Wynn kissed her back. "Good night, *babushka*."

Giggling like a little girl, the old woman clomped down the stairs. Wynn stepped into the room and took quick note of his patient now turned sister-in-law.

"How are you this evening, Marina?"

"Well, thank you." Marina settled against a fluffy pillow in the oversize bed. "I'm only sorry to have missed the ceremony. But the bride should not have to worry about a fainting sister."

"The important thing is you're improving." He moved closer to the bed. No sweating, clear eyes, pale cheeks, and full breaths. "A few days more and you might be able to move around a bit."

"I couldn't do it without Mrs. Varjensky's nursing. Svetka tries, but she frets too much." She yawned. "I know you'll be good to her. She doesn't think so, but she needs someone to take care of her. Good night. Brother."

Wynn had moved to the door but stopped at her words. Could he live up to them? He was going to try. "Good night."

Ascending to the third floor, which was designed as master and mistress suites with a shared common space between them, Wynn hovered outside his door. Should he change and then go see Svetlana? No. She would get the wrong impression if he appeared at her door in pajamas. He could knock on the door of their shared common room. No. That might appear too casual. Before he lost his nerve, he walked down to her door and knocked.

After several long seconds he was met with an, "Enter."

The room hadn't changed since he was a boy and his mother ruled as Duchess of Kilbride. Soft lavenders and creams, pillows on every available surface, and silver fixtures that reflected the glow of candlelight. The botany book he'd given Svetlana lay open on the small table next to the bed. To what page he could not see from where he stood in the doorway.

Svetlana turned from where she stood at the window. She'd changed from her wedding attire into a billowy dressing gown complete with out-of-date mutton chop sleeves. To his disappointment her hair remained pinned up. What had he expected? For it to be flowing intimately loose down her back?

He could hope.

She tugged the belt tighter about her waist. "The maid is soaking your mother's dress. She believes the wine will not stain."

"Mother hasn't worn these clothes in over twenty years. I doubt she remembers they're here. She'd be glad to know they came to good use, though I wish you could have worn the wedding dress you wanted."

"This was not a usual wedding. I could not have expected anything I wanted." Color bled to her cheeks. "Forgive me. That is not what I meant."

"I know what you meant, and you're right. It wasn't the wedding I wanted either, but it's done now."

"Yes, it's done now."

They stood on opposite sides of the room, but the space between them constricted to within the stroke of a single heartbeat. She was wreathed in golden light, illuminating beauty of another world. But she wasn't of another world. She was here, with him. Claiming his name, and the knowledge of it filled him with awed pride.

She fiddled again with the knotted sash at her waist, breaking the moment. Nervous.

"Won't you have a seat?"

Eager to put her at ease, he chose the most uncomfortable chair in the room that forced him to sit erect. No draping against pillows or velvet settees.

"Marina looks better this evening. I imagine she should be strong enough to take small strolls around the back garden in a few days."

"I missed having her at the ceremony today, but I'm grateful you allowed her to come downstairs for the feast. Important moments should be shared with one's sister."

"I wish I could have brought her to the church, if only to make you happy."

"I know."

He shifted against the chair's hard back. "I've written a cheque to be delivered to Sheremetev in the morning. He has no further reason to pursue the debt."

"What of his threat about the Bolsheviks? He's not a man to allow a slight to pass unheeded." She jerked on the sash, creating another knot. "I would rather face the Reds than marry him."

"You married me instead."

Her hands stilled as her eyes flickered to his. "Yes, I did."

He leaned forward, bracing his elbows on his knees in an attempt to appear nonchalant. He felt anything but on this, their wedding night. "As your husband I'm getting you out of France as soon as possible. You and your family will be safe enough on my family's estate in Scotland."

"Aren't you coming?"

"As long as this war rages and the injured are brought in, my duties remain here. I will come to you as soon as possible."

"What will keep Sheremetev from taking out his revenge on you? The danger you have put yourself in because of me—"

"Because you're my wife."

"I wasn't your wife three days ago when you proposed and inadvertently threw yourself into the line of fire."

"Hardly inadvertently. I knew from the first moment that any relationship with you would be difficult. You don't make things easy on a man."

Her eyebrow arched. "You claimed to be a man who appreciates a challenge."

He smiled. "True, but sometimes a little peace and quiet can be nice too."

"I seem to have brought anything but peace and quiet to you. You would have been better never having met me."

"I don't believe that."

"No? I've offered you nothing in this arrangement. Fake though it is, what good will our union do for you?"

He locked his fingers together as the conversation veered into territory he wasn't ready to dissect. "You've asked me that before."

"And you gave me a doctor's answer. Because I needed help. Any number of your patients can say the same thing, but you didn't marry any of them."

They're not as beautiful as you. Nor as fascinating or intellectually stimulating. You alone I wish to know all of me. He could tell her none of that. She'd run out the front door and never look back, and he'd never have the opportunity to woo her properly.

"As I told you the night I proposed, you may think of this as a business transaction offered to you because it was the right thing to do. I can offer you a good position in society where you will lack for nothing and enjoy the comforts to which you are accustomed. And despite your perseverance to convince me otherwise, I enjoy your company and wish to continue doing so."

"My part in this transaction is companionship?"

"Yes."

She watched him, waiting to cut apart his answers to find the true meaning behind his words. She'd lived in a shroud of secrecy for too long. Was it any wonder she craved the truth? He wanted her to count on him for that.

"Because I'm drawn to you."

A simple confession, yet he could not mean it more.

She turned away and faced the window. Whatever response he was hoping for, cold dismissal wasn't it.

He stood. "I'm sorry if I've offended you."

"You haven't." She turned back to face him. Her cool reserve dropped as faint pink dusted her cheeks. "In Russia we are not accustomed to sharing such straightforward sentiments. Forgive me if I do not always know how to respond."

"Honesty. That's all I ask. In return I'll be honest with you."

She nodded. "Honesty between us always."

Her simple wedding band winked in the candlelight. He longed to kiss it as affirmation of the vows he'd made to honor and protect her. He longed to kiss the tender inside of her wrist, trailing kisses up her arm and over the curve of her shoulder. He longed to press his lips to her throat, feeling her pulse increase as he moved to her jaw and finally to her lips. More than anything he longed to kiss her. His wife. He had every right to, but he wouldn't violate the tenuous trust between them. He would wait for her.

"Good night, Svetlana." Gathering his self-control, he crossed to the door.

"Wynn." He stopped and turned back. She didn't smile often enough, but now she did. And she was smiling at him. "Thank you."

Nodding, he stepped into the hallway and closed the door softly behind him, heart nearly beating out of his chest. His wife might like him after all. In the books, November the tenth would go down as the best day of his life.

CHAPTER 16

W here is all that noise coming from?" Svetlana got up from her chair, crossed to the window, and drew open the yellow drapes. Light flooded the bedchamber in a golden halo.

Marina roused in her bed. "Are we being invaded?"

"If we are, the citizens of Paris look quite jubilant about it."

A sea of humanity swept down the street in front of the townhouse with shouts of celebration and fluttering of blue, white, and red flags. Svetlana opened the glass door and stepped onto the small balcony. Canons shot in the distance as a wave of voices singing "La Marseillaise" rose higher and higher above the din. Tears and smiles glistened on the peoples' faces as they marched south toward the Place de la Concorde. This was no invasion.

She spotted Wynn's head weaving through the crowd. The only one without a hat. He looked up and saw her. A wide grin split his face, and he waved before shouldering his way to the front door. A few seconds later, feet pounded on the stairs. He bounded into the room and swept her off her feet, swinging her in a circle and laughing.

"It's over! The war. At eleven o'clock this morning. Our lads are no longer fighting."

Elation like she'd never known flooded her and she laughed along with him. The horrible nightmare that had swept the world into death had gasped its last destructive breath. Wynn set her on her feet but didn't let go. Pressed close to him, her face inches from his, the world and its celebrations narrowed to the space between them. For an instant she forgot about the happenings that brought them together, the vows that claimed her as his wife. All she saw was the deepened desire in his golden eyes, knowing it reflected in her own and drew her to him.

She stepped back, out of his arms, away from his pull, and clasped her hands in front of her for protection. Against his magnetism or her own unsettling reaction to it she couldn't decide. This was a business arrangement, a mutual companionship. Not a romantic fantasy to be swept away in.

"I'm delighted there will be peace at last."

The desire in his eyes flickered then snuffed out and a polite expression slipped in place. "They said it would be over by Christmas the first year. So far, we've had four Christmases pass, but this year we can finally celebrate." He walked to Marina's bed and grasped her hand. "How about that? Would you like to have a festive Christmas in Scotland this year?"

Marina nodded eagerly. A light no longer feverish danced in her eyes. "How wonderful! We can see if the *sochivo* sticks to the ceiling. After all this misfortune, I bet it will."

Wynn frowned. "You throw socks at the ceiling?"

"*Sochivo*. It's a porridge made with wheat, honey, and fruits. It's good luck if it sticks to the ceiling."

"The dining hall at Thornhill is near three stories tall, but I'll make a go of getting porridge up there if it brings us luck."

Marina laughed again, but it quickly turned to coughing. Wynn placed a hand on her back. "Breathe deeply through your nose. Good. Again." He poured water into a glass from the bedside table and handed it to her. "Small sips. We need to calm the bronchial hairs from agitating your lungs."

Marina's eyes widened over the rim of her cup. "I have hairs in my lungs?"

Wynn nodded. "When they get tickled, we cough." He tossed a wink in Svetlana's direction.

How effortless he made it all look. Never rushing but always moving with purpose and complete embodiment of his confidence. He was easy to get caught up in. If she wasn't careful, she might do just that.

Mama ran into the room, her hair still in rag curls and sleep blinking in her panicked eyes. "Has a herd of elephants come crashing in?" Her attention shot to Marina. "*Kotyonok!* What has happened? Do we need the hospital?"

Coughing less, Marina batted Mama away as she came at her with hands aflutter. "I'm well enough. We have our own doctor here."

Mama grabbed Wynn by the lapels of his coat, clinging to him like a scuff on a shoe. "I was resting—my nerves, you understand—when I heard a terrible noise like thunderclaps."

Wynn tried to loosen her grip. "Probably me running up the stairs. Or the captured German canons they're hauling down the Champs Élysées."

"I dreamed we were in Petersburg—I mean, Petrograd—again and the revolutionaries were coming."

"They aren't. No one is. The war is over."

Mama glared at his outrageous claim. "Do not tell me the war is over when those crazy men sit in the Winter Palace as if they own— What do you mean? Which war?"

"The Great War. The one the nations of Europe have been waging for four years."

"No one is dying?"

Wynn pried her fingers loose from his crimped lapels. "Hopefully not anymore."

"This is wonderful news! Why did you not tell me right away?" Mama clapped her hands. "We must celebrate. I'll have that maid fetch us chicken and beef, vegetables, fruit, and pastries, and anything left from the wedding feast yesterday. You really must hire a trained cook. I found part of an eggshell in my soup last night."

"Food will be rationed for some time to come, but I'll give her a few more coins to find what she can. We do deserve a celebration."

"And dresses. We must all have new wardrobes now." Mama twirled about the room with a dreamy smile on her face. A look that was always expensive.

"This is hardly the time to discuss such matters," Svetlana said.

Mama stopped twirling and pressed her mouth into a tight line. She never liked being told no when she was excited, and she certainly didn't enjoy learning from her past debts. Debts Wynn had paid off on her behalf.

"Another time then. I'll go and set a menu with that maid until a proper cook is hired. Heaven knows she's in need of a proper mistress. The French aren't known for hard work like the Russian peasants." With a sweep of her heavy skirts, pilfered from Wynn's mother's Victorian wardrobe, she left.

The room seemed to sigh in relief.

"I'm afraid that along with food rationing, I've more bad news," Wynn said. "I wasn't able to procure travel tickets. In fact, I wasn't able to make it to the ticket office at all. The crowds were too great to make it beyond three streets. Took me nearly an hour to walk the way back. I'll try again tomorrow."

"Won't the ships be needed to take the soldiers home?" Svetlana asked.

"Yes, but it's going to take weeks, months even for command to start making new orders. Everything will be in chaos for a while. I'll get you to Scotland. Don't worry."

She nodded to keep the worry from surfacing. She had no doubt he would do everything in his power to get them to safety, but every minute spent in Paris was another minute for Sheremetev to track them down. She walked to the window. The gloom had lifted from the streets, cast off as easily as a cold shroud upon the emergence of the heartening sun. Eyes no longer turned to the ground as if weighted by their own misery. Faces no longer tensed in hardship. Every miserable second they had endured for the past four years disappeared in the new day's celebration of peace. They could begin living again.

Laughter, tears, relief, unmeasurable pain, and disappointment sought footing on this new day. One could live many times over in such torrents of emotion. For some the agony would never end. For some like Svetlana, a war still raged in a distant country that no longer wanted her. She had been cast into the shadow, left searching for where the light might shine.

A face far below in the street stilled among the swarming throng as it looked at her. A face she had not seen in a very long time. A face that yet appeared in her dreams. Svetlana gasped.

Sergey.

She raced down the stairs and out the front door and was immediately swept into the pulsing crowd. Pushed and pulled, she couldn't control her own feet as the people carried her along. She twisted her head left and right. Where was he? Had she imagined him? She tried to call his name. The crush of bodies hemmed her in until she could hardly breathe. A foot clamped onto the back of her dress and she pitched forward, slamming into a man's back. She tried to push away, but the wall of bodies pinned her from moving.

Suddenly the bodies peeled back. Wynn's arm came around her like a shield while he used the other as a ram to shove through the crowd. In a matter of seconds, they were back on the townhouse's front steps.

"The next time you want to get yourself stampeded, give me warning." Wynn's fingers dug into her shoulders. His eyes scanned her face, body, and back up. "Are you all right? What were you thinking running out like that?"

She gasped against the racing of her heart. The faces in the crowd blurred. No Sergey. "I thought I saw someone."

"Who?"

"Someone, but he's not there. He looked right at me, but he's gone."

"Who are you talking about?"

"Sergey. He was right here."

Wynn scanned the crowd, then slipped his arm around her waist. "Let's go inside. If it was him, he may have gotten taken away by the crowd. He'll come back."

Inside, Svetlana hurried to the sitting room window that overlooked the front street to look for him. Wynn followed her. He stood behind her, his face reflecting in the glass. "Are you certain it was him?"

"No. I saw him only for a moment, but it had to be. He said he would find us in Paris, but then the Bolsheviks took him. How would he find us at this address?" The moment of unexpected joy fractured into pieces of a frightening puzzle. "He would have heard where the Russian émigrés have consolidated and gone there. Someone may have pointed him to Sheremetev. Sheremetev knows everyone and everything. It wouldn't be that difficult for him to track us here and use Sergey as bait to lure us out."

Wynn turned her to face him. His hands cupped her cheeks, large and warm and steady. "Don't even think that. That man is never coming near you—"

Knock. Knock.

Svetlana jumped. She couldn't help the pathetic reaction. The world, so bright and glorious minutes before, now closed in on her.

Wynn's thumb stroked her cheek. "It's only the hospital's message boy. Gerard must have sent him. Wait here and I'll be right back."

He left to answer the door, and Svetlana was abandoned to the swarm of fear. An animal trapped in a cage with no way of escape. She wrung her hands together. The unfamiliarity of her wedding band rubbed against her skin. What would Sergey think of her marriage? There was never a formal engagement between them, yet part of her felt guilty with betrayal. He would have to understand she'd had no choice.

That is, if she were allowed to explain first before being executed.

In that instant, she was done. Fear had reigned as master for far too long. She may not have complete control of her circumstances, but above all she could have control of herself and herself refused to cower any longer. She was a princess marchioness. Not a beaten animal.

She swept from the room into the foyer where Wynn stood. "Tomorrow I'm going with you to the ticket mast—"

A yellow telegram was clenched in his fist. The fear she'd overcome moments ago rippled into action.

"What's wrong?"

His fist shook, the knuckles stark white against the yellow paper. "My brother was killed."

CHAPTER 17

The Calais port was jammed cheek to jowl with Red Cross ships, makeshift hospitals, and ambulances. Wounded soldiers were propped against cargo boxes as they waited to hobble up the gangways while the more serious cases lay on stretchers with nurses dotting among them. The days of armistice celebration had waned to the excruciating task of transporting the weary combatants home.

The ship swayed gently as Wynn stood on the deck with Svetlana after seeing her and her family's things stowed safely in their room. It was cramped, but it would do to make the voyage from Calais to Portsmouth. Every other available space, including the deck, was taken up by wounded Tommies.

"Will you not come with us? Your mother needs you." Dressed in a black frock from his mother's wardrobe, Svetlana stood stark against the white bandages and stained uniforms surrounding them.

"I gave my word to the hospital to remain through the end of the year. I won't abandon my patients."

"You would not be abandoning them. You have a duty from your brother now as well."

"A dukedom I never wanted. My work was never at the estate carrying around those titles. It's always been in surgery." He snorted. "Little good that's done for my brother."

"There was nothing you could have done for him."

"That's because there was no body to repair. That shell obliterated everything. I have nothing to take back to our mother."

Heads turned their direction at the harshness in his voice. Wynn took a deep breath and gripped the rail. Rage and sadness spiraled through him until he could no longer discern up from down. Hugh had been killed leading a charge on some muddy field one week before the armistice. He'd escaped the war without a scratch only to be cut down by a screaming shell. His commander had written a glowing report of Hugh's heroism and selfless leadership that served as an inspiration to his men. Hugh had always been the shining example. His memory was the only thing left to shine, and the loss pierced Wynn to the core.

Svetlana stepped closer, blocking off the curious stares. "Your desire to stay is admirable, but responsibilities often take us from where we would like best to remain. You cannot hide forever."

"Is that what you Russians call grief consolation?"

"Russians console their grief with vodka. It makes for miserable funerals."

"And here I thought it was the deaths."

"I can tell you from experience that hiding will not make your sorrow disappear." She rested her hand on his arm. Her wedding band made a slight bump from under her glove. "Come with us, Wynn. See to your mother. Honor your brother. Tend to the wounded who are arriving in Britain every day."

He wanted to say yes. Wanted to leave behind the death and destruction that clung to the very air here. He wanted to take his new bride home to meet his mother and show her the peace he knew as a boy growing up at Thornhill. Who was he kidding? There was no peace to be found there now. Every rock and blade of grass would remind him of Hugh and the legacy Hugh had left him as the new Duke of Kilbride. To return would be a severance from everything Wynn had worked so hard to achieve medically. He might as well cut off his right arm.

The whistle blew, signaling all non-passengers to go ashore. Around them, nurses tucked in blankets and said final goodbyes to their patients, reassuring the men that new nurses would be waiting for them in Blighty. Svetlana looked down and shuffled her feet. Nervous. And why shouldn't she be, embarking on this journey to an unfamiliar country? She was capable of overcoming any obstacle that might arise, just as she'd done escaping Russia, but he didn't want to abandon her to the unknown. On their wedding day he'd sworn to protect her, and he had every intention of keeping his word as a husband and a man. The only way he knew to do that was to send her away.

"You'll be safe at Thornhill. Mother will teach you everything you need to know about the estate as its new duchess."

"I would prefer you to teach me."

The whistle blew again. A high, lonesome sound marking their final moments together. There hadn't been enough time between them.

"All ashore who's going ashore," called the porter as he walked up and down the deck swinging a bell. "Last call."

Svetlana looked at Wynn with an expression he couldn't discern, as if she wanted to say something but didn't know how. What should he say to her, his wife of two weeks? Good luck? Don't be a stranger; write me sometime? Will you miss me? Can I kiss you goodbye?

She reached into her handbag and pulled out a small gold coin with a pistol slug smashed into the middle. "My father's. He was shot while fighting in the Balkans. This kopek saved his life. I've kept it sewn in my clothes all this time." Taking his hand, she placed it in his palm and wrapped his fingers around it. "He carried it everywhere he went as a talisman. May it bring you safely home as well."

Wynn leaned forward to kiss her, then stopped and pulled back. "Goodbye, Svetlana."

Heart heavy for more reasons than he cared to count, Wynn strode down the gangway. Away from her, away from the memories of home, and toward the bleakness stretching before him.

"Wynn! Wait." Svetlana hurried toward him and kissed his cheek. "May God bless you."

Then she was gone. A black smudge standing at the rail of the ship as it grew smaller and smaller on the choppy waves of the Channel. All that remained was the warmth of her lips on his cheek, the weight of the coin in his hand, and an unbearable loneliness.

───────

The townhouse was a shell of a ghost that haunted Wynn with memories at every turn. Svetlana's skirt rustling down the stairs. A wedding feast scattered across the dining table. His mother and father dancing in the sitting room when they would come to Paris in the autumn. Hugh sitting with a stack of books next to the fire. Bittersweet images seared into Wynn's brain. His brother should be here; they should be toasting together the end of the war and taking on the world as only brothers can. Anything Wynn did now would only be half a success.

A month ago he put his bride on a ship and sent her off to the wilds of Scotland while he stayed behind to wrestle with his grief. He'd thrown himself with abandon into the saving work of surgery. As if by piecing together broken and splintered bodies he could piece himself back together.

He grabbed the last of his papers from the study and shoved them into his suitcase. That was the last of it. He could leave these claustrophobic walls and not come back until the ghosts were gone. If they ever were. As he stepped outside, a chill frosted his face. The war had ended by Christmas, but its devastation lingered like gangrene in the open wounds of the city. Hospitals overflowed with patients, the walking wounded shuffled along the streets, and citizens struggled to rebuild their lives. Hardly anyone noticed it was Christmas Eve.

Fitting the key into the door, Wynn locked it. The streetlights flickered on behind him. His heart rate spiked. No. It was all right now. German night devils didn't fly anymore. The City of Light could shine once more. He leaned down to grab his suitcase and saw it.

Scratched into the door was a star with red streaking down it. Not blood, he would know that in an instant, but red paint. Fresh. He whipped around and scanned up and down the street. Two men dressed all in black with hats pulled low over their faces watched him from a darkened doorway.

Keeping his eyes on them, Wynn started down the steps. The mystery men ground out their cigarettes and followed. Wynn forced his pace to remain even but gripped his suitcase tighter. It was heavy enough to use in a pinch. Mayhap it was time to start carrying a blade more damaging than a scalpel. He crossed the street. The footsteps followed. There was only one explanation to why he was being tailed.

Sheremetev. The debt was paid—nearly twice the amount actually owed. All that was left to be angry about was Svetlana. Was this the man's recourse when denied what he thought was his? Brute intimidation?

The Russian had chosen the wrong man if he thought that would work.

Wynn hurried across a busy intersection and looked back, readying himself for confrontation. Nothing but ordinary people going about their business. Senses on full alert, he hailed a passing taxi and climbed inside.

"Hospital du Sacré-Coeur, *s'il vous plait.*"

The auto lurched into gear, throwing Wynn back against the seat as they dodged around a horse-drawn carriage. There on the street corner were the two men watching him from under the shadows of their hats as he passed. By the time he arrived at hospital, his blood pressure was sky high. It took several minutes before the familiar scent of antiseptic and bleached linen took hold and provided its comforting effect. As difficult as the task had been, he was relieved he'd sent Svetlana away when he did. Now he had only himself to worry about.

"Something wrong?"

Wynn jerked from his reverie. "No."

Gerard frowned at the clipboard in Wynn's hand. "Then why are you reading that upside down?"

They stood in the middle of the post-op ward with patients asleep all around them as the lamp from the nurse's desk glowed softly in the corner. As comforting to a physician as the stitching of skin and mending of bone, the silence worked its healing magic in the lost hours of night.

Wynn flipped the clipboard around. "Lost in thought."

Gerard peered over his shoulder at the patient notes. "About a fractured tibia? Has married life softened you that much?"

Hardened him, more like. Those thugs looked more than ready to break his legs if given the opportunity. "More like painted a target on my back."

"What do you mean?"

"A target for bad jokes. Forget it." Wynn hung the clipboard at the foot of the bed and continued his walk down the aisle with his ear cocked for labored breathing or moans of pain from the recovering men. "Don't mind if I move back into the bachelor quarters with you, do you? Too quiet rattling around in that old house by myself."

"Sure. The missus won't care? Hate for her to think I'm corrupting you back to the days of a single man. It's a shame you lovebirds couldn't spend more time together as newlyweds."

Not having much experience with women for himself, Gerard was always quick to think a mere handshake between a man and woman was akin to a declaration of love. After Wynn sewed up the bare skin on Svetlana's leg that long-ago day, Gerard had them written together in the stars. Wynn hated to burst his friend's notion of romance, but he hated him believing a lie even more.

Putting a hand on Gerard's shoulder, Wynn led him to a quiet corner of the ward away from curious ears of VADs, who were fueled by rumors at teatime.

"It's an arrangement of mutual convenience. Svetlana needed help, and I couldn't turn my back on her."

"Never could ignore the cry for help. Either way, you landed yourself a real lady." Gerard scratched a hand through his orange thatch. The corners of his mouth turned farther and farther down. "You said it was mutual. What are you getting out of it?"

Svetlana had asked him the same thing, and he'd told her as much truth as he dared. Because he was drawn to her in a way he'd never been drawn to another woman. She challenged him to do more, to be more. How could he not fall for a woman with such strength? Time would tell if he was to fall into her arms or a rocky bed of loneliness. Knowing his preference, Svetlana would be the one to decide his fate. If he couldn't say all that out loud to her, he certainly wasn't confessing it to Gerard in the middle of a sick ward.

Stalling, Wynn crossed his arms and stared down at the floor. The once expensive hotel carpet had been trampled threadbare from patrolling nurses and trolleys wheeling about.

"I don't know yet."

"What do you mean you don't know? Did you wake up one morning and think, *Gee, guess I'll get married today. Nothing better to do.* You at least like her, don't you?"

"Yes, of course. Most of the time, when she's not trying to freeze me out, but if you can get past that you can see how special she is. I've never met anyone like her."

"I do believe that you, Dr. MacCallan, are smitten."

"Don't tell my wife. She's already suspicious of me, and that's on our good days."

"Isn't your wife the one person you're supposed to tell?"

"I don't want to scare her off this early in the relationship. I need more time before I spring it on her."

"A wooing. How perfectly romantic."

"Have you been reading the nurses' dime novels again?"

"Sometimes there's not much to do on these long shifts, and I have to keep myself occupied, but don't change the subject. How do you propose to woo your wife and capture her heart when you're in two different countries?" Gerard tapped his pointy chin. "Come to think of it, in *Letters to a Sweetheart*, Millicent and George find love via writing letters. Like pen pals. Now that was a satisfying read."

It wasn't worth the repeated argument to question his friend's reading taste. Gerard would storm off only to return with an armload of books to prove his point that *Lost Together in Venice* and *Capturing the Untamed Heart* were as important to read as any medical journal. Wynn could barely keep a straight face when he started orating on sheiks and lost desert princesses.

"My stint here in Paris is over by the end of the year—a week from now. Then it's a Blighty ticket for me. I've already written to a few hospitals in Glasgow inquiring about a position."

"Wish I was going with you, but it's a few more months until I see England again. I suppose you're eager to get home and set up Svetlana as the new duchess— Oh, I'm sorry, mate. Didn't mean to sound crass in the wake of your loss." Gerard ducked his head, berating himself under his breath. "A terrible thing for me to say."

Pain stabbed Wynn's chest as Hugh's ghost flitted before him. He'd written to Wynn at the beginning of summer saying he hoped to find a wife once the war was over. His preference was a brunette. Wynn had written back saying they would scour the breadth of England until he found his brother the perfect wife with a postscript not to discount blondes.

"Svetlana will make a grand duchess. She was born for it." He swallowed against the tide of emotion threatening to take him under. "One of us had to be."

"Aw, Wynn. You're not giving yourself enough credit."

"That's because the second son never had to. Not when it comes to running an estate. I'm not a title; I'm a surgeon. I've put my entire life into medicine. It's the only thing I want to do."

"Who says you can't?"

"It's not the way it's done. Lords of the manor are expected to be just that and nothing more. Overseeing property, collecting rent from the tenants, heading up charities. A lifetime of servitude to duty." The knowledge of what awaited him at Kilbride extended its shackling weight day by day. By the time he reached his beloved shores of Scotland, would he be able to lift his feet, or would the weight drown him? "If anything good could come of this war, I hope it's a break in the chains of tradition where men are allowed to carve out their own paths instead of adhering to those laid for them. If a clergyman's son like you has the right to become a renowned physician, why not a duke?"

Gerard blushed to the roots of his hair. Too many in their profession looked down on him because of his humble roots, but Wynn saw that it kept him grounded and pushed him to work harder than all those who lived life on a silver platter.

"Careful with that talk or they'll have you pinned as a zealot. Next thing you'll be campaigning for women's votes."

"Women make up half of the world's population. They should have a voice in how it spins."

"Come off that talk. Bad enough the entire medical board is buzzing like hornets about your cardiological theories."

"The heart must be made into its own specialized study if we ever want to achieve proper understanding of its anatomy and physiology for the betterment of treatment."

Gerard threw up his hands in surrender. "No need to lecture me. I was there when you set them all off."

"Not all. Dr. Lehr has been sending me case studies of undiagnosed pulmonary—"

"I know. The folders have toppled onto my desk now. Including that request for an interview from the *British Medical Journal*. You still keep in touch with Harkin?"

Wynn nodded. "He's back in London now. I wrote and asked if he would like to be part of the interview with me. It could offer a unique and often overlooked view from the patient that's imperative for surgeons to understand."

The ward door opened, and one of the junior doctors fresh from school stuck his head in. The new ones were easy to spot. Their noses twitched the air like mice stepping outside for the first time in six years. He scurried over and dropped his voice to a whisper.

"Dr. MacCallan, those X-rays are ready for you to view." They were also sent on errands that senior doctors shrugged off to the nurses, like conveying messages between the floors.

"Coming," Wynn said. The young doctor scurried off and Wynn turned to leave. A dripping red star flashed in his head. "Sure you don't mind me bunking in with bachelors again? That townhouse is too big for me, and I'm hardly there enough to justify keeping it open." Open where ghosts were left to roam and strange men prowled in the shadows. Neither would he mention to Gerard. His friend had the heart of a lion, but it was an unnecessary burden to put on him. If there was trouble, Wynn could handle it without endangering his friend.

"Sure. I saved your bed for you. It'll be like old times."

Wynn offered a smile, but it soured in his stomach.

"Like old times." Except that everything had changed.

CHAPTER 18

Rain drizzled down the diamond-paned windows of the library where Svetlana sat on a bench seat staring out at the waterlogged afternoon. All it did was rain in Scotland, churning the rolling landscape to a blur of gray and green. Though she missed the refinement of city life, there was something about this wild land that eased the tension from her bones. On a rare day when the sun breached from its sleeping habitat behind the thick clouds, she could almost feel a sense of peace. But even that peace could be overtaken with restlessness.

She'd been greeted at the train station as Her Grace, the Duchess of Kilbride, and whisked off to her new home at Thornhill. By Scottish standards the castle was considered substantial with its towering walls of beige sandstone and turrets that reflected its sixteenth-century style, and while it boasted modern amenities and comforts, it was rather utilitarian compared to the opulence of Russian palaces. Her own Blue Palace had three reading rooms designed for nothing beyond the pleasure of whiling away hours reading next to enormous marble fireplaces. Thornhill, on the other hand, had an entire weapons wing lined with ancient armor, shields, swords, bows and arrows, and all other manner of intimidation for killing one's enemy. And she once thought Russia had a war-infested history. She'd spent the first few weeks wandering the halls and grounds—weather permitting—

familiarizing herself with what had become her new duties, yet she felt adrift without an anchor to keep her steady in the changing currents.

"Good gracious. Studying again." Wynn's mother, Constance, breezed in with the tails of her gossamer black scarf flapping behind her. Wreathed in mourning, the fluid lines of her gown enhanced her endless motion. "I don't believe this room had nearly enough attention until you came along."

Svetlana closed the book on her lap. A history of the county she now called home and its natural resources. Not to mention the vast fortune accrued under the MacCallan name. Wynn had never told her precisely how wealthy they were.

"I want to learn all I can about the MacCallans and Thornhill. The customs and expectations are different from those in Russia."

"My dear, when you are foreign, you are judged on an entirely different scale than the native population. When my mother came from America as one of the dollar princesses to marry the ninth Duke of Kilbride, the locals didn't know what to make of her with her optimism and individualistic thinking. She was a fast learner and did quite well, if I do say so myself. And so will you."

Svetlana ran a finger over the worn leather binding, so similar to the ones lining her father's study in the Blue Palace. An ache swelled inside her. They used to read them together after dinner. *"Treat your people fairly and they will do the same for you,"* he would instruct. *"Always seek improvement."*

"I've been reading on the advances made on the estate over the years, many of which have helped it continue operating when so many great houses are going under due to the economical strain of war. As chatelaine, I should like to continue the work of mutual benefit for Thornhill and our tenants. According to the account books, they've been struggling of late— Oh! Forgive me. I did not mean to imply—"

"Save your breath to cool your porridge, my dear, as the Scots would say." Constance held up a hand and smiled kindly. "I'm perfectly aware that my housekeeping abilities are atrocious. I love this house and the people here, but it's never been in my blood to stay rooted for too long. Too many wondrous things out in the world to explore. Which is why I'm so delighted you're here for me to pass the mantle to."

Svetlana nodded. She'd been preparing for such a mantle her entire life. The Scottishness of it was a bit of a twist, but the foundations of running an estate remained the same no matter the country. Why then did she feel the drowning waters of uncertainty lapping close to her head? Wynn had offered this course of direction to her life as if it were the most natural one to follow. All other options had closed to her and so she'd followed him into marriage to find safe harbor amid the raging storm. Secluded now in that harbor, she was missing the compass that had pointed her here. The anchoring compass that kept her from drifting back into the storm.

She glanced down at the simple gold band wrapping around her finger. He'd bound everything he had into that ring and offered it to her. His name, his money, his protection, his home. He'd given her so much and she'd not returned anything. She covered the band with her fingers, the cold metal warming at her touch. That changed now. She would make herself the best Duchess of Kilbride she could be and bring honor to his name.

Constance swished herself onto the window seat next to Svetlana, crinkling the corner of the open plant book between them, and took Svetlana's hand. The gold band winked between them.

"When I received Wynn's message saying he'd married, I was overjoyed. He's always been a man to love and be loved. I knew he'd never be completely content with a set of scalpels in his hand. He needed a woman to round him out, and here you are. I couldn't be more proud to have a daughter-in-law such as you." Tears shimmered in her eyes. "I'm only sad to have missed the wedding."

Alarmed at the sudden waterworks, Svetlana tried to edge her hand away, but the older woman clung tight as emotion rolled across her face. Should she offer a hankie or a pat on the shoulder? What would Wynn do? Offer a joke. No, she wasn't good at those. He'd summon courage and meet the discomfort head-on.

"We missed having you there, but with the war on it would have been too dangerous to send for you. It all happened so quickly."

"As I often told my husband, when you know, you know." She nodded and sniffed. "Though I don't think any of us could have known how all of this would come to pass." Her glassy eyes lifted to a painted family portrait hanging over the fireplace. The brothers looked very much alike, but Wynn held a familiar twinkle in his eyes while his brother's gaze was calm and steady.

"Was Hugh very different from Wynn?"

With a short laugh Constance finally released Svetlana's hand and swiped an errant tear from her cheek. "Good gracious, yes. Where Hugh was contemplative, Wynn was inquisitive. Where Hugh nodded and agreed, Wynn questioned. Where Hugh consulted his books, Wynn simply knew on a hunch. But they were brothers through and through. If one was in trouble, the other was right there next to him."

"Wynn spoke fondly of him."

"They were the best of friends, but from the beginning they had their roles. Hugh always knew he would inherit one day and modeled that role of responsibility to a T. Wynn, on the other hand, was left to enjoy his freedom. I confess, we may have spoiled him a bit, but he was never one to sit around and wait to be petted. He always had to do. Still does. He'll never give up if there's a path worth pursuing."

"In Russia we call that having the head of a bull."

"One of his most endearing qualities, but then I suspect you already know that."

"I've noted it a time or two."

"I don't know the circumstances of your marriage to my son. Perhaps the whirlwind of a wartime romance that I hope you'll tell me all about one day. I want you to know how happy I am to have you in our family. With you, the MacCallan name and legacy will live on and Thornhill will thrive once more. These halls may always carry a sadness for me, but you, my new daughter, have brought the beginning of happiness."

"Happiness," Svetlana repeated as if the word were foreign to her. It certainly was not a concept she had dwelled on of late. Revolution, murder, and survival tended to block out any pretense of the notion, but coming to Scotland in this new life had swept away the old fears. Happiness and the ability to pursue it no longer had to be denied.

Constance must have noted her hesitation as she patted her arm in understanding. "We all merit a go at it, do we not? Life is too short to let the uncertainties haunt us, and a woman of your strength deserves reasons to smile."

Warmth rushed through Svetlana. "Thank you, Mother Constance. I hope I am worthy of your praise."

Her mother-in-law patted her hand, and Svetlana didn't pull away. "Just be yourself, dear. I can't ask for more than that."

"Ask for more than what?" Mama appeared in the doorway, eyes slanting between Svetlana and Constance. She wore a purple gown. Not having personally known Hugh, she declared full black mourning was unnecessary.

Svetlana withdrew her hand from Constance's and smoothed the black velvet of her skirt. She'd ordered an entire trousseau befitting her newly married station from Glasgow but her mourning clothes from a local seamstress. The woman's eyes had nearly popped out of her head to have a princess patron her shop. Svetlana decided to place more orders through her in the future to boost the local economy.

"Acceptance into the family."

"Oh. The Dukes and Duchesses of Kilbid."

"Kilbride."

Mama waved her hand as if batting away an unpleasant thought. Wrapping her colorful shawl around her, she meandered into the room and glanced around at the bookshelves and paintings dotting the paneled walls, careful not to touch anything.

"It's a nice enough title. Dating back to the sixteenth century, did you say? The Dalsky titles were granted by Ivan the Great. Back then such honors were only given to those who performed memorable deeds in the name of Russia. Other countries seem to give them away like candy to greedy children."

Constance smiled placidly. "How fortunate your family was to acquire one. Or rather, your husband's family."

Mama's eye glinted at being outmatched. Outmatched perhaps, but not outdone. Crossing herself, she drooped onto the velvet settee angled in front of the fire.

"My poor husband. Whatever has become of him? A loyal man who stayed behind to fight to the death so that we might escape. My poor Dmitri. I fear I shall never see him again this side of Heaven." She crossed herself again.

Svetlana came to her feet and clenched her hands together to keep from shaking her mother. "Mama, please stop doing that. We don't know that he's dead. Nor Nikolai. They are the best soldiers in the army."

"The tsar's army, which is no more thanks to those murdering zealots." Mama touched a trembling hand to her head. "To think about it is more than I can bear."

In a soft rustle of satin and swishing scarf, Constance glided to the bell pull hanging between two potted ferns. "You're shivering. Allow me to ring for you a pot of tea. It does wonders for the constitution."

"How kind of you. You do not know the comforts of having servants about once more. All manner of wild ways we've been forced to adopt since fleeing our beloved homeland."

A few minutes later, a footman dressed in a liveried kilt carried in a gleaming tray with a porcelain teapot, cups, saucers, and a small plate of what the British referred to as biscuits. He poured the fragrant brew with expert precision, inquiring as to the preferred amount of sugar and milk, before passing a prepared cup to Mama with his gloved hand.

Mama took a sip and sighed. "How delicate you make your teas here. I suppose that's to be expected from using those odd pots instead of a proper samovar."

Constance shook her head as the footman offered her a cup. "Yes, but then it's a practice from one of the many nations we've ruled over the centuries instead of isolating our traditions behind our frozen walls. If you'll excuse me, I have a few letters to write. The Charity for Wounded Soldiers is meeting here next month and I've yet to make a guest list. Svetlana, dear, let's plan a time after the rain to inspect those overgrown flowerbeds in the back garden. I think your idea for a dacha garden sounds intriguing." With a twirl of her floating scarf, she left.

Svetlana dismissed the footman, watching the door close behind him with a weary sigh. She wasn't in the mood for battle, but sensed it coming anyway.

Mama didn't disappoint. "To think, my daughter has married into that family. How else must we demean ourselves? Dacha garden indeed. You are a princess, not a country farmer."

"Perhaps I would like to do more with plants than arrange them in pretty vases with my pretty princess hands." Svetlana took a deep breath. Mama always knew where to prick her. "Constance is a lovely woman who has done nothing but generously invite us into her family."

"She's American." Mama gave her a pointed look as if to say that explained everything wrong in the situation.

"Half American, and it's not as if we have much leg to stand on. Fugitives with no home." Svetlana poured herself a cup of tea and moved to stand closer to the fire. The brew was fragrant and warm and tasted of comfort. Unlike that awful concoction she'd prepared for Wynn in Leonid's apartment. She smiled at the memory. Did he ever think of that day when he'd held her hands?

"*Au contraire.* You've brought us to this place we're now supposed to call home. As if anyone could live here and like it with all the rain and cold. The weather seeps straight through the stone walls and settles into my bones."

"Russia was cold."

"Yes, but we had furs to keep us warm. There it is a crystal cold that sharpens your lungs and brings you to life. Here it wearies the soul to bleakness. Not that you would know much about my troubles. You spend more time with that woman and in this library than you do with me. Even Marina has abandoned me for that old *babushka*. She had no business coming with us."

"Mrs. Varjensky has been good to us. I will do no less by her."

Mama harrumphed and scooted down into the pillows, cradling her steaming cup of tea. "Of course, but why listen to me? I'm not but your mother who raised you as a princess to live in palaces and ride in fine *troikas*. Surrounding yourself with musty old books is not the habit befitting the lifetime of training I have poured into you."

"Those days are over, and I refuse to cling to them as you do. We have the chance to start again. Not many of our people were given that."

"Start again. What does that even mean?"

The unfamiliar sensation of nerves trailed over Svetlana's next words. "We can rebuild our lives here. You, me, and Marina. Certainly it is different and many of the customs far from our own, but this is a chance to leave the hurts in the past. We cannot continue to carry our past disagreements and hope to thrive." The wall between them may not tumble in a day after years of sharp words and wounded pride reinforcing the mortar, but it was high enough and she grew tired from the bricks lobbed at one another.

Taking a sip from her teacup, Mama's eyebrows rose over the rim. "By *thrive* I am to assume you mean ingratiate ourselves with these people who have welcomed us into the bosom of their backwater hovels." So much for not flinging bricks.

Placing her delicate cup on the mantle, Svetlana swept an arm up and pointed a toe out in *ecarte*. She would work her way through an entire warm up in a corset if it meant staying calm.

"I am now Duchess of Kilbride. I must learn to find a new way, and that starts by reading all I can about this place and its people because they're my people now. My responsibility, and I will do what I can for them." And for Wynn.

"In Russia—"

"In Russia I was only required to sit perfectly, attend the opera, dance at balls, and offer light conversation in powdered drawing rooms. I want more than that. Here, the nobility are expected to participate in charities, provide benefits to their community, and ensure their tenants are looked after. I can make a difference here."

"Did your husband tell you all of this? To carry on the work while he's not here?"

Svetlana rose *en face*. Not a week went by without a letter from Wynn giving her all the details of his hospital and the declining rate of soldier patients as they were shipped back home to Blighty. Odd name for England. He'd also mentioned moving back into his old bachelor quarters with Gerard, which she was glad to hear. That townhouse was too large for him to rattle around in by himself. He needed the company of others. Never once did he mention Sheremetev, Leonid, or the White Bear. He always asked if she was settling in well, the health of Marina and Mrs. Varjensky, and a passing greeting to Mama. Every letter was signed "Yours, Wynn."

Yours. What did that mean? Yours in letter form? Yours most sincerely? Your husband? Yours in belonging? Which did she want him to be?

Toes aching, she lowered to *a la seconde*.

"Growing up, you instructed me not to bother my husband with trivial details of home maintenance while he was away. Those details belong to the woman's domain, you said, so that the man might keep his focus on more important matters."

"Sergey never would have dropped you in the middle of such a miserable existence only to abandon you. If he hadn't been dragged off the train platform in Petrograd, he would've been in Paris with us. Our lives never would have veered onto such a desolate path."

Positions forgotten, Svetlana whipped around with enough force for a *fouetté*. The heat from the fire seared up her back. "Wynn has not abandoned me, nor has he placed me on a desolate path. Every action has proved him honorable."

"So was Sergey's."

"Sergey is not here, and any future I may have had with him is gone. My future is tied to Wynn, and I will honor the agreement made between us."

Placing her cup down, Mama drew the edges of the shawl around herself and rolled her eyes away from Svetlana. "You sound like your father."

From anyone else it would have been a compliment, but not from Mama. She never appreciated a stance against her desire to bend wills. "Is that so terrible? Father is a good man. Honorable and strong."

"Most think so until it overshadows your marriage. Mark my words, you'll find out there is truth in my words soon enough."

The heat waving across Svetlana's back weaved into her blood. "Why do you dislike Wynn so? After everything he's done for us, you still treat him as second best."

Mama notched her chin up, still not meeting her daughter's eyes. "Wynn wasn't my choice."

"No, he's mine."

"Choice for what?" The deep male voice cut through the throbbing tension like a welcome shot of relief.

Svetlana spun around to find her dripping-wet husband standing in the doorway. Never had a sight been so joyful.

"Wynn. You're home."

CHAPTER 19

S hould she knock? Of course she should. What an idiotic question. But knock on this door or the one from the sitting room dividing their personal chambers? Svetlana stopped pacing. She was acting like a . . . like a . . . Well, not like a duchess. Throwing her shoulders back, she firmly knocked on Wynn's door.

"Come in."

He stood barefoot in the center of the room wearing nothing more than gray trousers and a half-buttoned pale blue shirt. His unhitched suspenders hung down by his legs. Rubbing a towel over his wet head, his muscles rolled in graceful movement the length of his exposed forearms from where he'd turned back his shirt cuffs.

"Hand me one of the ties from the dresser, will you?" Wynn's voice was muffled under the towel.

Tearing her eyes from the fit figure he cut, Svetlana crossed to the dresser and rummaged through the drawers until finding the neatly folded ties. Selecting a black one with tiny diamonds stitched into it, she handed it to him under the towel.

Wynn stopped rubbing his hair. "That's not Larson's hand."

"No, it's not."

Flipping the towel to the back of his neck, Wynn grinned sheepishly at her. "Good. For a second there I thought you were my valet and my eyes were starting to go." His fingers brushed hers as he took the tie from her. "And I'd hate not to see how pretty you are."

She took a step back, away from his clean scent of rain and washed cotton, away from the vibrations circling them, away from the distracting patch of skin below his throat exposed by his unbuttoned shirt. She steered her gaze away to focus on anything else but him. Anything like the dark walnut walls and wainscoting, rich green drapes and comforter, masculine furniture that culminated in a massive bed taking up most of the far wall. Dear her, no. Anything but the bed and his exposed throat.

"I trust your bath was well?" She held back a groan. That was what she came up with to keep distractions away? "I mean, you're refreshed from your travels?"

"It rained all the way from Calais to Edinburgh. I think I'll still be wringing myself out three days from now."

"It's rained for nearly a week here." Riveting. She might as well put him to sleep right then and there. She moved to the window and stared down at the soggy garden. The heart of winter and nary a color beyond gray and green to be found. Unlike the white nights of Russia where everything was singed blue and silver.

"Rain or not, I'm glad to have Scottish soil firmly beneath my feet again. Rocking boats aren't for me."

She traced a watery bead sloping down the pane. Unsteady in its descent, it stopped and stuttered, but never veered left or right as it continued in a singular direction. Much like her own path that hesitated and wavered yet with the gravitational force pushing her onward from necessity. Down the window drops collided and rushed onto a harmonious trajectory. Such was her life with Wynn, though time would tell if harmony was to direct their path. A path they had yet to discuss. Wars, revolutions, Bolsheviks, debts, and separation had demanded precedence in their whirlwind relationship up until this point. With no looming threats of disaster, what became of them now?

She caught Wynn's reflection in the glass. What were his expectations? Best to find out now so that she might adjust hers accordingly.

"Now that you're home, what will you do?"

"That's something I'd like to discuss with you."

She spun away from the window. "With me?"

His eyebrows lifted as if attempting to discern her confusion. "You're my wife and I value your opinion. You should have a say on the direction we go."

His wife. Her husband. Nerves tangled in her stomach. Husband and wife. That's how marriages worked, but Mama had never instructed her on the possibility of being asked her opinion. "*Your husband will tell you what to do,*" Mama had repeated. "*It is your duty to obey. Husbands and wives do not need a life together, merely ones that coexist.*" A wife was to be an advisor only when asked, and even then it was to be agreeable to whatever the husband had already decided. Svetlana had laughed at that. What was the point in asking then? Wynn had never been a man for placating answers. Insincerity wasn't one of his character flaws, and for that she was immensely grateful. It stood him apart from almost all other men she'd known.

"What would you like to discuss?"

Tossing his towel on the bed, he moved to his travel trunk and pulled out an envelope. "This came to me in Paris just before I departed. It's an invitation to work at Glasgow Hospital. Apparently one of their surgeons attended the cardiology lecture I gave and was impressed by the new thinking. He'd like to explore it further in their surgeries. I would be put on an observation period with the potential for residency."

"That's wonderful! Congratulations."

"They want me to come to Glasgow next week for a short interview and tour of the facilities. I thought you might like to come with me. See the city. Spend time together."

"If that's what you would like, then I'll be happy to join you."

"I want you to come because you want to come."

Svetlana couldn't stop the smile spreading across her face. "Then I'll come." His returning smile was all the confirmation she needed in knowing it was the right answer. And not because it was the agreeable answer to her lord and master, but because it seemed the right decision for them. Time together. Time to decide who they would be together in this marriage.

Of course, any conclusions would impact their duties as Duke and Duchess of Kilbride. The lumbering elephant in the room that could no longer be avoided.

"Have you given thought to Thornhill? A residency in Glasgow would take away your time needed here."

Wynn's smile faded. He turned and busied himself with stuffing shirts into a drawer. "Bruce Mackie is our estate agent. He's been helping run this place since Father was here. He'll keep everything in order unless I'm needed for the bigger decisions."

"As the duke I think you're needed here for more than just the big decisions."

"More than at hospital? Advances are being made every day to save lives through cardiology. I can't help bring about change stuck on an estate collecting rent."

Svetlana frowned. "There are responsibilities here."

"I also have responsibilities to my profession. I can't abandon one for the other. This is all new to me, trying to balance physician with landowner." He grimaced as if he couldn't bring himself to claim the title duke. "We'll figure it out."

He may have wanted her opinion on the direction of their life, but now was not the time for an argument. Besides, what would she be arguing for? Both responsibilities were important, and as he said, abandoning one would bring devastation to the other. Unless there was a way for them to coexist. It needed some thought, but in the meantime, they would see what the physicians in Glasgow had to say.

"I've been reading over your family and estate history," she said, shifting topics to regain the easiness they'd had moments before. Before he'd felt cornered. "The MacCallans have been well favored over the centuries. This land is said to have once belonged to the ancient Celtic gods who used it as hunting grounds."

Wynn laughed as he set his shaving kit on the bureau. Where was his valet to do the unpacking? Then again, knowing Wynn he wouldn't want the fuss.

"I'd nearly forgot about those stories. Our horse master used to tell us about them, claiming he got them from his old gran who once served as a Druid priestess. Back in the old days before the earth rounded and stags and wolves big as mountains roamed the wild woods. It would take arrows as tough and long as oak trees to bring them down. Where they fell they left valleys."

"We have similar stories in Russia, but with bears. They, too, were tall as trees."

"Did you ever see one?"

"Once at the Peterhof Palace. He wasn't as tall as a tree, but his fur was thick and black like coal. There were also zebras, an elephant, two tigers, peacocks, and a camel. Russian nobility loves extravagance." Or did. Those days were long over. Whatever became of the poor creatures?

"We don't have elephants or camels, but I can show you where the king of red stags supposedly fell and all the Druids in Scotland came to mourn him and curse the hag who shot the arrow."

"What kind of curse?"

"They turned her to the stone of a mountain and now she cries great waterfall tears to create Loch Dunwan. It smells like sulphur. I wouldn't advise going near it, but the valley is splendid. Come June, the heather is thick enough to walk across. In winter, ice crystals collect on the ferns growing near the river. As the water rushes over them, the ice thickens and drags the branches to the bottom."

"How beautiful. Seasons paint masterpieces on nature, always changing. Yet remaining the same year after year."

"I'll take you to see it once the rain stops."

"I'd like that." For the first time in months, possibly since she'd left Russia, her heart danced in delight. Memories of happiness in simple pleasures had been suffocated beneath the terror of survival for so long, she had doubted they would ever surface again. Much less the possibility of feeling so happy. Yet, once more, Wynn offered her hope.

Before she could dwell further on the meanings behind that thought and the warmth it stirred within her, she crossed the room to the door.

"I better allow you to finish dressing before you catch pneumonia."

"You can't catch pneumonia from being cold. It's an infection that fills the lungs with fluid."

"Chills, then."

"At the moment I don't feel any chills."

She wasn't either with the way he was looking at her. Silhouetted against the orange glow of the fireplace behind him, he seemed larger than she remembered, shoulders wider and chest broader with arm muscles filling out the sleeves of his shirt. She remembered feeling those arms around her, holding her close, protecting her against the onslaught of fears. With the way he looked at her now, she knew he wouldn't deny her stepping into his embrace once more. A darkening of the eyes, a parting of the lips, a concentration of the brow. It was a look to be recognized by a woman in a man and within her power to do what she willed with it.

What did she want to do with it? She'd become his wife under duress, but now that the danger had passed, they found themselves treading unfamiliar waters. Should she ignore the pulling look in his eyes and swim back to the shallows, or give in to the swell of emotion and strike out to deeper waters with him? She was no longer sure where the boundary of safety tethered. With a desperate need for stability, that uncertainty was enough to frighten her.

Her hand fumbled for the doorknob.

"You can use the other door." He pointed to the door that connected his chambers to hers through the private sitting room. The desire stirring in his eyes blinked away.

She tried not to give in to the disappointment at his polite change in expression. She had made the decision to step back, and like the gentleman he was, Wynn was respecting it. Would she mind so terribly if he threw politeness to the wind and closed the distance between them?

"I didn't want to make a habit of entering your room that way. That is, I mean to say, I don't wish to intrude on your privacy." She twisted the knob. She needed to get out before her rambling carried her away.

"You'll never intrude, Svetlana. Not at my door. It is always open for you. All you have to do is step through."

She did step through. Out and into the hall before he carried her right into those deep waters where she no longer knew if she was drowning or floating.

CHAPTER 20

Glasgow teemed with life and new purpose as the city unrolled itself from the fog of war. Battle scars remained in the wearied faces of its townsfolk, but businesses and shops were beginning to reopen as life resumed, though at an altered pace.

"Any more shops you wish to look in?" Tucking a newly purchased maidenhair fern against his chest, Wynn held tight to Svetlana's arm as they crossed George Square in the biting January air.

Like the other bit of Scotland she'd witnessed, a wet cold clung to the air as mist rose from the nearby River Clyde and reminded her of Petrograd winters. People bundled into their coats as they scurried under the midmorning shadow of the towering Scott monument while Svetlana lifted her face to inhale the icy air. Winter had always dressed Petrograd in frosted finery, and she, like a true daughter of Russia, reveled in the snow crystals of brilliance.

She shook her head, careful not to unpin the new felt and quail feather hat Wynn had insisted on buying her yesterday, their first day in the city. She'd been looking for a traditional fur *shapka*.

"You've bought out most of them already."

"My beautiful wife deserves to be spoiled. No more rags or ill-fitting castoffs for you."

Ignoring the temptation to run a gloved hand over her fine wool skirt, Svetlana squeezed his arm instead. Buttery soft kid gloves, warm woven wool, delicate lace at her throat, and real silk undergarments. It was like returning to a long-lost fairy tale after living in a nightmare for so long. Yet while she had been restored to a castle, many still found themselves in the trenches. Or in an overcrowded, infested basement lost in Paris. In this new chapter of tales, she would not forget what it was like to go without.

Wynn hefted the young fern, its delicate stalk wrapped in protective burlap. "Should we find another florist and see what they have in the way of trees? Or those decorative herbal plants you were telling me about?"

"No, I think this addition will be perfect for now. It's the wrong time of year to plant them, but I think he'll grow nicely in the solarium where I can control the temperature better." She touched one of the small green leaves sprouting from one of the dozen stems as the faint scent of dirt wafted under her nose. Spotting it in the florist's shop window a block over, she knew the plant begged to be taken home to Thornhill. A beautiful life to grow and care for all her own in any kind of vase she chose. No finely cut empress's vase required for this little one.

Running feet pounded on the pavement behind them. Shouting filled the air. Fear froze Svetlana to the spot. Bolsheviks.

Three boys chasing a ball streaked by.

Wynn's worried face hovered in front of her. "What's wrong?"

"I thought . . ." She pressed a shaking hand to her chest. Her heart thundered for release beneath her restrictive corset. "Sheremetev."

"You don't ever have to worry about him again." Wynn grasped her arm and gently squeezed. "You're safe now. No one has followed us here."

Safe. He kept saying it, yet the first time she returned to a city the memories of burning Petrograd and hunted Paris rose from the ashes where she'd thought them buried and dead.

"I'll take you back to the hotel," he said.

"No. If I run at every scare, I'll never stop." She took a deep breath and forced herself to look around boldly to scare back the shadows threatening to creep around her. "I'm tired of running."

Crossing the square, they turned down Hanover Street. The smell of coffee and bread lingered among the eateries as the last of the breakfast dishes were cleared away in time for lunch. A woman in a shawl with threads unraveling at the ends stepped out of a café and wiped off the tables. Her eyes widened at Svetlana as she passed before quickly dipping her head. Svetlana tried to acknowledge the curtsy, but the woman wouldn't meet her eye. No doubt she was freezing in that threadbare wrap.

"Before we leave, I would like to find Mrs. Varjensky a new shawl," Svetlana said. "She's very fond of the peasant ones they wear back in the villages, but hers is tattered. Perhaps I'll get her two. A sturdy wool for every day and a more delicate one for special occasions."

"I'll get her a brooch to match. It's time she used something better than a safety pin for decoration."

"She's not the extravagant kind."

"You told me all women appreciate jewelry."

"Yes, that's true, but nothing too grand. She would never wear it."

"What if I have one made into the image of that doll you told me about? The kind her husband used to carve as a toymaker."

"*Matryoshki* dolls. Yes, I think she would like that." As a child, Svetlana had several of the nesting dolls that decreased in size. She would spend hours placing them one inside another until only the largest one remained. Hers had all been painted as Russian tsarinas, but Mrs. Varjensky said her husband carved his as animals, flowers, soldiers, and fairies. How she would have loved to see such whimsy.

"Good. Tomorrow morning I'll find a jeweler to have one commissioned." Wynn frowned. "There's one problem. I don't know what they look like."

"I'll make you a sketch."

His eyebrows rose, inching his gray fedora up his forehead. It shaded his eyes to a soft brown. "I didn't realize you drew."

"All accomplished young ladies do. One of the few acceptable parlor pastimes, but I'm not very good at noses so don't laugh when you see my attempt."

"I promise not to. Too much." Promise or not, the edge of his lip curled up. It only added to his rakish charm. Yes, she thought her husband charming. The fashionably cut coat and knotted tie did little to restrain the vitality exuding from him, as if life's problems met their end in his presence.

Many of hers certainly had.

Yet he was not immune to troubles. They sought him by way of sickness, Russian crime lords, runaway princesses, wounded patients, and the death of a brother, but through it all he remained grounded. Never allowing the circumstances to overwhelm him, instead, meeting them as new challenges. It was a trait she was starting to find irritatingly irresistible.

"There must be something you're not perfect at," she said.

He jerked to a halt. "Who told?"

"A wild guess."

"My handwriting is atrocious. They test you in medical school. If it's legible, you fail."

Svetlana laughed and tugged him into walking again. "I already knew that from your letters. Try again."

"I can't boil an egg."

"Neither can I."

"I think you just want to see how many things I can come up with. Let's see." His gloved fingers tapped an off-cadence beat on her hand that was tucked in his elbow. "I can't sing. Dogs howl when I open my mouth."

"I'm sure they do not."

"Let's find out." He opened his mouth wide.

Svetlana clamped her hand over it as the first note gurgled out. "I believe you." She giggled, actually giggled right there in broad daylight for all the public to witness. Who was this woman she was turning into, the one only Wynn seemed to bring out? The more time she spent with him, the more the layers of loneliness and self-protection seemed to melt away, releasing the coldness she once harbored.

His warm breath seeped through her glove, filling her palm. He gently took hold of her hand and pulled it away from his mouth but didn't release it.

"I love hearing your laugh."

There he went again. Effortless. Earnest. With a deep voice that wrapped around her like the White Nights of a northern summer. It caressed her senses, teasing her ears and tempting her heart.

"You are easily won over, sir, to find my crinkling nose an amusement. To laugh is considered undignified for a princess, but to have my nose scrunching at the same time is beyond humiliation."

"Despite your best efforts to prove undignified, you are the singular most intriguing woman I've ever met. Princess crinkles and all."

"If they weren't the crinkles of a princess, what then?"

"You know I don't care for titles. Titles muck things up from their true essence. That truth is the most fascinating. What I see is a radiant woman smiling at me. Nothing else matters."

She'd known of his distaste for titles since first they met, but to hear him state it once more confirmed him as a man apart from all others. She didn't have to be the perfect princess with him, nor bring him wealth or standing in the noble ranks as had been her expectations since birth. She could be Svetlana, who got lost in a pair of honest hazel eyes that saw deep inside her when no one else bothered looking.

Voices in that indecipherable Glaswegian accent vibrated in her ear.

"Standin' there all day, are they?"

"Might be goin' somewhere private, aye."

"'Tis the middle of the day, for goodness' sake."

"'Tisn't a proper distance they be keepin'."

She and Wynn stood in the middle of the sidewalk. People swerved around them, twisting their heads back to gawk.

Svetlana tried to take a step back, but her hand remained captive in his. "Wynn, please. You're embarrassing me." Embarrassed. Warm all over and wishing there weren't a hundred curious people milling around them like a circus spectacle when all she wanted was for him to lean forward and kiss her.

"I'm complimenting you. There's a difference." Offering no kiss, which was probably for the best as a priest had stepped outside of his church to squint at them through his spectacles, Wynn readjusted her hand in the crook of his arm and continued down the sidewalk, the fern swaying merrily in his other arm. "If I'd wanted to embarrass you, I'd keep singing."

"Then I would be forced to leave you here like the *pomeshanniy* you are."

"What does that mean?"

"Lunatic. Crackpot."

"Sounds better in Russian, Lana."

"What is this Lana?"

"My name for you."

"My family and friends call me Svetka. Or Svetochka, Svetulya, Sveta. It's common for Russians to have several diminutive versions of their names, but I've never heard Lana."

"Good. I don't want to sound like everyone else."

"I don't think you could even if you tried." This outing was proving to be more daring than she first imagined. If she wasn't careful, she'd let the magic of it sweep them into the middle of the street for a dance. Weren't they supposed to be doing more serious things instead of giggling like children and almost kissing like lovers? The hospital! Yes, that was their purpose. "We should go or you'll be late for your meeting at the hospital."

He stepped toward the curb and lifted his arm to hail a passing motorized taxi. There were no horses left in the city after all of them had been sent to France for the cavalry. "I'll have you taken to the Willow Tearooms. Mother is a friend of the owner, Miss Cranston, and says it's the only acceptable place to have tea in Glasgow. Renowned artwork of some kind inside. I'll meet you there after my meeting."

A taxi swerved over and they climbed inside to the worn black leather seats. It was no warmer than the frigid January air outside.

Wynn shut the door and scooted close. "Willow Tearoom—"

"Glasgow Hospital," Svetlana said, taking her fern from him and propping it on her knee where the bright green tips could trail down her skirt.

He looked at her with brow puckered. "You can't come with me."

"Whyever not? The decisions made at this meeting will affect both of us. I see no reason for me not to lend you my support on such a momentous occasion. Glasgow Hospital, please."

The driver twisted his head to look at Wynn. "Off to where now, aye?"

Wynn settled back against the seat next to Svetlana, an amused smile twisting his lips. "You heard the lady. Glasgow Hospital."

———

"We have ten surgeons on staff and four operating theaters. All are located on this floor for the best advantage of natural light coming through the windows." Dr. Neil, chief of administration at Glasgow Hospital, led the small tour group delegated for Wynn's visit down a wide corridor lined with symmetrical doors on either side. Iodoform and its disinfecting properties clung to the air in a familiarity to all hospitals. It smelled almost like a bouquet of flowers compared to the warfare casualties of blood, putrid human flesh, and filth-soaked uniforms that had choked the Parisian hospitals months before. They paused before the last door. "This is our largest operating theater."

Opening the door, Dr. Neil gestured for Wynn to step inside first, followed by the trailing staff and doctors. Wynn could barely contain his surprise. This was no field tent caked with mud, nor a converted hotel dining room with glass chandeliers dripping with crystals. It was a large room specifically designed for the fixing of broken bodies.

Light poured in from the wide windows and glistened off the sterile white tiled floors. Tiered seating took up an entire wall in the traditional fashion of allowing medical school students to observe the remarkable feats happening in the center of the room. Shiny instruments and equipment surrounded the operating table like servants before a throne, awaiting their glorious moment to serve.

Wynn ran his hand over the table, feeling the invisible current running through it, offering a chance to live for whoever laid upon its sacred surface. So, too, did the surgeon's tools as they had been lined up perfectly as soldiers in their trays. Deadly looking with their hooks and blades, but nothing could be further from their true purpose.

"I see you've incorporated the vacuum-assisted closure." Wynn pointed to the apparatus designed for continuous wound irrigation. The procedure hurt like the dickens, but it was an effective way to prevent infection from setting into open wounds.

One of the other physicians stepped forward. "We have, Your Grace."

Wynn tried not to flinch at the imposter title aimed at him. The usage was meant with the best of intentions, but it didn't belong to him. Not really.

"Dr. MacCallan, or Wynn, please."

The man paled, which was impressive considering the already pasty pallor of most doctors. "Apologies, Dr. MacCallan. We pride ourselves on providing the newest technology and studies that may benefit our patients. The war cost us much, but advancements in life-saving procedures have been made possible because of it."

"Something we hope you can help us continue in the burgeoning field of cardiology," Dr. Neil said. He enunciated each word with Oxford-based precision, as if to overcome his humble Dumfries origins. As if knowledge cared a sixpence about a person's birthplace. "I've read over your transcript from the speech you gave to the medical board in Paris, along with Dr. Lehr's notes on the matter. It's a radical approach, but one we in this room are eager to deploy. Too many in our profession stick their heads in the sand or cry heresy when methods are challenged. We aren't ostriches here at Glasgow Hospital."

Wynn grinned. For all his nervousness about coming here, he'd never felt more at home. "You don't know how relieved I am to hear that."

"Well, gentlemen. I believe we are all in agreement." Dr. Neil glanced around at the other men as they all nodded. "We would like to offer you a position here at Glasgow Hospital, Dr. MacCallan. You would be placed on a trial basis for six weeks as is standard, observing our techniques and assisting the other surgeons. At the end of your trial period, we will convene again to decide if you are to be offered a full-time position as head of the new study for cardiology. Do you find these terms acceptable?"

Stifling a loud whoop, Wynn gave a more professional nod. "Yes. Thank you for the opportunity. I only hope I can be an asset to the work ethic and studious minds you've cultivated here."

"I believe there's only one outstanding concern we have. How will your duties as duke affect your duties as physician? A surgeon cannot be allowed to leave during an operation if there's a ribbon-cutting ceremony."

The other men followed Dr. Neil in a hearty laugh, but Wynn's came out dry and brittle. Must he always chose one over the other? Duke or doctor. Was he selfish to believe there truly was a choice anymore? Day after day his new mantle grew in weight, a weight that had been borne so well on Hugh's capable shoulders. For Wynn it was a shroud burying him alive.

During the war he was perfectly in line with his calling. There was no time for lords and manors. All that mattered was the shattered soldier on the table in front of him. Wynn had never felt more alive, more purpose coursing through his being—a purpose he could use to alleviate pain and suffering. A duke's days were spent crawling through piles of estate accounts, tenant rents, commissions for this, speeches for that. Father had the diplomacy for handling those responsibilities; doing so breathed life through his every fiber. He was born to the title. As had been Hugh. Now Wynn was expected to cast aside everything he'd built his life toward and fall into a role he was never equipped for.

His only solace was that times were changing. The war had forced it. Could he not look after Thornhill and its people while also serving his medical oath? Oversee the larger issues and plans while entrusting the day-to-day business to Mackie? Or Svetlana. His wife had grown up in a palace, and he had the fullest confidence in her abilities. Was it naïve to believe it could work? He wanted to believe. Only time would tell.

"I see no reason why one should interfere with the other," Wynn said. "My priority is to those in need."

Apparently it was the correct answer. Dr. Neil bobbed his head in approval. His entourage nodded along. "Delighted to hear you say that. Now, shall we return to my office? I'd like to speak with you more about this heart theory regarding electrophysiology."

Leaving the theater, the other doctors allowed Wynn and Dr. Neil to carry on alone. The two retraced their steps back down the corridor as nurses in starched aprons bustled by. Wynn peered at the surgery schedule posted by the doors, eager to see his name on rotation.

"We have the ancient Chinese to thank for laying the foundation of arrhythmia theories," Wynn said, "but only recently have machines been created to detect the electrical phenomena of the heart. Disorders can be identified—"

An orderly popped up in front of them like a jack-in-the-box. He held out an envelope. "Dr. Neil. A letter for you."

Dr. Neil waved him off. "Put it on my desk. I'm in conference with Dr. MacCallan."

The boy's nervous gaze flickered. "I was told to hand it to you with urgency, sir."

"Very well." Dr. Neil snatched the envelope from him and tore it open. "Excuse me a moment, Dr. MacCallan." Scanning the letter, his eyes widened until they looked ready to fall out of his head. He refolded the letter and tapped it against his palm for several seconds. Finally he cleared his throat and looked at Wynn, his face pinched with displeasure. "I do not know how to say this but right out. You are familiar with a Lieutenant Harkin?"

Uneasiness curled in Wynn's belly. Why would he ask that? They'd been speaking of Harkin only an hour before. "My patient in Paris."

"The one whose heart you rotated for object extraction. It seems he has died due to surgical complications."

The unease balled into a fist of shock and socked Wynn square in the middle of his chest. Harkin. The scared soldier who was nothing more than a lad. Who had trusted Wynn to keep him safe. Dead. It was always a possibility. Anytime a person went under the knife was a gamble with death, but the rationale was lost in a flood of guilt. Each death left a jagged crack through his Hippocratic oath.

Wynn pushed a shaking hand through his hair. "I was going to visit him in London next month. He'd written to me a fortnight ago saying how well he was doing." The shock of the news spread numbly through his veins until his mind could only focus on a single thought. "It's more important than ever to advance the cause of cardiology so incidents like this can be avoided. If we have the tools in place, patients like Harkin—"

"Yes, something to consider in future. I'm afraid we must part ways here. We'll be in touch should we decide to continue the prospect of you joining our hospital."

"I don't understand. Minutes ago you offered me a trial position."

"Your Grace—"

"Dr. MacCallan."

Dr. Neil sighed through his nose. A common physician's reaction when a patient refused to comprehend the diagnosis. "In light of this unfortunate development, the hospital's president feels it would not be in good taste or standing to hire a doctor with a besmirched reputation. We were quite willing to listen to your newfound theories, but seeing as they cannot be considered safe—"

"No surgery is safe."

"Be that as it may, we have our patients to consider. No one will wish to be operated on by a physician who is already under the displeased eye of the medical profession at large."

Heated anger avalanched through the numbness, scorching all ability for diplomacy. "A man has died. A man who entrusted himself into my care after being knocked down by a machine gun in service to his country, and all the president cares about is how it will make him look?"

"An investigation is being launched. The authorities will be in contact for your statement." Dr. Neil placed a hand on Wynn's shoulder. Another well-meaning physician's gesture that did little to nothing. "I'm sorry."

Wynn was left standing alone in the corridor. An hour before he'd been welcomed with enthusiasm as a golden boy, and now he'd been deserted like a pariah. The desertion he could deal with. Even the hot-cold treatment of so-called medical professionals he was accustomed to, but the death of a patient was something he would never shake off. A patient he had promised to do everything he could for. In trying to prove his own gut instinct of what was needed, had Wynn sentenced Harkin to death on that operating table? Had he stopped to consider all the possibilities before rotating that heart? If he'd not been so rash, would Harkin still be alive?

No. He'd done what he thought was right at the time. No surgeon had time to second-guess himself in the moment. Or was that his arrogance defending itself again?

Wynn tore down the stairs as the demons of doubt clawed at his heels. He needed to get out of there. He needed to retrace every step and action he'd taken that day when operating on Harkin. Had he done everything he could to prevent death?

He rounded the front reception desk. "Where is Her Grace?"

The nurse looked up from her files of paperwork. "I believe she was taking a tour of Wing A. If you'll wait a moment, I'll have one of the junior nurses show you—"

"No need. I'll find it."

He'd been in enough hospitals to understand the general layout at a glance. It took him approximately ten seconds to locate Wing A, and fifty seconds with several wrong doors before he located his wife. She sat in a waiting room filled with families. Most noticeably the men were former soldiers, if their missing limbs and facial injuries were any indication.

Weaving his way to her side, Wynn gently grasped Svetlana's elbow. "Apologies for interrupting, but we need to be on our way."

Svetlana smiled up at him like the sun coming out of hiding, but he couldn't feel the warmth due to the numbness lingering in his bones like an ill-fated chill waiting to freeze him out.

"Wynn, I'm so glad you're here. This is Mrs. McDuff, her husband, Mr. McDuff, and their children. Mr. McDuff lost his leg in . . . Marne?"

Clenching his worn hat in his hand, Mr. McDuff pushed to his feet using a crutch for support. "Yes, ma'am. I mean, Duchess."

"They have to travel over four hours every month to come here to the hospital only to sit for hours in the waiting room. Most of the other patients find themselves in similar distressing circumstances because adequate care isn't available where they live in rural areas."

Wynn tried to focus on what Svetlana was saying, but the words garbled together in his ears as it hit the thickening fog of numbness. She was looking at him. They all were. Waiting for him, the great surgeon, the lofty duke to say something. "It's a problem everyone is facing. Hospitals and medical staff are doing what they can."

Mr. McDuff bobbed his head while his wife dipped into a curtsy with tears in her eyes as if Wynn had spouted ecclesiastical revelations. It twisted the guilt of wretchedness like a knife. Svetlana thanked the couple for sharing their story with her and said goodbye to the others in the room. All Wynn could manage was a wooden nod.

Outside, Wynn hailed a taxi and they climbed inside. "Grand Central Hotel."

Svetlana paused in untangling her fern fronds and frowned. "I thought we were having tea at the Willow."

"No. We're leaving for home."

"Is everything all right?"

"A former patient of mine, a Lieutenant Harkin, died."

"Oh, Wynn. I'm so sorry. How terrible for his family." Her gloved hand rested lightly on his. Any other day he would have thrilled at her touch, but he felt nothing beyond the guilt. "I'm sure we can return another time for you to meet with the hospital board."

The whole truth spilled to his mouth, but he clamped it behind his teeth. How could he tell her about the rejection? The one accomplishment he prided himself on had now been tarnished, and those esteemed opinions he sought to change for the betterment of patient treatment now turned against him. It was enough to cripple the pride of any man.

Besides, she'd witnessed enough suffering and disappointment; he didn't want to add one more thing to burden her shoulders. Not after he'd vowed to defend her against further woes. He would take the troubles on himself if only to spare her. One day he would tell her, as he'd promised honesty on their wedding day, but not until the storm had passed.

He gently slipped his hand out from hers in a move made to look like he was adjusting his hat. Her hand was too trusting, and the weight of such responsibility was more than he could bear. Glasgow's gray cityscape passed in a blur outside the taxi window, but he saw only his failure in the eyes of a dead man. "Another time. Perhaps."

CHAPTER 21

Svetlana eyed the bundles of laundry stacked in the corner of the cramped hovel and tried not to breathe through her nose. A cauldron bubbled over a fire in the center of the room, its pungent smoke wafting through a hole in the thatched roof.

"'Tis the peat that be givin' off the smoke. Best not to keep yer eyes open too long without a blink, aye." Mrs. Douglas, mistress of the hovel, busied herself at a rickety table set near the middle of the room. A plain woman with dark hair streaked in silver and creases lining her face, she wore the expression of a hard life, but she couldn't have aged past forty.

"I have never heard of this peat. Is it common to Scotland?"

"We've it all over here in the bogs. All the dead 'uns scamperin' or growin' round get compressed right down together and sealed in tight with water, so they do. Good for heatin'. Burns long too." Mrs. Douglas poured water into a teacup and stirred it with a wooden spoon. "Me man cuts peat for the distillery near Bothwell. Or did afore the war took his hand. They give him work when they can, but who be needin' a one-handed man for cuttin' and stackin'?"

"Too many of the returning soldiers find themselves in similar circumstances."

"Aye. Go off to fight for king and country, they do—only their country canna use them no further when they get home. What thanks is that I ask ye after what they sacrificed?" Placing the cup and saucer on a wooden tray, Mrs. Douglas brought it to where Svetlana sat on a bench, the only seating in the room besides the bed crammed against the far wall. "Drink that right down, Yer Grace. Warm ye up, it will."

The lady hadn't poured a cup for herself. The few pieces of mismatched bowls and plates sitting on a shelf behind the table suggested the teacup was the only one of its kind in this humble abode. Though chipped on one side, great care had gone into painting little purple flowers on the sides.

"What beautiful artistry."

Pink brightened Mrs. Douglas's rough cheeks. "Me mam was fine with a brush. A real talent she passed on to my lassies."

Svetlana took a sip of the tea. Mrs. Douglas hovered anxiously. Svetlana swallowed and forced a smile so as not to insult her gracious hostess. "What an unusual flavor."

"'Tis heather. Same as painted on the cup. A great many uses here in Scotland."

Svetlana took another polite sip. It wasn't terrible, but it wasn't the sophisticated Russian taste she was accustomed to. Like so many other things, it was a difference she needed to learn and accept if she had any chance of being received in the community.

"I find myself amazed at the never-ending resourcefulness of the Scots. Russians tend to limit our creativity to music, dance, and architecture."

"Been an age since anyone had reason to dance 'round here. Too busy survivin'. 'Twas lucky enough, I was, to take on extra services as a laundress." Mrs. Douglas hooked her thumb at the piles of laundry. "And me man returned. Not all the wives can say as much."

"Are the widows able to find work?"

"Some, aye, but not enough for the little mouths they need to feed. Many of them were forced to be givin' up their jobs to the returnin' men. I suppose 'tis the way, but some of the lasses don't want to be returnin' to the kitchen now they've a taste of the freedom."

"It sounds as if they need opportunities to earn their own way. Especially if they are left as the sole provider for a family."

"Aye, but take Katie MacKinnon livin' three doors down. Her

man came back, or what's left of him, and now she's tendin' the bairns and him. Savin' every coin she can to pay for his medical bills whilst hirin' herself out as a scullery maid down at the pub."

The back door banged open and in shrieked a pandemonium of four dark-haired children under the age of ten. Like hounds to the scent, they rounded the table and fell on the gift basket Svetlana had brought.

"Out, ye wee rascals! None of that for ye at the now." Mrs. Douglas tried to shoo them away, but the children ignored her as they tore into wrapped sweets.

"What's this?" The smallest girl with a long plait swinging down her back held up a wrapped parcel of cookies.

"Russian sweets. Tea cakes, *pastila*, *khvorost*, and *sushki*. Mrs. Varjensky, a lady who came with me from Russia, made them. No heather, I'm afraid." Svetlana rose and joined the children at the table. She lifted out two small jars filled with pastes. "She's also a skilled healer. I don't recall what she mixed these with, but the green is for cuts and bruises, and the yellow is for headaches and fever."

Tears shimmering in her tired eyes, Mrs. Douglas took one of the jars as if it were a golden scepter. "Thanks be to ye, Yer Grace. And thank Mrs. Var . . . Var . . ."

"Varjensky."

"Aye, be thankin' her too. We ain't never had anyone think of us like this."

"You are most welcome. Now, I must be going as I do not wish to take up any more of your valuable time."

"Blessed me. To think I've had a real princess in me home."

"I do hope you'll allow me to come again."

"Our door always be open to ye and yers." The woman wobbled into a curtsy and flapped her hand at her children for them to follow suit. It wasn't protocol, but Svetlana returned the gesture. Mrs. Douglas deserved it and every other recognition for her stalwart perseverance.

Svetlana stepped outside, grateful to breathe fresh air void of smoke once more. Wynn rounded the corner with a lanky man missing his left hand. He could only be Mr. Douglas.

"I'll send a few men over on Tuesday to get that barn wall repaired," Wynn said. Dressed in high boots and tweed trousers, he looked like he'd been wading in muck. "The hole is big enough for the cow to slip through."

Not a large man by any measure, Mr. Douglas swelled with pride, bringing him nearly to Wynn's towering height. "Appreciate yer help, I do, Yer Grace, but I can manage without troublin' ye."

"It's no trouble. You're a good tenant, as was your father before you. We take care of our own."

Such a good man. Always seeing to the needs of others and never making a promise he didn't keep. The honesty of his heart was a thing of unfathomable beauty. He had the intellect, wealth, and station to use those beneath him to elevate himself as so many of the so-called nobles did. Not Wynn. He shunned the pretentiousness of titles in favor of doing good and what was right. Even marrying a runaway princess when she had nothing to offer in return. Thank goodness for his stubbornness in pursuing her. She hated to think where she'd be without him.

One of the children, the older boy who looked to be around nine, streaked out of the hovel and planted himself in front of Wynn. Barefoot with dirt smearing his round face, he didn't appear the least bit fazed to be standing in front of a duke.

"I heard ye fix broken men."

Wynn squatted so he was eye to eye with the boy. "I do my best."

"See lots of blood?"

Mrs. Douglas gasped as she hurried out to join them. "Charles Edward Stuart Douglas. There's nay need for such talk."

Wynn leaned closer to the boy. "Plenty, but it's not good to talk about in front of the womenfolk." He caught Svetlana's eyes over the top of Charles's head. Humor flickered in his eyes for a moment, then lost to a sweep of sadness. Though he'd never mentioned it after their departure from Glasgow nearly a week ago, Harkin's ghost seemed to haunt him.

"Are ye goin' to help my da?"

Mr. Douglas grabbed Charles's shoulder and shuffled him away. "That's enough, lad. No impertinence to His Grace."

"I wasn't pertinentin'." Charles swooped under his father's arm and stared at Wynn. "He lost his hand fightin' those Hun. Can ye give him a new one?"

"I'm afraid that's not my field of specialty—" Wynn worked his jaw back and forth as if trying to decide how much medical information to pass on to a nine-year-old. Standing, he ruffled the boy's hair. "Never say never."

The Douglas family waved goodbye as Svetlana and Wynn rode off in the back of their chauffeured Renault motor car. Wynn absently tucked a wool blanket across her lap before turning to gaze out the window at the bleak landscape. Hills rolled by in winter colors of gray, brown, and frozen green as the reluctant sun did little to grace them with its warmth.

"These war wives and widows feel displaced now that the fighting has ceased. A circumstance I all too well understand." Svetlana angled the fox fur trim of her coat out from underneath the blanket so it wasn't crushed. "The armistice may have been signed months ago, but these families are still fighting the repercussions. War has dictated their circumstances, and they must find new ways to survive. I should like to help them."

"Hmm." Wynn continued to stare out the window. His long, capable fingers tapped against a dried patch of mud on his knee.

"Perhaps a teaching center where they might learn useful skills or trades outside the home, but then who would care for their children when they're not at school?"

"Yes, good idea."

"The other issue is leaving behind these jobs for days at a time because the only medical help to be found for the injured men is in the larger cities."

"Hmm."

Svetlana plucked at the tassels dangling from the edge of the blanket. "Mrs. Douglas gave me an interesting cup of tea. Heather, she said. I believe it's making me sprout a horn. Like a unicorn. Is that common, being the symbol of Scotland and all?"

"Hmm, yes."

"Wynn!"

He turned to her, eyebrows raised as if he'd been caught off guard. "Did you say something?"

"Yes, but you haven't heard a word. Where are you?"

"Sitting next to you in the back of the auto."

"Mentally you are somewhere else. Have been since Glasgow."

He flinched, pain washing across his face. If only she could draw it out of him like he did so many times for those hurting. Slipping off her glove and the vulnerability it sheathed, she reached across the distance between them and took his hand. The coldness in her fingers was lost to the warmth of his. How simple a thing touch was, often shared by those wishing to establish a connection. She'd never understood the need for such unseemly indulgences and thought them best left to those of weaker character. She prided herself on solitary fortitude where everything was self-contained. She had been in control, but she had been alone. Holding Wynn's hand, she was no longer alone. She was exposed and unprotected, but he engendered trust and faith. She would gift him the same.

Curling her fingers around his, she drew his hand to rest on her lap. "Is it Harkin?"

He jerked as if the name were a needle to him and tried to pull his hand back. She held it tighter.

"Please tell me."

His jaw worked back and forth as he pondered his response before discarding it to consider another. "It's never easy to lose a patient."

A carefully selected reply that answered without answering her. Very unlike Wynn. He customarily charged into statements with the confidence of a *prima ballerino* on center stage.

"I imagine the sadness stays with you forever. I know you did everything you could to help him, but the control of some things remains beyond our grasp no matter how much we wish it otherwise."

"Your faith in me is touching, though a bit off base in this case."

"Tragedy often shakes our confidence. Once you start your work at Glasgow Hosp—"

"Glasgow Hospital has decided not to expand their cardiology department. They don't want their sterling reputation besmirched by questionable practices." Taking his hand from hers, he crossed his arms over his chest. With the added layers of winter clothing, his breadth was twice as large and doubly formidable. To all but Svetlana. She saw the tucking in of himself to a defensive position after having his pride pricked.

"Oh, Wynn. I'm so sorry. How terrible for you and how short-sighted of them to deny people the advancing treatments they need."

"You sound like you've been reading medical journals."

"You leave them all over the house."

"Careful or you'll be touted a radical."

"If my husband can stand for surgical improvements, then so can I. A person would have to sit on their brain not to see that these studies and procedures are needed. In fact, I read the other day about a Harvey Cushing who worked as a neurosurgeon during the war and helped to reduce the mortality rate of brain injuries from 50 percent to 29 percent. Something the article called 'brain wound care.'" Journal diagrams of the dissected brain flashed through her mind. So many parts. So many incidents waiting to go wrong. "Not that I wish you to indulge in brain work. The complications sound increasingly more than cardiology."

"I don't think I'll be performing any type of surgery in the near future."

His pride may have taken a blow, but she wasn't about to let him stay down for long. There would be other opportunities. He was like a caged bear, useless to his true purpose, when his skills weren't being utilized.

"Pay no heed to Glasgow. There are plenty of other hospitals in need of your skills. We only need to apply to them."

Wynn took a deep breath, then slowly exhaled. "In the meantime, Thornhill will become my priority. After Father died, Hugh had a list of improvements to be made, but then the war . . . It's past time attention was paid the estate. As duke it's my responsibility. Why are you frowning? I thought you'd be pleased after claiming I was deserting her."

"I never said that. I merely do not wish to see you abandon one responsibility for the other."

"I haven't abandoned anything."

"You are both a duke and a surgeon. I want to help you find equal footing as both."

He rotated on the seat to look fully at her, pinning her like one of his patients strapped to the operating table under the bright light of inspection.

"Why is it so important to you that I strike this balance?"

"Because there is much good to be done without the seal of approval from a medical board. There are so many people right here in need of help, some of the same people that stuffy medical board refuses to lift a finger for because they are deemed untreatable or lacking in funds." She bristled at the memory of those families waiting in Glasgow Hospital and the Douglas family scraping to get by. "We have the responsibility to ease the suffering of those around us. Perhaps not in a fine city hospital, or with the blessing of your colleagues, or even for accolades, but that does not mean the endeavor is any less worthwhile."

"That's one of the things I fancy most about you. Cut to the heart of the matter." He half smiled, then looked down at his hands. "Do you think I've allowed my ego to overshadow what good I'm supposed to be doing as a physician?"

"I think if you are not careful, pride may overcome what is right by your patients."

"If it hasn't already. Being a physician was all that mattered to me, and now . . ." He spread his hands in an aimless gesture. "I never wanted this mantle of duke, you know."

"But it is yours to bear now. All you must decide is if you will smother yourself in it or use its generous folds to help others. A privilege, I believe, that also exists in the hands of a physician."

"You seem to have given this a great deal of thought. More than me, I'm ashamed to admit."

She studied the pattern of lines and checks on the blanket. They started smooth and unbroken until bisecting with opposing lines to weave a new pattern. Much as the threads of her life. They'd woven a silken path until revolution knotted her to a different line twisted with war. Another pattern. And then there was Wynn, striking bold and straight to tie up the loosened threads into an unexpected weft. She traced the thick blue line that drew the eye beyond all other drab colors.

"You have given me so much with no payment asked—"

"You're my wife. No payment is required."

"I wasn't always your wife. Now that I am, my gratitude can better be expressed in ways of supporting you."

"And I wish you would stop thinking of our marriage as a series of transactions and payments."

"A difficult request considering it's all I know of marital matters. That, and I am to smile and oblige you in all situations."

His hand stole over hers, his fingers twining between hers. "Let me guess, your mother told you that as part of the perfect princess training."

"All mothers tell their daughters this. It makes for a smoother running household."

"Since when has anything between us run smoothly? You've never withheld your opinion from me before. I don't want you starting now."

He was rotating her wedding band, and her thoughts were spinning right along with it. They blurred faster and faster until her carefully attached reservations cast off and the guarded questions to which she only ever surrendered in the loneliness of silence rushed out.

"Then what do you want from this marriage?"

If her bluntness surprised him, he didn't show it. Nor did he take long to consider it.

"A chance to move forward. With you." His eyes darkened, like the glowing heart of an emerald under moonlight. Mesmerizing and tempered on the cusp of passion. "What do you want, Lana?"

She took a shaky breath that mimicked the tripping of her heart. Surprisingly, she didn't need long to consider her own answer as the words came from her heart without complication.

"I think I would like that too. My whole life has been rooted by obligation and expectation, yet I tire of the stillness. I wish to see what exists beyond the borders. With you."

The back of his fingertips traced her face, blazing a path from her cheek, along her jaw, to her chin and curving around the other side. With each pass he closed the distance between them, leaving mere inches between his lips and her need to claim them.

"After meeting you, it's a good thing I specialize in heart troubles. I feel I'm about to lose mine."

In that instant the strength of his emotions overwhelmed her, plunging her to heady yearning. She gathered her courage to receive them as the tide swept her away to deeper currents from which he beckoned. He was not for the faint of heart. She'd never fainted a day in her life, but she felt light-headed.

She tilted her head as his warm breath fanned her face. His green eyes dissolved to desire, taking her right along with him. Finally, she would know what it was like to kiss her husband.

The auto jerked to a stop and the door opened to a blast of frigid air. Svetlana jumped, knocking Wynn in the face with the brim of her hat. Embarrassment scorched through her, but she quickly cooled it by flicking the blanket from her lap. No one, aristocrat or servant, was about to make her feel guilty about the almost kiss. Proper decorum was too cumbersome for the back of an auto. Especially when one's husband looked as Wynn had.

"Welcome home, Your Graces." A footman stood holding the door open with his eyes staring politely ahead.

Grunting, Wynn unpeeled his arm from around her and whacked away the stiffened peacock feather threatening to take his eye out.

"Impeccable timing, McNab." He glared at their chauffeur. "Drive slower next time."

McNab bobbed his head from the front seat. "As Your Grace wishes."

Wynn climbed out and offered his hand to help Svetlana down, then hooked her hand into the crook of his elbow. They crossed the gravel drive to the gloriously imposing presence of Thornhill. With the tumultuous gray skies behind her, the castle resembled a medieval lady rising on her solitary throne of steel.

"Did you mention something about war widows and wives?"

So he had been listening. Or partially listening. Svetlana lifted her heavy black skirt and stepped over the mud puddling at the front entrance.

"Perhaps a charity ball. We'll send invitations to the neighboring gentry and all proceeds will go to the war benefit."

"It's not feasible to write all the affected families a cheque."

"No, but perhaps it can ease their immediate suffering while helping to establish a more permanent venture. Such as a training center. Of course, that only alleviates half of the problem." It would take time and thought to devise a more concrete plan of action, particularly time when her thoughts weren't consumed by wanting five more minutes in the back compartment of the Renault.

They shrugged out of their overcoats, hats, and gloves and handed them over to the waiting servants who would whisk them away to be brushed free of possible dirt and stored among cedar closets lined with lavender sachets. It felt good to be wearing tailor-made, clean clothing again. Any scuffs were buffed out. Holes were immediately mended. Inches taken in or out. How had she survived last winter with barely a shawl on her back? A patched shawl that too closely resembled Mrs. Douglas's. First thing in the morning Svetlana would put together a donation box of warm items to be distributed in the village.

Their butler, Glasby, glided across the floor of the Stone Hall, so named for the smooth river stones lining the three-story space that always set guests' jaws dropping. He held out a post platter stacked with several envelopes.

"Her Grace the Dowager Duchess is having tea in the library along with Princess Marina and Mrs. Varjensky."

"My mother has not joined them?" Svetlana asked.

"No, Your Grace. She claims a headache and is resting in her chambers."

"Another protest at the lack of a proper samovar, no doubt. Thank you, that will be all."

Inclining his head, Glasby glided away as Wynn filed through the post. Svetlana scanned the addresses on the envelopes, hoping against all odds that she might see a familiar script written from Father or Nicky telling her they were alive. Or Sergey. She'd all but convinced herself that she'd imagined seeing him on Armistice Day outside the Paris townhouse. But no letters ever came for her.

She brushed off her pang of sadness. "Shall we go into the library?"

"I'll join you later. I have a few things to attend first." Wynn strode toward his study with a thick cream envelope stamped with a London address clenched in his hand.

"Is anything the matter?"

Entering his study, he closed the door without a backward glance. The sound of the shutting door reverberated among the river stones, echoing back the loneliness of the hall in which she was left.

———

The paper dropped to Wynn's desk as if the report were written in damning lead ink. All feeling drained from his legs, and he sagged into his chair like a boneless bag of abject emptiness. The slivers of hope he'd clung to on the precipice of despair had sharpened to knives with each word of the report, twisting deep and thoroughly gutting him.

A glutton for agony, he read the damning words again.

Coroner concludes death of Lieutenant Harkin caused by operative trauma under care of Dr. Edwynn MacCallan with crisis arising several months post operation. Ill-advised surgery was undertaken without physician gaining further consent from supervisor and patient.

Despite agreed upon medical practices of the hospital, Dr. MacCallan proceeded to his own advantages and ensured his reputation for aggressive and malignant theories which prove detrimental to the sacred oath of caretaking.

"Aggressive and malignant." Daggers into his soul.

They now thought him an arrogant butcher with no care of destroying those entrusted to his care, as if his Hippocratic oath meant nothing. As if he didn't mourn every life that couldn't be saved. Did they truly think his arrogance stripped him of human decency in the delicate balance of life and death?

He dragged his hands through his hair as his mind railed against the accusations. Harkin had shown no signs of post-op complications, although many could lay dormant for months. Wynn yanked open the desk's bottom drawer where he kept correspondences and pulled out the third envelope down. A letter from Harkin dating two weeks before his death stating that the physicians at St. Matthew's Hospital in London had cleared him with a full bill of health. Surely if a complication had lain dormant, they would have discovered and diagnosed it.

Despite the letter's false claim, Wynn had made sure to gain Harkin's permission before the operation. He had been scared, as most patients were, but never once had he voiced disagreement.

A thick absence of feeling coated him from scalp to foot, blocking sound from his ears and sight from his eyes. All sight except the black words. Their tyranny could not be hidden from the cold light streaming in through the window nor the slamming closed of his eyelids. They taunted him in the darkness, searing into his brain. If only Hugh were here. *Where are you, brother, when I need you most? We always looked out for each other and now the wolves are set to devour me.*

"Wynn?"

Wynn's eyes shot open. Svetlana stood in the doorway.

"I am sorry to disturb. I did knock." Head tilted to the side, eyes softened, corners of the mouth slightly pulled down, hesitation in the stance. She was worried. About him. "Is everything all right?"

He wanted his ice princess with her haughty expression and raised eyebrows. The glacial slant of her nose where woes dared not fall lest they slip off to their deserved doom. The arctic chill in her eyes that frosted demeaning circumstances and stamped them beneath the ice where they belonged. That beguiling creature would at least challenge him to exert all his willpower to thaw her with a smirk here and a teasing comment there.

Instead, his willpower was nearly crippled by her look of near pity. He would not be that to her. Whatever it took, she would not witness him crippled by his own arrogance and failures.

"The coroner sent his final report on Harkin. A formality." The words slipped out before he could stop them. He grabbed the letter and shoved it into the bottom drawer.

Sadness and relief flitted across her face. Wynn's stomach twisted. What did it cost the soul to lie? Mere fragments breaking off until its existence was nothing more than a hollow shell? Could he learn to live on the meagerness that remained? Could his future with Svetlana exist on it? Would he be able to survive the guilt?

But so much had been taken from his wife; he could not bear to see her suffer further because of him. One day he would tell her the whole truth, but to do so now would only cause her unnecessary pain. He believed she would understand the reason for his conceal-ment when the time came. She had not agreed to become his wife in exchange for a life of disgrace. He had wanted only to save her from that in promise of a good life. He would salvage whatever remained of his reputation and force his feet to tread the path demanded of him. He would give Svetlana the life of happiness she deserved.

"Will you come and have tea with me?" she asked.

"Nothing I'd like more." Coercing a smile, Wynn stood and shut the drawer, but not quick enough to erase the letter's final lines burn-ing him with shame.

Edwynn MacCallan is thereby stripped of his medical services and doctoral titles pending a formal investigation of actions.

CHAPTER 22

Every chandelier in Thornhill blazed with light to warm the stone walls and walnut floors like an ancient oil poured out as anointment for the charity bazaar. The elegant tapestries and glowing candles wrapped the affluent guests in rich comfort as they entered from the frigid night. Gift-laden tables set out for the silent auction were available to peruse while a small orchestra played lively tunes from Tchaikovsky, Stravinksy, and Rachmaninoff. The world may still eye Russia with distrust, but Svetlana wasn't about to allow the same for its music. Such superiority needed to be heard by all.

Svetlana slipped among her mingling guests and into the dining room where delicacies from shortbread and some kind of oat flattened cakes called bannocks—which Constance assured her were a must at any Scottish gathering—to Russian peasant savories of *vatrushaka* and *pelmeni* covered the long dining table in artful arrangements.

Marina came to stand next to Svetlana. With her curled hair pinned atop her head and pearls dangling from her ears, Marina had bloomed overnight into a woman. If they had been home and life had continued as planned, her baby sister would have been presented in court before the tsar and tsarina with suitors standing in line to beg for the first dance. Such things belonged to dreams of the past, but at least they had awoken to a future together.

"I believe Mrs. Varjensky has found her true calling. She was destined to be a caterer." Marina tilted her chin to indicate the small figure across the room.

The old woman was dressed in a simple but elegant black gown with no adornment other than the lacey shawl Svetlana had given her held together in the front with the *matryoshka* brooch from Wynn. Standing next to the table, she snagged whoever went by and pointed out all the food choices to them while loading up a plate and practically shoveling the food into their mouths. If the person didn't immediately groan with taste-bud ecstasy, Mrs. Varjensky would reach for another sample to force on them.

"I found her offering Lord Barrow an oil to massage the lump on his forehead," Svetlana said. "She claimed the protrusion was caused by a kiss from the devil. Thank goodness he didn't speak Russian."

Two women dripping in jewels strolled by and congratulated her on the splendid evening. Svetlana thanked them for coming before allowing herself to take in the other fashionable guests. Smiles and laughter rippled through the soft strains of music and clinking plates. Perhaps they had only come to see the new Russian princess curiosity, but they had come and that was as good a starting place as Svetlana could hope for.

"They're right. Everything looks splendid tonight. You've outdone yourself, Svetka," Marina said.

"Mama's party-planning sessions have finally paid off. I've been able to put my skills to good use."

"Anyone with enough money and wine can put together a party, but you've done something more. You've created an event that exceeds its premise. The guests are excited to be here, unlike all those painted-on expressions of regal boredom drowning in the palaces back home."

"You forget: we were those bored people."

"Not anymore. People are having a good time." Marina's smile encompassed the room.

"I think they're all simply curious to see the *russkiye*. Maybe I should have hired Cossack dancers to really give them a show."

"No, I think they're here to see the new Duchess of Kilbride. This mysterious princess from the east with her strange accent and even stranger family in tow. 'Do they really dine on bear and cabbage?'

they're probably asking." Horror flashed across Marina's face. "Mrs. Varjensky didn't make bear and cabbage *pirozhki,* did she?"

"With the way people are going back for seconds, I doubt it. Then again, they are Scottish, and Wynn informed me the cuisine here is all based on a dare." Svetlana absently plucked at the cream lace on her sleeve, her thoughts drifting far beyond questionable food. "I only hope this evening reflects well on Wynn. He hasn't been the same since his brother died, which is understandable, but then the death of his patient too. He needs something to lift his spirits."

Grief touched souls differently, often lingering longer in some. She was by no means an expert on Wynn's handling of personal sensitivities, but she sensed a change rooting deeper than the loss of his brother. Tension marked his moves and smiling seemed an afterthought. More than once she'd caught him staring off into the distance as if a war raged in his mind. When she asked him about it, he would shake his head and assure her nothing was amiss. But the smile he offered wasn't from the Wynn she knew.

Since that day in the auto so many weeks ago, he hadn't tried to kiss her again. In fact, he hadn't done more than brush her shoulder in passing. Was he regretting his hasty declaration of wanting to move forward with her? Without the stresses of wartime binding them together, was he regretting their marriage? Was that the change he was hiding from her? An ache filled her chest as the fragile foundation they'd built continued its shift.

"I'm certain this party is just the thing to lift his spirits. Think of how much money you'll raise tonight for the training center," Marina continued. How blessed was youth without adult worries to tint its optimistic view. "I can't wait to help with the nursing courses. If there's one good thing that came from that wretched influenza, it's knowing we need more nurses on hand. Do you think they'll let me qualify early?"

"Hospitals have their age requirements, but don't worry. I'm sure they'll still need nurses when you turn eighteen."

"What good is having a top surgeon for a brother-in-law if he can't bend the rules a little?" Marina grumbled.

"Patience, *kotyonok*. Your time will come."

"Time for what? Cats?" Wynn materialized as if summoned. His hair, customarily waved and loose in opposition to the dictates of fashion, was slicked to the side with a sheen that darkened it to brown, with his eyes following suit.

"Kitten," Marina corrected with a giggle as she eyed Wynn's knee-baring ensemble. "More important, what is that?"

"A kilt. It's traditional Highland dress for formal gatherings."

Svetlana frowned. "We are in the Lowlands, are we not? Perhaps I do not understand the boundaries of your country as well as I presumed."

"No, you're correct." Wynn adjusted the thick material pleating over his shoulder. "Traditionally, Lowlanders follow English standards of dress, but a few decades back, when King George became the first monarch to visit Scotland in nearly two centuries, organized by Sir Walter Scott, I might add, his regal vision was assaulted by tartan pageantry. The visit was a roaring success, blurring the lines between Highland and Lowland and declaring the plaid and kilt part of Scotland's national identity. It's a grievous sin now not to wear one. Thus, I am the tartan-draped man before you."

He wasn't the only man wearing one, but he certainly outshone all the others with his air of captured ruggedness. He tugged on the finely cut black jacket with its shining gold buttons, setting off the crisp white shirt and black waistcoat beneath. Svetlana had glimpsed the national garb worn by his ancestors—with great swaths of material looped over their shoulders and long eagle feathers blooming from their caps—in the portraits hung along the upstairs corridors. Seeing it in person was a thrill she could not anticipate. Men wore nothing like this in Russia. If they did, they would most certainly freeze. Hardy indeed were the men of Scotland. And this one was hers.

"I haven't worn this rig in ages and now I remember why, but it befits a duke, I suppose." A cloud passed over his face. It lasted but a second yet long enough to show the varying facets of his inner struggles.

Not knowing how else to show her support, Svetlana took a step closer and brushed her arm against his. "Very handsome."

At her touch his expression softened as he looked at her. "And very bonny, as we say here in Scotland. The MacCallan colors suit you."

A blush rose to Svetlana's cheeks as she smoothed a hand over the shoulder sash woven in blue-and-green tartan pinned to her purple dress of half-mourning. "Your mother suggested it. As befitting the Duchess of Kilbride."

"She was right." His gaze warmed over her face. Butterflies pirouetted through Svetlana's stomach. He'd looked at her this way before, but each time deepened the degree of intimacy, as if each time he unlocked a new part of her for his eyes only.

"Ahem. People are starting to stare." Marina cleared her throat, effectively clearing Svetlana's light-headedness. "Little wonder. You look stunningly perfect together."

An old familiar grin crossed Wynn's face. "You're right. My wife is stunning. What say we shame all the other couples on the dance floor as well?"

Taking Svetlana's hand, Wynn led her across the Stone Hall and into the Grand Hall with its polished dance floor and mirrored walls. The vaulted ceiling provided the perfect canopy to catch the orchestra's swelling notes and float them back down to the dancing couples. Wynn swept her into his arms and around the floor to a minuet in A-flat. The last time she'd danced to this was with a Bayushevy prince from Moscow. He'd lumbered like a bear in the middle of hibernation. Wynn wasn't the lightest on his feet, but her body moved as one with his as if it had been waiting for his direction all along.

The composition moved to Tchaikovsky's waltz from *The Sleeping*

Beauty. With no addition of brass, the strings and harp awoke from their slumber to unearth soaring melodies of longing and love's first blush.

"I danced to this at my first ball," Svetlana said as the hem of her gown floated around her ankles like flower petals on water, drifting her away to another time and place where memories misted with romance.

"You were enchanting."

"You weren't there."

"I didn't have to be. Your beauty needs no bearing of witness for me to know the spell you wove." He angled his head so his mouth brushed her ear. "If I'm not careful, your magical feet will carry me right out of here."

His soft breath feathered along her ear and down her neck, encouraging her to brush her cheek against his, but it was his voice, low and raw, that spiraled through her insides until she hummed with every word.

The music bounced in the background as other dancers blurred around them. Her hand tightened on Wynn's shoulder. "Carry you to where?"

"Let's find out."

He whirled her off the dance floor. Holding hands, they slipped between guests, who cast curious looks after them. Svetlana kept her expression serenely neutral despite the urge in her feet to take flight, to leave behind these people tethered to the earth and dance among the stardust with Wynn.

"Wynn. There you are." Constance's voice snagged them as they turned from the Stone Hall. Dressed in an ethereal half-mourning gown of mauve chiffon, she glided from the library with a rotund man on her gloved arm. "This is Mr. Dixon. He's on the administrative board at Edinburgh Hospital and heard a great many things about you while serving in the African campaign during the war. Mr. Dixon, allow me to present my son and his wife, the Duke and Duchess of Kilbride."

"My dear Duke and Duchess. An honor." Voice booming as if he were still in the war and trying to overcome gunfire, Mr. Dixon swept a low bow, or as low as he could, considering his protruding belly. With round, red cheeks and whiskers sweeping down his jaw, he resembled a Dickens character. "Fought in the war, did you?"

Svetlana tried to tug her hand back and stand in a more proper position, but Wynn held tight. "No, sir. I served as a noncombatant doctor in Paris. My brother, Hugh, fought."

"Ah, yes. I recall reading about him in the paper. Wretched shame that. Too many fine losses. My condolences."

Wynn's mouth pressed tight for a second, a telltale of the sadness prickling him. "Thank you."

Mr. Dixon sipped his port and waited a polite beat of silence. "Would have liked to have been in Paris myself, but the army sent me where they needed me. Hot, dry, and unintelligible languages thrown at me from all sides. Last time I put on an army uniform." He laughed, straining the buttons down his waistcoat. It was a wonder he'd been able to don the uniform to begin with. "Then again, we medical men go where care is needed most. Am I right, Your Grace?"

"You certainly are."

"While I was down there sweating my—" Mr. Dixon coughed at Constance's raised eyebrow. "Well, being uncomfortably hot, I read about the surgery you performed on that lieutenant. Harper, was it?"

Wynn's hand clenched. "Harkin."

"Harkin, yes. What a revelation. A breakthrough that you credited in your write-up to having first been performed during the Battle of Cambrai. Do you realize what this means for the future of medicine? Components we long considered a mystery to science are finally being explored with the importance they deserve. You, my dear boy, are the tip of the spear."

Dropping Svetlana's hand, Wynn crossed his arms. An invisible shield lodged into place. "Aye, well, I can only hope that the field of cardiology pushes onward as misconceptions are broken."

"It will! It most certainly will. What with men like you driving the charge. Those stodgy old dust bins have had their time. We need fresh blood to take risks, to give patients a fighting chance. Edinburgh Hospital is poised to take its rightful place among the greatest in the country. We need a man of vision like you to push our skills to the edge of capability. What do you say? Come and work with us. Be our tip of the spear."

"I thank you for the compliment of asking me, but I must decline. Forgive me." Jaw clenched, Wynn pivoted on his heel and receded down the darkened hall.

Svetlana's heart ached after him, but she kept a polite smile on her face. "Mr. Dixon, you and your hospital do my husband a tremendous honor. Perhaps upon further reflection he will reconsider your offer. In the meantime, please enjoy yourself. We have a wonderful selection of delicacies and fine wines in the dining room, and don't forget to make your bids in the silent auction. There is a pair of Spanish crafted basket-hilted swords that may be of interest. Excuse me, please."

Leaving behind a puzzled Constance and Mr. Dixon, Svetlana swept down the corridor as apprehension hammered her heart. That wasn't Wynn back there. That was a stranger who had stood with wounded confidence instead of seizing an opportunity of passion presented to him on a golden platter.

She found him in the solarium. An addition made to Thornhill when Constance was first mistress, the octagonal space was fitted with glass walls stretching to a central high point. Cold starlight bathed the room blue while the scent of potted ferns spiced the air, her maidenhair prize among them. It had taken happily to its new home, spilling its bright green fronds over the pot rim and stretching its roots deep into the rich soil she'd layered around it. It would take time before it was fully grown, but with enough care and solace the plant would flourish.

Wynn stood against the far wall, his arm leaning against the glass as he stared into the darkness of the moor rolling behind the castle.

"I've made my decision." His breath fogged the glass.

It was foolhardy to ask him to reconsider. Once his mind was made up there was no changing its course. If nothing else, she'd learned that about him from the start. Of course, there was nothing stopping her from telling him what a fool he was for turning the offer down, but even that honesty died as she stepped farther into the room and noticed the downward slant of his shoulders. Shoulders that had always been carried erect and with purpose. It seemed he'd shrugged purpose off.

All her questions narrowed to one. "Why?"

"I'm not the man for the job."

"Clearly they believe you are."

"Then they're mistaken. There are plenty of other well-qualified surgeons who could take on the position."

"The hospital would have gone to them if that were true, but they came to you because you are the best. You do not fear what is right for your patients when your colleagues would leave them to the fickle hands of Fate and old medicine. As if castor oil did anyone any good."

His blunt fingertips tapped against the glass. "You must have missed the article in *Medical Now* about the ten benefits it provides."

"I doubt it can cure a bullet to the heart." She moved closer, the thin heels of her shoes ticking across the flagstone floor. "Why did you say no?"

"It's no longer my path."

"Surgery has always been your path."

His fingertips tapped harder. "And now being Duke of Kilbride is. You said it yourself."

"I said you cannot abandon one for the other. This has nothing to do with taking on a title. Something happened to you the day you discovered Harkin died. You shut yourself off, and now you are trying to force yourself into a mold that you would rather not be cast in."

He whirled around. The blue light slashed across his face, digging into the hollows and hardening the planes until they looked sharp enough to cut.

"But I don't have a choice, do I? This title is what I am now."

"It is not all you are. You are a surg—"

"It *is* all I am."

Anger crackled through her. She flattened her hand at her side to keep from slapping sense into him. "What has happened to you? What has caused you to turn your back on the very thing that gives you purpose beyond all else?"

"You couldn't possibly understand."

"Then tell me! Help me understand. Ever since we returned from Glasgow I feel as if I have been dancing a *pas de deux* with a shadow partner." As soon as the words tumbled from her mouth she realized the truth in them. She didn't want to stand solo any longer, posture erect and footsteps precise as audiences waited for her to tumble under the spotlight. She wanted this man to whirl her onto their own private stage.

"I don't know what a paw de doe is, but I've been right here all along."

"In body, perhaps. Every other part of you exists somewhere I cannot reach. As if no one can reach you. What troubles take you so far away?"

"My troubles are not worth burdening you."

"But I have been burdened, have I not? I simply do not know with what."

"What is it you wish to hear?" He paced away, slashing a hand through his combed hair. "That my brother's death has left a gaping hole in me? That I'm not the surgeon I once glorified myself to be? That any time I hold a scalpel there's fear of a Harkin repeat?"

"Your brother's death will stay with us always. There is nothing to be done but grieve and remember him. As for Harkin, what happened was not your fault."

"He was my patient! Everything that happened to him was a result of me."

"This God-like complex does not serve you well. Have you stopped to consider that the operation went perfectly and an unrelated event caused his ultimate demise? If you think everything ties back to you, you're more egotistical than I originally credited you with."

She'd never witnessed this side of him, and while it terrified her, she saw the pain of an infested wound oozing from him. One he seemed unable to patch himself, and that difficulty most likely hurt him all the more.

"A blow has been delivered, Wynn. Several. Reeling from the shock is to be expected, but you cannot stay that way forever. At some point you need to pick the pieces back up and move on, otherwise it is a life half lived."

The pleats of his kilt flared as he pivoted on his heel, dark shadows breaking the fall of blue moonlight. "And if this is the life I now choose?"

"I do not believe that. This is the life you're wallowing in. A pathetic submission that is below your standards. You try to hide your misery, but I see it in the cracks of your smile. The dullness in your eyes where fire once shone. Even your banter has fallen flat of late."

"No need to kick a man when he's down," he mumbled.

"I am not trying to kick you. I am trying to help you."

"By pointing out everything I'm doing wrong?"

"By pointing out that you do not need to hide. Not from me." She stepped in front of him. He flinched at her closeness but didn't move. She took that as encouragement. If the truth was coming out, it might as well be all of it. "When we first met, trust was a nonnegotiable after the things I had been through. I feared for my life every second, jumping at the slightest noises, waiting for the black gloves to seize me in my bed at night. Then I met you. Kind, considerate, and always trying to make me smile all the while I eyed you with suspicion. I fought against it, but you earned my trust, and now I can rest knowing I'm safe. Because of you, Wynn. Will you honor me now with your trust?"

Pain still trembled in his eyes, but his waves of anger stilled. His shoulders sagged as he looked to the floor. "I don't deserve you."

"I know, but here we are."

His gaze flickered up to catch her smile. He raised his hand and drew his thumb across her cheek and along her jaw. "I cannot stand to lose you, not now, but if you truly knew— If you truly knew, I fear you might think less of me. My pride as a man could not handle that, and with that confession you can see how fragile my ego is." He tried to laugh, but there was no humor to be found in the admission.

"What is pride between us as long as there is trust?" She touched his hand, holding it to her cheek. "I wish to know all of you, as you have seen me. Even the fearful parts."

He took a deep breath, summoning the words. "In Glasgow—"

"Pardon the intrusion, Your Graces, but the auction is about to begin." Glasby stood in the doorway, polished shoes reflecting the moonlight. He'd kept to his impeccable white tie and black tails instead of donning a kilt.

Wynn raked another impatient hand through his hair, standing it up like quills. "Stall them. Bring out more wine and whisky if you have to. I need a moment with my wife."

"I would, sir, but the duchess's mother has other ideas."

Dread flooded Svetlana, drowning all concern for what Wynn had been about to say. "What has she done?"

"It's more what she's threatening to do." Glasby's expression remained professionally bland. A credit in this unusual household. "Princess Ana wishes to make a speech. I believe she has sampled each of the bottles of scotch."

"We need to stop her before she finds a captive audience."

Wynn must have realized the state of his hair, for his hands flew to it, attempting to squash it back into a semblance of order. "How much damage can she do?"

"Do you remember that time you had to carry her from the carriage to the church in Paris? That was on one bottle of champagne."

"I see your point."

They hurried out of the solarium and into the Stone Hall where Svetlana's mother stood three steps up on the grand staircase flapping her arms as if to entice the drawing crowd closer. Having declared it unnecessary to mourn for a man she'd never met, she'd dressed in green silk with emerald accessories liberally borrowed from Svetlana's jewelry box. Jewelry Wynn had presented her with as duchess.

"Ladies and gentlemen, or in Russian we say *damy i gospoda*, welcome to Thorphill. Pardon, Thornhill. Home of the dukes of my son-in-law." Mama smiled with the generous cheer of spirits. "I hope you all have been having a splendid time—I know I have—but there is one question I have for all of you. Why must it rain here so much? In Russia I do not recall it raining nearly as much. What you lack in pleasant weather you more than make up for in drink." She tipped a crystal-cut tumbler to her red-painted lips.

Wynn covered the three steps in one long stride. "Thank you, Princess Ana. Always a delightful addition to any gathering."

Mama elbowed him. "I wasn't finished welcoming our guests."

Wynn ignored her. "If everyone would like to grab a final glass before we start the auction, now is the time to do so. Otherwise, please be patient while the tallies are made. Remember that all of your generous proceeds will go toward new construction on a training center for education and work experience for those most affected by the war's suffering."

Applause rounded the room, echoing off the smooth stones that amplified it to thunder. Svetlana eased a tremulous pent-up breath.

What a tremendous moment for their community, one she was so delighted to share with Wynn. A task they were taking on together. He may have deceived himself into thinking he was no longer vital to the medical world—a view she was determined to change—but in no way could he deny the good he was doing this night. May it prove to be the push he needed.

A disturbance rippled from the back of the crowd. A head bobbed closer and closer until the press of guests peeled back to reveal a ghost. Curly hair black as a Siberian night, trimmed mustache, tall and slim with long limbs accustomed to climbing in and out of carriages before palaces. Eyes so dark Svetlana could drown in them. And they were pinned directly on her.

"Sergey?" Mama called as if from a long distance away, barely registering as Svetlana fuzzily tried to piece together the apparition before her. It wasn't possible.

Sergey's ghost strode toward her. Svetlana didn't have time to speak before his arms were around her, dipping her backward, and his mouth devouring hers, proving he was very much alive.

She froze. This wasn't happening.

Righting her, Sergey pulled back and beamed a smile that outshone the moon.

"Hello, Svetka. I told you I would come, *lyubimaya*."

"My love." Disorientated, Svetlana shook her head as her gaze skittered around the hall in search of Wynn. Where was her unchanging mark as the night slanted sideways? Around her the crowd of guests murmured with what was surely to be tomorrow's gossip. How could she explain?

She frantically searched the crowd. At last her eyes slammed onto her husband standing rooted to the steps. She caught one glimpse of the horror paling his face before the crowd surrounded her and Sergey, swallowing them whole.

CHAPTER 23

The guests had dispersed home amid the last drops of wine and buzzing with gossip of the duchess and her unexpected paramour. Another revolution could have sprung and Svetlana would not have noticed as she sat on the settee in the library with her arms wrapped tightly around her middle. The room had been a sanctuary when she'd first arrived with its overstuffed pillows and pages to pour through that recounted exploits of her new home, but she saw none of it now. Not even the blazing fire could stave off her chills, which had little to do with the formidable Scottish weather.

For his part Sergey appeared not the least concerned with the spectacle and ensuing fallout it caused as he recounted his tale.

"The Bolsheviks dragged me to one of the many buildings they had commandeered and threw me into the basement with the other loyalists they'd managed to capture that night you escaped." He paced slowly in front of the large fireplace, the flames burning bright orange behind him to elongate his already lanky shadow. "When they weren't interrogating me, I was beaten and starved. Brutal tactics by beasts."

Sitting in a chair opposite Svetlana, Mama dabbed a lace hankie to her eyes. "What information could they possibly hope to gain from a gentleman?"

"I'm a known loyalist to the tsar, as is my family, Princess. It was not always information they were after. More often it was punishment for my allegiances."

A tear slipped down Mama's cheek. "Where is your family now? I cannot imagine your gentle mother and sister enduring such horror."

Sergey dropped his eyes as if the agony could not allow him to look at another human being. "I do not know their fate, but I pray they are alive and well. I am only glad my father did not live long enough to see this. The Reds would have made an example of him."

"As they did to you instead."

"For months it was the same. Yelling, beatings, scraps of food to fight over. So many died. Then one night the guards came in taunting us and firing their pistols into the ceiling. They were celebrating the news of the imperial family's execution. To add to their merrymaking they decided to kill us, too, so we could continue to serve their highnesses in the great beyond."

Sergey paused and gripped the mantel. A knot bobbed in his throat. "They marched us to the edge of the city and forced us to dig our own graves before they shot us. I was hit in the arm and fell into the pit. They forced the village peasants to cover us with dirt, but one of them saw I was alive and saved me."

"Oh, my poor brave boy."

"Eventually I made it out of Russia and to Paris. I looked everywhere for you. Asked everyone I encountered."

Mama sniffed. "Svetlana kept us hidden. She didn't trust anyone to know who we were."

"It was safer that way, Mama," Marina said from her chair.

"Then on Armistice Day, I found you." Sergey looked to Svetlana. Anguish rippled across his face. "It was a moment, but I saw you. Standing at the window with your hair shining silver in the morning light. I tried to get to you, but the crowd pushed me on. By the time I managed to break free I was blocks away."

With a cry Mama lurched to the edge of her chair and stared accusingly at Svetlana. "Why did you not tell me you'd seen Sergey? How could you keep it to yourself?"

Having sat silent since they entered the library as the initial shock settled into acceptance that this was indeed happening and Sergey was standing before them, Svetlana roused herself to respond.

"At the time I didn't know for certain. I rushed out the door to find you, but then the letter came informing us about Hugh." She pushed away the memory of that awful telegram. "I thought if it had been you, you would return."

Sergey nodded sympathetically. "I mapped my way back somehow, only to find two shadows stalking me."

Marina gasped. "The Reds?"

"Whoever it was, I didn't feel safe leading them straight to you, so I left and laid low for a time. When I finally returned to the address it was locked up tight. The neighbors said you'd sailed to Britain."

"Where you've finally found us. As you promised." Mama's tearful voice cracked as if she were apologizing for their absence, as if their safety had been a secondary inconvenience.

"I would never break my promise to you." Sergey's eyes combed over Svetlana as if fitting the puzzle of her to the memory he'd held when they last parted.

She couldn't help doing the same. He was leaner than before, like a reed shaved down to its sparest form. The hair and mouth and mannerisms were the same, but there was an edge to him now. The easygoing manner so finely tuned to parties and afternoons riding in *drozhkies* had coiled into a bound energy that vibrated just below the skin. Yet when she looked into his dark eyes, she saw the same young man who had come to play cards with her on Sunday afternoons, who had taken her ice skating when the freeze set in, and whom she might have married. But the revolution had changed things, had changed them. Could he see the differences in her as well?

Differences or not, it was a wonderful miracle to see him again. Alive and safe. A piece of her life returned.

"I can't believe you're really standing here."

Sergey knelt in front of her and held her hands between his. "Believe it, *kroshka*. I told you I would find you and I have. The thought of returning to your side was all that kept me alive since we parted over a year ago." His eyes glistened with fervor as he pressed his lips to her fingertips.

The library door slammed shut, startling them. Wynn stood there, his face held in shadow as the firelight dared not touch that far across the room.

"The guest chamber is being prepared."

Svetlana withdrew her hands from Sergey's and tucked them in her lap. First that kiss and now this. She'd done nothing to contribute to either, but shame filled her nonetheless.

Ever the courtly gentleman, Sergey rose and smoothed the front of his worn black jacket.

"Thank you. My sincerest apologies for placing a burden on you with no advance warning."

"No trouble at all." Wynn strolled to stand near the end of the settee. His expression freed itself from the darkened shadows, but what was revealed was nothing resembling lightness.

Svetlana dug her nails into her palms to keep from twisting the silk fabric of her skirt. The charity event had been a great success, but this night was going down as the most chaotic she'd ever experienced.

"Of course it's no trouble when Sergey is a dear old friend of our family." Mama beamed as if Sergey had hung the sun and stars. A belief she'd always attributed to him despite having her own son to dote upon. Then again, Nikolai always had more heart than polish. "If not for him, we never could have escaped Petrograd. We owe him everything."

"As we do Wynn for all he's done. If I had a glass, I would toast you both." Svetlana smiled up at Wynn. "Sergey was telling us of his imprisonment and eventual escape from the Bolsheviks. It was him I saw that day in the crowd." Armistice Day. The day of worldwide rejoicing. The day their lives had changed forever when that telegram arrived announcing Hugh's death.

From the look on Wynn's face, he remembered it all too well.

Shifting his weight, he smoothed his expression to pleasant blandness once more.

"I'm amazed you were able to find the princesses in Paris. The war turned it from one of the most vibrant cities in the world to a pot of mass chaos."

"It wasn't easy, I grant you," Sergey said.

"How did you find us?" Svetlana asked.

"I knew you probably wouldn't be using your titles, so I made discreet inquiries that led me to the Russian part of Paris. Who knew such a thing existed? Seems I barely missed the influenza epidemic, which decimated our people, forced as they were to live like rats in basements."

"The entire world has been affected. They're saying the number of deceased victims may be greater than those lost during the war." Svetlana's throat constricted as she looked at Marina. "We had our own scare."

Sergey's hand flattened to his heart. "Dear sister. How glad I am that you survived. A true miracle."

"Another blessing Wynn gave us," Svetlana added.

Wynn's lips cracked into a soft smile. "It was the attention her doting nurse gave her that saved her life."

There it was again. That subtle look that passed between him and her like an exhale of breath. Soft, undetectable, yet laced with possibilities. What might have happened if they'd been able to continue their dance earlier? Would they finally have known what it was like to share a breath?

Sergey cleared his throat, drawing attention back to him, and resumed his recounting. "From a few of the survivors who remembered your descriptions, I was able to trace you to an Alexander Nevsky Cathedral where the priest said he'd married you in November. Imagine my surprise."

His lips pinched beneath his black mustache. Longing and sadness mingled in his eyes as they lingered on Svetlana, hundreds of hours of memories spent together lost in them.

"I would be a liar to say I was not shocked and saddened at the news that your precious hand had slipped from mine, much as it did that day on the train platform, but I forced myself to overcome my own feelings and rejoice that you were alive. That is all that truly matters to me."

The past held too many what-ifs and Sergey's sudden appearance brought them all rushing back to the surface. A future she had once been destined to. She could no longer afford to mourn. Life had moved on.

With this new life came suspicion of the old one trailing her. "Do you recall the names of the people you spoke to?"

"Peasants mostly. I didn't bother asking their names. Why do you ask?"

"I only wonder if it was some of the same people we lived with at the church." Or a crooked club owner who sheltered the evilness of communism to his own advantage. "We left rather in a hurry."

"So the priest informed me when he gave me your address."

Wynn stepped closer, the dancing flames shadowing havoc across his impassible expression.

"We didn't give the priest our address. Considering the name Dalsky is being hunted by the Bolsheviks, it was best to keep such information hidden."

Sergey dipped a finger behind the folds of his necktie to his scratch at his neck. "Pardon me for misspeaking. What I meant was, the priest told me you were a physician at the hospital, so naturally I went there. One of your colleagues was able to send me in the correct direction, but as I was telling the ladies, my timing proved to be a stroke of bad luck, and I was forced to continue my journey to Britain. Once here, there was little difficulty in finding the Duke of Kilbride's estate. I'm only sorry to have disturbed what appeared to be a remarkable evening."

He tried to cover his pain, but the half-hearted smile fluttering across his mouth wasn't an adequate mask. Guilt sliced through Svetlana. Once she might have shared a life with him. A marriage of companionship and understanding and comfort, which was more than most couples could expect. She might have tried for more, to love him, but she never would have fallen in love with him. Now friendship and refuge were all she could offer him. With Wynn, however, something wonderful stirred between them, something promising more than mere companionship.

"You must be exhausted from your journey," she said, her words falling flat against the startling surprise of his arrival. "We'll speak again tomorrow, but for now I'll have you shown to your room." She rose to ring the bell pull for Glasby, but Sergey waved her back down.

"I'm afraid there's one last thing I must impart. My heart dreads the telling, but if there is anyone who should tell you, I hope you find comfort that it is from an old friend." Eyeing them each in turn, he fidgeted with the buttons on his jacket. An unusual tic for one so confident as Sergey.

"On the night you escaped Petrograd, the White Army made a stand at Palace Square in front of the Winter Palace. The man I was imprisoned with was there when it happened. He told me what he saw. The soldiers fought bravely but were not enough against the Red Army. Those not killed in action were dragged to the river and executed. Colonel Dalsky and Nikolai among them."

Mama screamed and wilted into her chair. Marina sobbed. Svetlana sat unable to move as the blinding force of devastation sank through her like a stone. In her heart she'd known. She'd tried desperately to hold on to bits of hope despite reconciling herself to never seeing her beloved father and brother again this side of eternity. Yet to hear her deepest fear spoken aloud was enough to flay open her raw heart.

A tear slid down her cheek. Then another. She dashed them away and tucked in the lashed strips of her heart to tend at a later time when she could allow the sorrow to drown her. Rising, she crossed to her mother and slipped her arms around her.

Mama rocked away with a wail. "Dead! I always knew it. Gone forever."

"Mama, you must calm down."

"I will rage if I wish! Just because you do not have the heart to mourn for love doesn't mean I don't."

Svetlana bit back an angry retort as tears scalded her eyes. "Marina, help me get her to her chambers."

Tears streaming down her young face, Marina took hold of their mother's left arm while Svetlana took the right and together they hauled the sobbing woman from her chair.

Sergey hovered like a bird with wings unsure of its flight. "Can I do anything?"

Svetlana didn't answer. She didn't have the soundness of mind to think on what he could do. The edges of her mind blackened down to a single focal point of preservation. Get her mother upstairs, see to her family first, and then and only then could she crumble.

Turning she found Wynn standing next to her with arms open at his sides. As if he were waiting for her to find him. He took one look at her face and dropped his arms.

"Get her settled. I'll bring laudanum."

It was like wrestling a boneless cat up the stairs as it screeched and howled on each step. Once in her chamber, Mama flung herself onto the bed with a wail, clutching her cross necklace. Svetlana and Marina sat on either side of her, but their mother curled into a ball like a child and cried with great wracking sobs. They had to hold her down as Wynn administered the laudanum, Marina crying the entire time.

At last Mama's sobs quieted to a pitiful sleep as she still clutched her cross. Silvery tracks of tears shone down her face and blotched her silk bodice. Svetlana pulled a coverlet over her mother before turning to gather Marina into her arms. Her sister's fresh bout of tears soaked through the front of Svetlana's dress. Helpless, Svetlana held her tight and murmured nonsense words of comfort that fell coldly across her own embattled soul.

Pressing her cheek to the top of Marina's head, Svetlana found Wynn standing quietly at the foot of the bed. Solid, sure, unmoving. A tear trickled from her eye. Wynn moved toward her, his arms reaching out.

"Please don't," she whispered.

He stopped, expression pained, and dropped his arms for the second time that night when she needed him most. She couldn't allow him to touch her. If he did, she would give in to the overwhelming tumult of sadness and splinter apart. She had no doubt his arms were strong enough to catch all of her dissolving pieces, but not now. For a short time longer, her pieces must remain intact to comfort what remained of her family.

He left, quietly shutting the door behind him. Svetlana hugged her sister tighter, and as Wynn's footsteps faded away, a piece of her heart broke away and shattered.

Snow fell heavy from the sky, blotting out the weakened rays of sun creeping over the distant horizon. The white drifts thickened around the castle walls to muffle the early morning floor creaks and crackles of glass frosting over. Wynn stood outside Svetlana's chamber with every thought centered on the woman within. His hand raised to knock.

"Please don't," she'd said.

His hand flattened soundlessly against the cold wood. She'd stood there with the fire behind her burning around her edges and her face cold as marble, a juxtaposition of raging pain and cool control as she upheld her loved ones drowning in grief. The pain of losing his own brother had ripped through him afresh. Would their family never be able to enjoy peace?

He wanted so badly to gather her into his arms and carry her sadness. To run his hand over her smooth hair and whisper that he had her. She'd ordered him to stay put, but he saw the forbidding plea for what it was. A shield on which she carried others to safety before allowing the tending of her own wounds. He saw the cuts on her heart and the sorrow wailing in her soul. When the time came, he would bind her back together.

He knocked softly on the door. When no answer came, he pushed carefully into her chamber so as not to disturb her if she'd returned and managed to fall asleep while he'd been downstairs in his study. The room was dark and cold, and the bed empty. She most likely remained at her mother's bedside in the east wing of the castle. The opposite wing of the master and mistress chambers, and a wholly separate floor from the bachelor quarters, where he'd sequestered that Russian ex-lover, or childhood friend, or whoever he was supposed to be.

Wynn moved to the window and braced his hands on either side of the cold panes. The temperature bit into his palms and drew out bits of heated anger. The fact was Sergey had a past with Svetlana that at one time may have become a future together, but as far as Wynn could tell the man held no sway over her heart aside from what existed as fond memories. It mattered not how many times Ana cooed over the man or how many references to their Russian life were made, Svetlana was Wynn's wife now. Nothing could change that. Not even when that greasy mustached weasel kissed her standing in the middle of their home in front of all their guests, claiming her as a husband would. Claiming her in a way Wynn had not yet been able to do.

Then again, could Wynn blame him? There had been an under-standing between Sergey and Svetlana for years. The man had escaped death only to discover his good-as-fiancée had wed another man. But to tackle her and force his lips upon hers like that . . . It had taken every ounce of Wynn's restraint to keep from knocking the ill-wanted Russian's block off. Wynn was not a man often given to jealousies, as they were the result of flagging confidence and weak minds, but he couldn't deny the shaking of his own confidence. What if having Sergey returned to her made Svetlana regret her hasty marriage to Wynn? What if the man's reappearance ignited romantic feelings long repressed?

Shoving off the window, Wynn crossed through their joined sitting room and into his chamber. A small fire had been lit, its orange glow of heat extending a small radius before chilling at the night's blue touch pooling through the window. Why had the drapes not been drawn?

Crossing the floor, he stopped in the center of the room at the sight of the figure on his bed. Curled on her side, Svetlana still wore her gown from the previous evening, but the pins in her hair had been removed and the strands tumbled like ribbons of silver across his pillow. He moved quietly to the side of the bed, careful not to wake her. At his approach her eyes fluttered up to meet his and he saw that she hadn't been asleep at all. Tears rolled down her cheeks and splotched the pillow. A quiet sob trembled between her lips and fair to broke his heart. He was on the bed in an instant, pulling her into his arms.

"Lana, my darling. I'm here."

She clung to him, face buried into his chest and fingers twisting at his shirtfront as she cried out the pieces of her cloven heart. Wynn gently stroked her hair, murmuring inane comforts as he willed the ability to absorb her pain into himself. But that ability was beyond his limits. All he could offer was holding her tight to catch the falling pieces until her body depleted itself of sorrow and she lay limp and heavy in his arms.

"There now, my heart. I'm here."

CHAPTER 24

What comforts Thornhill had offered now stood listless among the grief, like a bright burning lamp that once cast its glow on all who drew near but whose light had shivered into shadow, its purpose extinguished. Svetlana wandered the halls, her black shawl pulled tightly against the cold air knocking on the windows as her heels echoed in lonely staccato against the stone.

Four days. That was how long it had been since her hope and prayers had died. Papa and Nicky were never coming back. They had died for the Russia they loved, their strong presence no longer felt this side of eternity. She had lived with the possibility for well over a year now, a period in which a hundred lifetimes had passed, time enough for the eventuality to plow a dull rut through her heart with a hurt so wide that only numbness could ease it. Was detachment preferable to the sharp sting that felled Mama? Or the quiet sadness yet brave smile of Marina? Grief struck with oddity. Svetlana's one consolation was that Papa and Nicky were killed swiftly and not destined to languish in a prison cell, subject to torture and prolonged deaths drawn out by the minute. They had died honorably as soldiers, befitting who they were.

Feet given no direction, she drifted to the solarium. It glittered like a winter palace under the falling snow with thousands of ice crystals dancing across the glass panes and white drifts crowding the window corners. The heart of winter had always been her favorite time of year. With its cleansing beauty of white blanketing the bareness left in autumn's wake, its crispness snapping the air, and its ribbon of rainbow of light shining across the northern night sky, winter seeped into her bones with a vitality held dormant in warmer seasons. Others decried the coldness as a plague to be endured, but where they saw brittleness, she saw beauty. Where they turned from the harshness, she fell into the seductive hold. Winter was an exquisite lady, bedecked in her elegant ice and dripping icicles. She was carved with an artist's hand, fragile yet strong. Delicate yet deadly.

Or at least that was the memory Svetlana held of winter. Today she felt none of that. She wandered around the solarium, a few dried leaves from the potted plants crunching under her feet. Their crushed earthiness drifted up like a lingering perfume from autumn's glory. Having taken fully to its new home with delight, her fern's tendrils cascaded down the sides of its pot like a frothy waterfall. The plant had nearly doubled its size since the night of the charity bazaar.

A lifetime ago, when the world held promise of safety and she had encouraged the possibility of a marriage in more than name. They would have kissed that night. She knew by the intuition women were born with when it came to a man desiring them. More than that, she desired him as well. Then everything had gone topsy-turvy.

She poked a finger into her fern's dirt. Still moist. It had been hesitant to grow for her at first, even drooping in despair once she planted it in the new pot. She'd fallen into a mild panic at the thought of killing it but quickly learned that all living things hurt when they're uprooted. Only once they are made to feel safe and cared for do they allow themselves to thrive. The double realization had not gone unnoticed with the changes in her own life. In Scotland her seized roots had unfurled into a richness she never could have expected. All because Wynn gave her the freedom to do so.

She longed for the hours to tick by so she could once again sit with him before the fire in their shared sitting room. It had become their ritual these past few nights since she'd cried in his arms. By day he administered laudanum to Mama, ensured plenty of hot tea was brought up to Marina, and apologized profusely for it not being brewed in a samovar. Svetlana divided her time between the two in an effort to rally their spirits while also trying not to suffocate under Sergey's hovering. He was trying to be of help, and she couldn't bring herself to tell him he was smothering her. At night when the house finally settled, she and Wynn would find one another and silently settle into the unspoken need to be together before the comforts of the fire.

The night before he had broken their silence by asking if she needed anything. What could she say? *Yes, I need you to take me away, far from this pain to a place I can no longer think beyond the length of your arms?* The words failed to come just as they had the night she'd wept against him, and so she simply laid her head on his shoulder in answer of a silent dance they were making all their own after being off step for so long.

A tiny splotch of darkness lifted from the corner of her heart. Yes, all their own.

A masculine tread announced itself in the room. Wynn. Svetlana dashed the tear from her cheek.

"Oh, Wynn. I'm so glad you're—" She turned around and stopped. "Sergey."

Resplendent in a black jacket and trousers with a gray silk waist-coat, he cut a fine figure for one who had donned a mourning armband. He'd always been handsome in a sleek manner, sleek in every way save his curling black hair, which often drew many female looks of envy. His months on the run had cut away the softness from his aristocratic lifestyle to showcase the immaculate bone structure beneath. Striking to gaze upon, but not the face she longed to see.

"Here you are, *lyubimaya*." Those striking bones softened with compassion. Sergey came to her with arms wide and pulled her against him. "This week has been terrible for you. For all of you. I'm sorry I was the one to bring you such pain, but please allow me to overcome this and bring you comfort." Speaking in their customary French with the Russian endearment crooned in, he gently pressed her head to his shoulder. He still smelled of expensive spice and cedarwood, the notes stirring up memories of a ballroom waltz and the first time he offered her his arm for a stroll in Alexander Garden.

Svetlana gently pulled away. Those memories, while sweet to dwell upon, belonged in the past. "Seeing you again, dear friend, is great comfort indeed."

Mustache twitching, his dark eyes swam with emotion. "'Dear friend.' How I used to delight when you called me that. Now I hear a distance in the phrase I once treasured."

"I hope you treasure our friendship still."

"I treasure any relationship I may have with you, Svetka."

Stepping back to put distance between herself and the sentiments of memory his eyes tried to pull from her, she wriggled her fingers between the fern fronds and plucked out the dead leaves near the stem's base.

"My apologies as hostess for not seeing to your needs these past few days. I trust you have been well cared for."

"Do not think one minute for me. Your absence has been well justified and your staff more than gracious to my intrusion. Even the master of the house has offered me the hospitality of your stables should I fancy a ride during my stay."

"You've spoken to Wynn?" Had they discussed Sergey's embracing kiss in the front hall for all their gathered guests to witness? Or was everyone playing ignorant and forgetful about it? At least Sergey didn't sport a black eye.

"Briefly. He was on his way to repair a peasant's roof that had collapsed. Do you not have estate managers to see to such menial tasks? Most other days the duke has spent in his study, though in truth I do not mind the solitude after my harrowing travels."

The images of a burning city and fleeing through dark woods scrolled through Svetlana's mind. She could feel the heat burning overhead and the scratch of tree branches on her cheek. She sank onto a wooden bench with Celtic knots carved into the back.

"The horrors you've been through. What you did to save our lives. We will forever be in your debt of selflessness."

He slid onto the bench next to her, gliding his arm along the back rest. "My deep affection for you and your family could allow me no less. I would change nothing to ensure your safety. The Bolsheviks are from the very pits of the devil himself, but no amount of their inflicted pain compares to what I would have felt if you had been captured. They have razed our beloved Russia to the ground."

Svetlana shivered and pulled her shawl tighter about her shoulders. "Is there no hope of ever returning?"

He shook his head. A black curl slipped over his forehead. "It is our home no longer. The Reds have turned it against us into something sinister. Something unrecognizable." He pushed the errant curl back into place with a smooth hand. "Would you ever consider going back? If the country were to be returned to its former sanity, that is."

"I should very much like to see Russia again. I miss the comforts of familiarity there and the white summer nights. There is nothing in all the world like her, but life has moved on without my permission. Decisions had to be made, and I cannot allow myself the remorse of looking back. My home is here now with a life I'm looking forward to with Wynn."

His black eyebrows spiked. "In this barbaric country? It does not suit the entitlements of a princess." He gestured sharply to the land beyond the frosted windows as if to point out the error in her assessment before frowning at the dead leaves curled in her palm. "Neither do dirty hands."

She tried not to allow his words to bristle her. Things were different now. She was different. No longer did she live in Petrograd with its confining rules.

"Dirty hands suit me in Scotland. The land is none so harsh after a time. I've learned to find a beauty in its wildness." She looked through the window to the rolling hills beyond. Come summer they would be covered in purple heather. Wynn claimed they could stroll across the tops, so thick was it. "The Revolution taught me much, and I will not take for granted my position again. If I can use it toward good, I will."

"You did good in St. Peters—gah, Petrograd. Will we ever grow accustomed to that new name? I heard talk of the Bolsheviks wanting to change it again to honor their leader, Lenin."

"The only good I did was self-serving or what reflected well in the social parlors so the Dalsky name glittered even brighter. What good did that do when the Revolution struck? It made me an outcast, a thing to be hated, starved, and flung out into the cold. I will never be that again, nor allow anyone in my care to be so."

On the back of the bench behind her, Sergey's fingers tapped an erratic rhythm as if his thoughts proved too restless for containment.

"That is a peasant's way of thinking. Share in the misery and all that. One must look out for themselves."

"A decent person does not look out only for themselves."

His fingers stopped as he considered her for a long moment.

"It seems the Revolution has changed us both. Me to hardness and you to tenderness. I think, perhaps, you are the victor in this metamorphosis, and I should heed your lead. I am your humble student, my lady." He placed a hand over his heart and bowed his head in courtly manner.

A half smile curled the edge of Svetlana's mouth. His gesture erased the years of terror, and they were once more sitting in her family's parlor at the Blue Palace jesting without a care. She'd missed his familiar friendship, a link stabilizing her through time when so much had been stripped away.

As he straightened, the light caught on a thistle stickpin with an amethyst for the purple flower nestled into the folds of his necktie.

"This is unusual for you to wear," she said. "The symbol of Scotland."

"Your mother-in-law was kind enough to offer me suitable clothes for my stay."

Consumed by her own sadness and keeping Mama from hysterics, she had barely given thought to others in need.

"I apologize for not thinking to offer them myself. I have been remiss in my duties as hostess and as your friend."

"Nonsense. Your grief is priority, and your mother-in-law has been most gracious. These belonged to a son named Hugh, I believe. She said he needed them no longer."

The dead leaves rested lightly in her palm, their musty scent of decay a pungent reminder of fallen life.

"He died in November. The war. He was Duke of Kilbride, but his death passed the title to Wynn, and now Wynn has a hole in his heart that can never be repaired."

"Then you have both lost someone dear to you. Would that I could give Nicky back to you. I shall take the greatest care of this for your husband in honor of his brother." Looking down, he fiddled with the folds of his necktie. The amethyst winked in and out of the silky material. "I cannot deny that such a piece would have proven beneficial on my travels."

Svetlana thought back to those nights racing through the woods, her corset weighted with valuables she had sewn in for safekeeping.

"We had to sell so many of our precious gems along the way for food and clothing. What we had left was stolen in Paris." She cast an eye over his fine clothes. At complete odds to the rags he had arrived in. "How ever did you afford passage from Paris?"

Eyes kept on the stickpin, he twisted it back and forth. "I managed a few odd jobs before I saved enough to buy a steerage ticket. The poor souls in the Russian quarters of the city were more than happy to help their fellow countryman in his time of need."

Strange. The doors of Paris had slammed shut on her in her hour of need—both French and Russian. Only one dared to crack open with exception and show her kindness. And a second with a man who loved nothing more than to take advantage of her kind.

She crushed one of the dead leaves in her palm. The brittle pieces crunched under her thumb. "Did you ever come across a Sheremetev?"

Sergey's fingers stilled for the briefest of moments. "As in the Muscovy Sheremetevs? Who ruled half the shipping and trading on the Black Sea before the Revolution? I don't believe so. Why do you ask?"

"The man who rules Little Neva—the Russian neighborhood in Paris. His presence was everywhere, particularly at a club called the White Bear."

"I kept my profile low and away from places like that. Any inquiries I made were with discretion and never with names."

"One of Sheremetev's greatest abilities is using discretion to his purposes." She watched for any flicker of recognition on his face. And why should there be? This was one of her oldest friends in the world who had sacrificed himself for her well-being. She had no reason to believe he would lie to her. Had the Revolution and scraping by to survive turned her so cynical? It had turned her desperate and look where that got her. Straight under the thumb of the vilest man on earth. She glanced down at the band of gold wrapped around her finger and covered it with her other hand, safe and protected. Without it she would still be under that hideously fat thumb. "Wynn tried to warn me."

Abruptly, Sergey stood and paced away. "The duke proves himself invaluable on more than one occasion. How fortunate for you to find such a man." Though he pulled his lips into a smile, it didn't mask his clipped words.

A mingling of sadness and guilt weighed on her heart. "I know my marriage was a shock to you. It was to me as well, but times were desperate. I'm sorry for any heartache I may have caused you."

"We were never formally engaged, it's true, but I felt as if there was an understanding between us. As a gentleman I cannot hold you accountable for my fault in not proposing when I had the chance. Are you happy with your choice?"

"Wynn is a good man. He's kind, and generous, and brilliant."

"You avoid my question. I asked if you are happy."

She'd once told Wynn happiness was a foreign illusion to Russians. Their national inclination was given to sadness and stoic reality. He'd laughed. Of course he had. It made her see the lightness missing from her life. A lightness that had stolen into her to make her realize she didn't miss the stoicism quite as much as she thought she would.

"Despite the hardships and sorrows, yes, I've found happiness."

"Do you love him?"

"Sergey! That is not an appropriate question to demand of a lady."

He fell to his knees in front of her, knocking the dead leaves from her hands and scattering them about the floor. She moved to clean them up, but he blocked her.

"Leave those for the servants to clean. As you did in the Blue Palace. I fear your time here has altered you."

"If by altered you mean I take more responsibility, then yes. And that starts by not creating messes for others to clean."

Still, he did not move. "I apologize. My feelings have led carelessness to overtake me." Anguish roamed in his dark eyes. "I ask this as a friend. As a man you once cared for. Has your love slipped from me to another?"

Apart from the wild impertinence of the question, Svetlana couldn't bring herself to tell him no, she'd never loved him. In her own way, perhaps, knowing that most marriages started without the sentiment but with hope of growing into love, but that deep, head-over-heels thrill of exhilaration had never consumed her when it came to Sergey.

"I did have affection for you, Sergey, that I can never deny—"

"Then don't!"

"But it is a feeling that belongs in the past. Wynn has become my future."

"Your future was planned with me. There's still time to make it so." He grabbed her hand, cradling it between his own. His fingers were long and cool, matching the iciness of hers. Unlike Wynn's warm ones, which could immediately draw the coldness from her.

"Come away with me. Now. To a place where no one can find us."

She withdrew her hand from Sergey's. "I am Wynn's wife. I pledged my loyalty to him."

"But you didn't want to." Sergey's eyes flickered over her shoulder, then back to her as he leaned closer. "We're destined to be together."

Svetlana opened her mouth, but promptly closed it. She didn't need to explain herself nor defend her decisions. She regretted the forced haste of her union, but not once had she had cause to regret marrying Wynn.

"Apologies for the interruption." Wynn spoke from the open doorway behind them. Svetlana spun around and spied a telegram in his hand and a cool expression icing his face. "I'm off to London for a few days."

The telegram. Svetlana shot to her feet, brushing Sergey out of the way. "What's happened?"

"I've been called to speak before the medical board." His gaze flickered to Sergey, then back to her. "If you'll excuse me, I need to pack to catch the two o'clock train." He turned and left.

Svetlana hurried down the corridor after him. Despite her long legs, her pace was no equal to his.

"Has it do with Harkin?"

"Most likely."

"But you've given your statement." Her words hit his retreating back.

"They want it again."

"Has something in the report changed that they need you to

292

verify? Why so many inquiries over a single death when your profession deals in tragedy every day?" She had not been privileged to see the business side of medicine for long, but what she had glimpsed consisted of mounds of paperwork, hidebound old men, and red tape. So many rules on how and when to save a life. If a life was lost due to a broken rule, the fury of repercussions would be great indeed. And if that life had been unnecessarily put at risk— "Do they suspect he was killed?"

"There's been no mention of foul play."

"Then I am coming with you."

That stopped him. He turned around to face her. "No, there's no need. I'll be back in a few days. Besides, your mother needs you."

"So do you." She swallowed against a charge of emotion. She needed him to know that *he* was her choice despite events threatening to persuade him otherwise. "It meant nothing. When Sergey kissed me. Nothing has been reciprocated on my part."

The coolness melted from his eyes and pooled to soft green. He trailed his fingertips along her jaw like a sculptor admiring his creation. Svetlana leaned in to his touch, marveling at his ability to center her as the one woman in his world.

"You're so beautiful. Have I ever told you that? Looking at you, I lose my bearings between heaven and earth." His husky voice ached with desire. Svetlana laid a trembling hand over his heart to show him she felt the same, but the movement shifted something in his eyes. The molten gold cooled and his touch dropped from her face. "Even if the moment is a fleeting indulgence."

He was retreating from her again. Pulling into himself while keeping her at arms' length. Too much separation and they might never find a way back together.

"Please allow me to come with you to London."

His gaze swept over her face as she saw his mind whirling with conflict. *Yes* formed on his lips, but at the last he shook his head. "I need you to stay here. When I get back, I'll explain everything. I promise."

Unease sprang to her heart. "Explain what?"

"Will you trust that I have only your best intentions in mind?"

"I trust you completely. As I hope you do me."

In answer he leaned down and brushed his cheek against hers before pressing a kiss to her skin. He lingered for the briefest moment before walking away. Svetlana cupped her hand over her cheek, longing to hold a part of him close since she could not hold the man himself. Steps apart again.

If she wished to close the distance, she would have to take matters into her own hands. That started with getting to the bottom of the medical board and their continued harassment of her husband. To do that, one needed to know the right people, and as before in Russia, she had begun to cultivate her own notable list in her new country. Striding with purpose to the library, she sat at her writing desk and pulled out a crisp slip of cream paper with the Duchess of Kilbride seal embossed in gold at the top. She may not be able to solve the torment in her husband's mind, but she could try to bring peace. She dipped her nib in the ink and set it to paper.

Dear Mrs. Roscoe,

I deeply appreciate the rose bulbs you included in your last package. They shall make a splendid addition to my garden come spring, and I hope you will accept my invitation to see them in full bloom on an extended stay at Thornhill.

If I may be so bold, I wish to shorten my pleasantries in order to bring a matter of great importance to your knowledge and perhaps request a favor of the most generous kind. I understand that your husband has recently taken the position of hospital administrator at St. Matthew's in London . . .

CHAPTER 25

R ain slashed down the windows of the Royal Medical Academy in east London. It turned the mounds of snow into gray slush that clogged the footpaths and splattered the buildings with icy sludge from each passing motor car. Situated on the corner of some highbrow street crossed with a priggish lane, the RMA had towered as a goliath in all its white limestone and colonnade glory since 1684, presiding over the health and advancement of medicine for mankind. More correctly, advancing the field when the governing old whitebeards deemed such advancements worthy of the cut. Everything not worthy was immediately thrown out like yesterday's chips or newspaper.

Which was precisely how Wynn found himself sitting on a bench outside the delegation hall staring at his bullet-punched kopek. For nearly five days he'd sat in that tomb of a chamber under the grilling eyes of the medical board directors and answered question after question about his education, training, experience during the war, political leanings, religious beliefs, readings, and everything else they could think of to suss out whether he was of sound mind to perform surgery.

The implication of such a finding should have been the single point to occupy his mind, but it wasn't. His thoughts remained fixated on Thornhill, or rather within Thornhill. The instant that telegram arrived to summon him to London, he'd gone in search of Svetlana.

And found that weasel kneeling at her feet. The same weasel who had barged into their home, wrapped his arms around Wynn's wife, and kissed her for all the county to witness. She'd said it meant nothing to her, but that didn't stop Wynn from wanting to beat the miscreant black and blue.

Guilt hit Wynn hard and quick like a punch to the rectus abdominis. Was he wrong to have married her when she waited for Sergey? A man she'd known for years, another Russian? Wynn braced his arms on his knees and hung his head. If given the option, would she wish to free herself of the marital contract and leave with Sergey? She had grounds to obtain an annulment. Wynn squeezed his hands together as his fingertips turned cold. Could he let her go when she'd come to mean so much to him?

"Not going to be sick, are you?" Gerard. His old friend had finally returned from war-torn Paris only to find a summons waiting for him to give a report on one Dr. Edwynn MacCallan, with whom he assisted in surgery that fateful day last summer. After giving his testimony of the events, Gerard had sat in the upper galleys as Wynn's moral support.

"No."

"Thinking about what's going on behind those doors?"

"No."

"Then why do you look like you've diagnosed your dog with one week to live?"

Wynn heaved a sigh and pocketed the coin. "I'm in love with my wife."

"Oh. Hard time that."

Wynn lifted his head and stared at his friend. "How would you know?"

"I've got brothers, haven't I? They're always going on about the misery of the old ball and chain, then follow it up with adamant declarations of love. Which is then followed up with a pint." Gerard plopped on the bench and scratched a freckled hand through his ginger thatch of hair. "Do you need a pint?"

"No."

"You might after today."

Wynn jerked upright, every nerve on edge. "Why? Have they said something?"

"No. At least not while I was in there. Bickering back and forth. It's enough to make a man's head explode." Gerard's thin shoulders sagged as he rolled his homburg hat between his hands. "The truth is, mate, they don't know what to do with you. Half the room is for tossing you in the tower, and the other wants to reinstate you with a formal apology by saying death is a part of our practice and you've always been a man to uphold your oath to do no harm."

"And if my arrogance overtook my oath on that operating table? Would Harkin be here with us? You always told me it would get me in trouble one day."

"I also said you were bloody brilliant."

Wynn snorted. "Aye, bloody brilliant at disgracing myself."

"Aha! That right there is where a pint will help. After a few you won't feel disgraced anymore. You won't feel anything anymore."

"I'm not a drinker. You know that."

"And you know I am. Come on. You can keep me from falling off my barstool while telling me all about your blue devils. As a physician I'm obligated to keep confidential whatever a patient tells me."

Gerard stood and slipped on his overcoat, then donned a hat that slid down over his ears. He never could find a fit to complement his scrawniness. "Come on, Your Grace. Those old toads dismissed you for the day. Sitting out here punishing yourself won't do a bit of good."

Did he truly want the best for his patients, or was he in it for the glory? The question burned on Wynn's tongue. He'd been too afraid to ask it, but his pride was trampled by the misery of needing to know. The walls of the ivory tower he had built of his medical achievements began to quake. "Do you think I caused Harkin's death?"

"I think we do the best we can as physicians. The rest is in the Almighty's hands. And Him you are not."

"They've taken everything from me. If I can't be a surgeon, what am I?" How pathetic he sounded. A more degrading state than having his license revoked, and one he'd never suffered before. It left him disoriented like a body of tissues and organs with no bone structure to keep him upright.

Gerard set his hand on Wynn's shoulder, drawing Wynn's gaze up. There was no derision in his friend's face, but empathy as only another physician could understand.

"You'll be my good friend Wynn MacCallan, duke of the northern Pict lands, champion of the weak, and fighter for extraordinary causes. Fighters don't sit around feeling sorry for themselves. So get up and squire me to the pub."

The rain had turned to a more Londonesque drizzle by the time they traversed the hall of mazes in the RMA and stepped out onto the street. A few brave souls hurried by, tucked under the safety of their brollies, while black taxis idled on the street corner in hopes of a fare.

Gerard started toward one of the taxis. "I know a good place in Mayfair—"

"Somewhere closer." Wynn flipped up the collar of his coat. "I need to walk."

"In that case, the Unholy Friar's it is." Gerard waved off the eager driver who scowled at Wynn. Whipping out a black brollie, Gerard plunked it over his head and followed Wynn. "Why must you Scots always insist on walking in the rain?"

"Clears the mind."

"Brings about sinus pressure and soggy shoes, is more like it."

Wynn dodged a slushy pothole. "Shall I carry you, ye wee softie Englishman?"

"I hope you're not as insulting to that lovely wife of yours."

The thought of Svetlana's soft arms wrapped around his neck and her sweet breath near his ear sent Wynn's heart thrumming. "She'd be more fun to carry, that's for sure."

"Why is she not here to curb your acerbic mood? I could certainly use the reprieve."

And just like that all thrumming stuttered to a halt. He'd wanted her to come, had nearly said yes when she asked. The black velvet of her mourning gown washed out her face and dulled the purple beneath her eyes, but her wraps of sorrow did nothing to diminish the strength that had drawn him from the beginning. He should have taken her in his arms and kissed her senseless until there was no doubt how much he wanted her near him.

Then he'd seen Sergey hovering behind her with his declaration still ringing in Wynn's ears. *"We're destined to be together."* How could Wynn take her to London as half a man? That was how he truly felt of late if he were being honest. He wanted to return to her and lay his reinstated license at her feet, clearing all dishonor from the name he had given her on their wedding day. All while begging an apology. If his time in London proved a failure, he would still tell her. Either way, she deserved the truth. Their marriage deserved the truth because real marriages were built on trust, and more than anything he wanted a real marriage with Svetlana.

"She remains at Thornhill," Wynn said at last.

"Oh, that's a pity. I should like to have seen her, then again, I know sitting through that interrogation day after day would have been rather distressing to someone of her regalness."

"She doesn't know."

"Doesn't know what?" Gerard tilted his brollie in defense against a spitting gutter over a bookshop. In an instant he whipped around, knocking Wynn's hat askew with the tip of his umbrella. "You haven't told her, man?"

"Let's cut down the explanation and blame it on pride." Wynn jammed his hat farther down on his head and hurried on.

Gerard dashed to keep up, splashing water on the back of Wynn's legs. "Pride or not, you must tell her."

The rainwater from Gerard's splashing soaked through the back of Wynn's trousers, clinging the material to his calves. He'd look no better than a drowned fish by the end of the day if this kept up. Par for the course. He felt about as low as one.

"I will. I wanted to before I left, but then . . . I'm telling her everything as soon as I return." He needed to start practicing knee exercises. Groveling wasn't a position he was accustomed to being in.

"You better. Woe to you if she finds out from someone else first."

"For a man who hasn't had much experience with women, you seem to know a lot about them."

"Those novels I read happen to be very informative on the subject and anything they leave out my married brothers are quick to fill in. More than once they've found themselves sleeping on my sofa after a row with the wife. I've heard it all, and as an outside party can dispense advice without prejudice. My advice for you is this: talk to her before things get worse. Miscommunication laced with ego is the major downfall of most marriages."

"Have you been reading those Freud theories again?"

"Jung actually, and psychoanalysis is not something we should ignore simply because it's untested, much like your cardiology."

Wetness slithered down the back of Wynn's neck, dampening his collar. No matter how he tried to cover himself against the elements, they managed to find a crack.

"I only wanted to protect her."

"I know you did, Wynn. That's who you are."

Rain slipped down the shop windows, coating them in a fine layer of gray mist. A white light twinkled through the gloom. Wynn moved to the storefront and stared at the beckoning display. His breath fogged the glass, but it didn't dim the finely cut rocks' glow with sparks of rainbow shooting through the centers. If ever Svetlana's essence was embodied in an object, it was within these gems.

If she opted for an annulment, it would break his heart to watch her leave, but he wasn't giving up without a fight.

"Go on to the pub, I'll meet you there," he said to Gerard as he opened the door to the shop. "I need to do something first."

CHAPTER 26

Night wrapped the castle in dreamless slumber as Svetlana wandered the halls in solitude. Her fur-trimmed velvet robe trailed behind her, swishing softly with each of her slippered steps. Roaming had become a nightly ritual as restlessness chased her from bed to find contentment by less filling means. So far, she had yet to find said contentment. Its finding would only come when Wynn returned. Until then, planning a meeting with the people of Glentyre to discuss improvements for the village and wandering Thornhill like a proper ghost at night were her best options.

It was lonely—*she* was lonely—without him. When had he overtaken that chamber she'd secreted off, even upon occasion denied its existence? He'd strode in and set it ablaze. Every look, every laugh, touch, and smile fanned the flames. She could no more douse them than she could return to the isolated woman she'd been before.

What if he was stalling because of the scene he'd witnessed in the solarium with Sergey? Svetlana's stomach twisted. Wynn couldn't possibly think she still entertained feelings for Sergey, not after she'd told him otherwise. Was that another cause for his secrecy and standoffishness of late? Perhaps seeing Sergey in the flesh had triggered doubt in Wynn's mind. As if romantic feelings for her old friend could be rekindled when her heart had passed into the possession of her husband. Did Wynn seek reassurance from her? Odd considering his confidence bordered closer to arrogance by the hour. Then again, confidence rarely held court over affairs of the heart. Even for a heart surgeon.

Like other specters calling to her from a night filled with music,

Svetlana found herself in Thornhill's Grand Hall as the shadows of falling snow danced in the blue light spilling across the polished floor. Deprived of music and revelry, the room held a silent breath as if patiently awaiting the next time it would be summoned to life for its grand purpose. In that quiet breath she remembered kilted lords and shimmering ladies, violin strings, piano keys, laughter, clinking champagne glasses. A carefree night sprinkled with stardust.

At the Blue Palace the ballroom had been her favorite place, aside from the outside flower garden, which spun its own delicate magic. As any proper Russian aristocrat, Svetlana was brought up in the art of dancing. The waltz, allemande, galop, mazurka, and quadrille. She could perform them in her sleep, but late at night when everyone was abed, she would slip down to the ballroom for the dancing that set her free. Intricate *pirouettes*, *grand jetés*, *assemblés*. Starting off in delicate movements of the adagio where her limbs flowed from one position to another like water, then faster and sharper to the allegro until her energy was spent and the lyrical music in her head would crescendo to an end.

Constance's phonograph sat untouched in the corner of the room, silenced due to mourning. She'd brought it back from her latest trip to America. Crossing to it, Svetlana rifled through the stack of disc records as an urgency rippled through her like the slow flap of birds' wings. Fast and faster the wings flapped until she thought they would burst straight out of her.

She'd been in mourning far too long. For Russia, for her life lost to the Revolution, the hardships, and deaths. Not since Sheremetev had she brought herself to dance again, and then the peace of moving had been tainted by his twisted usage. She wanted to feel alive again; she needed to feel herself come alive to the music and steps and an unyielding floor beneath her feet that transported her to a stage of magic and stardust.

Slipping the disc onto the machine, Svetlana touched the needle to the black grooves. The haunting harmony of Wagner's *Tristan and Isolde* floated out the tale of the foretold lost lovers in delight. Svetlana stretched her arms out to greet the chilled air in a dancer's embrace as her feet slid to fifth position with opposite toe to opposite heel. A tremble ran up her legs, swirled around her stomach, lengthening along her spine until her scalp tingled with anticipation. Weighted burdens fell away as she came into herself. Her slippers glided effortlessly across the floor, the velvet fold of her robe rippling around her like water rings on a pond's surface as the music's rhythm flooded her soul.

Svetlana closed her eyes and gave herself to the stardust.

─────────

"Ye'll be wanting me to ring for Glasby, aye, Yer Grace?" The old stable master took the horse's reins from Wynn and gave the animal a pat on its sleek neck. Snowflakes puffed from his mane.

"No. I'll manage." Wynn unstrapped his small valise from behind the saddle. The handle was cold and wet from the snow. "I left my trunk at the train station. Have one of the grooms run to fetch it tomorrow morning."

"Should've called for us and we'd've picked ye up instead of ye riding through the night hours." Judging by his hastily tucked shirt and hair standing on ends, the man had been fast asleep when Wynn decided to ride home unannounced.

"I'm sorry for waking you. After the London rain and stuffy train compartment, I needed the fresh air on my face. Been too long since I've ridden."

"London be for the stuffed shirts." The stable master scrunched his nose in contempt. No love was lost for their neighbors past the southern border. "'Tis glad we are to be having ye back, Yer Grace."

"Always glad to be back."

Gripping his travel bag, Wynn strode across the well-tended yard pearlescent with freshly falling snow. Thornhill stood quietly in midnight shadows with a blue moon striking against its familiar corners and turrets. A welcome sight after his week of failure. The medical board had come to no conclusion and decided to reconvene at a later date when tempers weren't raging. Many of the highly respected physicians in attendance had resorted to name-calling and vilifying the mental stability of one another. Horrifying as the scene had been, Wynn was grateful to have been forgotten in the melee. For good or bad, cardiology got people to talking.

Wynn slipped in the kitchen door and immediate warmth embraced him from the cooking fire, smoored down to its last embers of cherry red. Wynn squatted in front of the hearth and held out his frozen fingers. Leather gloves were well and good, but slushy winter air had a way of penetrating to a man's bones.

Feeling returned to his extremities and he moved to the worktable where Cook had left out bannocks under a wire dome, per Scottish tradition. Apparently it was to keep the fae hungrily occupied instead of roaming the castle at night for mischief. Wynn had never heard of that tradition, but then, he didn't hail from the deeply superstitious Highlands like some of his kitchen workers did. If there was one person in the house he wanted to keep happy, it was the cook and so the bannocks stayed. Except for the one he stuffed in his mouth to feed his growling belly. London was a long train ride.

Trudging up the servant's stairs, he came out into the Stone Hall and sighed with relief. Home. Music plucked his ear. Was someone up at this hour? Dropping his bag on a bench beneath an ancient targe and broadsword, he followed the strains of the recorded melody. He'd always appreciated music but never had the ear for it; he could never tell the instruments apart. At the double doors of the Grand Hall he stopped dead in his tracks at the ethereal sight floating across the floor.

Svetlana dancing.

No, not dancing. It was more than that. She moved as if her skin and bones had peeled away to release her very soul. A piece long laid dormant was resuscitated as her arms circled high over her head, stretching herself into existence. Her pale arms and legs extended in graceful arcs with the airy folds of her robe wrapping and unwrapping around her movements like butterfly wings. Moonlight weaved between the strands of her plaited hair, refining it to pure silver. The music surged. Faster and faster she spun until she was no more than a ribbon of silver.

The air clenched in Wynn's lungs. In that single moment his heart was irrevocably and irretrievably lost with no hope of ever reclaiming it.

The music ended. Svetlana stilled on the points of her toes. Her eyelids fluttered open, and her eyes locked onto his. Slowly she lowered her feet flat to the floor. Her position settled into one of familiar cool reserve, yet there was a rawness lingering along her edges, a shimmering residue of her soul that had yet to be drawn back in.

A smile played about her lips. "You're home."

Her voice drowned his battered ego and flamed a desire to come alive as she had been. To come alive with her. The war, the medical board, pride, and death fell away until nothing stood before him but her. The one he loved.

He crossed the distance between them in a matter of strides and took her face between his hands, hesitating long enough to inhale her gasp of surprise before covering her mouth with his. She tasted of mint, soothing yet with a sharpness that pierced through every part of him. Her body eased against his as she responded to his touch with equal fervor. She stole into him, lighting fire to his veins, and blood, and bones until he was wholly consumed with her brightness.

Svetlana pulled away. Cool air brushed across Wynn's heated lips. "Is this how you greet your wife?"

"Would she rather I didn't?" His voice came out ragged.

"She would rather you had done it sooner." Her fingernails dragged across the back of his neck.

It was all the encouragement he needed. Pouring every unspoken word and tenderness into the kiss, he held her as he'd dreamed of doing for so long. Never would she doubt the way he felt about her, how much he wanted her, how much he needed her. For so long he thought she called to a lost part of him, but he now realized it had never been lost, merely half formed. She gave him promise of being whole.

"I'm glad I didn't stay in London one more night." He touched his forehead to hers, savoring her nearness.

"I was expecting you to send word on when you were to return. I should have remembered your need to surprise me at unexpected moments."

The past week came rushing back, the full weight of it no longer to be ignored. He leaned back and steadied himself. He loathed to break the moment, but it was past time to confess.

"My days in London—"

She placed a slender finger against his lips. "Shh. There is plenty of time to tell me later."

"I need to tell you what really happened—"

"Tomorrow. Can we not have tonight?"

If they were ever to move forward, honesty must thrive between them. To hold back the truth was selfish. Or was it selfish to cleanse himself of his lies and ease his conscience when she pleaded for one single night together? How could he deny her?

"Wait right here." He jogged out to the hall and rifled through his valise to pull out a thin leather box and a velvet pouch. Back in the Grand Hall, he placed the box next to the phonograph and crooked his finger at Svetlana. "Hold out your hand."

He cupped her offered hand in his and felt the delicate bones tremble. Such a simple thing to touch another's hand. He'd touched hers often enough, but never like this, with each brush of skin creating a new sensation of intimacy. He turned the pouch upside down and out tumbled the sparkling contents. Earrings in the shape of cascading stars.

"Lana, you fell from heaven and straight into my life. What a lucky man I am."

Unmoving, she stared down at them. Uncertainty shifted Wynn's surge of confidence. Had he done something wrong? Was it too much too quickly? "I know you're more accustomed to imperial jewels—"

"These are more precious than any royal jewel. You gave them to me." Tears studded her long lashes as she looked up. She fitted the earrings into her ears, the largest star resting at the top as the smaller stars dangled along her jaw.

Wynn touched one of the trailing stars. "*Prekrasnaya.*" *Beautiful.* One of the first Russian words he'd learned from his lessons with Mrs. Varjensky.

"*Spasibo.*"

"I have one more thing." He popped off the leather box's lid and took out the record. An impulse purchase from the newly opened music store next door to his London hotel. Shiny and black, this record had been propped in the display window waiting to catch his eye. Waiting to be played for its rightful master. Placing it on the turntable, he lowered the arm and touched the needle to the grooves. Tchaikovsky's *The Sleeping Beauty* waltz filtered through the horn. "Will you dance for me?"

A smile curved her mouth. She stepped slowly back from him, her eyes never leaving his as she pulled the ribbon tie from her hair and shook out the mass of silvery waves reaching nearly to her waist. Wynn sucked in a breath. He'd never seen it entirely loose before. She became a candle flame dancing in the breeze, alive and carefree, spinning about with her gaze seeking to find him in the blue darkness. How amazing was the human form when given to the creativity of its abilities, but none so mesmerizing or alluring as her in this simplistic beauty. Limbs stretching out, spine curved, neck elongated. His living fire. Would he be consumed if he touched her?

Svetlana spun to a halt. Waves of hair fell over one side of her face. "This was originally intended as a *pas de deux*. A dance for two."

He went to her and slipped his arms around her waist. Her chest pumped up and down from the exertion of her lungs. Without thinking, he lowered his lips to press a kiss to her pulsing carotid artery just under her jaw.

She shivered. "Is this how you check a woman's heart rate?"

"Not usually, no. But then, I can't help myself with you."

"You've been remiss in your duties, Doctor."

"Apologies for the delay, my lady. A misstep that I should like to remedy as often as possible."

Her eyes slanted up to him. The brightness burned into him, carving out the hidden recesses. "We seem to be out of step more times than not."

From the day she'd limped into his hospital it seemed. Just off balance from one another yet stable enough to keep them wobbling instead of fixing themselves to firm ground. All he'd ever wanted was to keep her steady.

"When we first married it was for convenience, and I told you I wanted nothing in return, but I do want more. I want you. Always. Because I love you." Heart pounding, he touched his forehead to hers. Time was created for this moment. Where nothing existed beyond her and him. "Will you have me, Lana?"

Her hands moved up his chest and cupped his face. "Yes."

Wynn swept her into his arms and turned to the grand staircase. The soft blackness of the sleeping castle wrapped them in anticipated embrace as *The Sleeping Beauty*'s music faded behind them. Svetlana's star earrings brushed his cheek as her warm breath caressed his neck, and his heaven for the moment was gained.

CHAPTER 27

Sunlight filtered through the partially drawn drapes, spotting hazy orbs around the room. Svetlana rolled over and stretched in bed, feeling light and heavy all at once. Touching one of the star earrings still dangling from her ear, she turned her head to gaze around the unfamiliar chamber. Wynn's room. Her nightdress trailed over the arm of the leather chair. One slipper had landed near the fireplace while the other lay forgotten by the closed door, and her robe had disappeared altogether.

A note with her name scratched across the front lay on the bedside table next to her.

> Lana,
> You looked so peaceful in my bed that I didn't want to wake you. Wait for me. I'll be back shortly.
> Wynn

The handwriting was barely discernable, but she smiled anyway. Lying back on the pillow that still carried his scent, Svetlana held up her left hand and smiled as her wedding band glowed with new appreciation in the morning light. She had finally become Wynn's wife. His true wife in all manner of the name. It had been a night of revelations and discoveries, tenderness and passion. She had lain in his arms wrapped in love as a new beginning stretched before them.

Again and again he'd told her he loved her. She'd reveled in the words, never having heard them before. It wasn't a phrase commonly used in aristocratic Russian families, and she'd certainly never allowed a man to say it to her. Oh, some had tried, but she'd cut off their flowery words before they embarrassed themselves in dribbling nonsense. Wynn was the only man she wanted to hear say it and the only man she wished to say it to. Last night she hadn't out of fear. She wasn't accustomed to allowing her emotions so close to the surface, much less confessed out into the open, and panic had seized her. It was past time for fear. Today was the day. This morning she would tell Wynn she loved him.

Swinging her feet out of the large bed, she ignored the soreness and went in search of her robe. Somehow it had been flung on top of Wynn's bureau next to the gifted Fabergé egg from Leonid's name day. She slipped on the robe and tied the sash about her waist as ideas for the day bloomed in her head like spring flowers after a long, bleak winter. Upon Wynn's return she would confess her love and he would kiss her. Her eyes darted to the bed and heat rushed up her cheeks. Afterward they might go for a walk in the snow and visit one of the lakes—no, he called them lochs—nearby. Maybe go ice skating or on a sleigh ride. She would need to ask if he—*they*, she corrected herself with a pleased smile—owned a *troika* or other snow-appropriate conveyance. They could begin the honeymoon they'd never had.

She pirouetted around the room, neatly refolding her nightdress on the chair, arranging her slippers next to the shoes Wynn had kicked off by the fireplace. Taking his crumpled jacket from the floor, she gently shook it out while humming to herself. A yellow telegram fluttered to the floor. It was none of her business, but the sender being the Royal Medical Academy piqued her curiosity. It was dated the day he'd been summoned to London and addressed to the Duke of Kilbride. Odd. He usually requested his colleagues refer to him as Dr. MacCallan.

Your appearance is required before a medical board of your peers. Stop. Hereby to determine fault of surgical

procedure and death of Lt. J. Harkin. Stop. Physician
title and license remains withheld until inquest
concluded. Stop.

Fault of procedure. Death of Harkin. License withheld. The meanings battled through Svetlana's brain as the words ran together before
her eyes. Was Wynn being accused of killing Harkin because of the
surgery? She knew he'd been questioned about it, but never to this
degree. Never to the point of stripping away his medical license. An
ache throbbed at the base of her skull. All this time. Why had he not
told her?

The door opened. "Good morning, my beautiful wife. Or I should
say, *lyubimaya*? Did I get that one right?" He shuffled in behind her
and closed the door.

"How long?"

"I was only gone about thirty minutes. Luckily Cook already had
the oven heated for the scones."

Clutching the telegram, she slowly turned around. She tried to
ignore the mussed hair falling across his forehead and the undone buttons at the top of his wrinkled shirt where a few golden hairs smattered
across his wide chest. She tried to block the memory of resting her cheek
against that warm chest and clenched the condemning paper tighter.

"How long?"

The pleasantness evaporated from his face as he glanced at the
telegram. Very carefully he placed the breakfast tray on the foot of
the bed. He'd brought her golden toast with butter, scones with
clotted cream, sliced apples, and thin cuts of ham. Somewhere he'd
found three snowdrops blooming early in the season and put them in
a small vase next to a steaming cup of tea. His thoughtfulness cut to
her wounded heart.

"Since Glasgow," he said quietly.

The cut sank deeper. "Thank you for not lying to me. Again."

"I was going to tell you. I tried to—"

"When? You've had weeks. What would deem me, your wife, worthy to know of your troubles?" Her voice grew cooler with each word as she stepped back into the familiarity of distance and reserve even as pain poured into her widening wound. She folded the telegram precisely in half and dropped it on the table.

"I started to tell you the night of the charity bazaar, but Sergey arrived with news of your family, and my troubles were nothing in comparison to your loss. I tried again last night, but then . . ."

"Then what? You became distracted by falling stars and music under the moon?"

"You asked me not to say anything and if we could have one night for ourselves. I tried to think clearly, not to be selfish, but how could I deny you?"

"This is my fault?" She hiked an eyebrow, daring him to accuse her.

"No. It's mine. I should have told you from the beginning, but I wanted to try to salvage things. My name and career were being dragged through the mud. They still are. I wanted my name to free you from disgrace, not tarnish you."

"Did you not think I had a right to know? After all, it is my name now. Or was your plan to patch it all up before I ever found out? Blissful are the ignorant after all."

"I wanted to keep you safe from one more bad thing happening. To keep you from hurt."

Had she not proven her strength time and time again? "I am not some fragile piece of glass threatening to shatter at any moment, unlike your ego." The sharpened words recalled from that night in the solarium during the charity bazaar hit their mark squarely. She wished she hadn't.

Wynn's expression darkened to a shade of brewing thunder. He crossed the floor to her in three long strides, stopping close enough for her to see the unloosened storm.

"How easy do you think it is for a man to admit failure to his wife? Everything I have ever worked for has been snatched away. My honor and reputation have been slandered because a young man died on my operating table for a procedure fueled by my arrogance to prove a point. Patients die every day. It's part of a surgeon's cruel reality, but I'm the one they've chosen to crucify in order to prove that methods cannot and should not be changed. Every hour I wonder if they're not right about me, but intuition gained over years of experience is quick to swoop in and reassure me that everything I did in that operating theater was for the betterment of my patient. So yes, my ego, my pride is to blame. My savior and my destroyer. Is that what you wanted to hear?"

The full gust of his anger blasted across her, revealing a man raked of his dignity struggling to piece himself together with the tatters that remained. She should go to him, comfort him, tell him she understood. But she couldn't. He had promised honesty but betrayed her instead. Oh, how she missed her armor of isolation and self-preservation. She may not be able to slip back into it, but she would not be caught defenseless again.

She gathered the folds of her velvet robe and tightened the sash. "If it is the truth, yes. What other lies have you told me?"

"None, I swear. I was only trying to protect you by keeping this from you."

"What kind of protection is lying?"

"The kind that loves you. That wants to spare you any further hurt in this world and provide you with an honorable name so you can wake up each morning without worry." He reached for her.

She stepped back as the disappointment and pain grappled in her heart. These months together as man and wife had become some of the best in her life as she discovered what it meant to take comfort in another. They had shared in the joys and agonies, but now to discover she and Wynn were not as she'd thought them to be hurt her in a way that would not have been possible if she'd remained invulnerable.

"How can you speak of love and honor when you've withheld something so important? I may not be well-versed in the subject, but I know deception holds no place in true affection."

His arms dropped, hands clenching at his sides. Each word that came out was clipped with restraint. "Aye, I kept the truth of Harkin's death and my revoked license from you, but never doubt my affection for you. Never. Everything from last night was the truth."

"I do not wish to discuss last night."

"Last night was the most honest moment of my life. I love—"

"No! You justify yourself and expect me to follow along blindly, which I did. All I wanted was for you to rely on me as I have on you, and now that reliance lays scattered between us in broken pieces." *Like my heart.*

The thunder dissipated from his eyes, churning them to the unsteady brown-green of the ocean after a storm. "My greatest concern has only ever been for your welfare. I've made mistakes along the way. Not telling you the truth of my troubles from the beginning being the biggest, and for that I'm truly sorry. I wanted the burden on myself. Never to fall on you. You have become too precious to me to be crushed under the weight of my failure."

Precious. That was how she had felt held in his arms hours before, but the feeling crumbled as her heartache suffocated all in its wake. She felt foolish and exposed. This was what came from vulnerability and giving one's heart to another.

"After everything I went through escaping Russia and being forced to secrecy for fear of my life, I fought against allowing anyone to see my vulnerabilities ever again. Even you. Until you convinced me you were trustworthy. You became my one true north as the rest of the world spun on an axis of chaos." She pressed her lips tightly together, gathering the strength to defend against the anguish in her soul. "You have broken that trust."

Pain twisted his face as if she'd struck him. "Let me earn it back."

"I don't know if you can."

"Have you never made a mistake? Or have you been so cold for so long that you've frozen out what it means to be human?"

It was her turn to feel struck. The accusation she'd heard too many times to count, but never from him. And that made the sting all the sharper. "That's right. The Russian princess is cold and heartless. At least that way I can avoid disappointments."

"Disappointments are a part of life, like the one between us now. I'm sorry for what I've broken between us, but I swear to you, I will prove I am a man deserving of your trust."

His arms reached to circle around her. Oh, how she wanted them to. She wanted to end the struggle and find peace together again, but her need for self-preservation tightened, choking off any means of acquiescence as her body stiffened at his touch.

"Lana, don't cut yourself off from me."

She brushed past him toward the door connecting their chambers. "'Lana' belonged to a dream that disappeared somewhere between the stars of last night and the cold dawn of today."

"So that's it? Something breaks and you toss it onto the rubbish heap because it's no longer good enough for you?" The dejection in his voice pleaded after her, begging her not to cut the fragile threads binding them together.

Svetlana blinked back the threat of tears and twisted the doorknob. She'd allowed her pragmatism to be clouded by hope. If betrayal was all hope offered in the end, she was better off without the burden. "Better alone than trusting a man who doesn't keep his word."

Sweeping into her room, she closed the door behind her as the first tear fell. Followed by another and still more. The weeping of her heart slipped down her cheeks as silence enveloped her in its lonely embrace.

CHAPTER 28

Brooding. That was a good if not accurate word for Wynn's current state. He'd never considered himself a moody man, rather enjoying jokes and laughter too much to spiral into sulking solitude. Standing on the wide hill behind Thornhill with a cloak of descending night above him and the sweep of wind from the moors below, he had no need of jests, so brooding it was.

It was no better than he deserved. A liar and deceiver. Not to mention possible murderer and utmost fool. How did he ever manipulate himself into thinking that not telling Svetlana was for the best? Because he was a fool, that's how. He never should have allowed his desire to take her to his bed to overcome his duty to tell her the truth. But then she'd kissed him and begged him for one night together and he'd been helpless to stop himself.

He flicked his thumb across the pierced kopek he always carried and paced across the grass. The dead stalks crunched under his boots. He had a fine mind to grind them to dust beneath his heel. The memory of that precious night, of holding her in his arms in the ways he'd only dreamed of, was now tainted by the crushing weight of his lie. Four days she had shunned him after he tried again and again to see her, even speaking through her closed door. She answered him in silence and avoidance. He had only himself to blame.

"I knew I'd find you up here. At your spot." His mother crested the hill and stood next to him. She'd ditched her customary scarf and diaphanous gowns and instead opted for sturdy boots and Father's thick plaid drawn around her shoulders. "You've always come here to think."

"It's peaceful."

She nodded, looking down the hill to Glentyre, nestled among the fading shadows of the rises beyond. "What has you troubled to seek peace?"

"Nothing too concerning." More lies. "Hospital duties."

"Duties you'd rather attend to than the ducal ones." Mother held up her hand. "Ah, don't give me that look. I know perfectly well which you prefer."

"I'm sorry, Mother. I'm trying."

"I know you are, but being duke wasn't the path for you. You were always meant to be a great surgeon."

His gut twisted. If only she knew. "It seems that path is now lost to me."

"Nothing is ever truly lost if we fight to hold on to its importance. Being duke is a great responsibility full of trials and frustrations, but also fulfillment in helping those dependent on you. I believe your duty as a physician is much the same. Like every man before you, titled or not, you must find the balance between duty and personal desire."

Wynn ground his toe into the frozen dirt. There was nothing left to balance after he'd mangled his go at being a surgeon. "Father and Hugh made it look so effortless. Duty was never a question for them because it was a role they were born to. I can never be Hugh."

"No one expects you to be. Hugh was my stalwart sun, ever constant, but you, my dear boy, are my shooting star. My sons are both brilliant in their own unique ways, and I would never change that." Tears glistened in her eyes. "You must find your own path forward and be sure to avoid the pitfalls of defining yourself as one thing or another, duke or physician."

"That is who I am."

Scoffing, she blinked away the tears and fluffed the plaid around her throat. "I shall pretend I did not hear that most pretentious claim and cling to the knowledge that you are smarter than to believe that. People are not mere titles, dear. Why, if I went around believing I only existed as your mother, life would be quite boring for me."

"Have I not given you enough excitement as my mother?" He nudged her shoulder, eliciting a glimmer of amusement.

"More than enough for two lifetimes, and while I love you more than life itself, being a mother is only part of who I am. Don't be a one-sided bore, Wynn."

The truth of her statement dug into his core. He'd made an ivory tower of his ambitions, and when the walls had shaken loose, the bricks fell around him into a heap of disappointment all because he'd put the definition of himself into this one edifice. When the dust settled, he would have two choices. Let the bricks crush him flat on his face, or drag himself from the rubble and start building another life. Svetlana had done it, and if there was anyone to learn from about grace from ruin, it was her.

"I'll do my best, Mother," he said at last.

Reaching up, she patted his cheek. "I'm so glad you've returned home."

"Me too. I only wish I could have returned Hugh to you." He kissed her hand, then slipped his arm around her and drew her to his side. "I miss him. Somedays I look up and expect him to appear around the corner, or I go look for him in the library. Then I remember he's not here."

"His spirit is here now. At least we have that. And each other."

They stared out over the dipping slopes and huddled wood-lands dotting their estate. Far beyond Thornhill's borders, the river rippled under the dying sun's rays. Life still moved on, oblivious to the world's woes.

"I should like to erect a monument for him. For all the boys who didn't return. I believe it could help our people find peace with the losses we've suffered. So many of us never got the chance to grieve over a body." Mother sniffed and wiped at the corner of her eyes with the plaid. "We need a place to honor them."

"A fine idea. And very fitting. I think Hugh would wish to be remembered with the men he fought beside."

The scent of burning peat rustled on the breeze as families settled into supper and their warm fires against winter's chill. Wynn breathed in deeply. It was a unique scent, one he'd never particularly cared for, but it was of Scotland and therefore of home.

Mother shivered and drew her plaid close. "I best get back inside where it's warm. My half American blood still has trouble appreciating this cold."

"The cold lets you know you're alive."

"Spoken like a man who has the internal temperature of a furnace. Though I'm sure your wife appreciates that commodity, coming from a frozen land herself."

The mention of Svetlana lanced pain across his heart. "The cold doesn't bother her as much."

"She's a unique woman. Her manner may be a bit . . . stiff at times, but she has a kind heart, looking after her family and seeing to the tenants. I'm glad you've brought her to our family."

The pain boiled and spilled down his insides, scorching him with regret. He'd been raised to honor the truth. Mother would be ashamed to know he'd broken his promise of honesty to his wife in the so-called name of honorable protection.

"Your approval means a great deal to me."

"Then you have it and my support. Both of you. Be good to one another and the love will never die." Burrowing into her plaid, Mother started her way down the path she'd come. "Don't stay out here too long. Mrs. Varjensky is making something called goulash. It sounds dreadful, but the smell from the kitchen is divine."

Wynn turned back to the hills. If Mrs. Varjensky was cooking, the offerings were likely to be delicious, but only he, Mother, Marina, and *babushka* would be sitting down to enjoy it. Svetlana had chosen to eat in her room these past few nights. No doubt the sight of him would give her acid reflux.

He flipped the kopek in the air, head over tails, and caught it. A choice to be made, fifty-fifty either way it landed. He'd never had difficulty choosing before, the path always confident under his feet, but the ground had shifted. He could no longer look at the world through the same lens with his future balanced on the edge of a scalpel because unwittingly he'd put that same blade in the hands of his peers. And for what? To prove to himself how great he was? To prove to them how much they needed him?

He flipped the coin again. When had this monolith of success entered the competition against the human beings he had sworn to care for? His patients and tenants didn't require him to be the best in his field, and they certainly didn't care a bit for the arrogance toted around with self-proclaimed prestige. Perhaps a tiny part of it had been for the glory, but what real change did glory mark in the universal scheme when he failed to put his talents to good use on the people entrusted to his care? His talent may never change the history books, but he could change lives worth far more than the opinion of a board of white-haired old men. Hang their opinion and his need for their approval. It wouldn't stop him from serving those in need whether he received the praise or not.

At least that was one perspective he could change. Svetlana would take a wee more finessing.

Not brave enough to face that bitter pain yet again, he pocketed the kopek and hunched his shoulders against the coming darkness as the temperature fell around him.

CHAPTER 29

Mama, you must eat." The spoon in Svetlana's hand hovered in front of her mother's mouth, but the aging princess turned her face to the lacey pillow and stared out the window. The chamber had been shrouded like a tomb when Svetlana first entered, but she'd peeled back the heavy drapes to let in the sunlight at great protest from the room's occupant. The words were some of the few her mother had spoken since the news came of their terrible loss.

Wiping off the bits of sugared oatmeal seeping over the spoon's rim, Svetlana tried another tactic: her mother's vanity. "Your figure will waste away."

Mama's only response was a slow blink, as if her lashes were too heavy to hold up. Silver threaded between the dark blond strands of hair hanging past her sunken cheeks. She had always been meticulous about her appearance and aging cover-ups, but grief had woven a tattered spell of carelessness, leaving in its wake a stripped layer of the woman who once was.

Across the room, Marina shrugged at the daily battle. They'd taken turns coaxing their mother to eat at mealtimes, but Svetlana was never successful. Mama preferred Marina's administrations, and even then it was hardly more than a nibble or sip. Svetlana could hardly blame her. She wasn't pleasant enough company for herself these days. Not that it made a difference to her mother. She'd never found her eldest daughter's company more than tolerable, closing off her affection to shower upon her other children instead. Svetlana had never questioned it, merely accepted it.

Staring down now at the once vibrant woman shriveling to a gaunt shell of herself, Svetlana realized she never really knew her mother beyond the fancy gowns and tittering parlor room laughter—a laugh she claimed to have first caught Dmitri Dalsky's attention. It was one of the only claims Father had never refuted, so Svetlana knew it must have been true. A rare connection between her parents when she'd witnessed so few.

"Father would not wish to see you like this."

Mama slowly shifted on the pillow. Her eyes stared with unfocused lucidity as if searching for a ghost on Svetlana's face. Inch by inch, she raised her head and took a bite of the oatmeal. Eating four more bites, she tapped a brittle nail against the teacup. Svetlana poured the fragrant brew into the cup and held it up to her mother's lips. Mama took a sip, grimaced, and fell back to the pillow.

"I know it's not from a samovar, but we must make do." Wrapping her fingers around the delicate cup, the more obvious problem became clear. "It's cold. I'll ring for a fresh pot."

Marina jumped up from her chair near the fire, the book in her lap clattering to the floor. "I'll fetch one. My legs could do with a stretch." She took the tray from Mama's lap and smiled. Sadness still clung to her eyes, but she was doing her best to put on a brave face. "I'll see if I can find a few mashed cherries to put in the bottom. I know how much you like those. Makes it feel a bit more Russian."

As Marina left, Svetlana set about straightening the coverlet across the bed, smoothing the drape pleats, and retying the pink ribbon on Mama's nightdress after noting one loop on the bow was bigger than the other. Anything to occupy herself, for it was in the listless moments that the unwanted thoughts and feelings found her. The notes of a midnight waltz. The scent of wool and aftershave. The warmth of arms holding her at night. The stab of betrayal and heartache of lies. It all made her feel too much when she preferred the escapism of numbness.

"You're like him."

The scratchy voice turned Svetlana from the vanity table where she was aligning a tray of hairpins to find her mother watching her.

Svetlana slid a fingernail between a pin's blades, the metal cool and rigid like the shining medals pinned across Father's chest. He'd taught her the name of each one and allowed her the honor of pinning on his Order of Saint Catherine when he was decorated by the tsar.

"Organized, you mean?"

"Coldly efficient."

After all those years it shouldn't have stung, but it did. Svetlana nudged the silver pins into straight lines. "A soldier's trait."

"Prince Dmitri Nikolaiovich Dalsky, Captain of the Imperial Forces, with his resourceful mind and steadfast demeanor, and me with my wit and charm. The Dowager Empress Maria herself said we would make the perfect match." A soft smile curved Mama's pale lips as her thoughts drifted from the room to a happier time. Svetlana had heard the story of the matchmaking dowager more times than she could count, but it had always been told in a manner of boasting, never with this reminiscent fondness. As if an egg had cracked open to reveal its sweet, runny center, kept unspoiled all these years within its shell.

Desperate to assuage the earlier sting, Svetlana cradled the image in its delicacy. One false slip and the rare moment of vulnerability between mother and daughter would shatter. "You always looked smart together."

Mama toyed with her cross necklace, running her finger over the slanted bottom bar. "There's nothing more I love than a perfect match of anything. I tried so hard to please him, but I quickly learned there was nothing more he loved than order. I was anything but. No matter how many pretty gowns I wore or opulent dinner parties I threw with all the right attendees, I never pleased him as much as watching his soldiers drill or aligning his army boots in the closet."

"I assumed most husbands and wives held their own interests

independent of one another. Grand Duchess Xenia was often quoted as it being the only way to sustain a peaceful marriage."

"Because you have been taught to think no differently, as all properly brought-up young ladies are."

"Yet you wished otherwise, yes?"

"For a time, when I was young and naïve. Each passing year erected a brick around my heart. A growing wall your father never sought to scale. His eye was caught by too many other battles. He was a good man, but he made loving him nearly impossible."

"You're like him." The delicate moment of intimacy crackled apart and in blew the bitter cold wind of truth. "Is that what you think of me? I'm impossible to love?"

Mama's expression shuttered. She turned her face to the window once more. "Where is your husband?"

The denial of an answer and change in topic was like a slap to the face after having been spat in the eye. Unlovable and unable to love. In the days passing her fallout with Wynn, Svetlana's bones felt of ice, as if she were no longer a part of her body. She listened for Wynn's voice constantly but prayed her steps would not lead her to him. Her emotions were too raw to be reliable. Like a cord of beads strung on one after another with no intent of purpose. The lack of control was nearly as debilitating as the crack in her heart.

But this weakness she would never allow her mother to witness, not to be seized upon and brought down to Mama's level of insecurities. Svetlana tapped the hair pin tray parallel to a silver-handled brush. "His time is occupied of late with matters from the medical board."

"About that soldier who died under his knife in Paris?"

Svetlana's attention snapped up. "Lieutenant Harkin did not die under Wynn's knife. It was some time after the operation. Where are you hearing this information?"

"One of the maids has a brother who worked as an orderly in

the London hospital when that sergeant—lieutenant?—was there." Wrapping the necklace chain around her finger, Mama gave her a pointed look. "I have to get my information from somewhere when my own daughter won't tell me."

"That's because there is nothing to tell. It was tragic that the young man died, but Wynn did his best to save him. As he did—does—with all his patients." They may have been in the middle of a marital tempest, but no one could falsely accuse Wynn to her face and remain unchecked. He was a good man and a brilliant surgeon and would rather throw himself in front of a firing squad before seeing harm come to another person.

Had he not done just that to protect the woman he claimed to love? Her head pounded. Yes, he had. With a lie.

The sound of metal zippering over a chain filled the stretching silence. Mama's cross pulling back and forth on its chain. "The maids also tell me they've been lighting the fire and making the beds in both of your separate chambers."

Svetlana crossed the room in an undignified two strides and glared at her mother from the foot of the bed. All pretense of civility vanished at her mother's gaming attempts to needle her. "The intimate information of my sleeping arrangements is none of your concern."

"It tells a lot about a marriage. Particularly the early days."

"I'm sure you'd find more delight to hear of me slipping into Sergey's bed."

Mama jerked upright. "There's no call to be crude."

"I'm sorry, Mama. I didn't realize there was a more delicate way of stating whose bed you'd rather see me in than my husband's."

"Good heavens. I did not raise you to speak this way."

"It's the only thing ladies of the court discuss."

"Not in front of their daughters."

"Behind the back is preferable? Or only with the maids?"

"This is not—that is not why I asked. Always twisting my words around to make me a harpy of the worst kind." Lips pursed, her mother inhaled several times through her nose as her hands scuffed over the bed linen. Ever the victim. Ever so slowly, the high color on her cheeks receded. "I ask because . . . Well, what does it matter now? You're your father's daughter."

The angry dart flew straight and true at Svetlana's heart, but it was too late. She'd armed herself since the first attack. "I once felt special when you told me that. Now I know you never meant it as a compliment."

"There you go again, knowing all. Whatever would we mere mortals of imperfection do without your insight? Apparently we would have starved, been thrown out into the streets, or killed without you to guide us. I've yet to see one lasting ray of hope since we left Russia."

"I've done the best I can to keep us safe."

"I'm sure you think so."

With the covers pulled up high on her chest and the pink bow at her throat, her mother was not the bitter harpy she accused Svetlana of making her, but rather a selfish, scared child who knew no better than to lash out when she was hurting. Nothing hurt more than being denied love.

"Did you love my father?" *Did you ever love me?* Svetlana burned to ask but held back in fear of what the answer might be.

"I did, but it was too exhausting keeping up with that much perfection," Mama whispered, clutching her cross and slumping into her pillows. "Go away. I'm tired."

Svetlana turned, crossed the room, and opened the door. Marina stood there precariously balancing a fresh tray of steaming tea. The scent of apples lingered in the strained leaves.

"Oh good. I didn't know how I was going to get the door open holding this." The smile dropped from her face. "Svetka. What's wrong?"

"Mama is tired, but I suspect she'll feel revived after her tea."

"We didn't have cherries, but I strained a few of the chamomile petals you've been drying from your herb garden. You don't think she'll mind?"

"Of course not. Your thoughtfulness is always appreciated."

"Do you know when Sergey will return? He left rather unexpectedly, and I worry for him in this strange country."

Sergey had left not long after their last conversation in the solarium—where he had so brazenly declared himself to her—claiming he needed a few days alone to gather his thoughts while searching for new accommodations. It would be a lie to say she did not feel relief from his temporary absence. She had too many upsets to deal with, and summoning small talk for the man she'd rejected was not one she had the fortitude for.

"I'm not certain. Perhaps he needed time to clear his head. We Dalsky women can be overwhelming in our plights."

Marina stepped close and touched a gentle hand to Svetlana's shoulder. "Mama will get better, but it'll take time. We'll help her. There's no sense in you worrying so much about all of us."

The naïve sweetness on her sister's face—thinking it was their mother who caused the only trouble—slipped a knife into Svetlana's heart. "Part of being the big sister is to worry, *kotyonok*."

"Then it's good you have Wynn to look after you. He's the only one strong enough."

The knife twisted. Svetlana walked away as the pain swelled in her chest, culminating in the prickle of tears.

"Are we still conducting that village meeting later today?" Marina's voice trailed down the hall after her.

"Yes. Be ready to leave by three o'clock." Svetlana rounded the corner and threw open the nearest window. Icy wind rushed in and froze the tears cresting her bottom lashes. She swiped them away with a decisive flick of her hand before closing the window and continuing on.

The Glentyre schoolhouse was a sea of worn faces all bundled together against the chill rapping against the lead-paned windows. Women in headscarves held tightly to their red-nosed children while the men stared solemnly ahead. Men with missing arms or legs, scarred faces, limps, and haunted expressions of weariness. One might easily despair of their pitiable conditions, but that was a fool's take. War had pillaged and destroyed with its ravenous appetite for death, but it had not claimed its final stake in this village. There was still a fight to be had, and the overwhelming attendance that day was a rallying cry.

Svetlana stood before them with a world map hanging behind her. Countries, mountains, and oceans were marked in English and Gaelic, the ancient Scottish language she was determined to learn if only a few words for greeting.

She'd taken care to wear a simple black dress of mourning with a silk rosette of blue and green pinned to her lapel. MacCallan colors. Today, above all, was about unity.

"War has mastered our circumstances these past four years and now we must find new ways to survive its aftermath. Together. I stand before you not as a princess or duchess but as one of you. As one who has lived through bloody horrors, mayhem, and death. Left forever scarred, but in no way defeated." She took heart in the nods circling the room. "So many of you have shared your stories with me and for that I am grateful and humbled. I have felt your loss as my own."

"Feel our loss, do ye, Yer Grace?" A wiry man with fading red hair and a bandage around his left ear stood up from the back row. "What'd ye ken sittin' up in yer bonny castle wi' yer fine furs and jewels to warm ye. Ye dinna speak fae us."

Svetlana clasped her black lace–gloved hands together and offered a polite smile. "I do not believe I've had the opportunity of meeting you before, sir."

"'Twas lain up in a frog hospital fae neigh on five months wi' half me brains leakin' out this hole in me heid." He tapped the bandage. "Boyd Beardsly's the name."

"How do you do, Mr. Beardsly. Hopefully after our meeting we might have a private moment to speak, but for now I shall tell you that I was forced to flee my country as my home was burned over my head. My people were and still are hunted like dogs. My father and brother were murdered because of a sworn allegiance to their rightful king. I have begged in the gutters for scraps of bread to eat. All of my worldly possessions have been sold or stolen, leaving me only with the dignity of my name, which some would gleefully kill me over.

"So, no, Mr. Beardsly, I do not claim to speak for you. Merely as one who has shared a great loss, as you have." Her steady words belied the pounding of her heart. Her endeavor and acceptance rose and fell with these people. They never asked her to come and situate herself as their lady, but she was determined to gain their trust. If that meant opening this private piece of herself, then so be it.

"God save you, Your Grace!"

"Bless ye, Yer Grace!"

"She's not a toff, Beardsly! She's a MacCallan."

Beardsly scowled at the echoing voices around him before offering Svetlana a reluctant sniff. "Reckon ye hae at that. On wi' yer speech then." He waved a dismissive hand and plonked back down on the bench.

From the front row, Constance beamed while Marina sent her a sly wink. They, too, wore black and matching rosettes. If nothing else, she had their support.

Buoyed by the audience's desire not to shun her, the nervous whirling in her stomach ceased. "Thank you, Mr. Beardsly. As I was saying, our most pressing need is medical assistance. At present you are required to travel to and from Glasgow for exams and medications, wasting valuable income and days away from your farms and shops. I propose we open a medical facility here in Glentyre with trained nurses and a dedicated physician knowledgeable in the latest advancements to treat returning soldiers."

"His Grace kens about all that," said a man missing his left arm. A Mr. Grover, if Svetlana recalled, who farmed sheep. Next to him sat his wife clutching two children. They had been due a third child, but recently lost the baby.

Nerves tripping back into place, Svetlana pinched her fingers together. Wynn was the last thing she wanted to talk about, but he might as well be the proverbial elephant in the room. "His Grace has many responsibilities requiring his medical skills and duties for the estate. He is in full support of this proposition."

"His support, aye, but what o' him tendin' us as a healer? No every day there's a duke what can stop a bleedin' man." Mr. Grover's gaze softened to look at his wife. "Or woman, fae that matter."

"The duke's greatest desire is to serve the people of Glentyre, but in doing so he is forced to decline a commitment as permanent attending physician." Truth, but not the whole of it. "In addition to a medical facility, we will also have classes for those wishing to learn viable skills, open to both men and women, fourteen years of age and older."

Murmurs rippled around the room. Women bent their heads together while several of the men perked up.

"Ye're proposin' we pay fae this how? What few spare coins we hae left? Hospitals isna cheap," Mr. Grover said.

"The old weaver's mill is the prime location candidate. Repairs and renovations are at no cost to you, and we will be taking applications for tradesmen to work the site with priority given to Glentyre men. Classes and training sessions will be free of charge excluding any supplies needed. However, medical appointments and prescriptions will be your own expenses as per arrangement by the newly founded Ministry of Health and the Army Medical Board."

Medical Board. A collected tomb of cranky white-haired old men,

Wynn had called them. She instinctively scanned the room for him, her stomach fluttering with disappointment at not finding him. Her search found a small man dressed all in black hovering near the back corner. Sallow skin, greasy hair, and a pointed nose gave the repugnant image of a rat. The hairs prickled on the back of her neck as the memory of men dressed in black with red armbands dragging Sergey from the train platform trampled its horror over her once more. Some nights she still dreamed of them coming for her.

And like the instant waking from a dream, the man slipped behind the crowd. An expectant audience stared back at her.

"Thank you all for coming today," she hurried. "Before you leave please enjoy the pies and *vatrushkas*."

Constance and Marina moved to where Mrs. Varjensky stood with the baskets of food spread across a row of desks against the far wall. Svetlana weaved through the crowd in search of the rat man. Only by looking him in the eye could she put her nightmare to rest.

"Yer Grace. How ever can we be thankin' ye?" Katie MacKinnon, whom she'd first heard about while sitting with Mrs. Douglas, wobbled into a curtsy in front of her. She waved at her three little children to follow.

"Mrs. MacKinnon, a delight to see you." *If not a little untimely.*

The woman's chapped cheeks glowed pink. "An answer to prayer, this is. What with me man laid up 'tis hard to find proper work."

"I hope this will ease a burden weighing so heavily on our community."

"'Tis braw hearin' ye say 'our community.' We've a real princess championin' us, but my only hitch is what's to become of the bairns if'n I should take a class? Their da canna manage them on his own."

The three children's tattered clothes barely brushed their exposed ankles, but their hair was neatly combed as they stared at Svetlana with hungry eyes. When was the last time they'd seen a full meal on their table?

"I see the dilemma. This will take thought, but I give my word something will be managed."

"Oh, thank ye, Yer Grace. A godsend, ye are." Mrs. MacKinnon wobbled another curtsy. Over the top of her bowed head, the rat man stared at Svetlana. Nose twitching, he scurried into the outer hall.

"Excuse me, please. Be sure to sample the *vatrushkas* and take some home if you like." Svetlana hurried after the rat as people reached out to talk to her. She waved them off as politely as she could. It wasn't a co-incidence that man was here. If there was a threat, she needed to know.

Charging into the outer hall lined with coat hooks, she smacked into Sergey.

"What's all this?" He grasped her shoulders, holding her steady.

"You've returned."

"I could not stay away for long. You must know that."

Wasting no time deciphering that comment, she wriggled away just as the black flap of a cloak disappeared outside and the door banged shut on a gust of wind. She ran after the intruder. The wind whipped across her face and scattered the leaves around her feet as she scanned the schoolyard. A few tired horses and one fine gray from Thornhill's stable dotted the area, but not a soul to be seen.

Dead grass crunched beneath Sergey's polished boots as he joined her. "What's the commotion?"

"Did you see him?"

"See who?"

"A man. All in black." She stared down the single road leading from the schoolhouse and into the village. "You must have seen him in the hallway."

"I saw no one but hunched over villagers stuffing their faces." Taking her arm, he propelled her back inside. "It's much too cold for you to be standing in the elements."

"I'm Russian. My blood is made of winter's ice." She peered past him to the peep window squared out of the school's door.

"Tell that to your red ears and cheeks."

"He must have walked right by you."

"I saw no one, I tell you." He looked down at her. Every single mustache hair was perfectly combed and softened with oil smelling of nutmeg. "Are you feeling yourself, *kroshka*?"

She'd never cared for nutmeg. "I am not your little crumb."

The corners of his mouth turned down and he took half a step back, locking his hands behind his back. "Forgive my old habit of informality, it's only that I worry for you. Perhaps you spend too much time around these *muzhika*."

"They are not peasants."

"They might as well be for the social divide between us and them. As a gentleman and your oldest friend, I urge you to reconsider circulating among them so closely. It's not appropriate for a lady of your rank. They carry diseases."

This amount of idiocy was expected from her mother, but she never thought to witness it in Sergey. "I am not ill in the head if that is what you are suggesting, nor will I tolerate slander against these good people."

"Forgive me. I do not wish to insult you, merely to see you well looked after. Allow me to care for you, Svetka. The way you deserve. Far from this. Let me take you away. No one will ever find us. We'll be safe." He wrapped his arms around her, pressing her to the fine wool of his overcoat. Hugh's overcoat.

Mottled with anger at his bold persistence, Svetlana shoved him away. Something wasn't right. Sergey had never acted so out of character. "You forget yourself. Out of respect for the friendship we once held, I shall forget this distasteful notion while reminding you that I am a married woman."

"Married to a disgraced man standing accused of murder whom you never loved. Is that what you mean?"

"How do you know about that?"

"How do I not know when you rightfully belong to me? My eyes are everywhere you are. I love you, Svetka. This is our last chance to be together or all will be ruined. Send him away and come with—" Sergey jerked backward.

Wynn stood there holding the back of Sergey's collar. Rage thundered across his face. "I've a suggestion of where to send you." He dragged Sergey outside and pinned him against the back wall of the schoolhouse. His forearm crushed against Sergey's windpipe. "Lower than a snake's belly, slithering into my home and trying to seduce my wife. I've a mind to send you straight back to the hole from whence you crawled."

Wheezing, the whites of Sergey's eyes bulged as his gaze skittered to Svetlana. "H-help."

Wynn leaned forward. Sergey purpled as the full weight of Wynn's bulk settled on him. "Pack your bags and leave the country. If I hear even a rumor of your name, I won't waste a second in breaking your scrawny neck."

Wynn dropped his arm and Sergey crumpled to the ground in a coughing fit. "S-so much f-for y-your oath to d-do no harm-m."

"That oath was for humans. It said nothing about evil beasts. Go."

Sergey grabbed at the rough stone wall and hauled himself up. Red blotched his slim face as his dark eyes bored hatred into Wynn. Shuddering, he looked to Svetlana.

Wynn blocked him. "Last warning."

Panting, Sergey stumbled away to mount the fine gray horse and rode off. He looked back only once.

Svetlana trembled, but not from the gusting cold nor from the violent scene. Somehow through it all she'd felt utterly calm watching Wynn's barely restrained fury come within an inch of release, knowing he exerted complete control. Nothing was going to happen without him allowing it. Seeing him for the first time since their confrontation was what sent uncertainty shaking along her nerves. The ice crackled around her heart as it yearned for his nearness, while her head shouted for fortification around its beating vulnerabilities.

Hatless as usual, his hair waved unfettered in the breeze while the richness of his brown suit set off the gold in his eyes to perfection. Eyes that took her in with that efficient manner of his where nothing remained hidden. He reached for her hand. "You're shivering. Let's get you inside."

Exposed under that penetrating gaze, she angled away from his touch. It would undo her. "What are you doing here?"

His attention drifted from her face to her left ear. A hazy smile pulled at his lips. "Those are the earrings I gave you. I told you that I'd—"

"—captured a star."

"Captured a star that had shrunk in the presence of your beauty. I also said—"

"We said many things that night." Svetlana tugged at the curls she'd tried to cover her ears with that morning. A vain effort. Why of all her earrings could she not help herself from choosing these?

"I meant every one of them. I still do."

Another shard of ice fractured off her heart. She imagined the pain of his duplicity seeping into the crack, hurting her all over again. "Do not avoid the question with an entanglement of emotions."

"Loving you isn't an entanglement. It's a privilege."

"Then you should not have endangered it by withholding information vital to our future." Lies in a royal court or chandelier-graced parlor she could swat off with a flick of her glittering fan, but a lie from the man she had most trusted could not so easily be discarded.

He sighed. A weary, wordless sound that her tired soul recognized. "I wasn't going to come today. It might've raised too many questions, and I didn't want you put on the spot to answer them. Unfortunately, a summons from Glasgow forces me to crash your event." He scowled down the road where Sergey had disappeared. "Though not a moment too late."

She could not care less about Sergey at that moment. "The medical board?"

"Last hearing. They'll be making a formal decision at the end. I won't ask you to come, but I wouldn't say no if you wanted to."

Svetlana noticed his overnight valise strapped behind the saddle on his horse, tethered a few feet away. Her stomach dropped. "Are you leaving now?"

"It starts tomorrow morning. I think they like to let me know last minute in hopes I won't show up." He grinned, but it wasn't convincing. His life's work hung in the balance. "I know things have been strained between us of late and I take full responsibility. My pride and ambitions have hurt the people I care for most. My patients. Our tenants. You. I want to do what's best by all of you. For us."

She longed to hold him, to tell him she needed him and that she believed justice was on his side. Not because he was a surgeon or a duke, but because her life was incomplete without him. His words rocked against her anger, but pride bolstered her defenses and sealed off the confession.

"I believe you, but what has fractured between us cannot be mended so easily."

"But it can be mended. Tell me it can, please."

"I-I wish I could be certain."

"At least it's not a no."

He kissed her gently on the cheek, no more than a whisper of saddened regrets, and then he was gone. Svetlana stood in the schoolyard long after, impervious to the cold air. An ache swirled inside where her heart hung heavy in her chest like a broken pendulum.

CHAPTER 30

Svetlana padded along the corridor, the stone floor cold beneath her satin slippers. All of Thornhill was fast asleep as she found uncertainties troubling her mind after having received a reply from Mrs. Roscoe along with a sealed report from St. Matthew's. She would need to send it by special messenger to Glasgow first thing in the morning if it was to have any hope of reaching Wynn's trial in time.

Steering clear of the Grand Hall and its ghostly memories of dancing in Wynn's arms, she wandered into the far back reaches of the house where the floors and walls turned into a more contemporary wood style. Contemporary, at least, in comparison to the hodge-podge sixteenth- and seventeenth-century parts of the castle.

Descending a short flight of stairs, she followed the scent of baking bread to the kitchen. A large, rectangular room, its brick walls were warmed by cream paint and shining copper pots hanging from an iron rack over the worn worktable. Mrs. Varjensky stood in front of the enormous hearth stirring a black pot dangling over the fire. She refused to use a proper stove, claiming the old ways were better. Purer with no modern vapors to taint the food.

"No sleep?" the old woman said without turning around.

"*Nyet.*"

"Sit. Sit."

Svetlana perched on the only wooden stool next to the table. Apparently not much sitting was done in a kitchen. Bits of floured dough spotted the counter. "Midnight baking?"

"Cook woman. No let me come in day." She made a spitting noise over her hunched shoulder to ward off the devil. "My night secret."

There was a rivalry Svetlana had no desire to get caught in the middle of. Perhaps Mrs. Varjensky needed her own kitchen. The old gardener's cottage would be the perfect place for her to set up house-keeping, and as far as Svetlana knew there was no stove to taint the food with evil spirits.

"What are you making?"

"*Vareniki.*"

A dumpling with vegetables or in this case—Svetlana sniffed at the boiling pot—fruit. "My nanny growing up used to bring them from her village where her mother made them. She would go to visit twice a year, and Marina and I were so eager for her to return with the sweets."

"Twice year? That lucky. Most visit once every ten year. Or never."

Svetlana's memory had always seemed so quaint of tearing into brown paper–covered treats and devouring them without thought beyond the sweetness in her mouth. Peasant delicacies were never eaten among the rich soups and savory meats on nobles' dining tables. Her childish eyes never noticed the puffiness of her nanny's eyes or the sad smile holding back tears when Svetlana demanded to know why she had taken so long in returning—not to the poor woman's village home but to the Blue Palace that was anything but her home. How selfish she'd been as a child.

Mrs. Varjensky banged her wooden spoon on the pot and came over to the table. "You help."

"Me? I know nothing about baking."

"Two hands, *da*? You learn. Listen *babushka*. She show." With that, she proceeded to demonstrate how to knead the dough, dust it with flour to prevent it from sticking, and roll it flat. Using a thin, round piece of metal, they cut the dough into circles and filled them with the sugared berries stewing in the pot. Cook wasn't going to be pleased to find half of her sugar ration depleted come morning.

Once the first batch of *vareniki* was placed in the oven,

Mrs. Varjensky spit over the closed door to ward off the devil from the suspicious contraption and loudly complained about its inferiority to the brick ovens her people back home had used for generations. She made a quick pot of tea, squinting disapprovingly at it though thankfully avoiding spit this time, and poured a cup for each of them.

"Tell troubles."

Standing so Mrs. Varjensky could have the lone stool, Svetlana took a sip of her tea. A bit strong, but a spoonful of the sweetened berries softened the taste. "I have no troubles."

"Mama push away, other family dead, old suitor arrive, Reds still hunt, and husband gone. You troubled, *rebyonok*."

Svetlana choked at the bluntness and put her cup down. Plain white with a chip on the rim, this teacup was not from the set served upstairs. "When you put it like that, I suppose I do have troubles. Not one of them easily solved."

"Suitor banished. One solved." The wrinkles in the old woman's face burgeoned as she grinned.

When Svetlana had arrived home after the meeting at the school-house, Sergey was already gone. She'd managed to avoid an explanation to Constance, Marina, and Mama so far, but they would want to know of his sudden departure soon enough.

Mama. That was a whole other tempest waiting to whip itself into a storm. Svetlana tired of weathering them. The damage proved too painful and the broken pieces irretrievable.

"My mother, well, we both know that's an impossibility. She is who she is, and our relationship will never be more than a passing acceptance that we share the same blood and not much more."

"Fear make walls. Only strongest flower bloom over tallest wall. No stop climbing. Look at Reds. Build wall of fear and hate. Hate never win."

"Rumors circulated in Paris of the Bolsheviks coming after those fleeing to drag them back to Russia. I saw where they met in the back rooms. What if they find us here?"

"We kill them. My father butcher. I know use knife."

Well, that was terrifying and not the answer Svetlana had expected from the sweet old lady she'd come to see as a grandmother.

Mrs. Varjensky slurped her tea. "Now. Husband. That bigger problem." A bigger problem than wielding a butcher's knife? "Why you no with him?"

Svetlana stared down into her brew. Maybe if she stared hard enough an easy answer would bubble to the surface. "I . . . He has official medical business to see to."

"No care. Why you no go with him? Husband wife together. Always."

"It's not always possible to be together. Sometimes circumstances force you apart. Circumstances you didn't expect, and once they've come you have no idea how to recover what was lost."

"Nothing lost to those wishing in finding it."

"It's not that I do not wish to find it. Rather, I do not know if I can." Perhaps it was the warmth of the fire, or the smell of baking bread. Perhaps it was the comfort of the Russian tea, or the old woman's kind voice, but Svetlana could no longer suppress the well of hurt in her heart. A tear slipped down her cheek. "He lied to me, *babushka*."

"How?"

"Something happened to him that he decided I was better off not knowing. I only discovered the truth by accident. He claims he was going to tell me before and that he only sought to protect me. He wanted to try to right the wrong first. The trust between us has been broken by his betrayal."

Mrs. Varjensky let out a long cackle until tears wedged into the creases on her face. An unexpected response for the second time that evening. Were the midnight kitchen vapors upsetting her mental faculties? She swiped at the tears with the edge of her shawl. Wynn's *matryoshka* doll brooch was pinned above her heart. "Pride is stubbornness of youth."

"Trust is paramount in a relationship."

"So forgiveness." Pushing her cup aside, she laid a wrinkled hand over Svetlana's. It was worn with blue veins crisscrossing the tissue-thin skin, yet it pulsed with warmth. "Why he lie? Protect you. This come from love. Men none smart in proving love, but love all same."

"He should have told me his troubles from the beginning. I could have helped him. Supported him so that he wouldn't be forced to carry the burden alone." More tears came. "I've never been one for trusting. Trusting involves relying on others, and more times than not they prove unequal to the task. Then Wynn came along. He softens me in ways I never believed existed. Until him, I was buried under the misunderstanding that I am difficult to love, but he's made it appear effortless. I can simply *be* with him."

"One time he let down, you cut him out." Mrs. Varjensky made a ratcheting sound like ice breaking. "You have mistake. He have mistake. All us make mistake. Holding on to mistake is pride. Pride enemy to love."

Love. A four-letter notion allotted to poetry and music, yet its substance poured through the very threads of human existence. The poets dreamed of it, the scholars philosophized on its merits, the operas sang of it, and kingdoms rose and fell for it. She didn't want it to be a concept touted onstage for the amusement of audiences; she wanted it to reside within her. Within Wynn. Perhaps these threads were divided among lovers so that when they met the cords might become whole. If she were to look inside herself, would she find the cord whole? Yes, she believed she would. But she might also find it dangerously close to unraveling.

"Him you love?"

The truth refused denial under the old woman's probing gaze. Svetlana nodded, gaining strength with the small admission. "Yes."

"He love you?"

"He's told me so." From the very beginning of their marriage he'd told her how much he cared for her. He'd given her honesty when she craved it yet was too scared to accept it.

"All that matters. Love not something happens. Love builds little each day. Must care for, put effort. If no, love burn out. Let me tell wisdom: nothing colder than ashes after fire of love gone. We Russians too long cold."

Laughing, Svetlana dabbed the tears from her cheeks with her robe's lacey cuff. "I thought we were proud of that fact."

"Shh. No one need know truth. Secret we all cold. This why we need men keep us warm. Where yours?"

"Glasgow."

"That where you need be."

"But what if—"

"If, if, if. Questions for fools. You no fool. You kind heart admit or no." Wriggling off the stool, Mrs. Varjensky pulled the tray of baked *vareniki* out of the oven and set it on the table. A delicious whiff steamed off the golden puffs.

"You're wrong, *babushka*. My heart is mine no longer. Wynn took it long ago. I just didn't realize it until now." He had taken her heart over so completely that Svetlana was almost afraid to look further into herself lest she discover how little of herself was still joined to it.

"Go where heart is."

And with those words, she was free. Why had it taken so long? Svetlana hugged the old woman, kissing her soft cheek. "*Spasibo*."

Taking a square of linen, Mrs. Varjensky scooped up a handful of the puffs and bundled them into the makeshift sack. "Take. Take and give *golubchik*. He need eat more."

A bell sounded in the adjoining servant's hall. Svetlana ducked through the door and looked at the mounted board where the bell for the front door was rocking back and forth on its spring. Who would call at this late hour?

Svetlana handed the wrapped pastries back to Mrs. Varjensky. "Keep them warm for me. I'll fetch them in the morning before I leave for the train."

Hurrying to the Stone Hall, she was met by Glasby, dressed in his customary uniform of black coat and starched shirt. Either he never slept or he went to bed fully dressed, otherwise he could not have beaten her to the door.

Unaffected by the ungodly hour of the surprise visitor, he notched his chin up and opened the door. "May I help you?"

Icy air swept past the opened door and swirled around Svetlana. She drew her robe closer about her and tried to peer past Glasby's shoulder from where she waited in the shadows. It wouldn't do to have the visitor spot the lady of the house in a state of *dishabille*.

The man outside was thick with a fine coat buttoned about him and a hat shadowing his face. He spoke too low for Svetlana to hear him.

"We have no lady here by the name of Angel, if a lady she be," Glasby intoned. "There is a place one village over where you might have better luck."

The man tried to push his way inside. "Mac!"

Svetlana rushed from her hiding place. "Leonid? What are you doing here?"

Leonid Sheremetev, looking more wan than when she'd last seen him in Paris, brushed past Glasby and grabbed her by the shoulders. "Blessed holy God, you alive, Angel! I come tell you. You and Mac in danger."

CHAPTER 31

A solitary circular window perched high on the wall like the all-knowing eye to the official proceedings instigated within its domain. Its singular existence emitted a pale shaft of mid-morning sunlight that mocked the inner stale air with nature's brilliance. Wynn would endure the shatters of glass cutting his skin if he could hurtle himself through that window and escape the droning from the pasty old men seated in front of him.

His fate would be decided today. A doctor or a duke. Like any man before the gallows, he wished a swift end to this torturous waiting.

Glasgow's Medical Hall was none so grand as the Royal Medical Academy, but among the offices, laboratories, and classrooms a chamber had been reserved for said torture. What it lacked in thumb screws and iron maidens it made up for with a long table occupied by seven serious-looking men sitting in severely uncomfortable chairs. The defendant's chair, the one Wynn occupied, was most likely fitted with a loose spring if the pain at his left backside was any indication.

Dr. Stan, a retired optician, took the seat of precedence at the center of the table. Adjusting his eyeglasses, he looked across the table at Wynn.

"Dr. Lehr's character reference, along with several other key witness testimonies from Hôpital du Sacré-Coeur in Paris, have provided this review board a great deal to contemplate. As you know, Dr. Lehr is a trusted physician and his word goes a long way—"

"Get on with it," came the voice of a disgruntled orthopedist from farther down the table. He'd called Wynn a quack from day one and made no bones about the relish with which he would strip Wynn's license for good. Orthopedic surgery had been around for centuries, and those old boys didn't much care for the newfangled ideas associated with cardiology. A straightforward bone was more their game while blood made them squeamish.

Dr. Stan glared at the interrupter. "As I was saying, such high recommendations do not weigh lightly on the decision of this board. They are a great marker in the testimony of character of Mr. MacCallan. No! Pardon me. His Grace, the Duke of Kilbride."

Wynn didn't know which was worse. Being called by his name or his title. Above all he was a doctor.

"It is unfortunate anytime a patient succumbs, and we all as oath-taking physicians understand the risk of such loss. The only reason this review is being conducted is because you proceeded with a technique not consented to by your superiors from which your patient later died due to post-op complications."

"An unethical operation," huffed Orthopedic Man.

"A new operational method with lifesaving possibilities," Wynn corrected, rubbing his sweating palms against his thighs.

Dr. Stan nodded patiently. "Yes, all of that is here in the typed report. I am only repeating the charge as a formality. Before the board's final recommendation is voted on to reinstate His Grace or permanently revoke his medical license, are there any final words that wish to be said?"

Wynn shook his head. He'd said all he could from the truth as he knew it. Whatever the outcome, he would rest with his conscience clear, knowing he'd done the right thing by his patient at the time. It was all any physician could do.

"Very well. All those in favor of reinstating His Grace with full exoneration and medical rights as obtained by all licensed physicians in Great Britain—"

Bang. Bang. Bang.

All eyes swiveled toward the door as scuffling and angry shouts sounded from the other side. The door burst open. In strode Svetlana dressed head to toe in icy blue followed by none other than Leonid Sheremetev.

A junior physician scampered in behind them. "You cannot be in here, miss! The sign says no admittance." He made the mistake of trying to take her arm.

Leonid grabbed the back of Junior's jacket and tossed him out the door like a sack of meal. "No ever touch Her Serenity the Princess, weasel man. I make ham sandwich from you." He slammed the door shut on Junior's cry of outrage.

Having heard the title of nobility, the men behind the table rose confusingly to their feet. "Pardon, Your Royal Highness, but you cannot—"

Svetlana's slim eyebrows spiked beneath the froth of her hat veil. "I am not a royal highness. I am Her Serenity the Princess Svetlana Dmitrievna Dalsky MacCallan, Duchess of Kilbride."

Crikey, it was impressive when she rolled out her full title. Released from mourning clothes, she was terribly beautiful to behold. With her silver upswept hair, dress and hat the color of the sky reflecting off a glacier, she moved like a queen of the north. And she had come. Wynn was struck with wonder and fear at the same time.

He stood, but a low railing separated them as she glided up the central aisle.

"What are you doing here?"

She ignored him and kept her attention on the board members. "I have received evidence showing that the surgery performed by Dr. Edwynn MacCallan is not to blame for the death of Lieutenant Harkin."

Unable to sit in the presence of a standing lady, Dr. Stan shuffled from one short leg to the other. "Your Highness, er, Your Grace. A wife cannot testify against or in favor of her husband."

She waved a gloved hand at the inconsequential matter of law. "I have the evidence to prove that the purpose of this board is complete idiocy."

The board members harrumphed with indignation as Dr. Stan tried to keep the peace. "Be that as it may—"

"Do you not wish to hear the truth for yourself, or are you more eager to condemn a man, a well-respected physician, for doing what was required of him as a surgeon? Are you so petty in your antiquated mindset that you need to quiet any who might propose advancements in medical knowledge when the true culprit lies at the feet of no one save a German gun?"

One had to admire her technique. Straight for the jugular. But it could cost them everything.

"Svetlana," Wynn hissed.

She ignored his warning. "How many of you sitting there can boast of never having a patient die on your operating table? Or soon after due to complications unforeseen?"

"Svetlana."

The orthopedist sniffed. "*I* have never had an expired patient."

She ignored him too. "Lieutenant Harkin was a tragic case, but he believed in Dr. MacCallan's ability to heal him."

Sighing, Dr. Stan adjusted his eyeglasses as they slipped down his small nose. "As moving as your spousal support is, Your Grace, we simply cannot allow you to speak for your husband or to submit evidence that should have been turned over when this case first opened. It is against procedure."

"I received the letter only yesterday, so you must excuse the tardiness, though not the validity." Reaching into her handbag, she withdrew two slim envelopes. One was addressed in delicate script and the other carried the broken seal of St. Matthew's Hospital in London.

"It is against the law and holds no weight in this decision. More to the point, women simply are not allowed in these proceedings. Your word cannot be counted."

"Women indeed. It is no wonder your board proves incompetent." Sweeping aside, Svetlana motioned Leonid forward. "Then allow me to introduce Leonid Sheremetev, *boyar* of Muscovy. I don't believe you have the same qualms for *him* speaking."

Of Moscow Leonid might be, but nobleman he was not. The board members would know nothing of that, but it got their attention. His friend sauntered up the aisle in a finely cut suit that slimmed his pudgy waistline and stood next to Svetlana. What were these two up to?

"I Leonid Sheremetev." Leonid's boom knocked the white hairs back in their chairs. "This proof Mac no guilty. He true surgeon. He fix me after Reds shot in back alley." Fishing inside his somewhat wrinkled shirt, he pulled out a piece of metal on a chain looped around his neck. "This here bullet."

The extracted slug winked a dull silver as it spun delicately on its expensive gold chain above the thick turf of Leonid's chest hair.

"Congratulations on your recovery, Mr. Sheremetev," Dr. Stan said, "but I don't believe a bullet will drop the charges leveled against His Grace."

"Bullet no proof. I only show Mac fine handiwork." Leonid's lips flattened with derision as he tucked away the bullet and took the envelopes from Svetlana. He passed them to Wynn across the rail divider. "This proof like she say. Late or no, you take and read."

Wynn scanned the letters. Hope trembled inside him. "It's an updated autopsy report for Harkin. It claims he died from an undetected shell fragment lodged behind his right lung that became infected after my surgery. After he was cleared for release from hospital." He passed the papers to Dr. Stan. "It wasn't heart surgery complications that killed him."

Dr. Stan stared at the letters in his hands, uncertainty flitting across his face. If he took the letters as evidence, it would go against the law of the board, but if he refused he would be sentencing a potentially innocent man.

"I . . . How ever did you obtain this?"

Svetlana smiled coolly as if she'd been waiting for him to inquire all along. "I had the very great pleasure of meeting Mrs. Roscoe while en route from Paris to England on board a troop ship shortly after I was married. She had been visiting her husband in France, a Colonel Richard Roscoe, whom you may know better as the new head of administration at St. Matthew's Hospital, the very place where Lt. Harkin was recovering.

"We've kept in touch and she was quite distressed to hear of my husband's current circumstances. After she discussed the matter with her own husband, Dr. Roscoe was instrumental in ordering a more thorough autopsy that fully clears Dr. MacCallan of malignant surgery due to an unrelated and unseen fragment of shell." She pointed a gloved finger to the papers in his hands. "You may read the redacted and new report for yourself along with a personal note from Dr. Roscoe."

"But how did . . . "

"Women like to talk." Svetlana shrugged a dainty shoulder. "Shall I wait outside in a more appropriate area while you come to the obvious conclusion?"

Dr. Stan waved a distracted hand as he frowned at the papers in his hands. "Best if you did, Your Royal, er, Princess, er, Madame."

Wynn reached for her hand. "Svetlana, wait. What you've done . . . How can I ever tell you—"

"Say you love like she love you, Mac." Leonid apparently thought it wise to insert himself into the narrative once more.

Wynn's eyes didn't leave his wife's face. "Is that true?"

Beneath the veil, Svetlana's eyes swept to Wynn's. Pink stained her cheeks. Not in a restrained anger sort of way, but in a no forthcoming denial sort of way. Was that why she had come? Because she loved him? His heart soared. *Lana* . . .

"Love make later. Now I tell about *Papochka* and Bolshevik chums. You like I say chums? I pick up English words now. *Fish chip.*

Blimey. Spot o' tea." He shook his head as if to clear it. "It make no matter. You know my *papochka* never concern politics, only money. Whoever have money, they come to bar. So Bolsheviks come. Plot and plan and hunt for noblemen émigrés. Kidnap back to Russia for execution. *Papochka* mad when Angel left. She make much money for him. Now gone, he want revenge, so make deal with Bolsheviks take her to Russia and execute. *Papochka* get revenge while hands clean of dirty work. I there. I hear whole deal, so rush to warn Mac and Angel. They save my life. I return favor."

"Are the Bolsheviks on their way now?"

Dr. Stan frowned as he looked up from reading the new letters. "Who are these Bolsheviks and what is a popka?"

"Bolsheviks, Reds, communists. Murder imperial Russian family. Govern Russia now. My papa do business with if lucrative."

"If you have nothing further to add to this case, I must insist you, sir, and the princess remove yourselves out of these doors." Dr. Stan flipped open the folder in front of him and squinted between the filed papers and the new report in his hand. "In the meantime this board will suspend its vote. My apologies for extending your purgatory, Your Grace, but rather we should discover all of the truth than condemn a man for his duties as a physician. If you could but give us a few minutes more for discussion."

"Certainly." Wynn turned back to his wife, wanting with all his heart to leap across the low wall and kiss her senseless between words of love, but the impending danger outweighed all else. "Go to Savoy Hotel and wait for me in my room. You'll be safe there until we can decide what to do next."

The faintest hint of a smile curved her lips. "*We'll* decide?"

What was it she had said once? Russians were never ruled by their hearts because they were too fond of misery? Perhaps when they returned to Thornhill they could let go of the misery and put more effort into matters of the heart. Their hearts.

"Yes, because that's what *we* do. Together."

"No worries, Mac. I protect Angel with life until you arrive. After you arrive too." Furrows wrinkled Leonid's brow. "Never much like *Papochka* as criminal. I always want family go straight, own proper bar and restaurant. Money more interesting for him. I make new family with you."

With that inarguable proclamation, he offered Svetlana his arm and escorted her from the room. She glimpsed over her shoulder and smiled at Wynn, making his heart soar as the door swung shut.

Bam!

The gunshot echoed outside the door.

Wynn leaped over the divider and barreled down the aisle. Bursting into the corridor, he stumbled over Leonid sprawled on the floor in a thin puddle of blood.

Clutching the bleeding wound in his arm, Leonid fired off in rapid Russian, curse words if Wynn's ear picked them out correctly, before switching to English. "That way, Mac! Go!"

Wynn sprinted after the distant echo of feminine heels clicking down the tiled hall. He knocked past men in white coats and orderlies pushing trollies until the heel clicks vanished behind a slamming door leading to the back alley of the building. Ripping open the door, he raced out.

"Wynn!" Svetlana screamed as she was shoved into a waiting carriage.

Dressed in Hugh's stolen clothing, Sergey was wild-eyed as the devil himself as he leaped into the carriage after her and slammed the door. His accomplice, a man wearing all black and sporting a red armband, cracked the reins over the horses and the carriage shot off like a bullet.

CHAPTER 32

Svetlana stared at the man seated across from her in the carriage. A face familiar to her yet the man within utterly unknown.

"How could you do this? How could you turn traitor and become a Bolshevik? I thought I knew you better."

"I am not one of them. Whatever foul thoughts you may have for me at present, at least know that truth." Sweat dotted Sergey's pale brow. Gripping a gun in one hand until his knuckles whitened, he withdrew a soiled handkerchief from his pocket with his other equally strained hand and swiped his face. Never in her life had she seen him without a clean linen or with frayed cuffs. He had been living rough since he'd fled Thornhill, and the loss did not agree with him.

Quaking inside, she refused to let him see her fear. "Then it is well you cannot read my mind, for it is black enough to blot out all manner of niceties. How dare you turn a gun on me? Stop this carriage at once."

"There will be no stopping, at least not until we reach our destination. And do not think to take your leave early. The doors are locked."

The secured shades closed off all recognition of the passing landmarks Svetlana could use to determine their route. Any clue along the way for a means of escape. Without visual aid, she tried following the map of Glasgow in her mind, but as the carriage veered around corner after corner the map tangled into confusion. "Where might our destination be?"

"You are going home. To Russia."

"To be executed."

A sob escaped from Svetlana's mother who cowered against her

353

daughter's side. Dressed in a fine traveling ensemble of black and gray, she clearly had not been kidnapped. Her face had registered absolute shock when Svetlana was unceremoniously stuffed inside the waiting carriage.

Svetlana put her arm around her shaking mother. Whatever tension existed between them no longer mattered. "What did he tell you, Mama?"

"He told me you were in grave danger. That the Bolsheviks had found us and were lying in wait for you as you chased after Wynn. Little did I know it was he who was the Bolshevik."

"Do not call me one of them again!" The gun shook in Sergey's hand.

Mama bawled into her handkerchief before looking back to Svetlana. "I thought we were waiting in the carriage to whisk you safely back to Scotland."

"Where is Marina?" Svetlana demanded. "And how did you get to Thornhill? Wynn banished you."

"Your sister was in the village with that peasant woman you keep on a leash. I did not have time to wait for her to return, so you two will have to suffice. As far as that so-called husband of yours, he may be lord of the manor, but I'm cunning enough to slip past any arrogant roadblocks he set up. Particularly that watchdog butler."

Mama clutched at Svetlana's sleeve. Great fat tears rolled off her cheeks and plopped onto the material. "He told me Bolsheviks were watching the house and we had to slip off quietly. I didn't know, Svetka. I swear I didn't. I never would have gone with him if I'd known."

"It's all right, Mama. He might have tied you up and carried you out if he'd been forced to. Much easier to have a willing yet clueless victim." Svetlana leveled a cold stare at him. "Why? What have we done for you to turn on us, your dearest friends? Why go through the lies of trying to reunite with us in Paris?"

He shifted restlessly on the seat, squeezing the gun's handle again and again. The white of his knuckles pulsed like a heartbeat. "Because I *was* trying to reunite with you after fleeing Russia. When I arrived in Paris I had nothing. I was desperate, searching for you everywhere. One day I learned of the name Sheremetev and how he knew every Russian in the city, so I went to him begging for information about you. Your name sparked no delight for him, only cold-blooded hatred. He informed me that you had recently been married and no longer patronized his club with your dancing. I always adored your dancing, you know that, right?" His tone softened at the end. The tip of his gun wavered.

If he hoped to kindle good memories within her, he'd failed. "Sheremetev wants revenge for when I would no longer dance for him. He wants to murder me, Sergey, and all you care to do is spin compliments. How did you become tangled in his web?"

"He sold me to the Bolsheviks because of my connection to you. The Bolsheviks wanted to use my connection to seize you."

"So you have become the worker for their dirty deeds. But why? If we are indeed such friends, how could you turn on us?"

The carriage picked up speed as the scent of brine and seaweed dampened the air. They must be near the River Clyde that flowed through the city center. A good ten blocks from Glasgow's Medical Hall. And Wynn.

"Because if I do not bring you back to Russia they will kill my sister and mother." A knot bobbed in his throat. "They have already killed my father. I cannot allow the rest of my family to die. I am sorry, Svetka."

"Do not call me that. You do not have the right anymore. A true friend would never make a deal with the devil at the expense of those he claims to care for."

The panic of desperation cried in his eyes. "I tried to find other ways to save you! To run away together. To bribe Sheremetev to save my family and get them to Paris. Handing you over was never what I wanted."

Rage hissed in Svetlana's blood. Violent and hot, it screamed for release. The gun beckoned from Sergey's hand, taunting her to give in to the viciousness, but she remained still. Not from fear for herself but for her mother. She would wait until the opportune moment.

"You're nothing more than a pathetic rat. The honorable Sergey Kravchenko I know would never betray us."

"One does what one must for their family. Doing things they never dreamed possible for the sake of survival. You should know that yourself. Such as marrying a stranger." The desolation in his eyes receded to ice, a blackness set to swallow her whole. "But then I saw you with him. You had given your heart to him, and I knew it could never be mine again, that you would never run away with me to save yourself. I knew then that you were not the price for my family's lives."

In all his dealings, had Sergey not considered the most likely outcome? "How can you be certain the Bolsheviks will not kill you and your family anyway?"

The blackness in his eyes courted death. "Because if I do not turn you over, we are as good as dead. I have no option but to trust the devil."

"You low-lying snake! Fork-tongued, weasel, pathetic excuse for a man!" Claws out, Mama lunged across the carriage and raked her nails down Sergey's face. Ribbons of scarlet tore his cheeks.

Cursing, Sergey smacked her hard, knocking her back against the seat. Blood welled from her split lip. "Sit there and don't move or you'll get much worse." He pointed the gun at her leg. "The firing squad won't care if you stand or not."

Mama spit at him. Bloody spittle sprayed his white necktie.

Sergey flashed the gun to Svetlana's knee. "Last warning."

Grabbing her mother's hand, Svetlana fought against the rising tide of panic. Calm resourcefulness was their best chance for survival. As they'd had when escaping the threat of Russia once before.

The carriage wheels clattered over cobblestones, jostling the occupants like marbles in a box until they rumbled to a stop. Train horns whistled in the distance.

The door jerked open and there stood the rat man, his nose and mouth jutted out to a near direct point. His round eyes settled over Svetlana and Ana, but he said nothing as he blocked their escape to the busy sidewalk.

"Do not think to try anything. You will immediately regret it." Flashing his gun as a cautionary reminder, Sergey handed Ana out first to his accomplice, then Svetlana, keeping a tight hold on her arm. Blotting the blood from his face with a handkerchief, he placed a homburg hat atop his head. Made for a slightly larger crown, the hat slipped over his ears, shadowing the scratches on his cheeks. "Now, come along, ladies. We've a train to catch."

Glasgow Central Train Station. With its skeletal ironworks arching over the platforms, dark wood information desks, flashing indicator boards, and large hanging clocks overseeing the bustling schedule, the station chugged a chaotically precise rhythm familiar to anyone whirling from one place to another. A mere two hours before Svetlana had stepped off platform six with nothing more than Mrs. Roscoe's letter in her pocket and a winged prayer. By the end of the day she and Wynn should have started a new chapter in their life. A chapter full of promise that would begin with her confession of love.

With a cruel twist of fate, that chapter was ripped from her hands, its pages stained with the forthcoming blood spilled on Russian soil. Her blood.

She had to do something before that awful fate became her own.

People dressed in somber tones of black and gray that matched the outside dreariness bustled by with their eyes fixed on a destination far beyond the walls and steel tracks that had brought them here.

Svetlana tried to catch the eye of more than one of the station's uni-formed workers in hopes they would recognize her, but none seemed to take much interest in a lady on the arm of a well-dressed gentleman. They might have cared more if they'd seen the gun hidden inside his coat.

"Don't think of signaling to one of them," Sergey whispered in her ear. The tip of his gun pressed into her side.

"Or you'll shoot me? That would cause a scene I'm certain you're wishing to avoid."

They descended to a lower level where the crowds thinned and the air thickened with grease and coal smoke. Belching steel trains screeched along tracks and ground to a stop at the platforms where passengers crawled out like ants to scurry up the stairs or onto another platform. Shoulders and briefcases knocked against her, propelling her farther and farther into the belly of no escape. There, among the sea of unflinching black, a flash of red. Svetlana swallowed a cry of panic as she waited for the hands to grab her and yank her into the thrashing chaos of revolution. Mama cried behind her, Sergey's hand tight on her arm as they raced for the last train.

The red floated by. A man's scarf. Time snapped forward and out of the past.

"Brings back that last night in Petrograd." Sergey remembered too.

"It was the last night I thought you had a heart."

"Only to have wasted it on you, but unlike that night, I'll be going with you this time. A touch of sentiment in that, I think." He stopped to face her, and nothing existed in his expression to remind her of that awful night. Gone was the man who had kissed her cheek and thrown her onto the train to save her. In his place stood an unrecognizable man who chilled her to the core. "When I handed you onto that train in Petrograd, I knew it was the end of our beginning. A romance with-ered before it could bloom. This, however, truly will be the beginning of our end."

Her life had come to revolve around train stations as significant markers in time. Traveling on holiday to the Black Sea beaches with her family. Saying goodbye to Father as the army went to battle once more. *That* night of revolution. Sitting next to Wynn as they discussed his soon-to-be position at the hospital. Sitting next to Wynn in silence after the position had been snatched from his hands. That very morning's ride when the wheels could not roll fast enough to bring her to him. Now her last ride was to take her away from him. Perhaps there was poignancy to these bookending markers. A tragedy fit for Tolstoy.

At the far end near the very last platform was a bank of waiting rooms built for ladies to escape the ghastly smoke-soaked air. With the more fashionable platforms located upstairs to attract lady passengers, these waiting rooms appeared to be used more for storage. Finding an empty one, Sergey stuffed Svetlana and her mother inside. A single lamp hung from the low ceiling and rattled with each passing train.

"Find the conductor. Tell him we're here and give him this." Snatching off his oversize hat, Sergey tossed the rat man a bag that clinked with coin. "He'll get the rest when we change trains in London. Should be enough to keep his mouth shut."

The man shoved the coin bag into his pocket and scampered off, shutting the door behind him.

Nudging a crate out of the way, Svetlana helped her mother sit on a dusty leather bench. Leached of color and droopy, Mama moved like a brittle leaf blown far from its strength of branch and tree. She'd been the same when they fled Petrograd. She wouldn't survive another trip.

"Bribery and betrayal. How you've sunk in the world. The Bolsheviks must be proud," Svetlana said.

Sergey's mouth twisted into a cruel line. "I told you never to associate me with them."

"Then don't associate yourself! Don't do this, Sergey. I know you think there is no choice left, but there is still time to find another way. I can help you." If she could somehow reach the man she'd once known deep inside him, the man too fearful to come out on his own, then she would stop at no length to sway him.

"I understand feeling alone with all burdens weighted on your shoulders and only wanting to keep your loved ones safe. I have lived this horror for a year. Looking back, my actions make me weep for what I was forced to endure, but no matter how dark our circumstances, we cannot allow ourselves to give in to desperation when innocent lives hang in the balance. Please, if it is a Dalsky you require, allow my mother to go free while you take me on."

"It is too late for negotiation."

"It is never too late to do the right thing. We can save your family. We can make them safe far from Russia. Wynn has great power as—"

"Do not speak his name to me! This is how it will be. You and your mother will die for my family to live."

"How do you know your family hasn't been killed already? How do you know the Bolsheviks will honor their word?"

"Do you not understand? I have no choice but to trust them. If I don't do this, my family *will* die for certain."

Seeing nothing small enough to use as a club, she wielded venom as her weapon. "Then you are no different from these murderous Bolsheviks you claim to hate."

His eyes darkened to the fury of a winter storm thundering across the frozen tundra. He backhanded her across the face. The blow stung, juddering along her cheek bone and jaw.

The door squeaked open and the rat man slipped inside. He spoke in uneducated Russian. A village mongrel begging for scraps at the table of power. "We go in the fourth carriage. Other boxes filled with coal. Wait for the last call."

On the platform outside a man's voice carried over the hissing steam and shuffling feet. "Train six forty-two to London. All aboard!"

"If one of you so much as twitches in attempt to escape, I will not hesitate to kill both of you." Sergey touched the gleaming handle of his gun. "If your own death lacks incentive, know that I will personally return to finish off the last remaining Dalsky princess. Do I make myself clear?"

Svetlana stood erect, not bothering to comfort the pain throbbing the left side of her face. She had to remain strong for Marina's sake. Svetlana gripped her mother's hand and nodded. They couldn't simply jump from the train. They would have to take care of Sergey first. Terror pounded in her heart as her gaze slipped to the gun. She would take care of him, whatever it came to.

"Last call! All aboard!"

Sergey yanked the veil down over Svetlana's face. "Can't have someone recognizing you." Pushing open the door, he swept his hand with grand invitation. "Onward to destiny."

CHAPTER 33

Stealing horses was not an offense Wynn was in the habit of making, but today required an exception. He'd chased the carriage around the corner, but its four wheels and two horses quickly outpaced his two legs.

The horse stood before him like a gift from above. Shouting a promise to its owner to return it, he galloped off, swerving around wagons and motor cars, causing more than one near accident with his lack of fine horsemanship, but ever with the thieving carriage in his sights.

Far ahead, the carriage stopped in front of the train station. A figure in light blue stepped out. Svetlana. Wynn urged his mount forward, but the crush of pedestrians impeded his speed. By the time he reached the abandoned carriage, she was nowhere to be found.

"No luggage this time, Your Grace?" asked one of the station porters who had become familiar with Wynn traveling often to Glasgow.

"Have you seen Her Grace come this way? In a blue dress."

"No, but I've only just come on duty. Lemme ask one of the other lads—"

"No matter." Wynn jumped off the horse and tossed him the reins. "Hold this horse until I come back."

Sprinting inside, Wynn pushed his way through the throngs of humanity, uncaring of the disgruntled comments directed at him. He twisted his head this way and that in search of a scrap of blue among the black and gray. Nothing. If that black-livered dog hurt her in any way, Wynn wouldn't hesitate to choke the life from him.

People knocked into him. Hats blocked his view. He needed to get up higher. Shoving through the crowd, he leapt on top of a pile of trunks.

"Svetlana!" Attention snapped his way, but not a flash of blue. "Svetlana!"

"Your Grace." One of the station masters hustled over and did his best not to glare at Wynn. One positive thing about holding a title was that no one wanted to insult him directly or inform him what he was doing was wrong. "Might I ask you to come down from there?"

Wynn ignored the request. Politeness could go hang. "Have you seen my wife?"

"This morning I did. Bonny blue gown. So nice to be seeing her out of mourning—"

"Have you seen her again? Just now?"

"Let me think." The station master tapped his finger against his top lip for an excruciating second. "Aye, I believe I did. She was with two gentleman and a lady. Aye, I'm sure it was her. That blue stands out among all the black I see every day."

Wynn leaped down, snapping with impatience. "Where did she go?"

The station master stumbled back a step. "I, er, saw her that way." He pointed to a flight of stairs going down.

Wynn raced over and down the stairs, knocking people aside. The crowd lessened on the lower level as workers moved crates and trunks around the platforms. He ran the length of two passenger trains, scanning the windows, but Svetlana wasn't there. More trains chugged up the tracks, cargo carriers with grimy faced workers who saw more smoke than sunlight. He twisted his way through the trolleys of luggage and stacks of crates to where a final train huffed at its deserted platform.

A door among a bank of waiting rooms opened and out stepped Sergey and Svetlana, followed by her mother and a tiny rat of a man hustling toward the last train.

"Svetlana!" Wynn ran to her. Thank God he'd found her.

"Wynn!" Face alighting, she took a step to him, but Sergey jerked her back to his side as hatred contorted his face where angry red marks clawed down his cheeks. Someone had made a scratching post of him.

"Take care of him," he instructed the rat.

Releasing his hold on Ana, who appeared barely able to hold herself upright, the man charged at Wynn, head down and shoulders hunched. Having played a few seasons of university rugby, Wynn braced himself and sidestepped at the last second. His opponent whirled around for another go. Wynn hammered his fist into the man's face. Bone crunched and blood spurted. He crumpled onto a pile of boxes, clutching his bleeding, broken nose.

The vicious thrill of violent anger sang in Wynn's blood, but it wasn't enough. His ferocity demanded consumption in full. He turned on Sergey.

"Is that how you remaining Russians fight? No wonder all the intelligent ones fled your pathetic existence."

Sergey withdrew a revolver from his jacket and yanked Svetlana closer to his side. He caressed the gun barrel down the side of her cheek, mussing the veil covering her face.

His wife's whimpers of panic cut sharper than any finely wrought blade. Blood thundered into Wynn's curling fists. "Let her go."

"I never wished it to come to this." Sergey stroked Svetlana's cheek with the gun barrel. "I'm sorry, *kroshka*, but your execution will save my family. It will be a noble death."

Svetlana jerked away from the deadly caress. Fury snapped in her eyes. "Be a man and end it here and now. I'll never go back to Russia!"

Rage boiled in Wynn's blood, spilling into his veins as he stalked toward his prey. "Let her go now or I swear I'll kill you myself before you step foot on that train."

"Sadly, you'll never have the opportunity." The gun flashed up and pointed directly at Wynn's heart.

With a cry of alarm, Svetlana threw her arm up and smacked into Sergey's hand. The gun tumbled and skittered under a pile of broken trolleys. Knocking Svetlana aside, Sergey scrambled after the gun, but Wynn lunged and caught him around the middle, throwing him to the ground. They grappled across the filthy floor grunting and swinging limbs.

Sergey writhed like a snake as he jabbed Wynn in his ribs. Wynn used blunt strength fueled by murderous rage to pummel the weasel into a sniveling mess. Svetlana's screams, screeching wheels, and train whistles withered under the numbing instinct to kill. An instinct born into man and honed into a soldier to destroy any threat with primal viciousness. The battle peace, the Tommies called it. When the world fell away and calmness descended, allowing a man to do what must be done. Wynn no longer saw the bloodied face and black eyes of his enemy but Svetlana's terrified face, her cries of heartbreak, her feet dancing in the moonlight, her peaceful face as she slept next to him. He fought for her.

"Wynn!" And just like that, her cry pierced the blackening numbness, pulling him back before the last vestiges of his humanity disappeared over the edge.

Clutching Sergey by the lapels, Wynn rocked back on his heels as the rage in his blood hissed its restrained vehemence.

"You will hang for your crimes of conspiracy to kidnap and murder. I will personally wait until your legs stop twitching on that rope before I pronounce you dead, then have your worthless carcass carted off and tossed into a nameless cesspit."

Sergey grimaced, revealing the blood staining the crevices between his teeth. "I'd l-like to see you t-try."

The train behind them slumped forward, digging its wheels for traction against the steel rails. A long belch of black smoke erupted from its chimney stack. A beastly thing, it howled forward, tugging the cargo compartments behind it into motion.

Wynn stood and jerked Sergey to his feet. Sergey ducked his head and bit down hard on Wynn's hand. On instinct, Wynn released his grip and Sergey jumped out of reach.

He backed slowly toward the moving train, eyes darting for an open side door to lunge into. "I'll return for you. My family is worth more than you ever could be—"

A ball of black hurled into Sergey. He flew backward off the platform and disappeared onto the train tracks below. A scream tore, then a sickening thud. The train wheels picked up speed. *Thump. Thump. Thump.* The train pulled the last of its beastly bulk from the platform and the thumps silenced.

Ana, deathly regal in her travel suit of black and gray, stood calmly at the edge of the platform staring down at the track. Ever so slowly, she turned and clasped her hands calmly in front of her.

"He will not be returning." Her gaze settled on Svetlana. "You are safe now, Svetka."

Whistles, shouts, and pounding boots shattered the eerie stillness as the police came running. Leonid, gripping his bandaged arm, pushed his way to the front of the group.

"What is happened here?" He peered over the edge of the platform and stumbled back, crossing himself. "Holy Father of Heaven. Preserve us from evil."

"He jumped." Coming to her feet, Svetlana walked over to stand next to Wynn. She took his hand and pressed her shoulder to his, blocking her mother from view. "There was no place for him to go and he jumped."

Wynn threaded his fingers through hers and nodded. "He jumped."

Leonid considered them both for a long minute before finally adding his nod to the conclusion. "He jumped."

Like locusts, the police swarmed the area until their droning rose above the chugging trains on the upper level. The rat-faced accomplice was hauled from the pile of boxes where he'd been struggling back to consciousness and handcuffed between two burly sergeants.

"Looks like we'll be having a prime witness, lads," the chief officer said as the rat was taken away. "A good ol' fashioned interrogation ought to bring us a few more names to round up as we'll be having no red commies here. Your Grace, sorry to be pestering you after a trying day, but we'll be needing you to come down to the station for a few questions. Formality and all."

"I'll see the ladies to the hotel first, then happily answer all questions." Propriety or not, Wynn slipped his arm around his wife's waist. No chance on earth was he leaving her side anytime soon. Given their history, she might order him to, but he was of a mind not to listen.

"Right. We'll be seeing you there." The officer touched the brim of his hat in respect to Svetlana. "Ma'am."

The police milled all about Wynn and Svetlana, like rushing waves around an island. Her head was tilted down, the veil muting her features, but Wynn knew if he were to lift it he would see heartbreak and sadness.

"Are you all right, Svetlana?"

She turned into him and bent her forehead to touch his shoulder. "I thought you were to call me Lana."

Her voice was soft and fragile, like petals bruised on the ground after a bitter storm. One billow of wind more and they would crumble to fine dust, but even crushed petals linger with sweetness for he could describe her words as nothing but that. They wrapped around his soul as an intoxicating balm he wished to drown in. "Do you wish me to call you Lana?"

"Yes."

A single word, but, oh, the hard-fought victory in it. Wynn dropped his mouth close to her ear. "Then, are you all right, my Lana?"

Her face tilted so that her mouth hovered enticingly close to his. "I am now."

More than anything he wanted to kiss her and wash away everything that had driven them apart, but this was not the place. Not surrounded by barking policemen, morbid onlookers, and the stench of grease and smoke. Later, when death did not hover so close in memory.

Raising her gloved hand to his lips, he settled for brushing a kiss over her knuckles. "I'll take you to the hotel."

Svetlana pulled herself from Wynn's arms and walked over to put an arm around her mother. "Come along, Mama. We're free to go now."

Ana's shaking hand reached up to clasp the gold cross suspended about her neck as Svetlana escorted her toward the stairs. Gone was the avenging angel, returned once more into the aging princess who leaned into her daughter for support with a closeness never before encouraged.

The body, covered in a white sheet, was brought up from the platform. Blood speckled the cloth and a mangled hand with three missing fingers flopped out. Wynn choked back a sickened noise. He'd seen more than his fair share of death and broken bodies, but train tracks were a gruesome way to end a life. He tried to summon a sliver of pity for Sergey but found he had none while watching his wife and mother-in-law bravely walk away. That dog would have had them killed. Wynn may be able to find forgiveness for trespasses imposed on himself, but that magnanimity did not extend to those threatening his loved ones. A hypocrisy he was willing to live with.

Leaving the police to their grisly details, Wynn and Leonid fell into step behind the women and waved off the onlookers shouting morbid questions as they crossed the upper concourse of the station in search of the exit.

"How's your arm?"

"It heal like wound for hero." Leonid smacked a newspaper man out of the way as he tried to get them to stop for a photograph.

"Vultures," he muttered, ending with something in Russian that was probably best left unexplained. He leaned close to Wynn. "One day real story you tell me, Mac."

Wynn nodded absently. He needed to find that porter and have the borrowed horse returned. "One day."

"Next time ask first. I know how handle dead bodies. No one find."

"What is it with you Russians? Is disposal education part of your upbringing?"

Leonid shrugged. "Me, *da*, but no more. I honest path now. Unless you kill another patient, then I help." He slung his good arm around Wynn's shoulder. "Always need *druk* chum help bury body."

"I didn't kill a patient."

"*Da*, but if do."

Wynn shook his head as he placed a hand on Svetlana's back and steered her toward the door and the gray light beyond. These Russians were going to be the death of him.

———————

After two hours giving testimony at the police station, Wynn was ready to close the book on the day and then burn it. He hoped he never had to relive it again.

Dragging his feet down the hotel corridor, he stopped in front of the door marked 342. In 343 was his wilted mother-in-law, who hadn't spoken more than two words since they left the train station, and in 344 was Leonid, who had boasted an intent to order everything on the room-service menu. His appetite waited for no man. It was room 342 that Wynn was interested in, for that was where Svetlana was. Waiting for him.

He pushed a hand through his hair. It must be a mess, but if any day could excuse a lapse in grooming, it was this day. Ever since he'd left his wife here to complete the other orders of business, all he could think about was returning to her. Now that he was here, uncertainty plagued him. She'd asked him to call her Lana, but what if it had only been a desperate need for comfort in that horrible moment? Calmed from the ordeal, would she now regret her intimate actions of falling into his arms? How could he convince her that together was the only place they belonged? He didn't wish to live as man and wife separated, but ultimately the decision was in her hands. He wouldn't force his love on her if she didn't desire it.

Taking a deep breath to calm his jittery nerves, Wynn unlocked the door and stepped inside. She stood by the window bathed in the pearly gray of fading light. Unadorned with hat and veil, her hair was a silver sheen of curls floating over the iced blue of her dress. Dusk softened her lines, blurring her edges to the shadows behind her so he couldn't see the expression on her face.

He dropped his hat on a decorative chair next to the door and ran a hand through his hair again. "Svetlana, I—"

She moved so quickly he almost didn't see her. One minute she was at the window and the next her arms were wrapped about him, her face pressed into his neck.

"I love you. I am sorry for everything that has come between us. Sorry for the way I have treated you, for giving you less than you deserve when you have offered me everything with nothing expected in return. When you have cared for me from the very beginning just as you said you would. Will you please forgive me for my horrible snobbishness?"

Those were the last words he'd expected to hear, but thankfully his arms caught on quicker than his head. "Forgive you? If there is anyone to beg forgiveness, it's me. I lied to you and broke your trust. I should have told you the truth from the beginning, hang my pride." He held her close, glorying in the fierceness with which she clung to him as her words spilled through his mind like rushing water breaking through a barrier.

"My darling, you have been my rock and my salvation, keeping me from slipping into madness. You have taught me resilience, that simply because things are not as you wish or are taken from you does not mean you can't thrive. My power for good is not limited to the surgical tools in my hands because your strength has shown me how to use it elsewhere without need to fan my vanity. Will you forgive me?"

In answer she tightened her embrace as if willing herself to knit into him. Bones and breath and skin of one being until two no longer existed. Warm tears slipped down the side of his neck as her lashes brushed his skin like butterfly wings. He threaded his fingers through her hair, dislodging pins that pinged to the floor. Silken curls slipped free and tumbled down her back, caressing his arms as he drew her ever closer to feel the beating of her heart echoing in his chest.

Time no longer held sway until the last tear trickled down his neck and she took a shaking breath. With excruciating slowness, she leaned back in his arms, mere inches but enough to finally look at his face. Wetness clung to her lashes and the tip of her nose was red.

"I feel we have been on the wrong foot since first we met. Always one, or two, or three steps out of place from one another. I should very much like to change that. May we start over again?"

Finding it difficult to breathe when she looked at him like that, he brushed the remnants of a tear from her cheek. "Only if you allow me to court you as you deserve to be courted. With all the wooing of flattery and flowers and serenading that goes with it."

"No serenading. I've no wish to alert the hounds." A smile played about her lips as he imagined her recalling his last attempt to sing when they walked the streets of Glasgow. He had no thought for singing but for her lips he had an irrepressible desire to kiss.

"Flowers and chocolates it is."

"Those are insignificant to me when all I desire is you."

"Then you shall have all of me, especially my heart. It's all I've ever wanted to give you."

"I gladly accept."

He kissed her with every unspoken word gathered in his heart, emotions he could express in no other way. Words of longing, of desire, of promise, of love that she responded to with an aching all her own. He had found a life for himself in this woman. A woman he could fight for and fall with and create meaning alongside. Her lips melted beneath his, branding his with need, her arms a lock about his neck from which he never wished to break free.

Her mouth slowly curved into a smile and he pulled back as much as he dared to witness his handiwork molding those delightful lips. "If we're to start over again, does that mean you wish to take back the 'I love you'? Because I have to tell you, that's not something I'm going to let you forget. I've heard it and you can't unsay it."

"No, I do not wish to take it back."

"So that means . . ."

Her smile widened as pink stained her cheeks. "That I love you."

"At last! The woman takes pity on this miserable wretch."

"There was no pity involved. Nor was it because I was lonely or lost. I fell in love with you because after coming to know you, I knew you would forever be a permanent fixture in my world."

A man's heart holds a secret chamber where only one woman may enter. A place shaped for only her to breathe life into the darkened recesses and drum out a unique rhythm never before heard. Wynn pressed Svetlana's hand over his heart, allowing her to feel the existence she thrummed into him.

"I promise to be there for you every day. To walk alongside you and stand firm beside you. I promise to give you shelter in the storms and wings to rise above them. My privilege will be to wipe the tears from your eyes and give you reason to smile again. You are the most precious thing to me and with these words I give you all my life . . . I love you, Lana."

Tears misted her eyes. In the fading light they were like the first gloss of stars across twilight. "You are an exceptional man, Wynn MacCallan. A good man, and I am proud to call you my husband. In this instance I believe my pride is a good thing and not to our detriment. I am humbled by your heart's offering and I shall treasure it until my dying breath." She blinked back the unshed tears. "Which thankfully was not today."

He pulled her closer and suppressed the utter despair of having nearly lost her that day. His life, gone. "You're safe, Lana. You, your mother, Marina, and *babushka*. You have nothing to fear any longer."

Cupping her hand around his neck, she nudged his forehead down to touch hers. "Will you do one thing for me?"

"Anything."

"Take me home. To our home. I'm ready to begin living our life."

He could have shouted for joy. He could have done a backflip. And seriously thrown out his back. But there was one thing above all others that he wished to do.

"On one condition." He slipped one arm around her waist, while his other hand took hers, lacing their fingers together. "That you dance with me."

Bending her head, she kissed their entwined fingers. "I thought you'd never ask."

EPILOGUE

ONE YEAR LATER

C arpets of purple heather bloomed in the growing twilight as the Rolls Royce pulled up to the newly constructed entrance of Harkin Hospital, the county's first and only self-sustaining medical center. Svetlana stepped out of the back of the motor car and smoothed the front of her white-and-green striped dress. She was still growing accustomed to the ankle-revealing hemlines, but women all over the world reveled in the looseness of post-war fashion. There was even talk of doing away with corsets altogether, but she wasn't quite ready for that. A woman needed her shape, after all.

She stared up at the freshly painted limestone building with a surge of pride. They had done it. She and Wynn had accomplished something greater than themselves, something they never could have done on their own. It had humbled them both to gratefulness.

Inside, the white tile floors gleamed brilliantly under the newly installed electric lights as the unique smell of disinfectant and bleached linen permeated the air. Her eyes had watered at first from the strong concoction, but it was one of the many things she'd grown accustomed to as the wife of a physician.

"Good evening, Yer Grace," the front desk receptionist said. Dressed in pristine white with a smart cap atop her head, the young woman was one of the newly graduated nurses from the nursing course offered at the old sugar mill that had been remodeled into a learning establishment. Many of the village girls applied, and several had gone on

374

to be offered positions as far away as Glasgow and Edinburgh while more still opted to remain in Glentyre to be closer to their families.

"Good evening, Nurse Drummond. How is little Lorna?"

"Fine as dew on a lamb's ear, Yer Grace. Loving the children's wing, she is."

Another addition located at the rear of the hospital—an entire wing dedicated to children. The upper floor was for the sick, and the lower provided a nursery of sorts for children whose parents were taking courses or worked all day. It was headed by none other than Katie MacKinnon who had flourished in her training to become a shining example for superintendents. She had revolutionized the service into one of happiness and fun for the children and one of relief for parents who could now go to work unfettered knowing their children were well cared for.

"I'm delighted to hear that."

Nurse Drummond reached below her desk and pulled out a small posy tied with a red ribbon. "'Tis not much, and sorry we are without the grandness ye're used to, but a few of us mithers wanted to thank ye proper. The war took all we had, most of us our men, but we've a chance now to provide for our families. Ye championed us, Duchess, and we're ever so grateful."

Svetlana bent her head to smell the tiny yellow-and-white flowers, taking the humbling moment to blink back the emotion washing her eyes. "Thank you for the honor of allowing me to do so."

The nurse beamed, then remembered her station and grabbed a clipboard hanging from the wall. "Dr. MacCallan is still in the operating theater. Auld man McGillum ran a saw across his leg out cutting the wood. I'll be telling him ye arrived when he comes out. The doctor, not auld man McGillum."

"Thank you. He may find me next door at the Bear."

The Bear, Glentyre's newest pub, was connected to the hospital by an outdoor covered corridor that passed through a garden Svetlana had single-handedly planted with white roses, purple hyacinths, and yellow kingcups that perfumed the soft spring gloaming. A short wicker fence cornered off a back section for the dacha garden that provided the Bear and the hospital with fresh vegetables, which were rotated out according to season. Once unclaimed and without roots, the ground and its harvest now flourished to their own free will. As did she.

In the center of the garden stood Constance's monument dedicated to all the Glentyre Tommies who had served in the war, their names, including Hugh's, carved for all to remember.

Pushing through the Bear's heavy oak door, Svetlana stepped into a large room with thick stone and wood-paneled walls, flickering candles, and gas-lit sconces. A long bar ran the length of one wall, which sparkled with dozens of glass bottles ready for pouring. A fiddler and bodhrán player sat in a corner, plucking and drumming to the enjoyment of the patrons who sat at small round tables piled high with beer mugs and empty plates. Svetlana inhaled the rich scents of cabbage, venison, baked brown bread, and potatoes. Russia filled the air.

"Angel, you are here!" The Bear's proprietor, Leonid himself, barged out of the kitchen through a set of swinging doors. He'd grown thicker around the middle, but life exuded from his every pore. "Come! Come sit."

Svetlana weaved her way over to him. "I cannot. I'm waiting for Wynn."

"He is up to elbows in blood and knives. We wait. Sit. Sit!"

With no other option than to do as she was told, Svetlana accepted the offered chair he pulled out for her at their usual table. "Something smells delicious."

"New recipe." He turned and barked at one of the servers. None of his staff understood a single word of Russian, but all they had to do was serve their customers food and drink and their boss would be happy. As the server ran back into the kitchen, Leonid plopped into the chair next to Svetlana. "*Babushka* is making *pelmeni* with herring caught in the lake—loch? *da?*—she says addition came to her in dream. I think is vodka inspired, but you taste. Tell the truth."

"Don't I always?"

"*Da*, that is why you official taste test. You tell the truth. You I trust. Mac, not so much. Everything *babushka* makes he likes."

"Which is precisely why his trousers have grown too tight since you opened this place and took on Mrs. Varjensky to oversee the cooking."

"*Da*, my dream come true. Own place, own rules. No dead bodies."

"It's the only establishment in Scotland to serve Russian cuisine. You should be very proud."

Proud didn't begin to describe Leonid's attitude. His father had been arrested and the White Bear closed, but he'd had no desire to return to Paris and so had embarked on a lifetime dream of starting his own establishment right there in Glentyre. Everyone in the village knew him, though how anyone could not know of the larger-than-life Russian strutting about was beyond comprehension. He'd taken samples of his vodka and cabbage rolls into every shop until he'd made loyal customers out of each of them. Once they'd overcome their initial terror of him, that is.

"Where is goddaughter? Has been two days since seeing my *kroshka*. She will not remember me."

The little crumb had arrived three months and one week ago to the joyous delight of her family. Particularly Wynn, who was wrapped around Anastasia's tiny little finger. No matter how tired he was from a day at the hospital, he always made time for his wee girl.

"She is at home sleeping. Or she's supposed to be. Her grandmothers and aunt make her smile too much instead of keeping to a nap schedule."

"Stasia loves me best. I come tomorrow for visit so she no longer forgets me. I will bring name day gift."

"Her name day celebration is months away."

"I will bring gift then too. You want to know what I bring tomorrow?" His eyes widened like a child's at Christmas waiting for *Dedt Moroz*. "Proper samovar. Too long you are without. I have her name carved on it so all will know it belongs to Stasia from beloved godfather. She will drink proper tea now."

"I have no doubt she will treasure it always." The Lady Anastasia Edwynnovna MacCallan couldn't find the end of her nose, much less a teacup, but Svetlana wasn't about to spoil Leonid's joy.

The server came bustling back to the table with a loaded platter of sautéed dumplings and presented it to Svetlana. Peeling off her white netted gloves as per dining etiquette, she forked one of the delicacies and brought it to her mouth. Chewing, she tasted the fire-cooked fish flaked apart with a savory hint of rosemary. She set down her fork and dabbed at her mouth with a clean napkin.

"A dash of salt would bring out the smokiness."

Leonid slapped the table, startling the nearby customers. "That is what I say. 'Overwhelming the herbs,' *babushka* says. I let her in kitchen once and now she thinks in charge."

"Perhaps you shouldn't allow her in the kitchen anymore."

"*Nyet*. She is the best cook in Scotland. They eat sheep guts before we come."

The infamous haggis. Svetlana shuddered. Who would have thought Mrs. Varjensky, a self-imposed head cook who sold herbal medicines on the side, or often to inebriated patrons, would become the cuisine savior of Scotland?

The fiddler and bodhrán player finished their set and a vibrating balalaika came to take their place to the anticipatory applause of the drinking patrons. Leonid had traveled as far as London to find a Russian musician so the sleepy villagers of Glentyre could appreciate true culture. On Friday and Saturday nights the musician's wife joined him as a singer and dancer. What would begin as a tribute to Mother

Russia would eventually spiral into a wash of vodka and whisky for a rioting celebration of Celtic and Slavic proportions.

The side door opened and in strode Wynn looking more confident and content than she'd ever seen him. With Harkin's death ruled a tragedy of undetected slug remnants and not due to complications from surgery, Wynn's medical license had been reinstated with all honors and reputation intact. Hospitals in London, Edinburgh, and Inverness had warmed to his innovative surgery techniques, the same that had caused censure among his peers months before, and clamored for his services.

He'd turned them all down in favor of practicing at Harkin Hospital, where people came from all over the country seeking his skills. He'd also discovered a true gift for teaching. Many of the ordinary physician's tasks were given to other doctors on the roster while the major cases were placed under Wynn's skilled scalpel. Resigning himself only to the serious operations allowed him time for his other duties as duke. An imperfect balance when he'd rather be in surgery, but a balance all the same.

Greeting villagers as he passed, Wynn kept his eyes ever on Svetlana, making her heart pound with each step bringing him closer. He leaned over and kissed her generously on the lips, drawing a series of whistles from the nearby tables. The people had grown accustomed to the unusual acts of their duke and duchess, from public affection—which Svetlana tried and failed to chide Wynn from—and surgical duties, to eating among the commoners with their Russian friend almost as frequently as they dined in their castle.

"Had to do a resection of the pericardium due to end-diastolic pressure in the left ventricle. It's a new technique coming out of Frankfurt for heart failures. Mmm, what's this?" He grabbed a dumpling from Svetlana's plate and popped it in his mouth. The more surgeries, the more improved his appetite. "Fish? Tastes perfect."

"That is because you are *babushka's golubchik*." Leonid raised an eyebrow to Svetlana as if to say, *See what I mean?*

Ignoring him, Wynn grabbed another dumpling. "Where's Stasia? I wanted to show her the new gurney we got in the operating theater."

Svetlana swatted at his greasy fingers with her napkin. "Firstly, our daughter is three months old. She has not a clue of what a gurney or an operating theater is. Secondly, the last time you took her into that room, a removed organ was still on the table."

"It was a ruptured appendix. The patient no longer required it."

"Be that as it may, Stasia is much too young to stare at human organs, required or not."

"It's never too early to start her medical knowledge. Speaking of which, I ordered a new set of medical journals on the latest in surgical techniques—"

"They printed your article!"

"Not yet, but in one of the issues they mentioned improvements for strengthening weakened bones and misshapen muscles. A common epidemic among our soldiers, but it might also be useful to Alec MacGregor. You remember him and his wife, Lord and Lady Strathem? They hosted that charity gala for the continued care of convalescent homes."

"I saw mostly her. Lord Strathem, I believe, prefers his wife to shine while he keeps quietly to the back. A charming woman, but she laughs too much." She turned to Leonid. "American."

Leonid nodded in complete understanding.

"An American who married the surliest Scotsman in the country," Wynn said. "That should count in her favor."

"It does."

"You Russians and your need for the dismal."

After several more tasting rounds, Svetlana and Wynn bid Leonid good evening and walked back to the hospital. Wynn signed off his shift notes to Gerard who had come to work alongside his friend. He was proving himself most formidable with a scalpel, though with a caution that tempered Wynn's zeal.

Wynn shoved his arms into his jacket and plopped his hat on his head. "Should be a light load tomorrow. I'd like to examine a heart from a shell-shocked victim recently deceased. I have a theory about corollaries between inordinate amounts of stress and thrombosis."

Having not a clue what that meant, Svetlana slipped on her netted gloves. "As long as it does not interfere with talking to the estate agent. Mackie has an idea of turning the eastern plots of land into more viable revenue streams. And you wanted to do a walkabout to the tenants before planting begins."

"Which I have scheduled for tomorrow afternoon." Pausing next to the front door, Wynn pulled out a handkerchief and swiped it across the brass plaque that read:

> This hospital is dedicated to the
> memory of Lt. John Harkin.
> Let all who pass through these doors enter
> in the name of good and healing.

The burden of Harkin's death had scarred Wynn with unflagging pain as he blamed himself for not seeing the shell fragment that had grown infected after Harkin was deemed on the mend from his surgery. Every day he attempted to bury his guilt within these sterile walls, each life saved a recompense stacked against the judgment in which he held himself. Harkin was an innocent struck down by the lingering evil of war, but Wynn had done his best to see that the man had not died in vain. His memory would live on for as long as this hospital stood.

Twilight's purples had deepened to indigo with a night sky of spangled stars like dozens of diamonds broken from a necklace as their auto carried them home. The air tingled with the fresh waters of the nearby Cairnmuir River and the musky heather blooms as the welcome sight of Thornhill loomed in the distance. Svetlana snuggled contentedly at Wynn's side, his arm about her shoulder.

"My third favorite sight in all the world." Wynn's low voice hummed against her ear, making her drowsy. Or tempted to kiss him.

She traced a gloved finger over his muscular thigh. "What are the first two?"

"You and Stasia."

"Delighted to hear that. I was half expecting an open heart to be among the ranks."

His lips brushed her ear. "That's my fourth."

Turning her head on a giggle, she caught his lips. The world fell away into nothingness as she lost herself in him. His kiss, gentle and confident, yet possessive of every part of her, was something she could not live without as it stirred to life parts of her untouched beyond him. She was deeply, irrevocably, and hopelessly in love with her husband, and the surrender had never been sweeter.

"Ahem, Your Graces."

Svetlana pulled slowly, reluctantly away like a shell from its pearl. Their chauffeur held open the auto's door as light blazed from Thornhill's entrance. Somehow they'd arrived home without the slightest notice. Svetlana merely looped her handbag over her wrist and climbed out. It wasn't the first, nor likely the last, time he'd catch them in an embrace.

Stepping inside the entrance hall, Svetlana removed her hat and gloves and handed them along with her handbag to her waiting maid.

"I interviewed three more candidates for the ballet costume mistress position today. None suitable." Turning the last unused room at the old sugar mill into a ballet studio had been the perfect addition. It did not compare to the Bolshoi Theater, but dancing before the tsar and tsarina could not match the excitement of watching her little ballerinas *jeté* and *arabesque* for the first time. Her love for dance had finally found fulfillment. Fitted with mirrors, a barre, and a roster of potential pupils, her class of twelve was nearly ready for its first recital, but no seamstress had been found to create proper costumes of woodland creatures and flowers.

Wynn handed over his hat and jacket to the waiting footman. Despite proper dressing etiquette, he complained the sleeves were too restrictive and he would not be restricted in his own home. More likely, he'd grown accustomed to the looseness of a surgeon's smock. "That's because your standards are ridiculously high. Not everyone trained at the Imperial Ballet."

"They should have."

"Aren't our mothers sewing the costumes?"

Svetlana laughed. "They showed me yesterday what was intended to be a squirrel but resembled more of a lumpy sackcloth. There was not even a tail."

Wynn rolled his eyes, unconcerned with the catastrophe brewing. "I'm sure your class doesn't care if the squirrel has a tail or not. They're much too thrilled with learning ballet from a real-life princess."

Svetlana tapped a finger to her chin. "Perhaps I should put an advertisement in *The Lady's Journal*. There are enough Russians fleeing to British shores. Surely one is bound to have worked for a proper ballet company."

"Have your assistant send the advertisement. That is why you hired her. Poor girl doesn't know what to do with herself when you keep insisting on doing everything with your own hands."

"Why should I not perform duties that I am perfectly capable of executing? Duchess is not a title equated to lady of leisure."

"It should be. And I've a few ideas of leisurely activities starting now." He scooped her into his arms against her squeal of protest and started for the stairs.

Glasby swooped in out of nowhere and blocked them. With his formal black tails and starched white tie, he resembled a formidable penguin.

"There is a visitor for you, Your Graces. I've shown him into the library."

"Visiting hours are over. Tell him to come back tomorrow." Wynn moved to step around him, but Glasby didn't budge.

"I believe you will make an exception in this case. He has traveled a long way to see the Princess Svetlana."

"Traveled from where?" A spark of fear kindled in Svetlana's chest as Wynn set her on her feet. Months of calm had eased her anxiety, but more than once an unguarded moment had been seized by memories of horror. The past had found them again.

"The gentleman has requested to answer all questions himself." Despite Glasby's formality, the glimmer of a smile teased his lips.

Svetlana's apprehension eased. Bolsheviks would never elicit a smile. Glasby hurried to fling open the library door, by this time grinning widely.

Svetlana stepped inside the room. Her mother and Marina sat on the settee by the fire where a tall, thin man with silvery blond hair blocked the dancing orange flames. He turned and the light flashed across an unfamiliar black eyepatch, but he was unmistakable.

"Nicky!" Svetlana raced across the room and launched herself into her brother's arms. Her living, breathing brother. Tears coursed down her cheeks as they clung tightly to one another. "We thought you were dead."

Laughing, a sound that seemed rather rusted, Nicky pulled back. A sheen of tears watered his good eye. "Clearly I'm not."

He was still as handsome as a saint, though he'd grown painfully thin. As if the muscles of manhood had withered from his imposing frame. Svetlana gently touched the strap of his eyepatch. "What happened?"

"A souvenir from being a Russian nobleman. Turns out we're no longer welcome in our country."

"But how did you survive? We were told you and Papa were shot."

Nicky's mouth twisted with disdain. "Sergey seems to have spun all sorts of lies. Treacherous cur. Mama told me he threw himself under a train."

Behind him, Mama gave a slight shake of her head for Svetlana to keep quiet. Some secrets were best left unsaid.

Nicky held Svetlana's hands. They'd never been an overly affectionate family, but time had softened them, it seemed, for they held tight to one another. Perhaps afraid to let go and find the other gone.

"The Bolsheviks captured what was left of the White Army standing guard and shot us next to the Neva River. Papa died instantly when he tried to defend his men. A bullet scraped the side of my face, knocking me backward into the river where I floated downstream. A goat herder found me and hid me for over a year. I searched for you and Mama and Marina all over Paris, but it seemed hopeless, so I took a ship to England with other white émigrés."

A smile lit his tired face. "In London I was reading a newspaper article about collecting lost items from Imperial Russia for an exhibit at the Royal Victoria and Albert Museum. Imagine my surprise at the organizer being none other than the Duchess of Kilbride, the former Princess Svetlana Dalsky."

"An astonishing story." Tears filled Svetlana's eyes and fell unchecked down her cheeks. "I cannot believe you stand before us."

Marina clapped her hands and jumped up to hug them. "Isn't it wonderful?"

Mama's arms circled around them. Tears flowed down her cheeks. "All of my children together at last. Never shall we part again." She motioned to Wynn, who stood by the door quietly observing. "I said *all* of my children."

Svetlana's heart overflowed with joy as her family's arms wrapped around her, locking her safely in their embrace. They had journeyed far and been lost to one another only to find themselves together again at last, this time stronger through the forbearance of their struggles.

Wynn's arms circled her waist from behind, drawing her close to his chest so that she felt the steady beat of his heart. That's what he had always been for her, the steady beat that gave her courage. A beat she would never have to do without again.

"I thought Russians were averse to displays of affection," he whispered into her ear.

"Shh. It will ruin our hard-earned image."

"Hate to tell you, Princess, but you shattered that for me long ago."

Svetlana smiled. "*Spasibo.*"

THE END

ACKNOWLEDGMENTS

First off, I want to thank Netflix for suggesting the show *Road to Calvary* after I finished watching *Seyit and Sura*. It's like you know me so well and make sure I'm always aware of the newest and best foreign period dramas to be absorbed by. The Russian Revolution and the sad fate of the Romanov family were nothing new to me, but this show gave me insight into the catalyst of those horrific years, how it affected the Russian people, and how the country was forced to pull out of the Great War in order to fight its own civil war. Thank you for broadening my horizons and sparking the voice for Svetlana's plight as one of the millions displaced from their home.

Netflix is not alone in deserving my gratitude. *Fiddler on the Roof*, *Downton Abbey* season 5, and *War and Peace* are wonderful visual tellings of this turbulent region and what it meant for people caught in the grinding wheels of prejudice. For a more in-depth study of Russia's history and how each event piled atop one another like stones until it built into the crushing boulder that was the Russian Revolution of 1917, Orlando Figes's *Natasha's Dance* was an invaluable resource and one I cannot recommend highly enough. Be warned, it is a heavy read, but well worth it.

Thank you to Rick Barry who was oh so patient in helping me understand the Russian language, the difference between *ovich* and an *ovna*, and offering suggestions to my vocabulary list. Without you my Russian characters would sound, well, not Russian.

I wouldn't be sitting here typing this list of thank yous if it weren't for Linda, my agent, who still puts up with me after all these years and never stops fighting to see me succeed. You're one in a million, lady.

To my team at Thomas Nelson, who are just as excited about these crazy stories as I am and work so hard to polish them into a diamond. Amanda, Jocelyn, Jodi, Kerri, Margaret, Laura, Matt, and everyone else working behind the scenes. Stories would not be what they are without your zest and commitment, and I'm so excited to be a part of your publishing family!

Last but certainly not least, to my family. Daisy, for your unwavering companionship and never-fail bark to alert me that the Amazon guy is here. Again. We'd be lost without your vigilant protection. Miss S for the rainbow of color you explode into our lives. And to Bryan, *my* constant. Love y'all.

DISCUSSION QUESTIONS

1. Why do you think Wynn has complicated feelings toward his title, and how does his chosen occupation reflect these feelings?

2. What does Svetlana learn about herself over the course of the story? In what ways have her altered circumstances forced her to change?

3. In 1917 heart surgery was not part of medical practice. In fact, it was said that, "Surgery of the heart has probably reached its limit set by nature. No new methods and no new discovery can overcome the natural difficulties that attend a wound of the heart," and that "The surgeon who operates on the heart will lose the respect of his colleagues." Given that this was such a radical procedure, would you have allowed Wynn to perform heart surgery on you?

4. After Svetlana and her family escape Russia, they must embrace new places and traditions in order to survive. If you've ever had to uproot your life, how did you cope? Were you resistant to your new home or did you welcome it?

5. What do Svetlana and Wynn admire about each other? In what ways do their personalities complement one another?

6. Do you think Wynn made the right choice to operate on Harkin or should he have consulted other medical advice first?

7. Dancing is Svetlana's passion and the only way she can truly express herself, just as Wynn finds his calling through

surgery. If they were never allowed to dance or be a physician again, might they have found true contentment in other ways? Or does the heart long only for its true passion, never settling for less?

8. Svetlana states time and again that Russians are not known for their optimistic outlook, citing the miseries penned by Tolstoy and Pushkin to be a true reflection of life. Do you think this contributed to her denial of happiness and love? Or was the Revolution more to blame?

9. Setting takes a large role in *The Ice Swan*, from revolutionary Russia, to war-torn Paris, and finally to peaceful Scotland. How are each of these places significant to Wynn and Svetlana? How does each location help them to grow, not only as individuals but as a couple?

10. Most often we read about rags to riches stories, but *The Ice Swan* provides the reverse. Svetlana begins as a princess with the world at her feet only to be cast down into a basement begging for food. What kinds of challenges might a person in this position face, physically and mentally? Would they truly be able to say that money doesn't buy happiness?

Get lost in another
sweeping romance
by J'nell Ciesielski.

 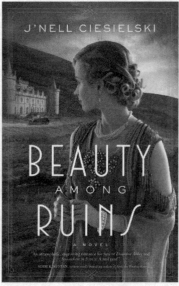

AVAILABLE IN PRINT, E-BOOK, AND AUDIO

THOMAS NELSON
Since 1798

ABOUT THE AUTHOR

With a passion for heart-stopping adventure and sweeping love stories, J'nell Ciesielski weaves fresh takes into romances of times gone by. When not creating dashing heroes and daring heroines, she can be found dreaming of Scotland, indulging in chocolate of any kind, or watching old black-and-white movies. Winner of the Romance Through the Ages Award and the Maggie Award, she is a Florida native who now lives in Virginia with her husband, daughter, and lazy beagle.

Learn more at www.jnellciesielski.com
Instagram: @jnellciesielski